SAVAGE GARDEN

Los Angeles Times **bestseller**
**A 2005 Finalist for Best Mystery,
the Southern California Booksellers Association**

"L.A. is as much a character as any person in *Savage Garden*. . . . Hamilton expertly plumbs the themes of jealousy, class differences, and identity."

—*Sun-Sentinel* (Ft. Lauderdale, FL)

"Decades after my introduction to Christie, I'm still hooked on crime novels. I love the books by Sue Grafton, Michael Connelly, Sara Paretsky, George Pelecanos, James Crumley, and Denise Hamilton."

—*USA Today*

"Eve Diamond is a go-getter without being feisty, vulnerable but not whiny, and she's good at her job."

—*The Baltimore Sun*

"Offering a noir-ish 21st century spin on Philip Marlowe's Los Angeles, Hamilton races the reader through its multicultural mean streets with . . . a central character who is edgy, smart, and credible."

—*Library Journal* (starred review)

LAST LULLABY

Los Angeles Times **bestseller and a Best Book of 2004**
USA Today **Summer Reading Pick**
**A Best Mystery Nominee,
the Southern California Booksellers Association**

"Sexy and exciting."

—Janet Fitch, #1 bestselling author of
White Oleander

"Eve Diamond is sympathetic and believable. . . . She also has the right mix of street smarts, sass and vulnerability."

—*Chicago Sun-Times*

"Engrossing."

—*The Washington Post*

SUGAR SKULL
Los Angeles Times bestseller

"Expertly crafted . . . a tale of lust, greed, [and] murder in the City of Angels."

—*Library Journal* (starred review)

"Denise Hamilton and Eve Diamond are the real deal."

—*The Denver Post*

"So absorbing that you don't want to stop reading."

—*Los Angeles Times*

THE JASMINE TRADE
Los Angeles Times bestseller
Edgar Award finalist   A Book Sense 76 Pick

"Gripping . . . intriguing . . . more than a good crime novel."

—Michael Connelly, #1 *New York Times* bestselling author of *Echo Park*

ALSO BY DENISE HAMILTON

Savage Garden
Last Lullaby
Sugar Skull
The Jasmine Trade

DENISE HAMILTON

PRISONER
OF MEMORY

POCKET STAR BOOKS

NEW YORK LONDON TORONTO SYDNEY

A Pocket Star Book published by
POCKET BOOKS, a division of Simon & Schuster, Inc.
1230 Avenue of the Americas, New York, NY 10020

This book is a work of fiction. Names, characters, places and incidents are products of the author's imagination or are used fictitiously. Any resemblance to actual events or locales or persons, living or dead, is entirely coincidental.

Copyright © 2006 by Denise Hamilton

Originally published in hardcover in 2006 by Scribner

All rights reserved, including the right to reproduce this book or portions thereof in any form whatsoever. For information address Scribner, 1230 Avenue of the Americas, New York, NY 10020

ISBN-13: 978-0-7434-9272-0
ISBN-10:   0-7434-9272-2

This Pocket Star Books paperback edition April 2007

10 9 8 7 6 5 4 3 2 1

POCKET STAR BOOKS and colophon are registered trademarks of Simon & Schuster, Inc.

Cover design by John Vairo Jr.
Cover photo by Holger Scheibe/Zefa/Corbis

Manufactured in the United States of America

For information regarding special discounts for bulk purchases, please contact Simon & Schuster Special Sales at 1-800-456-6798 or business@simonandschuster.com.

For Noelle, because her story is my story

PRISONER
OF MEMORY

CHAPTER 1

The mountain lion had marked his territory, powerful claws shredding the bark of a sturdy oak tree just yards from where the chaparral gave way to terraced backyards.

Standing on a hiking trail in Griffith Park, I wondered where the big cat was now and felt a primal twitch of fear. In the sudden stillness, every sound seemed amplified: the high, clear voices of children echoing off the canyon. The agitated bark of a dog. The drunken buzzing of bees harvesting the last dregs of nectar before winter settled in for good in Southern California.

Beside me, California Fish and Game tracker Jeff Knightsbridge fingered the bill of his baseball cap and cleared his throat. Placing my sharpened pencil against my notepad, I inhaled the tang of wood shavings and waited.

"He's not after humans," Knightsbridge said. "He's after the deer. Let me emphasize that, because I don't want to open my paper tomorrow and see a sensational story about mountain lions stalking hikers in Griffith Park. Your average puma goes out of its way to avoid people."

Knightsbridge scuffed a booted toe on the trail, and a plume of dust rose into the milky light. It had been a long, scorching autumn in the City of Fallen Angels, but the heat had eased into a brittle cold as the holidays approached.

"Can you tell how old those marks are? Or how big he was?" I asked.

The furrows started ten feet up the trunk. I imagined the mountain lion rearing up, muscles rippling under tawny skin, the explosive crackle of dry wood as he put his weight into it. What such claws might do to human flesh.

From far away, children's cries resounded off the rock escarpments. Bees droned, an atavistic murmur from the hive-mind.

Knightsbridge ran his hand along the defiled trunk. The deep scratches exposed the pale fibrous innards of the tree, its amber tears.

He shrugged. "Three days, give or take."

Lifting his chin, he scanned the brush. "Can you smell that?"

"What?" Looking up at the sky, where charcoal clouds were swiftly overtaking the blue, I wondered if he meant rain. As a hopeless city slicker, I'd benefit from a wilderness survival course that taught me to sniff out a storm and navigate by the North Star. But in my line of work, a martial arts class in self-defense was way more practical.

I was a journalist for the *Los Angeles Times* and this was my first day as a downtown Metro reporter. But instead of a juicy investigation, I'd drawn mountain lion patrol after commuters spotted a big cat grooming himself under the snowflakes and candy cane decorations of Hillcrest Avenue, where the asphalt met the urban wilderness of Griffith Park. In a city bedeviled by crime and corruption, distraction was a drug and now everyone was breathlessly fixated on a 160-pound feline. And I wasn't about to leave Griffith Park without a killer story.

"Not rain." Knightsbridge wrinkled his nose. "Like meat that's gone bad. I caught it again just now on the wind. Over there."

I turned in the direction of his outstretched finger and

took a deep breath. Through the dust we had kicked up, beyond the resinous scent of anise and sage, I thought I detected it, a faint, sweet charnel house smell.

"If it killed recently," Knightsbridge was saying, "the puma will hang around. And it will perceive anything that gets too close as threatening its meal." His hand went to the gun at his waist. "C'mon."

He set off through the scrub, and I scrambled to follow.

The buzzing grew louder. I paused, shrank back. There must have been a hive nearby.

Looking down, I saw the San Fernando Valley sprawl, arteries already starting to clog with afternoon traffic, commuters getting a jump-start on their holiday shopping. A thin layer of brown haze blanketed everything. Winter often brought the clearest light. But not today.

Knightsbridge had stopped too. He sniffed the air like a bloodhound. In the distance, a black cloud rose and swayed off the trail. The angry humming grew louder. I grabbed his arm.

"Are those . . . bees?"

"No," he said, his voice taking on an urgency I didn't like.

Knightsbridge set off for the cloud, with me tagging reluctantly behind.

He disappeared around a bend. Then came a disembodied shout. He came staggering back, face white, bandanna clasped to his mouth.

"What?"

But he only fumbled for a radio at his belt.

"Cat didn't do this," he said, his face a rictus of disbelief.

I pushed past him. I didn't care about getting stung anymore. The smell of decomposing flesh grew stronger.

As I rounded the bend, what I saw made me avert my

eyes and breathe through my mouth, but it was too late, the stench already seeping into my lungs. A body lay face-down at the edge of the dirt trail. A black cloud of flies hovered, swaying and rippling with each breeze. I couldn't look. I couldn't not look. Tearing my eyes away, I focused on the dirt trail and tried not to hyperventilate. Among the rocks and footprints and tread marks from mountain bikes, a bullet casing twinkled in the afternoon light.

A wave of nausea swept over me, and I bent to retch, but only dry-heaved.

It was the flies that put me over. That revolting black mass swarming over the head and nearby ground, dark where something had spilled and dried.

But even in my sorry state, I recognized that Knights-bridge was right. Mountain lions don't leave bullet casings behind.

I could hear him panting into the radio, announcing his coordinates, then a mumbled, "Oh Jesus, hold on," and a roar as churning liquid splattered. Then as he recovered, the matter-of-fact recitation.

"Griffith Park. Off the horse trail, on the Valley side. A half mile up the trailhead. Yeah. Don't worry, I'm not going anywhere."

Notepad still in hand, I steeled myself to look at the corpse. It's odd how the brain absorbs death in layers. At first I had seen an indistinct shape, my mind fastened in primal disgust on the flies. The second time I'd noted the darker stains on the ground, the bullet glinting like a malevolent jewel. Now I threw a rock, dislodging the flies, and took in the scene methodically.

Long, baggy beige cargo shorts, exposing tanned legs with golden hairs. Thin but muscular calves. A red, long-sleeve T-shirt with fancy lettering that said *Val Surf*. The body was scrunched where it had fallen. I saw a clunky metallic watch around one wrist. Short blond curls matted with dried black blood. Skin soft, hairs barely sprouting on his chin. Maybe seventeen.

I wrote it down. Knightsbridge hitched the radio back onto his belt and wiped his mouth with the sleeve of his shirt. Despite the cool air, sweat beaded his temples.

"Whoo," Knightsbridge said, flapping his arms. "Seen plenty of dead animals in my day. Do the autopsy, then head off for lunch. Never blink an eye. But this . . ." His hand twitched near his throat and he hunched his shoulders. I thought he might be getting ready to heave again. He took two shallow breaths, straightened. "Never seen a dead person before. Not used to it."

"You don't *get* used to it," I said, unable to resist the impulse to look around and make sure there was nobody crouched behind a rock or bush, pointing a gun at us. Some bozo out hunting human prey. In the Los Angeles hills, you had more to fear from two-legged predators than those on four.

"Homicide," Knightsbridge said.

I looked at the body on the ground. "How can you rule out suicide?"

"You see a gun?"

I looked around. Unless the kid had fallen on it, Knightsbridge was right.

The Fish and Game man again put his bandanna to his mouth and hiked closer. The flies lifted, hovered. He unzipped the boy's fanny pack and bent over it.

"Um, I don't think you're supposed to do that."

But I held my pencil ready just in case.

Do it.

"Oh." A disappointed pause. "I guess you're right." He straightened, backed away. "I just thought I'd call in his ID if I found any."

I shrugged. "Won't do him much good now."

"Somewhere he's got family. Parents. They'll be in shock."

"Who do you think he is?" I said.

Knightsbridge hiked to the edge of the hillside and looked down.

"We're about to find out," he said. "Here they come."

A woman and three men picked their way carefully along the trail. They hauled a stretcher, metal boxes, cameras and lights, enough to shoot a film. Two of them were armed. One wore a red Santa hat.

I walked over to Knightsbridge and we stood at attention. The crew fanned around the perimeter, marking off quadrants, putting up yellow tape, squatting low to the ground.

"Bullet casing over there," I said, indicating the chapparal, but Santa's helper was already bagging it. With its jaunty pom-pom, the man's hat seemed disrespectful, but I guess when you work around death all day, it's important to keep your spirits up.

"Hope we didn't mess up the scene too much," Knightsbridge called out.

An LAPD honcho walked up, squinting against the winter glare. I got the feeling he was sizing us up.

"Touch anything?" he said.

"Not me," I said.

Knightsbridge introduced us, told the cop how we had come across the body.

The cop turned to me, wrinkling his nose as though he

had just smelled something worse than the body. "Media, huh? Go give your statement to Jones over there," he said, pointing to a uniformed officer. "Then you'll have to leave."

I told Knightsbridge we could continue the tour another day and he bobbed his shaggy head in agreement.

For the next ten minutes, I answered questions about how we came across the body. The policeman said forensics would call if they needed an imprint of my hiking-boot sole and that I was now free to go. He went off to get a statement from Knightsbridge and I stood and watched the crime techs, hoping to pick up a useful tidbit for my story. They wore rubber gloves as they inventoried, carrying things back to a stainless-steel table they had set up to tag and bag evidence.

"What's the best way down?" I asked a uniformed woman.

Without lifting her head from the red lanyard key chain she was examining, she hooked a thumb back down the trail.

I wondered how she'd look with it tied around her neck in a big Christmas bow. Real tight.

I threw up my hands. "Look, I just don't want to disturb any evidence on the hike back."

One of the cops brought over the fanny pack that Knightsbridge had started to open. With gloved hands, he placed it on the metal table. Another tech reached into the pack and pulled out a purple-and-gray Velcro wallet with a lightning bolt across the front. Inside were four twenty-dollar bills and three ones.

"They weren't after money," I said, hoping to start a conversation.

But the woman was pulling out a California driver's

license. It showed a blond-haired boy with straight white teeth, freckles, and blue eyes smiling into the camera.

The woman put the ID on the stainless-steel table and filled out a form on her clipboard. I leaned in for a better look.

Dennis Lukin, it read, with an address in Studio City. I jotted it down and memorized it too, just in case. I looked some more. He did not have to wear corrective lenses. He did not have a class-A license that would allow him to drive an eighteen-wheeler. He was seventeen.

"Hey," the top cop said, walking over. "I thought I told you to get out of here."

"I was just asking for directions back down the trail."

He looked from the driver's license to me, then back again. He extended his hand.

"Give it," he said.

"What?"

"Whatever notes you just took."

I thought about saying no, then realized it didn't matter. Wordlessly, I tore the page out of my notebook and handed it over.

He glanced at my scribbles, snorted, then crumpled the paper and shoved it into his pants pocket.

I turned to go.

"If I see you at that house before we break the news, so help me God, I'll make sure you'll spend the rest of your career writing calendar listings."

"Don't worry," I said. "I'll be parked across the street until you leave."

I stopped to say good-bye to Knightsbridge so I could take one more look at the body, now framed and set off by yellow police tape.

I didn't know what I was searching for—needle marks or tattoos, piercings, brown roots to the blond hair, a school ring, hickies. Anything that would give me an inkling of who Dennis Lukin was. What teen tribe he pledged allegiance to. He wore a necklace made of tiny white shells. Puka. Add in the tan, the sun-bleached hair, and the shirt advertising a famous surfboard shop in the Valley and there was little doubt: Dennis Lukin was a surfer. My eye went to the oversize watch again. Probably one of those waterproof jobs for when he sat bobbing in the swells, waiting for that perfect wall of water. But what was that symbol on the face? I bent over the yellow plastic tape to get a better view and recognized the hammer and sickle. How odd. It was a Soviet army watch. I hadn't seen one in years, not since the USSR collapsed and flea markets around the world had been flooded with these clunky souvenirs of a dead empire. I frowned. Examined the boy again. Something didn't track. The surfer clothes. The deep tan and puka shells. This kid, who'd barely been born when the Soviet Union fell apart.

"Get away from that crime scene or I'll have you arrested," the head cop yelled, breaking my reverie. I straightened.

"Sorry," I said absently, filing this detail away for later. Maybe the kid had just come back from Russia on a student exchange. Maybe he collected timepieces. Maybe someone had traded it to him in exchange for weed.

I hiked down, glad I wouldn't have to break the news to Dennis Lukin's family myself. It was the part I hated most about newspapering. Let the cops be the bad-news messenger. My job was jackal.

Wheeling the car out of Griffith Park and onto the 101 Freeway, I called the City Desk.

"Feliz Navidad," sang José Feliciano's exuberant voice on the radio, wishing us a Merry Christmas from the bottom of his heart.

I turned it down.

"We found a body on the trail," I said when Assistant City Editor Jon Trabuco came on.

I heard the intake of breath, followed by the rapid click of keys.

"Holy shit, this is front page all the way. There hasn't been a mountain lion killing in L.A. County for years," my new editor said with mounting excitement. "Start dictating."

"It wasn't a cat."

"Then what the hell was it?"

"Unless mountain lions have learned how to use guns." I filled him in.

"Jeez, Eve. You had me all excited there for a minute. I was already writing the damn headline. Now it's just another dead body."

"Isn't a dead body still news in this town?"

"Yeah, but if the perp was a cat, I could have gotten you forty-five inches and a sidebar. Wildlife killings are huge. It upsets the natural order."

"So do dead teenagers. I'm on my way to talk to the family now," I said. "Be right behind the cops."

Trabuco grunted in approval. "By the way, some guy called and left an urgent message for you. He had an accent."

"This is L.A., Jon. They all have accents."

"He said he was related to you."

I winced, glad Trabuco couldn't see my face. I didn't have much family, and it was a sore point.

"He wishes," I said.

"Want the number?"

"Are you kidding?" I said. "I'm on deadline."

CHAPTER 2

Dennis Lukin lived on a narrow hill street in Studio City. It was south of Ventura Boulevard, where the money resides. From the road the house was unassuming—just another one-story contemporary flush to the curb. But I knew better. Beyond the front door I'd find a glass tree house, cantilevered over the hillside and supported by steel rails sunk into bedrock. Sliding doors would open onto a wooden deck perfect for barbecuing and sunset cocktails, the fey, caressing breezes of the San Fernando Valley fluttering chiffon scarves. Below there'd be another floor, bedrooms, perhaps, with views and more greenery.

The cops were already there so I drove past, gaping at the house across the street, where a glittering winter wonderland was in full swing. Fake snow covered the ground. Mechanical elves banged in toy workshops while an animatronic Santa Claus loaded the sleigh. From the roof, a speaker blared Muzak carols. All year long, the Valley's set designers and special effects wizards toiled away in the back lots of Hollywood. Christmas was when they staged *their* production, limited only by imagination and pocketbooks. Taking in the spectacle, I felt a twinge of sympathy for the Lukin family. While taste was certainly in the ear of the beholder, I knew I'd go batshit if I had to listen to "God Bless Ye Merry Gentlemen" on a twenty-four-hour loop after learning about my son's murder.

Nosing my car past the Lukin house, I continued up the hill. I had time to kill while the cops broke the news to the family. I took in the scenic views, the lovely Spanish houses mixed with new-money contemporary, a few unfortunate boxes that some ego-crazed architect had convinced a client would look daring and postindustrial. These usually featured black and white lights instead of the candy colors. One had eerie cobalt blue lights and looked like an alien landing pad. No winter wonderland for them.

Forty-five minutes later, I drove back down. Pulling onto a dirt shoulder below the house, I parked and hiked up.

The cops were just getting into their black-and-white.

"How is it in there?" I inclined my head.

"To save us all from Satan's power when we had gone astray . . ." sang the virtual choir across the street.

"They're taking it pretty bad." The cop stared, trying to shame me into something. I looked away. Fingered my notepad. Felt a drop hit my cheek.

I wiped it off, felt another, then five more. Looked up. The clouds were massing black overhead. It looked like a nasty storm. Damn, I thought. It's gonna wreak havoc on that crime scene.

"Talk to both parents?" I asked the cop.

"Yeah."

He sized me up like he was a big cat and I was a rabbit, about to meet my rabbit maker. But the important thing was, he was talking.

"They got any other kids?"

"Boy. Couple of years older."

"Could this be a drug thing? A gang thing? White gang, maybe?"

There were a couple of them in L.A. All that Aryan nonsense.

"Always a possibility," the cop said. "But the kid, his family, they seem squeaky clean."

"Quote you?" I leaned in to catch a name.

"No attribution," he said. "They don't like us talking to the press. You have to go through Media Relations." He shook his head. "Can I ask you something?"

"Yeah." Wary now.

"How can you live with yourself?"

I looked at him. He must be fairly new on the job. To wear it on his sleeve like that. The outrage. I wanted to reassure him that it would dull after a few years. He'd get over it. We all did.

"How can you live with *your*self?" I asked.

"It's different with us," the cop said. "We find out who did it, bring 'em to justice."

I broke a thin smile. "Sometimes we do too."

CHAPTER 3

I knocked. From beyond the door, I heard high keening. Then a murmur of words meant to comfort and soothe, but strung together in an unfamiliar cadence— long vowels and jumbled consonants. Then a staccato intake of breath, like babies get when they've cried too long. A nose being blown. The door opened.

"Yes?"

A man stood there, a nimbus of wispy white hair around a bald skull. I caught the accented *y* of the non-native English speaker, soft and mellifluous.

He wore a wool cardigan over a wrinkled Oxford shirt. He looked to be in his seventies, but his face was unlined. His eyes swam with grief, though another emotion was already flooding into them as he beheld me. From inside, I heard gentle sobbing now. And a Bach sonata, turned low. In the thin strip of open door, I saw floor-to-ceiling bookcases. A wall of family photos. The corner of an oil painting in a carved Baroque frame.

"Bozhe moi," the man said, the strange yet familiar words erupting from deep inside his chest. I focused on him once more. In the seconds I had looked away, the man's face had changed. The grief had given way to confusion. His cheeks flushed with color.

"Excuse me?" I said.

He gripped the door harder, passed a hand across his forehead.

"For a moment, there . . . I'm sorry, what did you say your name was?"

"Diamond. Eve Diamond. I'm a . . ."

"Yes," he said. "Forgive me. What a coincidence."

I paused, torn between asking what he meant and getting to the point of my visit. There had been a momentary shock of recognition in his face, naked fear and hope.

"What's a coincidence?" I finally said.

"It's nothing."

"We've met somewhere?" I probed.

"I don't think so." He waved his hand dismissively. Although he tried to hide it, he kept stealing glances at me.

"I'm . . ." I bit my tongue. "I'm sorry to disturb you at this difficult time. Are you Mr. Lukin?"

He lifted his chin. "I am he," he said, his Adam's apple bobbing in agreement. Against the black door frame, his hands were almost a translucent white, blue veins in high relief against the parchment skin. "They said a detective would come, but I didn't expect one so soon. Or one so young and . . ." He swallowed, turned away. "Please forgive me. . . ."

"No," I said. "It's me who is sorry. Mr. Lukin, I'm not a detective, I'm a reporter for the *Los Angeles Times*."

"Ah. My regrets then, Miss Diamond."

I was impressed with his civility, the struggle to keep his voice even and polite.

"My wife and I, we cannot talk to anyone right now. We need this time alone. You will respect our privacy, yes?"

He fixed me with those pale blue eyes. Definitely not American, I thought. The cadence of his words, the curious phrasing. The shape of his skull, the high forehead.

The rumpled, professorial look. Well-bred, educated, intelligentsia, cultured. Somewhere east of the Danube. My heart gave a little flutter. My father might have looked like this, had he lived. They were Russian, I guessed. That would explain the watch. Or maybe not. Most Russian émigrés had nothing but scorn for the Soviet system. So why would their son strap on a reminder of the hated hammer and sickle?

We stood there. I wondered which line would get me past the door but felt conflicted about manipulating him, now that there was a personal connection. I had touched something deep in him, even if it was only a case of mistaken identity.

"Of course, Mr. Lukin," I said. "I hope we can talk soon, though. I'm writing about your son for tomorrow's paper." I took a breath, plunged forward. "Did the police tell you I was one of the two people who found, uh, him?"

I had almost said "the body." But that would not do at all.

Lukin closed his eyes and his body swayed. A moment passed. When his eyes opened, they wavered unsteadily.

"They did not."

He turned and peered into his house, head and shoulders pivoting in the way of old men with stiff necks. I did a little step-glide with him and saw him examining the oil painting. I could see the whole thing now. Two young princes, dressed in ermine and crimson, stared out at me. Their skin was rosy; their golden hair caught and refracted the light. Thick metal crosses inlaid with jewels hung from their necks. One was on the cusp of adolescence, dangling between worlds. The other still a boy, mischievous and dimpled, his limbs steeled into repose, but ready to erupt again in kinetic energy the moment he was dismissed. I almost heard his laughter echoing down the hall as he scampered away, gleeful to be released.

The rich hues of the oil on canvas, the carved wood frame, the gathering shadows of a winter afternoon, all conspired to give the portrait a hushed and timeless air.

"My sons," croaked Lukin. "Denny is the younger one."

"Extraordinary," I said. "They look like children of a long-ago czar."

Lukin turned back, examining me with renewed interest.

"The artist is well known in Russia. As were his father and grandfather, all the way back to Catherine the Great. The lineage is unbroken. But it's all dust now. Ach. Dust and shadows."

His brow furrowed. I waited. My heart went out to this man who had just lost a child. He looked at his watch, muttered under his breath. And then he seemed to decide something.

"Won't you please come in, Ms. Diamond?"

CHAPTER 4

I stepped down into a sunken living room, wondering when—or if—I would meet Mrs. Lukin. The smell of buckwheat hit me, a warm, nourishing aroma. And meat frying with onions and spices. Pots bubbling on the stove. Because children come home hungry after a long day at school.

Lukin closed the door after me, bade me sit on a black leather couch. His shoulders hunched like a sad crow's as he walked with great effort to a chair and sat down. To avoid staring, I looked out the plate-glass windows. The view was stunning: hills stretching out to square grids, the bowl of the San Fernando Valley basin, more hills rising purple in the distance where Chatsworth became Simi Valley. The room shining with the ghostly winter light of late afternoon. This was the house of artists and doting parents. Sports trophies sat atop a grand piano. The furniture was a quirky mix of antiques and sleek modern, laid with heavy Turkish carpets. Around the extraordinary oil portrait of Lukin's sons was a series of photos. Long-haired blond boys on snowboards, sliding down pine-forest mountains. Lithe, tanned, sand-powdered bodies posed next to long boards, atop skateboards, in fluorescent swim trunks, their rib cages showing, their hair bleached white by the sun, holding up sea tortoises that craned long leathery necks and glared in annoyance. The spoils of a Southern California childhood. But my eye was drawn time and again to the Old World, almost regal quality of the oil portrait. The duality depicted here. Surfer boys with stained glass, Eminem and Pushkin. Duels at sunrise. Movies at the Galleria. Vassals and hounds.

Lukin sat in an upholstered chair next to me, crossed his legs in their baggy khakis, and clasped his long, pale hands.

"Tell me about my son."

Even though I had expected it, his bluntness startled me. This was the coin I had plunked down to gain entrance. But how could I tell him about the cloud of flies, the smell, the stained earth.

"What did the police say?" I parried.

His head bent like that of a babushka at prayer. He rubbed the inside of one white wrist until it chafed pink and streaky, as though he might dig the pain out of his flesh.

"They said he was found on the trail. That he had been shot in the head. They said . . ." His voice lowered. "They said . . . his body . . . it was eaten by . . ." He swallowed. The wattles below his chin quivered. "Oh God, forgive me . . . they said my boy, my child, that his body was eaten by animals."

Shock rippled through me. I hadn't noticed that. But then, I hadn't inspected him the way the forensics people had. I remembered the mountain lion's deep gashes in the oak tree and shuddered.

"It's like a grim fairy tale my grandmother used to tell me," he said in a hoarse whisper. "About the starving wolves in the winter forest, loping after the sled. And the family inside wrapped in fur cloaks, the snow growing thicker, the horses more weary. The wolves closer now, leaping and snarling. The loss of hope. And then finally, how they lightened the load. By one child. So that the wolves, able to feed, would fall back. That the rest might live."

Lukin hugged his elbows, and his eyes rolled inward to a landscape only he could see. In this hidden place, he now carried on a conversation, trying to soothe and convince an unseen person. "There, there. That was just an old tale to scare naughty children. Not something that really happened. Even in Russia. And certainly not in America."

His voice rose. "That's why we came here. To escape the wolves."

Slowly, his eyes focused. When he spoke again, it was in dull, mechanical tones.

"What else can you tell me?"

"I saw a bullet casing," I said, staring at my shoes. No, I would not tell him about the flies. There were things that parents of murdered children didn't need to know. I thought of the monstrousness of it, how murderers leave behind a vortex of suffering that ripples through the generations, tearing families apart. The Lukins had another son. I did the math. If Denny was seventeen, the brother must be about nineteen. Away at college, perhaps? Or comforting his mother in the next room? Or already blotting out the pain with drugs and alcohol and destruction? Would the legacy of violent death beget its own poisonous half-life in this family?

"And what caliber was it?" Lukin asked.

Startled, I looked up. "Sorry. I don't know much about guns."

He grew impatient. "But was it big, small? What color? The thickness. What do you remember?"

"I suppose you can get that from the police report," I said, struggling to remember. "It shone like brass. It was small, slender, like this." I put my thumb and forefinger about an inch apart.

"Were there any markings on his body? A note? Anything unusual?"

His voice grew more urgent. He was interviewing me.

"Not that I noticed. Nothing at all."

His body relaxed into the chair, though the grief did not leave his face.

"Is there anything else you can tell me?" he asked.

"He was wearing a Val Surf T-shirt and shorts. A puka-shell necklace. He had a fanny pack, like he was on a hike."

"A hike," Lukin said morosely.

"There was one thing."

"Yes?" he said.

"Was your son a surfer?"

"Yes." Annoyed now. "What does that have to do with anything?"

"Well, it just struck me," I said, "because he was wearing a USSR army watch. And I would have pegged him as a sporty-, high-tech-, waterproof-watch kind of guy. Salt water's hell on metal."

Lukin stood up. He walked to the chimney mantel. He raised a hand to a framed photo of his boys, ran his fingers along the glass. I thought I saw them tremble. There was a long silence.

His back still to me, he cleared his throat but said nothing.

The air in the room grew thick with waiting.

"Was it yours?" I finally said. "From your time in the Red Army? I mean, it was compulsory back then, wasn't it?"

Finally, he spoke.

"Yes. Eh, no. I mean, it wasn't mine. I despise all

things from the regime, I'd hardly keep it around as a memento."

"Hmm. That's odd, then."

There was a silence. Then Lukin's words rushed in to fill it. "But you're very shrewd, Ms. Diamond. It *was* a matter of contention between us. Denny, ah, got that watch at a swap meet several weeks ago. It was an act of defiance, a youthful rebellion. He knew I'd recoil at such a thing. What it stood for. Therein lay the attraction."

Lukin grasped the mantel and a shudder went through him. When he turned back, his face was creased into a horrible grimace.

"Imagine, the old man moves heaven and earth to escape communism, and then years later, safe in America, his son decides to thumb his nose at Papa with such a monstrosity. I tried not to show my distaste. With any luck, he'd have tired of it soon."

"Ah," I said, not at all satisfied. "Then please forgive me, I'm sorry to dredge up such painful memories."

I paused for what I hoped was a decent interval.

"When's the last time you saw him, uh, uh . . ." I stuttered, biting back the word, "alive?"

"Saturday night," Lukin said promptly. "He and a friend were going surfing early Sunday. He called when they got back. Asked if he could stay for a barbecue, spend the night, and go right to school Monday. Er, today. I gave my permission. I thought it was him when the police came. I wondered why he was knocking."

"Does your son like to hike, Mr. Lukin? Any idea how he ended up in Griffith Park yesterday?"

"Denny loves the outdoors. He walked neighborhoods for the Sierra Club. He cleaned up litter on the beaches. He brought home stray cats."

He gestured to two tortoiseshell bundles curled on a chair under a window.

"He was a gentle soul. He couldn't tolerate war, fighting. His moral compass was strong. He fought for the underdog."

Mr. Lukin put his head in his hands and rocked back and forth. "My son, my son," he said.

I waited. Then I asked, "What was this friend's name? What school did they go to?"

"Denny and Max are best friends. You don't think . . . ? I would vouch for him. We are close with the parents. Max's father and I, we have the white birches, the food lines, the commissars in common. . . ." He made a dismissive gesture with his hand: I could never understand.

"You mean you're both from Russia?"

"Yes. Though he's quite a bit younger than me. He didn't live through the worst of it."

Max, I thought. I've got to talk to him and his parents both. And for that I needed . . .

"What's the family's last name?" I asked.

"I gave it to the police."

"It would help if you told me, too."

I was on the scent now, like a truffle-hunting pig. But if I rooted too hard, I'd trample the delicate treasure. With that in mind, I drifted over to a side table, examined the photos. Saw one of the boys posed with their parents, proud and beaming. Noticed something.

"They're so handsome, and yet there's something ethereal, almost otherworldly about them. Maybe it comes from having older parents. You have more wisdom to pass on. By Russian standards, you started late."

A deep freeze filled the room that an icebreaker couldn't cut through.

I turned. Lukin was clutching his throat, and seemed to have gone even more pale.

"I had . . . there was . . ."

What a dope I was. They had probably tried for years. Or gone through the agony of fertility treatments. Or even adopted, for all I knew. And with my insensitive comment, I had . . .

"I'm sorry," I said. "That was crass of me."

Lukin struggled to speak, swallowed, then said, "You asked about Max, Ms. Diamond. And where my son went to school. I think you should get all this from the police." His voice trailed off as he followed my gaze to a gold trophy whose inscribed letters read: *Academic Decathlon Super Quiz. Third Place, Denny Lukin, North Hollywood High School*.

"All right," I said, turning away. Both of us knowing I now had a partial answer. North Hollywood High. The kids at school would tell me the rest.

Lukin's lower lip trembled, and he put a hand to his chin. I thought about his persistent questions in that hard, odd voice, and the pinprick of anxiety that I had shoved aside came roaring back.

"Did your son have any enemies, Mr. Lukin? What about you, your family?"

"Sasha," came a voice from the other room. It was a woman's voice, raw and wet. She had the same accent as Sasha Lukin. We heard the click-clack of heels moving with determination on hardwood floors. "Who's there? Who are you talking to, Sasha? Did the police come back?"

Then the owner of the voice appeared and I recognized Mrs. Lukin from her photo. She was tall and slender and wore a long skirt and a blouse with a ribbon at the neck.

Her wavy brown hair was held back by ivory combs, revealing tiny pearl earrings. Her eyes were swollen. She held a tissue bunched under her nose.

"It's a reporter, Irina. This is Eve Diamond. She found Denny's body."

There was a sudden intake of breath.

"I don't care," the woman said. "What on earth could have possessed you to talk to the press? Have you lost your mind?"

She shoved the tissue into the sleeve of her blouse and advanced toward me.

"How dare you? At a time like this. Get out."

Grabbing my arm, she marched me to the door over the gentle remonstrations of her husband. Her fingers were surprisingly strong.

Still in her grip, I turned and addressed her husband.

"Mr. Lukin?" I said. "You were going to tell me Max's last name?"

"Oh no, you don't," said his wife, jerking my arm with each word for emphasis. "Sasha, don't you open your mouth."

She looked at a grandfather clock solemnly ticking the time.

"We must go identify the body," she told me icily. "The coroner is waiting. Out."

Irina Lukin opened the door and released me. Her hand was on my back now, the better to push me out. What she saw waiting outside made her curse sharply in Russian.

CHAPTER 5

Two news vans were parked on the meager front lawn and a cameraman was clambering out as the TV antenna unfurled into the sky. The rain was coming down in a steady drizzle now. I wondered if anyone in TV news had ever gotten electrocuted. When the cameraman saw us standing in the open door, he hoisted the camera onto his shoulder, pointed it at us, and began filming.

"Sasha," Irina wailed behind me. "There's more of them. Oh my God, what a nightmare."

I felt a shove, then the door slammed behind me.

I stumbled, caught my balance, and tried to walk gracefully to the curb, self-conscious as the camera trailed me, the beefy, tattooed camera guy following.

"Mind if we do a little interview?" he asked.

"Wait, Billy," came a female voice from inside the van. "I'm coming."

A woman in a form-hugging red suit emerged from the passenger seat, carrying a microphone. She had the perfectly coiffed hair and pancake makeup of a TV news personality. With a ripple of irritation I recognized Samantha Moore, a local anchor and supersize airhead.

"Miss, miss?" she called, tripping toward me in ridiculous red heels, a flunky running alongside her with a red umbrella. "Do you live here? Are you a relative? Is it true that Denny Lukin was killed by a gunshot wound and his body eaten by animals as he lay on the trail overnight?"

Samantha Moore licked her collagen-stung lips and thrust the microphone into my face.

Somewhere behind me, a garage door whirred open. Samantha Moore craned her neck, panicked that she might miss something. I turned and watched a late-model Buick back out, only to stop as another news van rolled up, blocking the driveway and the Buick's escape route.

Trapped inside, the Lukins held magazines up to the car windows to shield their faces.

"Get them, Billy," Samantha said but Billy was already lumbering into position.

"Don't waste your film," I said. "They're just friends of the family. I'm Denny Lukin's older sister. My parents are already at the coroner's."

I was winding up now. "Just home from grad school for the holidays," I said. "Sure, I'll talk to you."

Behind me, the car revved, fishtailed to avoid the TV van, and screeched onto the grass, narrowly missing us.

"Let them go, Billy," Samantha muttered, loud enough for her cameraman to hear, but low enough to keep the rest of the media pack from baying over. "I need you over here, double-time."

The Buick jumped the curb, hitting the street with a loud scrape of metal on concrete. Then it was gone.

Samantha gripped her mike more tightly with one hand. With the other, she ran her fingers over her snow white teeth to make sure there was no lipstick dimming the 250-watt glow.

Then she spoke into the camera. "We're here in front of the Lukin home, talking to Dennis Lukin's sister," she said. Her face grew solemn, her voice soft with concern yet steeled to hear the worst.

"Tell us, Miss Lukin, did your brother have enemies?

Can you think of anyone who would want to do this to a young boy in the prime of life?"

The camera pivoted from Samantha to me.

"Well, actually," I began. Samantha nodded, giving me a look of intense empathy. I flashed her my most telegenic smile and said, "Denny doesn't have an older sister. I'm a newspaper reporter. But I hope you put me on TV anyway. I'm thinking of changing media, and this could be my big break. Be sure to send me the test reel."

I didn't wait for her reaction as I took off, jogging down the hill.

Once in my car, it took me ten minutes to reach Ventura Boulevard because I kept having to pull over to the shoulder of the narrow street to let more news vans up. The trail is cold, suckers, I thought.

As I drove, I dialed the City Desk, filling Jon Trabuco in on the new details, reconstructing Denny Lukin's last days, how he had gone surfing, then to a barbecue, then told his parents he was spending the night with a friend. Instead, he had gone hiking in Griffith Park. I relayed what Sasha Lukin had said as he fell apart, the gruesome detail that his body had been eaten by animals.

"Who's this friend?" Trabuco asked.

"Max somebody. He was about to tell me when the wife kicked me out."

"Find him," Trabuco said. "Or don't bother coming in tomorrow."

What a hard-ass, I thought.

"I'm working on it," I said.

I headed to North Hollywood High School. School was long out, but there were still students milling around. Thousands of kids attended this large and sprawling campus. What were the odds I'd find any who knew Denny and Max? At Magnolia and Colfax, I parked, walked around, questioning groups of students on campus and at the doughnut shop on the corner, slinking from awning to tree to overhang in efforts to stay dry. Some looked at me as though I were crazy. Others looked bored. Nobody knew anything. I was now completely wet.

"He Latino, man?" one kid with a shaved head asked. "Cuz I know a heavy cholo named Max."

"White boy," I said. "Russian, actually. Surfer."

"Sorry," said the kid, and he turned back to his friends.

Knowing a little about the campus ecology, I asked if the Russian kids hung out in any particular area. Nobody had a clue, but white kids in general were a minority. I walked around for another half hour, canvassing students, but had no luck. Finally I gave up and walked back to my car.

I turned my heater to blast, called the police, and asked for the name of the boy Denny had last been seen with.

"We can't reveal that information," the cop said.

"I know his first name is Max."

"No comment."

Frustrated, I drummed my fingers along the dash.

"Did the Lukin kid have enemies? Gang, drug involvement?"

"We're checking."

"Did he have a record?"

"Negative."

"What about his friend Max?"

"Negative."

I sat there, biting the inside of my cheek.

"Look," I said. "I know they're both from Russian immigrant families. The dad told me."

"That is correct," said the cop, laconic and bored.

"Is it possible there's a Russian Mafia connection?"

"We will be examining every angle."

"I wish you wouldn't be such a chatterbox," I said. "I can't write that fast."

"Don't waste my time, Ms. Diamond. My colleague has already gone through this all with another of your reporters."

"Who?" I said, my competitive hackles rising.

"Dunno," the cop said. "And he's on break so I can't ask. But this reporter was very thorough. They were on the phone a long time. Now, if there's nothing else—"

"Just one more thing. Denny Lukin seemed like a typical Southern California surfer kid. But I noticed he had a Soviet army watch on his wrist."

"They're from Russia, aren't they?"

"But the boy's dad hated the Sovs. That's why they came here."

I didn't want to go into everything Lukin had told me. I wasn't sure how relevant it was, and I didn't quite buy it. Lukin had seemed too agitated, his explanation too long and involved.

"Russian family, Russian watch. Whatever. The detectives get the police report. I'm sure they'll look into it," the cop said.

Uneasy, I signed off and wondered what to do next. People were getting home from work now; it might pay to visit Lukin's neighbors. Letting out the clutch, I put the car in drive and drove back up to the Studio City hills.

The media party was in full swing now, the street crowded with news vans. I parked low on the hill and hiked up, knocking at each house along the way, but either no one was home or they didn't have anything to say to a soggy reporter who balanced a newspaper on her head to ward off the rain.

It was getting dark. Lights were going on. Twinkling Christmas trees stood framed in picture windows. Mechanical deer lit with white fairy lights grazed on front lawns. Here in the L.A. hills, deer were considered more a hooved urban pest than a noble animal. They drank water out of sprinklers, trampled lawns, and breakfasted on the heirloom roses that Angelenos paid a small fortune for. And yet many folks put mechanical deer on their front lawns. I wondered whether the robotized deer confused their flesh-and-blood cousins. But in L.A., artifice always won out over nature, which held too many risks, too many variables. And so the mechanical deer bobbed and grazed, lifting their heads to blink at you.

It was growing colder, a clammy chill settling in. I wished I had brought a warmer jacket. Something with a hood. Or an umbrella. But native Angelenos never check the forecast. Ignorance and a sunny faith in the weather is almost a matter of pride. And since everyone has cars, it's not like we have to brave the elements very often. And when I rushed out willy-nilly this morning to meet Knightsbridge, I had no idea a storm was brewing or that I'd be out this late.

So now I was paying the piper. I talked to sensibly clad joggers and dog walkers. Some knew the Lukins, I could tell, though they claimed not to. Everyone was battening down the mental hatches in the face of yet another Los Angeles media onslaught.

I reached the Lukin house in time to see the reporters buzzing like the cloud of flies I had seen earlier. One chatty radio guy told me excitedly that a young man had just parked and gone inside, refusing to talk to the press.

Like all the others, my heart rose, then sank. It must be the elusive brother. How I wanted to sit down with him.

"He pulled up in this old-guy car," one of the male TV personalities chimed in. "I wouldn't be caught dead in that."

A thought occurred. "What car was it?"

"That Buick over there."

He pointed to a cream-colored car parked under a streetlamp, which was barely needed as the street was lit up bright as day with the TV lights. The same car that the Lukins had driven out of their garage two hours earlier.

"Yeah? Thanks. Oh well, guess I'll call it a night," I said.

I took a leisurely stroll along the media campsite, then made my way back to the Buick. I jotted down the license plate, intending to DMV it tomorrow, for whatever that might get me. I peered inside, looking for anything that might give a clue. But it was clean as a whistle, the rear seat empty, no receipts or anything in the well. Then my eyes went to the rearview mirror. People sometimes hung things up there, like racing dice, a good-luck amulet. But the only thing hanging from this car was a parking permit.

Parking permit?

I leaned against the car, pretending to get a better look at the house. Nobody paid me the slightest attention. I glanced into the front seat again, deciphering the letters on the parking permit. Rathburn International. Quickly, I looked away, stared up at the stars. My lucky stars. Now I had a lead. Someone in the family worked at Rathburn International. Sounded like a defense company. Tomorrow, I'd find out.

CHAPTER 6

At the bottom of the hill, I stopped at the red light, annoyed by the wait to get onto Ventura Boulevard. It was late and I was wet and wanted to get home. A sign in Cyrillic caught my eye. Below it were the English words *Market* and *Deli*. It was still open. As the light changed, instead of turning left, I pulled into the parking lot and killed the engine. I pictured Sasha Lukin, driving up and down his hill each day, seeing this place. A deli with food from his homeland? What were the chances that they knew him?

I walked in.

It was warm and smelled good. A teenage girl was behind the counter, skinning charred eggplants and mashing the flesh. She had pale skin and red cheeks, which were only emphasized by the white kerchief holding back her hair. When I asked about Sasha and Denny Lukin, she wiped her hands on a towel, said, "One moment, please," and disappeared into the back. A moment later, she returned with a bigger, jollier, older version of herself. Then she went back to her task, eyes downcast, though she moved with a deliberation that told me she was listening.

The older woman clasped her hands.

"Yes, please," she said.

I repeated my question.

"*Da*," she said, nodding enthusiastically. "Every week

he is here. He not buy much. Just for him and wife. He say children are becoming too American, only want tacos and pizza. They lose tastes of home."

"Russian, is he?"

She posed the question to her daughter. They argued for a moment.

"My daughter says yes. But I not sure," she said. She ticked off her fingers. "He buy Hungarian salami, Bulgarian feta, Armenian mouhamara, Russian piroshki. Never talk about old country. A lot of them like that. They either talk all time or don't say nothing. So long they come back, we not care." She winked, large and friendly.

A picture was emerging that was completely in line with the little I had seen today. A modest man, not given to grand gestures. Who kept to himself, bumbling and absentminded maybe. Quiet. Not gregarious like this lady. Still missing his homeland, but young enough when he got here to fit in, to learn idiomatic English with barely an accent.

"Where are you from?" I asked.

"Tbilisi," she said proudly. "But I am Russian. Though maybe there was Georgian grandfather hiding in the woodpile." Her eyes twinkled.

She saw me looking at her daughter, who was savagely mashing the eggplant.

"You would like try?" she said.

"Nah, that's okay." I swallowed my saliva.

"Moment," she said. She slid open the door of the refrigerated glass display case, pulled out a large bowl filled with a reddish-brown dip, and scooped generous spoonfuls onto a plate. Then she added a grape leaf, a knish, and a stuffed cabbage roll.

She handed it to me with a plastic fork.

"You like Russian food?"

"Yes," I said, my mouth watering.

"Sit down," she ordered imperiously.

She watched me eat, then busied herself doing things behind the counter. More people came in and ordered food to go. She served them, gossiping gaily in Russian, English, and another tongue I didn't recognize.

"Why you ask so many questions?" she said, plopping to rest beside me once the crowd thinned. "You KGB?" She laughed heartily at her own joke. I laughed too.

"Not even CIA," I said. "I'm a journalist."

"Something happen to him?" She got serious. Looked worried.

I swallowed the last bite, wiped my mouth, and pushed away my plate.

"No. But, unfortunately, something's happened to his son. He was found murdered today in Griffith Park."

The woman's hand rose, clasped over her mouth in horror.

"Bozhe moi."

"Those words. What do they mean?"

"It mean 'my God.' Which boy was killed?"

"The younger one. Denny. Did you know him? Did he ever come in here?"

Across the counter, the young woman had stopped mashing. Her mouth open in an O, she stood, fork poised midmash.

I turned in my chair to face her. "Did *you* know him?"

"No," she said. "I cut myself." She put her forefinger in her mouth and sucked loudly. "Oh, it stings. Please excuse me."

With that, she ran into the back. I stared at the swinging door, alarm bells going off. The daughter knew something.

"Crazy girl," the mother said. "Too many hormones."

"Was she friends with him? Girlfriend, maybe?"

"Not possible," the woman said stoutly. "She here at six-thirty each morning, making food before go to school. Come straight back after. Work more, then go home and do homework, go to bed. Too busy for boys."

But I wondered. I knew about teenagers, the secret lives they led, the ones the parents never knew about. My radar was out. I determined to come back here. But first . . .

"Where does your daughter go to school?"

"North Hollywood High," the mother said. "She is in magnet program. Smart girl. I tell her she study hard, she not have to work making food all life like me. I am old. But her life just beginning."

"So did you know the Lukin boy who was killed?" I persisted. This chatty grocer's wife must be a fount of gossip and knowledge about everything that went on in this tight-knit little community.

She waved an arm dismissively.

"Once or twice, he bring a young man, introduce as son. He not say much. Listening to his iPod."

"So you don't know anything about him, or anyone who would have wanted to kill him?"

She wagged a finger at me. "This is America, not Russia," she said. "Thank God when we immigrate, we leave troubles behind. When I first visit American supermarket, I am crying. Never before see so much food in one place. You want blintz now?" She beamed. "You tell your friends, good place, they come here."

I walked out about twenty dollars poorer, carrying plastic containers filled with food from eleven time zones. I might be striking out on the Denny Lukin front, but I would eat happy.

* * *

My phone rang as I got in the car. I turned on the windshield wipers and heater and answered it.

"Did you find Max?" Trabuco asked.

"No, but I found a girl who knows the deceased."

"It's getting late for deadline, Diamond," came his raspy voice.

"I can't talk to her tonight," I said, feeling my body starting to steam inside my wet clothes. "But we have a date at six-thirty tomorrow morning, though she doesn't yet know it."

"Good," Trabuco said, "because the cops aren't releasing Max's last name. On account of he's a minor. But they say he's a person of interest. There are inconsistencies in his story. We need to find him. Maybe this girl can help us."

No wonder the police had been so closed-mouthed with me.

"It's sad," I said. "This is an immigrant family. They come here, fleeing communism or whatever, thinking that their kids will have a better life in America. And this is how they end up."

"Los Angeles is not America," Trabuco said.

"Then what is it?"

"The seventh level of hell."

"If you really believed that, you'd be working for the *Boise Gazette*."

"I didn't say hell wasn't interesting."

"Well, this murder is plenty hellish. Who'd want to kill a young man on a hike in Griffith Park with no known enemies? Parents are totally freaked."

"You're breaking my heart," he said. "They got another son, don't they?"

"Ah, that's cold."

"No, Diamond, this is cold. You're no longer flying solo, I've given you a partner."

"I can handle it myself," I said, my fingers turning to ice. I did not want help. I had just gotten off a story where I had been roped into working with a new reporter named Felice Morgan whose ambition had nearly gotten us both killed.

"Brandywine just turned in a big take-out on nursing home abuses and he's at loose ends. I've assigned him to help you out. He's already gotten with the cops about this. That's how we know that little friend Max is a person of interest. There are too many leads for one person to follow."

"Of all people," I spluttered. So that was who the cops had been talking to! Joshua Brandywine was a second-generation journalistic aristocrat who had grown up in world capitals on five continents because his father was a foreign correspondent for *The New York Times*. Josh's keen intelligence and killer instincts were laced with a self-deprecating humor and I considered him a friend and sparring partner. But putting us on the same story was like tossing two tigers into a compound that held only one scrawny goat trembling behind a bush. We'd tear each other apart to get to it first.

"So if you're done mopping up in the field, c'mon back," Trabuco said. "Brandywine's sitting on long thumbtacks over here, waiting for you."

I looked at my watch. It was 6:45 on a cold and rainy night. My boyfriend, Silvio, was in Mexico, scouting promising new bands out of Monterrey. He was a concert promoter, and his immigrant father had built the family music business from a swap-meet stall into a multimillion-dollar empire by catering to the nostalgia of immigrants pining for the sounds of home. Silvio wouldn't be back until tomorrow, so I had no one to hurry home to. Au contraire, I wanted to work myself senseless to blot out my desire for his arms, the words he murmured in my ear, the scent of his body as his skin slid against mine. And now Trabuco was throwing down the gauntlet. You want to be a big-time Metro reporter, you put in the time.

"I would have been there five minutes ago," I lied, stifling a burp, "but there's an accident on the 101."

CHAPTER 7

Half an hour later I was hurrying into the lobby of the *Los Angeles Times*. It never ceased to thrill me that I was one of hundreds of reporters who put out a paper in the great metropolis every day, taking the pulse of this big unruly city that never sleeps. Sure, the tile floor was chipped and the Art Deco chandelier needed polishing, but being here made me feel that I was at the nerve center, the great pulsing heart, of an inky Leviathan. It was a heady feeling, to wend through the city every morning with my notepad and press pass like I owned the place, my nerves quickening with the hunt. Not only did newshounds have to catch the fox, but we had to bring it back, clamped delicately in our jaws, by 5:00 p.m., unbloodied and still alive.

It was what I'd been born to do. Being a journalist made me feel like a swashbuckling pirate, navigating through vast, uncharted oceans, where the tides were constantly shifting, the currents sluggish, then speedy, the waves tossing up new menace, characters, and clues. It was an adrenaline rush more intoxicating than any drug, and one of which I never tired.

Josh was scrolling through the wires when I arrived. I could see his wavy brown hair as I slid into a free cubicle, logged on, and scrolled through eighty e-mails. I had been off last week, vacationing with Silvio in the Yucatán before starting my new posting in Metro, and things had piled up. At least ten of the messages were from the San Gabriel Valley bureau—my old job—saying that a mystery caller had tried to reach me. He had sounded increasingly desperate with each call but wouldn't leave a message. This wasn't so unusual in my profession and I wondered if he was a crackpot. Hopefully I could pawn him off on Felice Morgan, the new hire in San Gabe now that I was on to bigger and more important things downtown. I scrolled through the other messages, but they were standard office stuff, reminders of meetings, updates on projects, and a few invites for drinks. I put those aside for later and read through the daily "budget," which lists the stories running in the next day's paper.

GRIFFITH BODY, read the skedline. "Police are questioning the family and friends of 17-year-old Denny Lukin of Studio City, who was found shot to death Monday on a trail in Griffith Park. Lukin was last seen leaving the home of a high school friend on Sunday afternoon. The friend, who is not being identified because of his age, told police that Lukin was headed home. But Lukin told his parents he planned to spend Sunday night at his friend's house and would see them Monday after school. The Lukins, immigrants from Russia, said their son was a good student, was not a gang member and had no known enemies. 35 inches. DEVELOPING. DIAMOND/BRANDYWINE with eyewitness descriptions by Diamond."

Ah, I thought. A double byline. Already it didn't belong to me anymore. A few more clicks brought me to the story itself. I skimmed over what I had called in, then moved on to Josh's contribution. He had zeroed in on the discrepancy between what Denny Lukin had told his family and what he told his friend.

There were a few quotes from the cops, confirming that

Denny's body had been gnawed at by animals. The caliber of the bullet casing, which should satisfy Lukin's odd curiosity. Confirmation by the cops and the family that Denny Lukin had no known enemies. Josh had even managed to reach a school official after hours at North Hollywood High who confirmed that Denny was a good student, not in a gang. And he had a quote from the coroner, too, weighing in with a preliminary report that gunshot had been the cause of death.

I sensed more than saw Trabuco walking over. My new editor ran six miles every day, could bench-press 210 pounds, and bristled with steely efficiency. He was more like a marine than an editor, but I didn't mind his gruffness. He was plainspoken and decent and I knew he'd have my back in a dark alley. It was the ones who played kissy-face and praised me to the skies that I worried about. You never knew what they really thought.

"Did you bring your birth certificate?" Trabuco asked.

I slapped my forehead. After 9/11, many federal agencies had tightened access and started demanding new government-issued press passes. The *Times* was applying for these en masse and tomorrow was the deadline to turn in the forms. I knew my birth certificate was buried in a box of my parents' papers, sitting on a high shelf in my closet. But I hadn't needed it in years. Nor was I eager to excavate the past.

"I swear, it's sitting on my desk at home," I lied. "I'll have it for you tomorrow."

His eyes narrowed. "You're pathological, Diamond. Why do you always leave things to the last minute?"

I grinned. "Because I'm a reporter. I don't feel alive unless I'm pushing drop-dead deadline."

Trabuco crossed his arms over his chest and inclined his neatly trimmed beard at the clock.

"Speaking of which, everything read okay on that story?"

"Yeah," I said. "But there isn't anything about the Max kid being a person of interest. Did the cops say anything off the record?"

Trabuco uncrossed his arms and pointed across the City Room to Josh's bobbing brown head.

"Why don't you go ask that metrosexual over there."

I closed the computer file and walked over to Josh.

He saw me, pushed away from his desk, and sent his chair rolling around to face me.

"So?" Josh said. A lazy smile skulked at the edges of his boyish good looks. A snub nose. Smattering of freckles. Thick thatch of chestnut hair. Round glasses. The way he had of speaking in italics, to underline the irony of his words. "*Comrades* in arms, is it?"

"I'm just grateful they let me breathe the same air as you," I said.

The smile widened. A dimple formed on one cheek, giving him an impish look that he'd still have when he was seventy and a grandfather. He knew when he was being mocked.

"Remind me to invite myself along next time you go hiking," Josh said.

I shrugged. "It was a little slow my first day in Metro so I thought I'd toss a body on the trail to liven things up."

He stood up, clasped his hands behind his back, and walked around the desk, inspecting me. Pivoted, came back. A professorial stroll. Negotiating a half-moon of skepticism.

"You wouldn't be the first journo to bend facts to your advantage."

"Aren't we all talked out on that tedious topic," I said, rolling my eyes. "So tell me what's *not* in tomorrow's story."

"Ladies first," Josh parried, eyes gleaming.

"Such a gentleman." I sighed. "Okay. One of the parents may work at Rathburn International. That's in Chatsworth. Sounds Department of Defense-y. I'll check it out. Also, I found a girl who knows Denny, another Russian kid, they went to school together, and I'm gonna hit her up tomorrow morning at six-thirty to get more. But here's the clincher. I think the Lukins are hiding something. The father asked me all sorts of questions, then the mom threw me out. It's not the usual 'won't talk to the press' routine."

"Squeaky-clean junior dealt a little drugs on the side?" Josh asked.

"Did the cops find any evidence of that? Any unexplained luxury purchases?"

"It don't mean a thing if it ain't got that bling? No."

"What about this friend Max?" I asked.

"Cops are playing mum."

"Trabuco says he's on their short list?"

"Max was the last person to see Denny alive. Told the cops that Denny got a call on his cell and headed out."

"Ah, that wasn't in the story, either. They ask you to hold off for now?"

"Yeah."

"It'll be easy enough to trace the call."

I saw Josh's look of pity, and thought fast. "Unless it came in from a pay phone," I added.

The pity turned to respect. "Right. Do you really think

the murderer would be so stupid as to lure Denny to his death over a traceable phone?"

"Probably not. But what makes you so sure he even got a call, smarty-pants? What if the Max kid is lying? Did they find a phone on Lukin's body?"

"No," Josh said after a pause. "And there *were* inconsistencies in his story."

"So they think Max did it?"

"For now he's just a person of interest. But the kid better hope he's got thirty witnesses to swear he was snoring in Calculus II study group while his buddy was getting offed."

"So how you finessing that for tomorrow's story?"

"Just say they were late into the night questioning Denny's schoolmate. And that police wouldn't release the name, blah blah blah, because he was a minor, but were probing what they called 'inconsistencies' in his story." He shrugged.

"That sure makes it sound like he did it."

"I don't think so. But the public can judge for itself."

"We've got to get his name. This girl tomorrow morning might know," I said, telling him about the deli.

Josh pulled out a cartridge pen and wrote *6:30 a.m.* on a legal pad. I didn't like the looks of that. Or what came next. "Pick you up at five forty-five, then. You still over there on Cove?"

"Um, I was kind of thinking I'd handle this alone. Don't want to scare her off."

Josh preened. "Teenaged girls love me," he said. "It's that older man, charismatic-writer vibe I give off."

"No, it's your great humility," I said, walking back to my desk. It was impossible to skewer him. He did it first, and better than anyone else possibly could.

Josh trailed behind me like a bloodhound. He crossed his arms and leaned against my desk. Just then, the computer beeped with incoming mail.

"Hold on a sec," I said, feeling a tingle shoot through me. I hoped it was Silvio. I was counting the hours until he got home.

My lover's words filled the screen.

Do you miss me, querida? I was sitting in a meeting yesterday and found myself unable to concentrate. All I could think of was that silk thing you wore to bed the night before you left, how the red set off your creamy skin. How hard your nipples felt through the silk. So sorry it ripped but I'll buy you a new one, that will be fun watching you try it on. I'm insatiable for you.

I flushed warmly, felt a pulse start up between my legs, and hit the screen-saver button, but not before I heard Josh's breath catch.

"It's just Silvio," I said with a sangfroid I didn't feel. "He's out of town."

"Red silk, eh," Josh said.

"You shouldn't have read it."

"You shouldn't have opened it while I was standing here."

"I was kind of anxious to know when he's coming back."

"Do you guys have, like, computer sex when he's gone?"

He stared into the middle distance, trying to pretend he wasn't totally titillated by what he had just read. It wasn't that I was immune to Josh's considerable charms. And working together under deadline pressure did make for an odd intimacy. But I had a boyfriend, and quaint holdover that I am, I believed in monogamy. But I was finding that throttling back what I felt for Josh just intensified the attraction.

"We even have it when he's *in* town," I said. "Like in the middle of the day at the office." I leaned forward. "And when I'm on deadline? It relaxes me, helps me focus. I just have to be careful I don't put steamy X-rated lines into my copy by mistake. Too many open windows."

"Really?" Josh licked his lips. He was breathing heavy.

"No, fakely. I'm pulling your chain. I can only concentrate on one thing at a time. Besides, you know I like to keep my work and love life separate."

This was a big joke, since I had met Silvio when I wrote a story about his family's business and helped solve his brother's murder.

"Well, if you ever change your mind about that . . ." Josh said huskily.

"You'll be the first to know."

Josh blinked and seemed to be harnessing all his willpower. And then, just like always, our banter was over and it was down to business, which was just as cozy in its own way.

"So how were the *grieving* parents?" he asked. For all reporters who covered crime in Los Angeles, such parents had, tragically, become a stereotype out of central casting.

"Devastated. But it was weird. The dad asked if they found a note or anything on the body. He seemed relieved when I said no. And he grilled me about the caliber of bullets. That's why I think there's something else going on here."

"Did you ask him?"

"That was when his wife kicked me out."

"Nice couple?"

"Wife's okay. I really liked the dad. Very Old World. And gracious, considering the circumstances."

"Think he's Russian Mafia? I've got FBI contacts we could call."

I remembered the steeliness in Sasha Lukin's eyes, but the dignity too. Something deerlike, alert but delicate.

"No," I said. "The Mafia guys I've seen are new Russians. Vulgar operators. This guy, he's got education. Class. House full of books, classical music going. Looks like a professor type."

Josh cocked his head. "The perfect disguise."

"I saw the inside of his house, Josh. He didn't throw up all those bookshelves to impress me."

"So crooks can't be educated?"

"Okay, so I'm showing my biases. But let me ask you, did the cops give you the impression this was a straight-on, all-American surfer kid?"

"Yeah, why?"

"Well, I thought so too, but he was wearing a Soviet army watch. One of those old-fashioned clunky metal things."

"So. You just said he was Russian."

"That's exactly what the cops pointed out. But I'm just wondering if they mentioned it."

Josh scribbled in his notebook. "No, but I'll ask. Though, frankly, it seems like a long shot. Those Soviet watches have been around for years."

"My point exactly. They're not in style anymore."

"Dad probably had it lying around."

"That's what I thought at first, but Lukin says the kid got it at a swap meet several weeks ago. Just to needle the anti-Communist paterfamilias. Think we could track down who sold it to him?"

"Doubtful," said Josh. "Those swap-meet people come and go. Different merchandise each week. The old Soviet Union must have made fifty million of those watches, and half probably found their way here. Good ole capitalism. I even had one."

I sighed. "Okay, Magritte. Sometimes a watch is just a watch."

Josh's intelligent eyes moved over me. "You mean Freud," he said. "Sometimes a cigar is just a cigar."

"Whatever," I said. "Put that in your pipe and smoke it."

CHAPTER 8

This business can make you paranoid. So each night when I come home, I check out the cars parked on my street. Make sure there are no shadows waiting inside. Tonight, the cars were clear. But there was a man sheltering from the rain on my front porch, illuminated by the streetlight. A bike was propped up behind him and he cradled something in his arms. So instead of pulling into my driveway, I jammed the gas and roared past. Curving up my winding street, I pulled into a neighbor's driveway and up the long road to his dark and shuttered house. I killed the engine and lights. Then I waited to see if anyone would follow. The high bluff hid me but offered a vantage onto the street below, lit by the wan light of the moon. Time passed. I smelled garlic and olive oil heating in a skillet. Listened to the hoot of an owl, the steady patter of drops. Strained to hear footsteps. The rattle of a bike chain, adjusting up the incline. But all was still. Slowly, my heart calmed as the adrenaline bled through my veins and dissolved.

A half hour had passed by the dashboard clock when I started the car and rolled back down, eyes alert for Bike Man. He hadn't moved. A wet and tattered knapsack lay beside him. Focusing now, I saw what balanced in his lap. It was a thick book. I didn't think that ninja assassins sat by street-lights, waiting for their victims in plain sight. They probably didn't read books either, literacy presumably being the gateway to a better class of job. But still. I pulled up slowly, keeping the car in drive, ready to speed away at the mere hint of a weapon. But Bike Man lacked the feral twitchiness of a killer. My street is quite narrow and I was close enough to see him. He had pale, shiny skin, a large nose that curved up slightly at the end, and thick, horn-rimmed glasses mended with duct tape. His baggy, acid-washed jeans had not been in fashion since the 1980s, and he wore only a thin shirt under a fake leather jacket whose sheen betrayed its petrochemical provenance. To ward off the rain, he had draped a plastic bag over a baseball cap. As I stared through the rolled-up window, he slammed the book shut with a sharp retort that made me flinch and jumped to his feet. Holding it up, he waved madly. I noticed the lettering was Cyrillic.

"Eve Diamond?" he called with a mixture of hope and excitement.

I rolled the window down two inches, my fear ebbing into annoyance at this obstacle that stood between me and a hot bath, my sheepskin slippers, and a Bill Evans solo cascading off the stereo.

The man waved again, and his hair, which was light brown and razor-cut straight, fell damply into his eyes, giving him the look of a slightly deranged schoolboy.

"She's not here. I'm a neighbor, from the unit below," I said.

"This is your house, yes? Why you are not parking?"

Because of you, buster.

"Who are you?" I asked.

A smile creased his face. He stood his full length and I swear to God that he bowed.

"Greetings, Eve Diamond. Here is Mischa Tsipin, your cousin from Moscow."

I shook my head to rid it of this hallucination.

"I already told you, I'm not Eve. She's away. Shall I tell her you came by?" Closing him down with exaggerated solicitousness.

He wagged a finger at me.

"You Americans are so suspicious," he said happily. "I know it is you, Eve. I saw your picture. I have your, how do you say, *num*-ber," he sang out.

"Your number is wrong. Now please get off our sidewalk before I call the police."

Exuberance dimmed from his eyes. Then a new buoyancy bubbled forth. He seemed to have a childlike faith in his ability to win me over.

"You are reporter for *Los Angeles Times,* yes? You are five foot seven inches, with red-brown hair and hazel eyes, yes? Age of thirty. You drive new Volkswagen Passat with California plates 4XRS 207?" He rose on his tiptoes, cast a significant glance at my car.

I tightened my grip on the steering wheel. A crazed stalker. Great. How did he know all that about me? I clamped down the urge to flee. I should get more information from him first, so the cops could go right to *his* door and nail him when I called. If he even had a door. The shabby clothes, the bulging knapsack, the bike I now saw was slung with plastic bags. It gave off the whiff of homelessness.

"In my country I am study computers," he said. "I very good hacker." He looked down at his fraying black Reeboks with grandiose humility. "Under communism, everything so difficult. Even Moscow phone book is state secret. But with Internet, so easy. I track down American cousin."

Ah, I thought. So this was the mystery man with the accent. And last week's caller in the San Gabriel Valley.

"I . . . E . . . Eve doesn't have any cousins," I said. "Not that she ever told me about," I added quickly.

"I know your, how you call, Social *Securitat* number. Visa card. How much money in your bank account."

A cold sweat began to drip from my armpits, trickling down my sides.

"You're kidding me, right?"

He scrunched up his eyes. "Let me see, balance today $3,782.95. With five checks standing out."

Darn if he wasn't right. I had just deposited my paycheck, and that's exactly what the teller had reported. I groped for the paper record in my purse, suddenly paranoid that it had fallen out and been snatched up by this lunatic who had then hatched an elaborate plot to lie in wait for me in front of my own house. But why?

He shot me a sly look, as though expecting a compliment. Then he smiled broadly.

"Have no fear, Eve Diamond," he said. "I am not using your credit card, which begins with numbers 5642—am I right? I am not buying diamonds or blying-blying, as your rap musicians say. That Puff Daddy, I shake my booty to him on MTV. I would like one of his fine Mac-Daddy suits, but not white one, because that would not be down with my complexion."

"You are insane," I muttered, wondering how long it would take to close my bank account and cancel my credit card, and whether it would do any good. "Really and truly, we are not related. It's not possible."

Roused from his hip-hop daydream, Mischa grew worried.

"Ah, now my cousin thinks me hooligan. Not good. Must find other data."

He put a finger coquettishly to his chin, squinted his eyes upward.

"*Da, da.*" He snapped his fingers excitedly. "Your grandfather name of Andrei, yes? His father and mother die in siege of Leningrad, I am right?"

I let out a long, slow exhalation and shook my head with disbelief. He might still be an utter crank. But here was something he could not have possibly pulled from a database. As far as I knew, it had only ever existed in the mists of obscure family lore. I barely remembered it myself. Feeling like I might levitate clear out of my body, I turned the car off and walked up to confront Mischa Tsipin.

"What do you want from me?" I said.

He stood, hands clasped monkishly to show how harmless he was.

"I want nothing. Only make acquaintance. We share bloods. Will you invite me your house? Yes, I am Russian, but is colder than ass of a well digger tonight, am I right?"

I cracked a thin smile. "Where did you learn that expression?"

He smiled too, happy to have passed this linguistic hurdle.

"I am big fan of your musician Tom Waits. From him I am learn this fine line and many else. So?" he said with a hopeful lilt, miming a wet shiver.

"Listen, buster, you could be a serial killer for all I know. Don't you have phones in Russia? Or how about writing a letter first, letting me know you're on your way, since you seem to know where I live?"

I thought about an editor I knew who had sponsored distant Russian relatives to come to the United States and discovered second and third cousins with a preternatural grasp of how to work the American system. They had immediately applied for multiple credit cards and charged up an orgy of debt before finding their true métier with insurance fraud. Others found relatives they no longer had anything in common with. Branches of the family tree grew in different ways after generations apart, taking on characteristics that made them almost unrecognizable. Is that what we had here?

"You never home," Mischa said accusingly. "I call but not want leave message. And work number I call many times. A place called Gabriel Valley. But you are not checking mouth-mail. Finally today a kind man direct me to your new employment in City Center. There I leave other message."

"I'll tell you what. Why don't you ride that bike of yours down to Glendale Boulevard and up two blocks and you'll come to a coffeehouse called Sumatra. I'll buy you a sandwich and all the coffee you can drink and you can tell me your story and then I'll decide whether it's fact or fiction."

Mischa licked his lips and another shiver seemed to pass through him. It occurred to me now that his jeans weren't baggy as a fashion statement; he had the gaunt, unhealthy look of someone who has lost a lot of weight in a hurry. His flesh hung loosely on his bones, and his face managed to be both drawn and jowly.

I wondered how he was getting by in the Promised Land and dreaded finding out. But at least we could do so in a public place, surrounded by all the late-night jitterinas that this town produces.

alf an hour later, I watched Mischa tear raven-
ously into his fourth sandwich of smoked
turkey with arugula and tomato pesto on focac-
cia. His coffee cup, long emptied, was now filled with
half-and-half, which he quaffed happily.

In the well-lit and cozy confines of the coffeehouse, he
didn't look so dangerous, and indeed could have passed for
any of the Silverlake denizens who congregated here to
work on their Great American Screenplay. With his scruffy
looks and squalid Eurotrash mien, he might have been any
singer/actor whatever, waiting for his big break.

I wondered whether he had any idea of the fantasy he
dangled before me, of an instant family, magically reunited across oceans and generations. Both my parents
were dead. My only brother had died when we were
teenagers. I was an orphan adrift on the Pacific tides,
yearning for a family to come home to. But at the same
time, I wasn't naive. Something about Mischa felt too
pat. And the fact that he should wash up in my life on the
very day that I started investigating the death of a young
Russian-American boy, well, I wondered about that, too.
My every instinct screamed that there was more at work
here than fate and a joyful family reunion. I would do
well to keep my wits about me. And not reveal anything
of my own past he could use to embroider his tale. Let
him supply the details.

Mischa finished eating and blotted his mouth with a napkin. He glanced hopefully at the deli case, but it was late and he had cleaned them out of sandwiches. Next he eyed the pastries. But since he'd have to ask me to pay again, his pride got the better of him. Instead, he helped himself to another cup of half-and-half.

"That's going to make you sick," I whispered when he came back. "It's pure cream."

He shrugged with a diffident air. As he dried out, a musty smell came from his clothes. He had taken off the cap, and his hair had dried at odd, wispy angles, giving him the look of an electrified imp.

"I am Russian," he said. "It is in my veins."

I wondered if he meant genes, or that his blood would soon clot from the richness.

"Suit yourself." I leaned back in my chair. "Okay, Mischa. Now tell me exactly how we're related."

"Yes, yes," he said. "I imagine you are killing to know. Our great-grandmothers are sisters. Of this I have proof."

He rummaged in his dirty knapsack, drew out a ragged envelope of obsolete Soviet make, and began pulling out documents, little passbooks and black-and-white photos with scalloped edges, spidery Cyrillic lettering running along the back.

These he shuffled like a deck of cards until he found the photo he wanted. Running his hand along the Formica table to swipe it clean of crumbs, he unfolded a napkin, laid it down, and placed the photo reverentially upon it.

"There," he said.

We both leaned in. I saw four girls of descending age posed in a clearing. Behind them stood a two-story wooden house and beyond that stretched a dark forest.

"That was taken at dacha, near 1900," Mischa said.

"You can recognize your great-grandmother. Very striking resemblance."

I peered in, looking for clues. The girls' hair was done up in ribbons and ringlets, they wore white summer frocks that fell down to their calves. Their almost translucent faces dimpled into frowns, as though they had been forced to stare into the sun while the unknown photographer took their picture. The oldest was about eleven. She stared at the camera with serious, appraising eyes. The youngest was a toddler, barely walking. They were all beautiful and regal, like little princesses, and from the looks of their surroundings, they had been raised in luxury. I turned the photo over and saw the inscription, *1904, Peredelkino*, and shivered, because I knew what horror lay ahead for these girls, one they, in the full bloom of summer and girlhood, could not have fathomed. And yet. There was something in the oldest one's steady gray eyes that spoke to me across nearly a century, a steadfast expression of serenity and self-composure that said, I will endure.

"That one." I pointed to the oldest girl.

"No," he said. "Here is Anya. She live to ninety-eight and die in Tashkent. Husband die from influenza in 1930s and she not marry again. Not enough men after Great Patriotic War."

I studied the other girls but none called out to me the way the older one did; they were too young and unformed. What a fanciful game we were playing, I thought. This photo could have been stolen from any historic trove or old pensioner dying in a Moscow garret. But here were the birch forests of Russia, the dacha, the girls with their clear gray eyes and lustrous brown hair. The straight, fine noses of my family. I began to get a chill.

"You give up?" Mischa said playfully. "Eve, what is your final answer? We have that show in Russia. For us it is a dream. Instant millionaires. Of course it is ruble millions."

I shook my head. "I have no idea."

"Here," he said triumphantly, pointing to the second-to-youngest child. I'm not good with little kids' ages, but she looked about seven, solemn as all the others, a clutch of violets in her hands, which were folded neatly in her lap. She had that same clear-eyed stare, but with a hint of mischievous glee. A small terrier curled at her feet, and she had slipped off one shoe and buried her toes in the dog's fur. Could this be my great-grandmother?

"Yes," Mischa said, nodding enthusiastically. "She is ballerina with Mariinsky Theatre. Like other sisters. Is very artistic family. But your great-grandmother not stay. She marry businessman who take her abroad during revolution. Give up career. My great-grandmother and other sisters stay. For them Russia is home. Is good life for them. My great-grandmother, she visit her sister, your family, in West, but always return. She tell us that West is not for her."

It rang the faintest of bells. But it also sounded like a fairy tale.

"All the sisters were ballerinas?" I asked, incredulous.

"They are dancers or singers, yes. Much culture runs through our family," Mischa said with approval.

"What happened to your great-grandmother who stayed behind?" I said.

"You must know," he said to me. "You are pull my foot, yes?"

I shook my head, flushing that I knew so little.

"But it is family history. It is the blood. How you can not know?"

"Mischa," I said heatedly. "Many people who came to the New World were fleeing war, famine, pogroms, dire poverty. They left all those memories behind. They started over. They didn't want to burden their children. It was a fresh start here. They wanted their children to be pure Americans. And that happened three, four generations ago. My parents didn't even teach me Russian. And when you're a kid, you don't ask. It doesn't occur to you. You just know that certain subjects are off limits. And then, when you're old enough to ask, sometimes it—" I stopped, realizing I was revealing way too much about myself to someone who just might be a charlatan. "Well then, it's just not possible anymore."

"Then I must inform." Mischa straightened up and folded his hands. "The war come. My grandfather is in boarding school outside Moscow, in line of German troops. They march, they get closer. Grandfather evacuate to Tashkent. Year 1941. After war, he learn his parents starve to death in siege of Leningrad."

"How tragic. We never knew. What about the other sisters?"

"One die also in war. One is lost in gulag. One is in West. Your great-grandmother." He gave me a beady look.

"Are there other relatives left over there besides you?"

Mischa frowned.

"Is possible. But I not know them."

This didn't sit quite right. He saw the look on my face and added hastily, "I am only child. My mother was orphan and my father has no brothers, sisters. We Russians, we not make enough babies."

"So you grew up in Moscow?"

"Yes. We hope that after communism, things get better. But very little jobs. I decide try my luck in America."

"Was it hard to get a visa?"

He made an embarrassed face. "I not need visa."

"Everyone needs a visa to get into America these days."

His eyes twinkled. "Government does not know I am here. My back is wet."

"You mean—"

"No, that is wrong." Mischa snapped his fingers. "What is word? Wetback." His voice rose triumphantly. "I am wetback."

At the next table, a young Latina with a pierced nose frowned at Mischa.

"You mean you got smuggled in from Mexico?" I looked at him, aghast. What had I let myself in for?

He took a thoughtful gulp of cream. "To tell you truth, I am in much trouble."

I put my elbows on the table and lowered my face into my hands, massaging my temples. "Why does that not surprise me?"

"Bad people are looking for me."

"Oh joy. And you've landed on my doorstep."

He kept going. "I owe much money to Russian Mafia."

I shifted uneasily. In the last half hour, I had gained a stalker, a relative, an illegal alien, and now a guy on the run from the Mafia.

"Aren't they the ones that pour acid on your fingers after they kill you so no one can identify your prints?"

He stared miserably down at the photo. "They are not bothering with acid now. Just chop off hands."

"Goddamn it." I smacked my own hand so hard on the table that Mischa jumped, upsetting the rest of his cream. It oozed out over the Formica and Mischa threw down napkins to stanch the flow.

"I am sorry."

"Look, bud, I doubt I'm related to a nut job like you. But this is where I get off. I'm glad you enjoyed the sandwiches," I said, standing up and throwing twenty-five dollars on the table. "It's been nice knowing you. But if you show up at my house again, I'm calling the cops. And they can arrest you and deport you back to Vladivostok or whatever tundra you came from."

"They have your number," Mischa said quietly.

For a moment, there was glaring silence.

When I spoke, it was in a very low voice.

"Who has my number?"

"At least I think they do. To call you about ransom."

"The ransom?" I practically screamed.

"For smuggling fee. I fly Moscow–Havana–Mexico City. Car come, drive us to Mexico-U.S. border. Guards, they look for people with dark skin. We say nothing, everything A-okay. They bring us to house in North Hollywood. So many people we must take turn to sit. We go to toilet one time each day. No food, little water. The smugglers call relatives. When they give *baksheesh,* people are release. Not many Russian mens. Most young women. A madam come for them. She talk on cell phone, say 'delivery' is soon. 'I not care what you do,' this madam say. 'Put them in chains, tie them, no matter. They belong like property.' When girls hear that, they scare. But what they can do? By third day, only forty-five people left. This is last week. I am calling your work each day, and home also, but you are not answer."

I thought back on all the messages the receptionist in the San Gabriel bureau had received. At least I knew he was telling the truth about that.

"I am afraid they kill me," Mischa continued. "I keep try, hope you can pay ransom. I am pay back, loan only, work hard, do anything. But next day police and INS raid house. We climb through windows and run very fast. Police are looking for Mexican people, not Europeans. No one think I have wet back."

At the next table, the Latina had had enough. Scowling, she packed up her laptop and stalked out.

"Will you stop using that term, it's derogatory," I said.

"But it is from American movies," he said in bewilderment. "In Russia I am studying carefully, making lists, to be down with idiom."

"I rest my case. So ever since then you've been on the run? How did you find out where I live?"

He looked down at his hands.

"Internet. There is no Eve Diamond on list but there are ways. So I am pedaling to the domicile of every E. Diamond. Eleanor. Everett. Ernest. Elizabeth. Erin. You are seventh. I 'borrow' bike to get around. I will give back as soon as I get job. America is land of compromise and opportunity. I am excellent computer programmer. I will show you. Perhaps your paper has need of me? I will work very cheap, very good, very hard."

I groaned. "It doesn't work that way. You need a green card. Even to flip burgers at a greasy spoon."

"But Mexican people tell me *dokumentat* is not problem. They give me address. One in City Center and also a place called Huntington Park."

"I have to go now," I said. "It's late and I have a big day tomorrow."

He seemed to accept this with dignity.

"No problem. I call you tomorrow?"

He looked downcast, and somewhat frightened. The milk mustache had dried, giving him the look of a sad clown. And I don't know why, but I relented.

"I'm awfully busy. There's a Russian community center in West Hollywood that can help you."

He got a funny gleam in his eye. "Yes, already they are helping me. With lodgings."

"Great." I paused, thought about the wet night. "Want a ride there?"

He peered out into the night. "No, thank you. Rain is very light now. I am pedal. I am full of coffee beans now and America is beautiful at night. 'Mischa by Starlight.' A song, no?"

"Not quite."

CHAPTER 10

O nce in my house, I remembered I had to find my birth certificate. I had long put off going through my mother's papers because I feared the bittersweet memories. There would be photos of my brother, who had died in an accident at thirteen, of the two of us as kids, of our family in happier times. My parents were gone now and family was one of those touchy things I preferred to keep in a locked box. But Mischa's tales had piqued my interest. Was he for real? Might I find confirmation in my mother's papers?

In the kitchen, I reached for a bottle of Zinfandel, almost knocking over the Stolichnaya. I paused at the colorful orange label, so familiar from my childhood. My grandmother always kept a bottle on the bathroom shelf. She used it to disinfect our childhood scrapes, and I recalled the strong smell of spirits as it glugged onto a cotton ball, then stinging needles against bare, scraped flesh.

After a short lull, the rain had started in earnest again. I hoped Mischa had made it to his West Hollywood lodgings. I poured a glass of Zinfandel, dark and peppery on a cold wet night, and stood at the picture window, gazing at the illuminated skyline. I lived in Silverlake, a neighborhood just ten minutes northwest of downtown but light-years removed from the corporate hustle. My 'hood was known for narrow winding hill streets, old homes, and a mongrel mix of people. In Silverlake, poor Latinos, upscale white yuppies, and Asian bohemians shared space with leather fetishists, former city councilmen, and B-movie actors from Hollywood's golden age. At the local coffee shop, you'd see animators from the Midwest, drag queens, eighty-year-old dowagers, and nineteen-year-old surrealists all chowing down on the $6.99 early bird special. It was a tolerant place with a sense of community that had long disappeared in most of the city, and we cherished it like a rare heirloom of our collective past. Even more so when it wasn't our own past, but a mythic one. I, for one, didn't have deep roots in L.A. My parents had both been immigrants, and I had no family here. Perhaps that's why Silverlake's sense of community was so appealing.

But now there was Mischa. His abrupt arrival in my life as the holidays approached brought on a melancholy tinged with longing. Images flickered inside my skull, like shadows thrown by a cave fire, stories I couldn't possibly remember but had heard so many times that they had become memories. Of a 1920s villa in the hills above Nice and all-night parties with glamorous guests. Furs and ivory cigarette holders and hot jazz from a hand-crank gramophone. And relatives who spoke Russian and wore jewels and drank tea from small curved glasses with cubes of sugar tucked into back teeth. There were loud arguments that fell silent as a child wandered in, only to be hustled out with a piroshki, a pat on the behind, and suggestions in artificially bright voices to go play outside. There was a beloved family dog named Bobbie with one gray eye and one blue one who destroyed Christmas Eve dinner while the family was away at midnight mass. As the house lay still and empty, Bobbie had crept to the groaning sideboards and gnawed his way through turkey, goose, and ham, sampling Beluga caviar from silver bowls and rustic *pirok* from aluminum pans. Then, in a grand finale of destruction, he had pulled down the floral curtains, wiped his greasy muzzle, and settled, tail tucked under chin, for a long nap.

And another scene, clear as an old Hollywood movie, of raised voices and hot splashed tears and recriminations.

"Stay with us, Natasha," the relatives cried to a beautiful woman in a silk gown. "Don't go home."

But the woman named Natasha turned away, her graceful back twisting.

"I must," she told the relatives. "Dmitri is there."

"He'll find a way to join us," they pleaded.

"They'll never let him leave," Natasha said. "He's their insurance I'll come back. Don't worry, dearest ones. Things will be better next spring."

"Each year it only gets more difficult," they protested. "Soon the borders will be sealed."

"Hush. Don't say that. This state of affairs can't last."

Natasha glided over and sat amid these relatives who loved her, absorbing their warmth for the cold journey ahead. Things were getting worse in Russia. Food more scarce, the fear more palpable. She and Dmitri were dancers with the Mariinsky Theatre. Natasha was good. Dmitri was a national treasure. But his gift was also his curse. They'd never let him go, and she loved him too much to abandon him. Yet she pined for her sister, who had fled to the Côte d'Azur during the revolution. The sister's cynicism about the Reds had served her well, while Natasha's need to believe in something exalted, a better world, had doomed her.

"I miss him terribly," Natasha said. "Without him I'm only half alive."

"Without you, we're only half alive," they lamented.

A click of the tongue. A slurp of tea. And their turbaned heads bent together, jewels clinking, perfumes mingling.

My grandmother had told me the story so many times that I could hear the words and phrases echoing through the big house, felt the mistral that blew across from Africa. I sensed the indignity of being hustled out by the grown-ups and felt the rough bark against my bare feet as she climbed the Persian mulberry tree and sat for hours, gorging on the fat purple berries, throwing them down to attentive, adoring Bobbie until his muzzle turned a ghastly crimson from the juice.

"But why didn't you *ask* them?" I demanded of her, seventy years later, in the arid reaches of a Southern California suburb. I was eight years old and we were playing double solitaire, a favorite pasttime on sweltering summer afternoons. And my grandmama had shushed me with one hand, fingers gnarled from arthritis and the needlepoint she did for hours during the war that destroyed her joints and her eyesight.

"In those days, they didn't tell children anything. That's just the way it was. But I remember Tante Natasha. She was young and beautiful, with auburn curls and green eyes. A dancer like Maman used to be. I loved her. And I remember that after I ate the mulberries, I crept into the parlor and listened to their argument. Tante Natasha saw me and she knelt and wrapped her arms around me and promised she'd be back. After that, we dressed up in pretty clothes and had a tea party."

"And what happened to Natasha?" I had asked, sitting on my grandmama's brocade couch with clawed wooden feet that had come with her across the Atlantic. I wondered if Natasha had sat on the same couch in a villa in

France seventy years earlier and agonized over what to do.
"Did she really go back to Russia?"

"Yes."

"But she came back the next year, right?" I held my
breath.

"For a while we got letters."

"She broke her promise?" My eight-year-old heart was
aghast.

"After 1927, even the letters stopped. We wrote until
our fingers bled. I stole pages of Maman's stationery and
sprayed them with perfume. I folded in quail feathers and
dried rose petals, all her favorite things. Still we heard
nothing. Then the war came, and everything was cut off.
Afterward, the letters started coming back, smeared with
inky stamps, big and official. 'Deceased in the Siege of
Leningrad.'"

"I hate her," I had screamed at my grandmama.

"Hush, child, it was more complicated than that."

And the blue-veined hands would reach out, jeweled
rings shooting off rays of light, and stroke my hair. Her
fingers were smooth and cool against my temples. But I
felt her fear of that great fortress in the East. A dread that
went unspoken and lived in the bones.

I took a sip of wine and heard the coyotes howling on
the next hill. Unbidden, another conversation came echoing back through time.

"After the war, we saw the Russian prisoners of war
lined up at the train station, waiting to go back, and we felt
so sorry for them," my grandmother said as she laid out
pickled herring and vegetables and black rye bread for
lunch.

"Why, Grandmama?"

"They were crying. My girlfriend and I, we were in the

Scouts, and we pedaled down and brought them bread and sausages for the journey."

The idea of grown men crying was disturbing in ways I couldn't articulate.

"Why were they crying, Grandmama?" I asked, a wet sniffle starting up behind my nose.

"They didn't want to go back. They knew what was waiting for them."

"What was waiting for them?"

But she only shook her head, and her voice hardened.

"We even knew people who went back. Not Red Army prisoners. White Russians who had settled in France during the revolution but never stopped pining for home. After the war, Stalin put out the word that all Russians should return. He needed their knowledge to rebuild the motherland. All would be forgiven.

"We told them not to go, but"—she shrugged—"people wanted to believe. And they were so homesick. I won't say we weren't tempted. But I had your mother and . . ." She stopped. Her face grew ponderous. "Our life was in France by then."

"What about Grandpapa?"

She examined her cards and frowned. "He died after the war," she said. "He was an idealist and it killed him."

"He wasn't a soldier, then?" I sensed tiny shifts in her posture, ripples in her jawline.

"The Germans took him to work in their factories. It was slave labor. He came back ruined in body and soul. For him the West had failed utterly. He died in 1946."

"So you and Maman didn't go to Russia, then?" I asked. I was eight then and it was as abstract as moving a chess piece on a board, this decision whether to go or stay.

"Of course not," she said with a sudden vehemence that scared me. "We weren't stupid. Nobody trusted Stalin. Stories had seeped out. Terrible stories. But with peace came new hope. And so"—she exhaled loudly—"many families sent one person to test the waters. They would go and report back. But everyone knew the mail was watched. If things were bad, they'd be forced to lie. So they made a plan. If it was a trap, they'd add a line to the letters. They'd say, 'The sun is shining and the butterflies are everywhere.' And then we'd know."

I could barely breathe. "You mean—not to come?"

"Yes."

"And what happened?"

"Every family got an enthusiastic letter urging them to sell all their belongings and come by the first available train. And every one of those letters said, 'The sun is shining and the butterflies are everywhere.' So they stayed and thanked God they hadn't been foolish enough to return."

"And what happened to the relatives in Russia who sent the letters?"

My grandmother slapped down a round of cards.

"They were never heard from again. When the families didn't come, Stalin knew the word had gotten out somehow. Later, we heard they were all deported to gulags or killed."

"But why?"

"Stalin thought that people who had been to the West were spies. He didn't trust them. Fifth columnists, he called them."

After that, I looked up Stalin in the encyclopedia, studying the bushy head of hair, the thicket eyebrows, the cold, calculating eyes that radiated power and evil. The bristling mustache that Osip Mandelstam would call a cockroach. Hungrily, I read about the purges, the power plays, the prison at Lubyanka where Anna Akhmatova had captured the cry of a frozen generation when she wrote about the search for her son, taken away by black-booted KGB in the dead of night. When my parents grew curious to see what their daughter was obsessing over, I slammed the book shut guiltily, as though they had caught me looking at dirty pictures. Every kid needs a bogeyman, and for most of my childhood, Josef Stalin was mine. My heart was filled with ice. When *The Gulag Archipelago* came out, I devoured that, too, a kind of pornography, an antidote to the easy life of Southern California. Ashamed, guilty for wallowing in it, yet unable to stop reliving a past that might have been mine.

And so was steeped my deep distrust for all things Soviet. When I was twelve, my Russian grandmama died. And with her died all the lore.

It was a turning point. Adolescence lured me into more youthful pursuits—boys and malls and beach parties. The past receded like a tide, leaving only jetsam that surfaced at odd, unbidden moments. When my parents died, it was too painful to revisit that world. And by then I had other challenges—school and work and keeping it together. Life narrowed down to the essentials. The memories, when they came, were hazy and indistinct, an old movie reel of someone else's history.

But I did remember my mother, the year before she died, waiting until my father was at work, then pulling out the silk hatbox she kept in the back of the closet, safe from thieves and my father's prying eyes. If anything ever happened to her, I was to go through the papers, get the key to the safety deposit box, and empty it of valuables. There were important documents and other things, she said.

She made me promise, but I was lost in teen languor and dismissed her as overly dramatic. How could I know that her need to scan the horizon for massing armies and plumes of smoke, to liquidate the valuables, to be ready at any moment to flee, had been transfused in her mother's milk from the war generation that came before?

And in the end, my father had gone first, and then a year later my mother had died of a heart attack instead of the cataclysm she had long feared. And I had gone dutifully to the bank to retrieve her jewels, obscurely disappointed, after all the buildup, to find only Art Deco rings and bracelets and brooches that she and my grandmother had brought with them from Europe.

Unable to bear living in a place inhabited by ghosts, I had sold our childhood home. As for my mother's papers, I slid the box onto my own closet shelf, too heartsick to sift through things that bore her perfume, her memories. One day, I kept telling myself. When I feel stronger. And I'd finger her filigreed silver earrings of Baltic amber that I wore on special occasions, and swear that the time was coming. And so more than a decade had passed.

Tonight there was no putting it off any longer. Without the strange events of this evening, I would have found my birth certificate and slid the box back onto the shelf. But Mischa's stories had piqued my curiosity. Was it possible my mother's papers and photos held proof of his claims?

Palms sweaty with the old unease, I dragged a chair into the walk-in closet, clambered up, and pulled down boxes of my own stuff until I came to the silk box. It gave me a pang to see it there, a relic from an era when women wore gloves and men wore hats and Red Car trolleys criss-crossed Los Angeles.

Sneezing at the dust I had disturbed, I took it to the kitchen table and sipped my wine. Revisiting the past was something best not done sober. I opened the hatbox and the smell of lavender hit my nostrils, sending me reeling. There were documents in manila envelopes stamped with red seals. The deed to their old house, long ago sold and bulldozed to make way for a McMansion. The last mortgage payment, with a note in my mother's round handwriting that said, *Paid in full.* Old expired passports. Locks of our hair. My parents' marriage certificate. A pill bottle full of yellowed baby teeth. Pictures of us as children, squinting into the backyard light, with freckle faces and gaps in our teeth. Composition books with painstakingly drawn alphabets. Book reports. It touched me to see the things she had kept. But so far it was all mementos from our life in America. I'd have to excavate deeper.

Suddenly, I was hungry to do so. Mischa had stirred up a cauldron of echoes in my head. I reached for a stack of letters and postcards, some in Russian, many in French. I'd have to get the Russian ones translated one day. I dug once more. There it was. My birth certificate. As I pulled it out, the corner caught on a yellowed envelope. I shook it and a sheet of stationery tumbled out, covered with spidery writing. A fountain pen, the ink faded on thick watermark paper.

Dearest Anya, it began. *Every day that we don't see each other is like a physical pain in me, a soul-sickness that I cannot abide. You are my light, my life . . .*

A wistful smile played around my mouth. My mother's name was Anya. This was a love letter from my father. Even with both of them gone, it felt voyeuristic to read such an intimate note. I slipped the letter back into the ivory envelope, found my birth certificate, put it in my purse. Time to clean up now. I picked up the love letter to put it back but instead I opened the envelope and took the letter back out.

I began to read, surprised at the banality of the lover's words, and also at the flowery language. I had never heard my parents speak like this to each other. My father was a tightly buttoned man who rarely expressed emotion. This provided a long-ago periscope into his psyche that I had never known. Fascinated now, I read to the end, only to be pulled up abruptly at the signature: *Your loving Luka.*

I stared at the name. A hollow roaring started in my ears. My father's name was August. This letter was not from my father. It was from another man. One of my mother's boyfriends, perhaps, long before she had ever met my father. But the letter wasn't dated. Again I heard her voice, imploring me to go through the box if anything ever happened to her. Maybe she hadn't been able to bear the thought of destroying it herself. Though I don't think my father would have cared. His love for her was stolid. Immobile. I pictured my mother in a light frock, doe-eyed with young love, pledging eternal devotion to a man who wasn't my father.

I looked back now, searching for clues.

"Last night when you came to me, I was filled with such love that I thought my heart would overflow," the mysterious lover wrote. "If I could only persuade you of the nobility and integrity of my intentions, then we could always be together. Do not say I am wrong, or misguided. I am passionately committed, and what I wish for, every waking moment of my days and in my dreams at night, is that you will join me in this life. Give me your answer soon, my love, and release me from these shadows where I now dwell in hope and fear and longing.

"Your loving Luka."

I got up, walked to the window, saw the neon archaeology of L.A. blinking like a Christmas tree. On either side, the dark, sylvan hills of my neighborhood settled into deep shadow. Everything I knew was disintegrating, burning up like tinder hit with a lit match. No wonder my mother had been so adamant that I go through the box. And I had only excavated one-third of the contents. What else lay in its depths?

In a trance, I walked back. I'd stay up all night if I had to, brew a pot of coffee. Again I picked up the envelope. It was addressed to my mother at 312 North New Hampshire Street in Hollywood. I remembered that she and my grandmother had lived there when they first came to America. At the top left was the sender's address: 2750 Cordoba Street, Hollywood. They had probably hopped on the Red Car to visit each other.

It was quite late now, but I logged onto the *L.A. Times* computer and looked up property records from the L.A. County assessor's office. When I typed in the address on Cordoba Street in Hollywood, no match came up for "Luka." The owners were Morris and Wendy Avila. The house had probably changed hands several times since Luka had owned it. I needed a last name and more information. Now I used the crisscross reverse directory and found a phone number for Wendy and Morris Avila. I wrote it down. I was getting somewhere.

I was so deep in thought that it took me a while to realize the doorbell had been ringing for a long time.

CHAPTER 11

I crept to the front door and looked through the peep-hole.

It was Mischa, looking like a drowned rat.

I opened the grate.

"What are you doing here?" I said, too shocked to be angry.

"I not tell truth about lodging," he said. "I am afraid to go to Russian center. They may have connections with people who look for me."

I didn't speak. More than anything, I wanted to get back to that letter and my mother's lover.

"I have no place to sleep," Mischa was saying. Drops of rain clung to his fake leather coat and dripped off his nose. "I may come in?"

I glanced back at the box. I felt like he had caught me red-handed, trying to piece together my past.

"No," I said quickly. "You can't stay here. My husband is asleep, he'd kill me."

"Eve?"

"What?" I snapped.

"I know you not have husband. I am read article online you write about St. Valentine and boyfriends."

He had certainly done his homework.

"How do you know I haven't married since then?" I said.

He held his hand up in front of his face and rubbed the notch of his ring finger.

"I'm a modern woman. I don't believe in rings," I lied.

He stared through the grate at me. "You may be modern woman, but you are old soul. It is Russian in you."

"Enough with the Russian mysticism! Why am I even talking to you? Even if I'm not married, I probably have a boyfriend and he's here."

"That is true." His voice was sad now. "Attractive lady like you. But it is cold tonight."

"You're Russian, you'll survive. You're used to the permafrost. Honestly, Mischa, you seem harmless enough, but I just can't do it. I can drive you to a shelter if you want, but that's it."

I stared back at my mother's hatbox, thought about those long-ago talks with my grandmother. And realized it was only luck and timing that had placed my relatives on the right side when the Iron Curtain came crashing down. What if my great-grandparents had been idealists like Natasha? Then it easily could have been me, making the pilgrimage halfway around the world almost a century later to stand on a distant relative's front porch and beg for shelter.

"Mischa, that great-grandmother of yours, the one who used to go visit her relatives in Fr— in Western Europe," I said, biting back the country, not wanting to give anything away. "What was her name?"

Mischa barely hesitated. That computer brain of his retrieved the information and spat it out on my doorstep, altering my life forever.

"She was Natasha. Her relatives lived in West. Let me remember. Yes! On Côte d'Azur."

"Hmm." I pretended to ponder this. But it reverberated like a gong throughout my body.

Slowly, I unlocked the door.

"Come in," I said, holding it open.

"Thank you, Eve," Mischa said, stepping inside. "Did your parents tell you about Natasha?" he asked, resuming our conversation as though it were the most natural thing in the world. "She was very beautiful."

"No," I said honestly. "My parents never spoke of her."

Mischa was looking with appreciation at my living room, especially the deep, comfy couch.

"Don't get too excited," I said. "You are going to sleep on my back porch. Don't worry, it's enclosed. You can take a shower first if you want, and I'll bring out a bunch of blankets. You won't be cold or wet. But tomorrow I'm driving you to West Hollywood and you've got to fend for yourself."

"No problem," he hastily assured me. "*Spasibo,* Eve. Our great-grandmothers would be pleased."

"Oh stop."

I felt rather ridiculous as I hauled extra blankets, quilts, pillows, and an old down sleeping bag out of my closet and dumped everything on the back porch. If he meant to do me harm, he didn't have to wait until I was asleep.

But Mischa bustled around happily, arranging his winter's lodging on my chaise longue with the diligence of an overgrown badger making a nest. Then he crawled inside the sleeping bag and began pulling blankets over himself.

It occurred to me now that this odd cousin wasn't the only one I had to worry about.

"Mischa, you said earlier that these Mafia people might have my phone number. They could easily find out where

I live. Don't you think they'll come looking for you here eventually?"

Mischa's head popped out of the down comforter.

"If that is happening, I am running away. I am not making problems for you, Eve Diamond."

Your very existence is a problem for me.

"Well, let me show you a back way out of this property. If anything happens, God forbid, you use it."

This time, we donned slickers with hoods, and Mischa followed me down the back stairs into the double lot that my landlady cultivated like a wild and savage garden. The grass was knee high in spots and brushed against my bare shins in a clammy embrace. We trooped through the sloping yard and past a handful of citrus trees. Seeing a tangerine tree whose branches hung almost to the ground with the orange neon fruit, Mischa gave a cry of wonder and ran over.

"No one in Russia will believe it," Mischa said, holding up the sunset globes. "Oranges you can eat right off tree. Just like in Raymond Chandler novel."

"Tangerines," I said. "Satsumas."

Properly dressed for once, with a sweater underneath, I didn't mind being out in the wet night.

Mischa didn't seem to either. He tore the peel off a tangerine and crammed the segments into his mouth. Juice ran down his chin.

"Like nectar of gods," Mischa said. He shoved ten more tangerines into the pockets of his slicker and wiped his hands on his jeans.

"Let us get down to the bronze tacks now, Eve."

"Brass," I said.

"What?"

"Oh, never mind. Here." I walked past an ancient

banana plant and showed him a wooden gate, overgrown with creeping vines. "Voilà," I said. "Escape hatch."

Mischa peered dubiously over the gate and into another backyard. At the far end of the yard stood a wooden house with a sagging porch and peeling paint.

"Past that house is Duane Street," I said. "There's no fence, you can walk straight onto the road."

"I see." Mischa stroked his chin. "Very clever. I am moving my bicycle behind tree now. For how do you say? Insurance. Which Soviet people did not have, until recently."

He walked around the banana tree to see if his bike would fit behind it. A moment later, he cried my name.

"What?" I said, startled.

"Come. This I truly cannot believe."

I hiked over. In his hand was something small and curved. For one nightmarish moment I feared it was a gun. When I realized it was green, I relaxed.

"You have bananas!" Mischa said.

"You can't eat them. They're not ripe."

But he was already peeling one and shoving the hard green cigar into his mouth.

"Is not bad, this California banana," he said, chomping in thoughtful reflection.

"It's inedible," I protested. "Bananas need a tropical climate to ripen. Trust me, your bowels will howl in protest."

But Mischa was already wrestling with a large, hanging clump of bananas. He tore some free and returned loaded down with booty.

"Fine," I said. "I'll leave you a roll of toilet paper and hope I'm wrong."

We walked back up the hill to get his bike, Mischa happily extolling the virtues of California produce.

"What a wonderful place is this land. Bounty from fertile earth. In Russia, we must forage for mushrooms and dig for potatoes."

He laid his spoils on the blankets beside him, caressed his tangerines and small green bananas.

"Take it easy on those bananas, I'm warning you," I said in parting, wondering how I would ever fall asleep with this lunatic camped on my back porch. Then I locked the kitchen door behind him and crawled into bed. I tried to steel myself into watchfulness, but the day's seesawing emotions tipped me into unconsciousness as my head hit the pillow.

CHAPTER 12

T he knock the next morning came at 5:30 a.m.
"Wake up," Josh's voice floated through the front door. "Bagels and coffee."

It felt like I had just gotten to sleep.

Outside, it was cold enough to see your breath. The rain had stopped but it wasn't over.

"Come in," I told Josh, then ran to the back. Throwing the kitchen door open, I bent down, shook the sleeping bag heaped with blankets. "Wake up, Mischa. Come inside."

From the nest, a rumpled head peered out, groggy with sleep. "Cousin Eve," he said, eyes crinkling into a smile. "I was dreaming about our family in Russia."

I shivered. "It's freezing out here. Come in the kitchen and meet my friend."

I looked at the thermometer: thirty-six degrees. It was a lie that L.A. didn't get cold. It was a semidesert, after all.

Mischa crawled out. He wore two sweaters under his fake leather jacket. His hair was standing straight up and a white line of dried spittle ran down his chin. He stepped into the kitchen just as Josh walked in with coffee and a bulging white bag.

They stared at each other like it was a shootout at the OK Corral, then Mischa extended an arm and said, "Here is Mischa Tsipin from Moscow. I am cousin to Eve. It is great pleasure to meet Eve's boyfriend. May I commend your choice of woman."

Josh put down the tray carefully and raised an eyebrow. He looked from Mischa to me, then back to Mischa.

"Well, this *is* a surprise," he said. "Josh Brandywine, pleased to meet you. Alas, I'm not her boyfriend." He cleared his throat. "Just her colleague."

"I see," Mischa said, nodding heartily. He spied the bag. "May I?" he said, already reaching in. "And coffee, on such a cold morning. *Prekrasno!* How wonderful!"

"This has got to be pretty mild for a Russkie like you," said Josh.

"Yes, indeed, Mr. Josh, but you see, I am not used to sleep outside."

"Outside?" echoed Josh, with a quizzical look at me.

Mischa had inhaled a bagel. Suddenly he bent over, grabbed his belly, and gasped. "You will please excuse me."

I knowingly pointed him to the bathroom and he darted off.

"I told him to watch those bananas," I said.

"No one is making any sense this morning," Josh said.

I told him about my unexpected visitor and his banana harvesting.

Josh sipped his joe. "Well, he certainly looks harmless," he said when I finished.

"Yeah, well, so did Ted Bundy."

"Why would he make all that up? Seems a bit far-fetched."

"Everything about him is far-fetched, as you'll soon see. But I've got a real problem here. What am I supposed to do with him?"

Mischa came bustling back. His hair was wet and his face looked freshly scrubbed.

"I have done my morning ablutions, as you say in America," he announced.

I shot Josh a look and he coughed.

"Let's hit the road."

"Anyone want a banana before we go?" I asked innocently.

A seasick look came over Mischa. He clutched his stomach.

I gave him an I-told-you-so look. "Get your things, Mischa. We'll drop you off after our appointment."

"Where?" he asked, affecting surprise.

"Wherever you want. I'll go with you to the Russian Community Center if you're nervous about showing up by yourself."

"But you are the blood," he protested.

"I can't have you staying with me here. I don't even know you. The center can help you."

"I will sleep on porch. I will be no trouble."

"I don't think so. We've got to get to this appointment and I'm not leaving you in my house alone."

"What about bicycle?"

"We'll put it in the back. Josh has an SUV."

I slipped into a wool coat and wrapped a scarf around my neck, then checked my e-mail while Josh loaded up Mischa's bike. I had sent Silvio a long, feverish e-mail from work last night and he had written back. Regretfully, he had to meet with the lawyers of a band he had signed and wouldn't make it back home today after all. I tried not to feel disappointed as my romantic evening dissolved into smoke. Silvio was flying in tomorrow instead. He wanted me to meet him at an airport hotel as soon as his flight got in. A Mexican rock star had raved about the place. He hoped I would wear something sheer and violet. I jotted down the address and wrote back that I'd see him there. I was flattered that he couldn't even wait until we got home. Besides, spending the night at a hotel would give me an excuse to avoid Mischa.

Crossing the lawn, hard frost crunched beneath my shoes. My breath came in billows of white steam. In Josh's car, I turned the heater to high, sipped coffee and came awake, thinking about tomorrow's rendezvous.

Mischa stretched across the backseat, looking right at home. He'd found a box that held Josh's CDs and was rooting through it.

"You have Eminem?" Mischa asked.

"Yeah," Josh said. "But I don't play that before noon."

"Oh," said Mischa, deflated.

Josh shot me a look. "Speaking of rap . . . I can't believe they transferred you out of the San Gabriel Valley just as it starts to get hip. Did you know that Snoop Dogg lives out there now? Big pad in Rowland Heights."

Rowland Heights was a ritzy new suburb, filled with Asian immigrants and big houses carved into rolling hills. The idea of a rap superstar seeking refuge there was ludicrous, and yet made perfect sense. It was suburbia at its most bucolic, light-miles removed from the urban mean streets.

"Cool," came an admiring exclamation from the backseat. "Have you interviewed this rap star?"

"No," I said. "But I hear he coaches his son's football team at the Rowland Hills park every weekend."

"You will take me to their practice?" Mischa asked. "I would like very much meet him. I have business proposal that Snoop must hear."

"No, Mischa," I said. "We're not going to pester him. Let the man have his privacy."

"Rowland Heights," Mischa muttered, memorizing the name. Snoop could run, but he couldn't hide.

I turned to Josh. "What you're seeing here is first-generation can-do capitalism at work." I shivered. "Damn, it's cold this morning."

"Poor Californian," Josh said. "Your blood is so thin."

"Give me a break," I said. "Didn't you grow up in Jakarta and Kinshasa?"

"When I wasn't in Helsinki and Biarritz," Josh countered.

Christmas lights blinked as we drove through the darkened streets. We pulled into the shopping strip at exactly 6:15. There was only one car in the lot and the stores were closed. Across the street, however, an open doughnut shop did brisk business. Mischa grabbed his backpack and said he'd wait there for us. When I handed him five dollars, he took it and murmured a sheepish thanks. We watched him go, then drove around to the rear of the strip mall. Light was shining under the back door of the deli. We got out and knocked.

There was no answer, just loud Russian pop music playing. As we stood there, wondering what to do next, the door opened and the girl from the previous night appeared, hauling a bag of trash. At the sight of us, she shrieked.

"*Shto? Shto?*" a male voice yelled from inside. The next thing I knew, a man burst out and Josh and I had our hands in the air, staring into the muzzle of a big gun. The girl was behind the man, sobbing, hiding her face. I don't know who was more scared, us or them.

CHAPTER 13

T he face above the gun was old and grizzled and lined, eyes dilated with adrenaline.

"Whoa, whoa," Josh said.

The man spoke in Russian and the girl abandoned her trash and slipped back inside the deli. Then he switched to thickly accented English.

"What you want?" His voice was harsh and guttural. He wore a brown jacket, dark pants, and blue tennis shoes, dusty with flour. His face was as jowly as a basset hound's.

"We're reporters for the *Los Angeles Times*," I said, not wanting to move my arms and show him my dog tags. He seemed so jumpy. Maybe we should have waited until they opened. But then the girl would be in school.

I inclined my chin to the dog tags around my neck and the man came forward, still holding the gun, and pulled them close and read them. I don't know if he understood but his body seemed to relax. Slowly, the man put down his gun. He took out a cloth and wiped his forehead, which was glistening with sweat despite the cold.

"What you want?" he asked again.

"The girl," Josh said, pointing to the now closed door. "We would like to speak to her."

His eyes narrowed. "Why you want speak my granddaughter?"

"She went to school with a teenage boy who was found dead up in Griffith Park yesterday," I said.

I could tell Josh had lost him. His English probably consisted entirely of interrogatory questions.

"My granddaughter good girl. Only school. Work. Sleep," the man declared.

"Yes, of course," Josh said. "But she may know the boy who was killed. Could we talk to her?"

We showed him our press passes again and he examined them at length this time, holding them so close they almost touched his bristly nose hairs.

When he handed them back, his gruffness fell away.

"Please come," he said, pulling out a key and unlocking the back door.

We walked into steaming heat, ovens blazing. The air was thick with the smell of sweet yeasty breads, savory pies, and sizzling onions.

He barked a command in Russian at several Latino guys in hairnets and they grabbed wooden paddles and got busy pulling things out of the ovens.

They were spinach pies with sharp cheese. Faintly dusted with flour, they slid off the wooden paddle and onto plates that suddenly appeared before us. Then came hot tea. Finally, the grandfather walked toward a steel desk in the corner, carefully stashed the gun in a drawer, then returned.

With a loud exhalation of breath, he sat down beside us, reached for a sugar cube, and tucked it deep into the left pocket of his mouth. Then he slurped his tea, exhorting us to eat and drink. It was amazing to see the metamorphosis from gun-toting thug to Mr. Hospitality. The deli now felt like a family hearth, heated by the blasting ovens and warm food. Outside, the sky began to streak and lighten.

"Lyuba," he bellowed, and the girl came in, wiping her

hands on an apron. Her brown curly hair was pulled back in a hairnet and she wore a white baker's smock that accented her pale complexion. The grandfather spoke in Russian and prodded her with a fat, horned finger. She gave a flustered smile and said, "My grandfather asks your apology. He is sorry if he frightened you and hopes you will accept our hospitality."

She waved at the food.

"No offense, Lyuba, but why did he pull a gun on us just now?" I asked.

She looked down and lines formed on either side of her thin mouth.

"He is jumpy. He is sorry."

"But why?" I persisted.

Lyuba toyed with a pastry that oozed feta cheese.

Her grandfather, sensing what was being asked, erupted in a rage. Spittle flew from his mouth, speckling his jowls. For five minutes he lectured us in Russian while Lyuba looked pained. I wondered what this all had to do with the dead boy on the wilderness trail. Then he fell silent.

The girl looked at her grandfather. He nodded his head and blinked slowly.

In a halting voice, she began.

"He says he has a right to defend his property."

"From who?" I asked. "Is he worried about getting robbed?"

Lyuba hesitated.

"Not exactly robbed. Gangsters."

Visions of tattooed, bandanna-wearing hoodlums sprang to mind. But I knew she meant something else.

"Gangsters?" I repeated.

"Russian people," she said. "My grandfather doesn't want me to tell you this, but I am ashamed of how he frightened you. You should understand that he is not a bad man. But he is afraid. Russian businesses must pay money each month. For protection."

"*Nyet*," erupted the man, launching into another tirade.

"He says I must not tell you this. He says they will come after us. But it is the truth." She raised her head in defiance. "Honest businesspeople have to pay a 'tax' to these hooligans. My grandfather thought it was them, coming to collect, when you surprised him at the door. And we don't have this month's payment."

Josh and I exchanged a conspiratorial look that said, *Good story, if only we can get them to talk.* But they'd be scared, fearful of retribution. From fellow émigrés who preyed on their own, as surely as cats prey on mice.

The grandfather raised his hands in an "all effort is futile but we must persevere anyway" gesture that Russians have probably been making for centuries. Then he shuffled off to the workers who were prepping the day's menu. I waited until his back was turned, then said, "What can you tell us about Denny Lukin?"

"Nothing," the girl said quickly.

"I don't believe you."

She sniffed. Her mouth hardened. She said nothing.

"Don't you want his killer arrested and brought to justice?" said Josh.

"Of course," she said sharply. She walked to a wicker chair and stood behind it, plucking at the white paint on the wood.

"I . . . I really didn't know him well," Lyuba said.

"But you knew him from school?" Josh said.

"A little." Her face seemed to soften.

"What were his favorite classes? Hobbies? Was he popular? A jock? Any details are helpful," I said.

"He was intense. Shy . . . like me." She looked up, nervous again.

"I bet you're not shy once you know someone," Josh said soothingly. He gave her a reassuring nod, and an electric kind of girl/boy energy radiated between them.

"Tell us more about Denny," Josh said, his voice a caress. And damn if it didn't work.

"He was into saving the environment. And surfing. He drew cartoons in his spare time. And played computer games. He told me once that he wanted to be a game designer. That outraged his parents. They had higher hopes for him. They gave everything to those boys."

"He was close to his family," I said.

"He loved them a lot. But it was hard on him. Denny just wanted to be a regular American kid. He didn't want to hear about all the sacrifices they had made for him. The guilt-tripping."

The emotion in her voice made it clear that Denny wasn't the only one who wanted to be treated regularly.

"Did he buy that Soviet army watch as a rebellion, to piss off his parents?"

Her face was blank. "I didn't hear about any watch."

"Didn't he buy one at a swap meet recently?"

She shrugged. "He might have."

"You didn't see it on his wrist? He never talked about it?"

"Not that I noticed. We're not, like, best friends or anything."

I was losing her. Josh stepped in, giving me a look.

"Where in Russia is his family from?"

"Moscow. Years ago."

"What did they do there?"

"I have no idea."

"Any idea why he was in Griffith Park Sunday afternoon?"

She fidgeted with her apron. "I haven't kept in touch lately. He's avoided me ever since . . ." she looked up, her eyes opaque, "since school began this year."

"That's not what you were going to say," I interjected.

She stared at the floor and twisted her apron into a knot.

"Something happened between you and Denny?" I said softly.

She said nothing.

"You were close once?" I persisted.

Still she was silent.

"Boyfriend?" asked Josh, catching her in his liquid-eyed tractor beam.

She blushed and pushed away from the chair. Striding to the cupboard, she pulled out textbooks. I followed, dogging her.

"There's something you're not telling us," I said.

"I've got to get ready for school," Lyuba said.

She turned, and the corner of her chemistry text jabbed into my chest. I thought she might have aimed.

"Excuse me," I said pointedly. "My fault. So were you and Denny, like, together?"

Lyuba glanced anxiously at her grandfather, but he was tossing a bowl of grated carrots, slick with sour cream.

She made a dismissive motion. Lowered her voice. "He had a crush on me. That's all."

"You don't want your family to know?"

She shrugged. "I'm not supposed to date. But we went out a few times," she said softly. "I didn't want to hurt him. He's a sweet boy. It's just that Max . . ."

She halted, frowned. Seemed desperate to get away.

She walked over to a backpack and shoved the books inside.

"The bus comes in five minutes," she said, her voice apologetic.

"What about Max?" Josh asked.

Ducking her head, Lyuba grabbed a pile of just-washed bowls and began drying them. In a few hours, they'd be filled with savory salads and dips. Her mother would ladle them onto plates and into take-away containers. An elixer to ward off homesickness. I followed her, more warily this time. I felt bad that we were tag-teaming her. But it was working; she seemed about to crack.

"What's Max's last name?" I said.

She half turned. Bit her lip. Bent over her bowls, rubbing so hard I thought the pattern would come off the ceramic.

"We know Denny spent his last night at Max's house," Josh said. "The police do too."

"Max didn't have anything to do with this."

The emotion surging through her voice made it clear—Lyuba knew the kid we were hunting for.

"How close are you to Max?" I asked.

She studied her clunky black shoes and didn't answer.

"When's the last time you spoke to him?" Josh said.

"He's not answering his cell. I've been trying ever since I heard that . . ."

Josh nodded knowingly. Max wasn't answering his cell because he was tied up with the police.

Lyuba saw the look pass between us. Her face grew apprehensive. "He's okay, isn't he? I mean, you're not here asking me questions because he's . . ."

"Because he's what?" Josh said softly.

Lyuba looked alarmed. "*Nyet*. Max's father isn't Mafia. He's a computer guy. Works all the time. Max wishes his dad made less money but was around more. But I guess he wants to give his family the opportunities he never had. All he talks about is how soft and spoiled we are here in America. He makes Max memorize four lines of Russian poetry each day. Can you believe that? On top of his regular schoolwork, it's so unfair. But he's not Mafia. He's in business."

She pronounced it "beeznis." In Russia, the word was often synonymous with Mafia. Even I knew that.

"So he's got his own computer company then?"

"Oh no," Lyuba said. "He just works at one."

Which meant he was probably just another silicon-stained wretch, not a criminal mastermind. I'd have to try another road.

"Did Denny and Max have a fight on Sunday?"

A violent crimson stain spread across her pale cheeks. "Why would they?"

"Did Denny have an argument with his family?" Josh asked. He moved closer to her. "His parents? His brother? How did they get along?"

She placed one foot on top of the other and balanced like a lovely stork. She seemed to be struggling with whether to tell us something. Or what lie to throw out next.

"We're working up a story for the paper," Josh said. "Any details you provide would help us show Denny in the best possible light. And maybe even catch his killer."

At that, Lyuba's eyes grew watery and she put her hand over her mouth and stifled a sob. She stood that way for a long moment. Then she took a deep breath and said, "Denny's father is some kind of scientist. His mother teaches music at UCLA. Denny's brother, Nicolai, is there. Studying Slavic languages. He wants to be a professor. They're gentle people. I can't imagine anyone would have wanted Denny dead."

"Does Nicolai live at home or on campus?" Josh's voice was elaborately casual.

"Dorm. We went there once to visit him for a party."

"Which dorm?"

She named it and I memorized it.

The grandfather looked up from the stove, realized we'd been talking intently. He walked over.

"Xhorosho?" he asked, clapping Josh heartily across the back. Lyuba smiled and her voice grew chipper and bright. She must be telling him that everything was fine. The grandfather spoke, stabbing at his watch.

"Da, da," Lyuba said. "I have to go now. School."

She heaved the backpack onto her shoulders, waved good-bye, and ran out the door with relief.

I scooped up a handful of spinach pies and threw fifteen dollars on the table.

The grandfather grew outraged, clasped his hands to his chest, demanded we take back our money. *"Gosti,"* he insisted. Guests.

"Please don't be offended," I said, "but our newspaper won't allow us to accept free food. It's just our policy."

I grabbed the bag of pies, patted his clasped hands, and smiled, a word from childhood springing unbidden to my lips. A word that meant thank you.

"Spasibo," I said.

CHAPTER 14

Do you think Denny rode off on his white horse to save the girl he loved and the Mafia killed him?" Josh asked as we crossed the street to the doughnut shop to retrieve Mischa.

"The girl's definitely hiding something."

"I didn't want to say anything in front of your cousin, but I spoke to the cops late last night. They wanted to keep Max overnight. Try and squeeze him. He's their chief suspect right now, not the Mafia. But the dad raised a stink. Got the kid all lawyered up. They were getting ready to release him when I went to bed."

"Did the cops suggest the dad might be mobbed up?"

"He's a computer guy," Josh said. "Not a whiff of impropriety."

We walked into the doughnut shop, looked around. Mischa wasn't there.

"That's odd," I said.

"I'll look in the men's room."

But Josh came back alone, looking perplexed.

Where could Mischa have gone? Would he now disappear from my life as mysteriously as he had arrived? I felt a stirring of hope. At the same time, I was obscurely disappointed. Mischa had detonated a bomb in my life, got me sifting through a past that grew more convoluted the more I learned.

"Now what?" I said.

"Let's get back to the office."

"What about Mischa?"

Josh grinned malevolently. "He found his way to your house once. I'm sure he'll do so again when he's ready."

"That's what I'm afraid of. But let's just give him ten minutes."

We ordered coffee and slid into a yellow plastic booth.

"I'm still hung up on this Mafia angle," I said. "You have FBI sources you can run this by, right? From that story on the little Asian girl?"

"Yeah." Josh reached into his satchel. He pulled out a black address book, rooted around.

"What're you looking for?" I said.

"Top secret."

"Oh, stop with the James Bond routine."

He groped another minute, then gave up. "Damn," he said. "I must have left my cell phone in the car."

"Here." I handed him mine.

"Oh no." He pushed it away.

"What?" I played dumb.

"This is *my* source. I call him on your cell phone, you've got the number."

I snorted. "It's not like the FBI's number is a state secret. I wouldn't even know who to ask for." Then I smiled. Letting the paranoia wash over him in soft, gentle waves.

I watched the muscles in his face tighten. Then relax.

"This guy wouldn't talk to you anyway," he said dismissively. "Be right back."

I sipped my coffee and watched him walk to the car. Behind the counter, the Cambodian family that ran the doughnut shop was bringing in fresh trays of crullers. The Cambodians had monopolized the doughnut business, even though their doughnut king who had started it all and loaned fellow immigrants money to buy their own franchises had fallen on hard times due to a gambling habit.

Josh slid back into the plastic seat and punched in a number. I heard him playing the hale-fellow-well-met game and telling his source there was something he wanted to run by him. "You got it," he said. "Two p.m."

"That's fast," I said when he hung up. "I'm impressed. Will you teach me that trick?"

"On your knees and beg, Lois Lane."

"You wish."

I looked around the doughnut shop and heard people speaking in five languages. The Cambodians behind the counter. Latinos in paint-splattered overalls across from us. Russian shopgirls wearing garish makeup. Armenians in boxy suits, heads hunched together over a yellow legal pad.

"L.A.'s the first great multicultural city, you know," I said, the caffeine jump-kicking a surge of love for my hometown. "And these are historic times. The flood of immigration. The Babel of languages, cultures, civilizations, even crime. It's all boiling down, being rendered, creating something so new that we can't even imagine what it's becoming."

Josh took a sip of coffee and stretched his lanky frame.

"It may seem new to you, pilgrim, but what's happening in L.A. is as old as history itself. Look at Shanghai in the 1930s. Odessa in 1917. New York in 1880. Go back to Constantinople. Classical Rome and Athens. Alexandria. They all had a stew of different ethnic groups, rivalries between outside powers. Great wealth and poverty. A thriving drug and criminal culture. A place to start again for refugees. Where the most threadbare immigrant can become a millionaire. L.A. is just being snotty to think it's the first."

"And on that note . . ." I stood up, tucked my cell phone into my purse, and noticed the scribbled phone number of the Avila family who lived on Cordoba Street. A sharp stab of memory hit, my personal life bleeding through work.

Then my phone rang.

"You are wondering where I am," a familiar, accented voice said.

"Mischa, yes, where are you? And how did you get my cell phone number?"

"Finally," said Josh, rolling his eyes.

"I hack into phone company," Mischa said offhandedly.

"How did you know which company to hack into?"

"No, is small joke. I see your number on display screen."

"Why didn't you stay at the doughnut shop like you said you would? We've been waiting here twenty minutes."

"I was in wrong mood for doughnuts. So I walk to Laurel and Ventura, where is Russian bakery name of Vrema. You must try turnovers with sweet farmer's cheese. Fantastic."

"We'll pick you up at the corner in five minutes."

"Ah, you must come inside," Mischa said.

"Why?"

"There is a bill."

And he doesn't have enough to pay.

"Oh, for Christ's sake, Mischa, this has got to stop."

"I know," he said meekly. "I will pay back. On my word."

I stabbed the "off" button and told Josh what was up.

"I'll wait here while you go get him," he said. "I want to call LAPD and see what's new."

When I walked in, Mischa waved me over with a smile. He had flakes of pastry down his shirt and the table was covered with crumbs. An empty coffee mug held the swampy remains of dunked breads.

The front door opened, the bell jingling as a blast of cold air swept in, followed by three thick-necked men with gold jewelry, black sunglasses, and ruddy faces. They wore leather jackets and too much aftershave and walked with a stiff swagger that might have been eased by looser pants.

As their gaze swept the room, they bunched up, like a pack of sharks that has seen a sea lion. One spoke Russian into a cell phone, then slapped it shut. The other two reached into their jackets. The girl behind the counter froze, her body arched over the display case, a rag clutched in midswipe. A look of dawning horror was on her face. I took a fast breath. A palpable air of menace had swept into the room along with the physical cold. What struck me most was their aggressive body language and wolfish stares that persisted long after Western decorum would have made them look away. It was a look that said, *I have raw power and firearms on my side, and I am not bound by societal niceties.*

I stepped back. Behind me, I heard the scrape of a chair and a scuffle, then the pounding of receding feet. I turned in time to see Mischa disappearing down the back corridor.

One of the men uttered an oath and fired a gun. I hit the ground, aware that the woman behind the counter had disappeared. I wondered if Mischa knew these men or whether, like me, he was simply reacting to a universal threat.

Within seconds, two of them pounded past in pursuit of Mischa and the third was pointing the gun at me. Then the other thugs came back and six hands pulled me up roughly, their faces red with rage. Stubby fingers stained yellow from nicotine poked the flesh of my arm. A sharp, acrid smell oozed off them, sweat and vodka-soused cologne, tobacco, and garlic. With that came the whiff of betrayal. Had Mischa set me up?

One of the men grabbed my hair and pulled me toward him, screaming in unintelligible Russian. I could see yellow incisors, the flash of steel teeth, an uvula pulsing with engorged rage. It became clear that he was repeating the same words over and over. I nudged my purse toward him but he swept it off the table with a curse. I groaned and pressed my hand over my scalp where the hair stretched horizontal in the air between us. He gave a vicious tug and I gasped.

"No Russian. American," I said. It was crucial that he understand this. He must have me confused with a Russian who owed him money, or had once betrayed him. But I was an American, raised on democracy, civil society, and the rule of law. We didn't go in for this kind of bullying. There would be a high price to pay. I tried to straighten, wanting to convey my indignation through the ramrod steel of my spine, but he had a shank of my hair between his fat fingers and I could only stoop.

He pulled me toward him, until our faces were inches apart.

"Who your friend?" he asked in thick, guttural English.

Again I heard the scrape of a chair, Mischa bolting, the gun going off.

"Friend?" I said thickly, my lips numb with fear.

The hand released my hair and I staggered backward, hitting the table and sliding to my knees. Pushing back up, I forced myself to look at them. They wore gaudily patterned silk shirts and leather jackets. There was an unformed quality to their faces, like dough that hasn't risen right, skin chafed red and angry where they hadn't taken enough care shaving. Slate gray eyes like dirty glaciers.

"Where he go?" The leader's pudgy ringed hand snaked toward me and I flinched, afraid he was going to hit me, but he grabbed my chin and jerked it up to drill me with those empty eyes.

I hadn't yet spoken to Mischa when they walked in. They had no way of knowing we knew each other. My head swam. Yesterday, I had been blissfully ignorant of Russian cousins. Today this new family member might get me killed. Should I tell them everything I knew and be done with it? For all I knew Mischa had led me into a trap. But what if he hadn't?

"I've never seen that guy before," I said. "I wanted to ask him what he was eating so I could order it too."

"Lies," the man yelled, letting me go suddenly.

I waited for blows to rain down. Instead, my interrogator took a step back. He crossed his arms and narrowed his eyes, studying me. Then he bent over, picked up a fallen chair, set it back on its legs, and made to dust off the seat.

"Please," he said with an oily grin. "My apologies. You sit."

I started to say no, then thought better of angering him again.

He sat down next to me, pulling up his own chair for an intimate chat.

"We have business with this man. Yes? For two days we are looking, looking. It is very important we find him. You understand?"

"Yes," I said, nodding frantically as I tried to figure it out. Maybe Mischa had told me the truth about escaping the Russian Mafia. At least that meant he wasn't in league with them. What on earth had I gotten mixed up in? I prayed someone would stroll in for a coffee and poppy-seed pastry, but busy Ventura Boulevard was ominously empty.

"You are relative, maybe?" the man said conversationally.

"No."

"American girlfriend, then?" The tiny eyes assessed me.

"That's ridiculous. I've never seen him before in my life."

Time dragged, and nobody said anything. They began a heated exchange in Russian. I feared they were arguing about whether to kill me. Then the leader silenced them. He studied me for what seemed like an eternity, then sighed.

"Sorry then, miss. Enjoy your breakfast."

He motioned to his accomplices and they fell grudgingly into line behind him like dogs that have been denied a bone. Halfway to the door, the leader turned, straightened his collar, and came back. He placed his palms flat on the table. Whorls of black hair curled out where his shirtsleeves met his wrists.

"If you are lying, we will find out. Many eyes and ears report to us. We will track you down. Next time we are not so nice."

He swiped a napkin from the table, crumpled it in one fist, and let it fall to the floor, leaving little doubt as to what he would do to me. Then he and his friends left for good in a black Town Car that pulled away with a screech of tires. Too late, I thought to look for plates.

I sat there for a long while to make sure it wasn't another trick, that they wouldn't drive around the corner and come back. There were still no signs of life behind the counter or in the back kitchen. Then I staggered out of the bakery, kicking the bunched-up napkin into a corner as I went.

Wrapping the last dregs of my dignity around me, I hiked with shaky legs back to the doughnut shop where I had left Josh. His car was gone. I looked at my watch and was shocked that only twenty minutes had passed. I was stranded. I thought of calling the police. I thought of calling Josh. Instead, I stood in the parking lot and thought about the danger Mischa had placed me in with his hare-brained scheme of getting me to pay off his smugglers so he could start an illegal life in America.

Just then, Josh's car tore into the lot.

"Where have you been?" he shouted through the window.

He looked at my disheveled hair, the alarm on my face.

"What happened to you? Were you abducted by aliens? And where the hell is your cousin?"

"So he didn't come running back here, huh?"

"No. Now what happened?"

"A passel of Russian hoods showed up for breakfast," I said weakly, then climbed into his car.

He gave me a disbelieving look, but killed the engine.

"From the beginning," he said.

"I can't believe it," Josh said when I finished. "We have to go to the police."

He saw the look on my face. "Don't we?"

"Those guys scare me," I said. "I don't know what I've

gotten mixed up in, but I think it's bigger than just me and Mischa. Besides, what exactly would I tell them?"

"What you just told me," Josh erupted.

"But then I have to tell them about Mischa," I said. "And explain why I let him spend the night instead of turning him in."

Josh looked at me with disgust. "It's your funeral," he said.

"Josh, what if he really is my cousin? He knows things about my family that I've never told anyone. That I barely remembered myself."

"You're making a mistake."

"He shows up on my doorstep, pressing all the right buttons. He's in trouble. And he says he's my cousin. The only family I may have."

"Fine. Tell him to go back to Moscow and apply for an immigration visa and list you as his next of kin. Nice and legal."

"How's he supposed to get back? And he'll still owe the Mafia for smuggling him in."

"Then take out a loan and pay off the slimeballs and make him work like a coolie to pay it off. He's still here illegally and subject to deportation if the INS catches him."

"I know," I said. "I've been over all of this. I don't know what to do."

"Try focusing on your job for a change." He put his hands on the steering wheel. "So," he said, his tone lighter, "you still up for a visit to the Feebs?"

"You bet."

"Good girl," he said, starting the car.

igging in my purse for a breath mint, I again pulled out the piece of paper on which I had written Wendy and Morris Avila's number.

"I have to make a personal call," I said as Josh wheeled the car onto the 405 freeway.

I dialed and a voice said, "Halloo?"

I asked for Luka.

There was a long pause. "Moment," the voice said, then after much shuffling the phone was handed to another person.

"Yes, can I help you?" came a Filipino-accented voice.

I repeated my request.

"Sorry, there's no one here by that name."

"Maybe a previous tenant," I said hopefully. "He'd be an older man. Slavic. Maybe Russian?"

I saw Josh start paying attention.

The voice grew more formal. "We are not tenants, miss. We own this house. Since 2002. Now who are you? What do you want?"

"I'm trying to locate this man, Mr. Luka. Maybe he sold to you?"

I realized how dumb this was, in a place like L.A., where property turned over every few years.

"We bought from a lady. Her job was transferring her to San Francisco."

"I see." I was getting desperate. There was an important thread that I had to retrace. "And before that?"

"We wouldn't know. Have you tried a real estate agency?"

"Thanks."

I hung up and called the *Times,* where I got Luke Vinograd. He was a senior copy messenger and friend who often undertook clandestine assignments for me. At forty, Luke was ridiculously overqualified for his job—with his razor intellect and keen memory, he should have been a star reporter or editor by now. But his insistence on seeing life as a playful adventure instead of a cutthroat boiler-room drama meant that his career path had derailed years ago, though he seemed not to care. By now, he had been at the paper so long that he knew its secrets better than most editors, which often served me well. I reciprocated by buying him drinks and feeding him scuttlebutt and we genuinely appreciated each other's company.

"How's tricks, Lukey?" I said.

"Not as lively as yours, judging from the byline this morning."

"Just wait till tomorrow. I'm en route to a rendezvous with the FBI as we speak," I said, winking at Josh, who rolled his eyes.

"I hope you get a special agent who looks like Kevin Costner in *The Untouchables.*"

"If so, I'll be sure to get his number for you. Say, Luke, can you do an owner history on a property if I give you an address?"

"Sure thing, missy. You know I've always had a thing for a man in a uniform."

"The Feebs don't wear uniforms," I said, giving him the address.

"They do in my fantasies. And they carry handcuffs and batons. But enough wishful thinking. I'll get back to you toot sweet."

"Wanna tell me what that was all about?" Josh huffed when I slapped the phone shut, still laughing. "What did he say about uniforms and handcuffs?"

"You heard that? Trust me, you don't want to know."

"But if it relates to Denny Lukin . . ."

"It doesn't."

"C'mon, Eve. What about that address you gave him? Who lives there?"

"I honestly don't know. This is personal. I'm trying to trace someone who knew my family."

"You have a personal life?"

I thought about it.

"Not really."

Luke called back ten minutes later, reporting that the house had been built in 1929. It was a one-story, two-bedroom, one-bathroom place. One man had owned it until 1941, when it was sold. It changed hands again in 1947, then not until 1965. Luke rattled off the names of the first owners and I jotted them down.

"And who bought it in 1965?"

I heard the clicks of the keyboard as Luke scrolled down.

"A Stepan Domashny."

My breath caught. Could this be my guy? "How long did he own it?"

"Oh, he was there a long time. Sold in 1989. Maybe he died. Probably raised his family there."

An odd pang went through me.

"Does it give a middle name for Domashny? Something along the lines of Luka, perhaps?"

"No middle name."

"Damn. Who did he sell to?"

"Winnie DeCarlo. Who sold in 2002."

Ah, the woman who had been transferred to San Francisco.

"Thanks, Luke," I said, signing off.

As Josh crawled south toward Getty Drive and the monolithic museum on the hill, I called San Francisco information and got a W. DeCarlo who lived on Thirty-first Street. Trying her number gave me a recording and a referral to a cell phone if callers needed to reach her right away.

Holding my breath, I punched in the number but got her voice mail again. I left a message.

"Hi, um, you don't know me, but my name is Eve Diamond and I'm trying to track down a long-lost friend of my, uh, late mother's. His name was Stepan Domashny. He might have gone by Luka, too. And I understand he sold you the house you once owned on Cordoba Street in Hollywood. I was wondering if you knew how I might find him. I'm not a lunatic or a creditor, honest."

"Subpar, Brenda Starr," Josh said when I'd hung up.

"What?"

"You sounded unhinged. I'm surprised. Tracking down people is what you do for a living."

I shrugged. "But this isn't work. Like I told you, it's personal. I can't hide behind the press pass."

At 1:45 p.m. we pulled up to the Federal Building in Westwood, where the FBI had its headquarters. There was the usual mayhem outside, a group of veiled women marching with protest banners and bullhorns at the corner of Veteran and Wilshire boulevards. Next to them, another group of veiled women held opposing signs and waved their fists at the first group.

"How'd you get so thick with the Feebs?" I asked Josh.

"One of them called last year to praise my brilliant reportage and we ended up going out for a drink. The rest is history."

"You lie!" I said. "Not in a million years would a Feeb call up the Great Media Satan."

"He would if they went to school together."

"Let me guess, that school of hard knocks known as Yale?"

"No, Miss Smart Knickers, that's CIA recruitment headquarters. I mean my alma mater, Princeton."

"From Princeton to the FBI. Jeez, what a comedown for his poor parents."

Josh grinned. "Not really. Lansing's dad was some big kahuna with J. Edgar."

"I'm liking this guy more and more."

"Don't hold him responsible for the sins of the father," Josh said.

At the Federal Building, we joined a throng of people looking for passports, immigration papers, and government assistance who were being cleared, one at a time, by uniformed guards with earpieces who gave us the evil eye. They scrutinized our IDs and put us through an airport-type security gauntlet including metal detectors, a personal pat-down, and metal wand massage.

After going through a second level of security at the inner lobby, we headed for a bank of brushed-chrome elevators and took a ride to the eighteenth floor, where a young FBI receptionist with black-rimmed glasses and a severe haircut sat behind floor-to-ceiling glass. We signed in and she called for Lansing, explaining we needed an escort to go inside.

Within several minutes, a man with slicked-back hair, a squat, muscular build, and ramrod posture stepped out to meet us. He wore a crisp white shirt, tie, and khaki pants with razor creases. He slapped Josh on the back and they did a faux ghetto handshake. Only when Josh introduced me did Special Agent James Lansing turn his probing brown eyes on me. We shook hands briskly and he told us to follow him, keying in a combination that opened the door to the inner sanctum. We walked along rows of cubicles with computers that faced away from the windows—for security reasons, Lansing said. I saw an older man bent over a keyboard, typing madly with two fingers. His face was ruddy and red, and he had the bloated body of a drinker.

Lansing saw me staring. He gave a little frown.

"That's Clavendish," he said, shooting a look at Josh. "Don't mind him. Russian expert. Does organized crime now. It's his last week and he's overdue for pasture. Sucks back three martinis at lunch. They've got them on special at Hamburger Hamlet across the street. Sobers up in time to drive to the poker clubs."

Lansing ushered us into an office, closed the door. He sat down, rolled his chair over to the desk, swiped a bottle of vitamin-infused water, and took a long glug. He exhaled, loud and virtuous. Grabbing a finger-pumping device, he began squeezing. "I spend *my* lunch at the gym."

He inclined his head toward Clavendish, whom we could see through the window, now flipping through a file cabinet.

"He's old school. Still fighting the Cold War, poor guy.

Doesn't understand that the world has changed. And then there was that scandal . . ."

Lansing trailed off delicately. Or was it salaciously?

"What scandal?" I asked.

He waved his arms. "Couldn't keep his hands off the help. But that's ancient history. This is the new FBI. We hew to a higher standard of professionalism. Frown on gambling, too. But never mind. Don't like to talk bad about a fellow who's down on his luck."

You could have fooled me.

Lansing leaned back in his chair. "So what can I do you for?"

"Did you read about that kid found on the Griffith Park trail yesterday?" Josh said. "Denny Lukin. Parents are Russian. Nice house in Studio City, right, Eve?"

I nodded. "Sasha and Irina Lukin," I said. "They on your Mafia radar?"

Lansing picked up a pencil, flipped it upside down, bounced the eraser on his desk.

"I can only talk in generalities, you understand."

"You mean you can't get specific about an ongoing investigation?" I said blandly.

Lansing raised his eyebrows and turned to Josh. "I detect a certain lack of finesse in your colleague."

"Don't mind her," Josh said. "She's used to brawling with local law enforcement."

"Ah." Lansing formed his fingers into a church steeple. A look passed between them. I resisted an urge to slap it off. Instead, I sat on my hands and radiated my best local-yokel vibe. The more he underestimated me, the more my power grew.

"Does that mean you are investigating the Lukin murder?" I said.

"I can't confirm or deny any investigations," Lansing said with mock patience. He jabbed his pencil at me. "Is that clear?"

"Absolutely," piped up Josh. "We'd be happy for whatever general background you can give us about the Russian Mafia in Los Angeles." I nodded, smiled, and got my notepad ready.

Lansing leaned back and hooked a thumb into his belt loop. For the next ten minutes, he regaled us with the history of the Russians in Los Angeles. The first big wave had been White Russians—intelligentsia and minor nobility who had fled the revolution in 1917. Hitler's rise had brought an influx of refugees, many of them brilliant artists, writers, and film people, and the end of World War II saw displaced persons, Holocaust survivors, and more political refugees. The next group to arrive were the Jewish refuseniks of the 1970s and '80s who won asylum for religious reasons.

"Emigration was pretty tightly controlled in the Brezhnev stagnation years," Lansing drawled. "You either had to be a refusenik or a dissident, and usually somebody prominent like Solzhenitsyn, although he settled in Vermont, not out here. The only others they let out around that time were spies." Lansing laughed unpleasantly. "You can ask Clavendish all about that."

It was a throwaway line, which I failed to jot down. Only later would it come back to me.

"After Gorbachev came to power in 1985," Lansing went on, "things changed fast. By the late 1980s, people with family and connections from all the Soviet republics were immigrating or coming as tourists and overstaying their visas. Most of them were law-abiding folk. But some bad eggs slipped in too."

"You mean Mafia?" Josh said.

"You bet. These were ruthless folk who had grown up in the gulags and had their own shadow economy to maneuver around the impossible Soviet planned economy. For them, ripping off the system was a way of life."

"And then they landed here."

"If they could function under a police state, well, imagine how easy they have it here. Good times. Even after nine-eleven, Slavs get a pretty free pass from Homeland Security. They're not on the no-fly lists. Did you know you can hire a guy in Moscow to come out and whack someone in L.A. for two thousand dollars? They arrive as tourists, buy a gun, take care of business, go home. By the time the body's found, they're drinking vodka on the Arbat.

"And Russia? Forget it. There are assassinations on the street every week. They target prosecutors. Judges. Duma members crusading against corruption. Businessmen who won't pay protection money. Even journalists."

Lansing leered at me, and I wondered whether he thought that was such a bad thing. "Remember the editor of *Forbes* in Russia? They took him out in broad daylight. And he was an American, for God's sake. So be careful where you stick your nose. Leave the dirty work to us."

Lansing winked at Josh.

I tried to ignore his condescending tone. Obnoxious or not, he was a source.

". . . they eliminate anyone who gets in their way," Lansing was saying. "Maybe that's what happened to your man." He referred to some notes he had jotted down, and I wondered if this was an elaborate feint and he really knew the case quite intimately. "This Sasha Lukin fellow. Maybe he crossed them somehow. Wouldn't pay protection money. Or got into debt. Human life is meaningless to them."

"It was his seventeen-year-old son who got taken out, not the father," I said, annoyed at Lansing's flippancy. "And he's not a businessman. He may work for a high-tech outfit in the Valley."

Lansing smirked knowingly. "That's probably just his cover."

I thought about Sasha Lukin, his world-weariness, his cultured demeanor, and it didn't fit. How could he be involved with such a cutthroat illegal business?

"That's why we're wondering if there's any whisper on the street that this was a Mafia hit," Josh said, ignoring Lansing's earlier *diktat* about not discussing specifics.

"We're looking into it," the special agent said.

"Especially since Eve here just got roughed—"

"What a view you've got," I interrupted, jumping up and stomping on Josh's toe as I made my way to the window.

"Eve got what?"

Lansing's eyes narrowed.

"I interviewed the dad yesterday, it was pretty rough," I said, emphasizing the last word. I did not want Josh dragging my thuggish encounter into this conversation.

Eighteen stories below, the veiled women moved like ants along the sidewalk.

"Does this sound like a Mafia hit?" Josh persisted.

"They'd kill the whole family," Lansing said immediately.

"So what are the Russian Mafia into?"

"Runs the gamut. Money laundering. Credit card and insurance fraud. Auto theft. Arms smuggling. Drugs. Extortion. Prostitution. Heavy into that."

I recalled Mischa's tale about the smuggled women. Lyuba's grandfather and his protection money.

Lansing rambled on about his latest case, how he had broken up an identity-theft ring that stretched across five states, and then the conversation devolved into Princeton gossip and I zoned out. Josh might think he had a wonderful source here but other than a primer on Russian immigration, Lansing hadn't told us squat.

On the way out, we passed Clavendish, still at the files. He gave us a quick look, then hunched his shoulders and bent over the cabinets. His wool suit looked shiny in places, its wide brown lapels all wrong. He was a big man, had a huge head with salt-and-pepper curls. But it was his eyes that got me. In that split second before he averted them. They were big and blue and liquid where I expected unflinching steel. He couldn't have been too good at clandestine ops with those eyes; they gave too much away. Or gambling either. But maybe he hadn't started out that way.

While Josh excused himself to use the restroom, I sat on a leather couch in the lobby, where I saw that the receptionist had a poetry collection by Aleksandr Pushkin propped up behind the glass. I could tell because unlike Mischa's book the night before, this one was in English.

The office door opened and Clavendish walked out. He did an exaggerated double take when he saw me, inclined his head in a solicitous nod, then swept past. At the desk he paused.

"Well, Janet, I'm off for an early lunch." His gaze fell on her book. "Pushkin, hmm? You really shouldn't bother. He's virtually untranslatable."

Taking a step back, Clavendish clasped his right hand over his left wrist and began to declaim in a schoolboy fashion. A Russian schoolboy. The words flew out of his mouth with fiery emotion, and his graying jowls quivered with the effort. After four lines, he stopped and smoothed his hair back.

"In the original, it's quite magnificent," he said. "Well, my dear, I suppose that's enough verse from me today." Then he turned on his heel and walked out.

"Bye, Tom," she called after him.

When the door opened, I expected to see Josh, but the big, leonine head of Clavendish thrust itself back into the room. He cleared his throat.

"I was just thinking, Janet. If you're determined to read in translation, why don't you try Tsvetayeva? It's all rubbish unless you read it in Russian, of course, but I believe you'll find her style infinitely more accessible."

CHAPTER 16

The next time the door opened it was Josh. "Ready?" he said.

Clavendish intrigued me. He was an exotic flower, clinging to life amid a desert of cocksure Lansings. He didn't fit in. He might never have, I thought, recalling J. Edgar Hoover's tough-talking, poker-faced G-men. But then I remembered Lansing's derogatory comments, how this was Clavendish's last week before retirement. Maybe he had just stopped trying.

Josh said he'd drop me off at my house. Then he was headed to an LAPD press conference where detectives would announce the latest in the Lukin case. I decided to try to track down Denny's brother at UCLA.

When we pulled up, Josh came inside my house to make sure Mischa hadn't slunk back with Mafia mobsters in tow. But the place was blessedly empty. So Josh unloaded Mischa's bike and waved good-bye. Soon I was on my way back west.

Outside the UCLA dorm where Nicolai lived, I waited until some students walked up then explained that I had misplaced my ID. I must have looked enough like a grad student or someone's girlfriend that they let me in. Then I popped my head inside one of the study rooms, asked for Nicolai, and was directed to the third floor.

I knocked and a boy in Bruins sweats and a flannel

shirt answered. It wasn't one of the faces that had stared back at me from the oil painting.

"I'm looking for Nicolai," I said.

He looked me up and down. "Nick isn't here."

"Know where I can find him?"

"Went for some air. Said he might end up at the Coffee Spot."

"Thanks. I'll try him there."

The boy seemed to realize he had been too free with the info.

"I'm Trent. His roommate. And you are?"

"Oh." Sheepish and sorry. Shuffling my feet. "Eve. An old family friend. We've just gotten the word . . ." I drifted off and let my silence do the talking.

Trent had been reared well. His eyes swept downward, mouth pursing. He exhaled noisily. "Oh man, I'm sorry for your loss," he said.

If he had a hat, he would have swept it off his head and placed it over his heart. He took another long breath.

"It's sick, man. Who would do a thing like that?"

Exactly what I'm trying to find out.

"Nick and his brother were real close," Trent continued. "They talked all the time. He was going crazy today, cooped up here waiting for his parents or the police to call. Media's camped out in front of his house, even his parents have bailed. Nick was doing laps around the room. I finally pushed him out the door. Told him a walk would do him good."

"The police?"

"Sure," Trent said authoritatively. "They need to interview the family and stuff."

"Did Nick seem nervous about that?"

"A little. Which was weird. It's not like he did anything. I told him to chill. But I think it's genetic."

"What's genetic?"

What did Nicolai have to hide?

"You know." Trent made his hands into circles, miming binoculars. James Bond, as interpreted by Austin Powers with a surfer haircut and flip-flops.

Trent leaned against the doorjamb, crossed his arms. "Commies. Spies. All that Russian blood. Nick's old man had a good line about that. He'd say, 'In Russia, everyone is guilty. It's just a matter of matching the person to the crime.'"

"So you don't think Nick had anything specific to tell the police?"

Trent pushed himself off the jamb. A smell of musty bedclothes, sweat, and chlorine wafted over, fanned by his open flannel shirt.

"You'll have to ask him. I'll tell him you came by. What did you say your last name was?"

"I didn't. But it's Diamond. Eve Diamond." I turned and walked down the stairs.

I asked some kids along Bruin's Walk where the Coffee Spot was, then picked my way through the meandering green campus until I came to it. Nick wasn't there, but after asking five groups of kids, I stumbled across one who knew him. He said Nick had come in earlier, then gone to the library.

Great, I thought, there are only about ten of them on campus. But then I remembered he was doing Slavic studies. That meant the URL—University Research Library. I strolled inside, found the Slav stacks, and wandered around, trying to conjure up the photos I had seen in the Lukins' living room.

Finally, I spotted a kid with dishwater blond hair reading at a cubicle. Subtract a few years and his features matched the photos. I walked over.

"Nick?" I asked. He was dressed in the SoCal uniform that seemed to prevail, no matter the weather—long cargo shorts, T-shirt, and flip-flops. In deference to winter, he had a long-sleeve white waffle shirt under the T.

Hearing my voice, the kid slammed the book shut, practically jumping out of his seat. Odd, you'd think that grief would slow the reflexes, emotion thickening like slurry in his veins.

"I'm sorry to startle you," I said. "Are you Nicolai Lukin?"

He looked up, and a wary cast fell over his eyes. "No." He paused. "But I know him. Is there a message?"

He looked away, ran his fingers through tousled hair, and waited. I knew it was him, but didn't want to let on. My gaze dropped to his book. It was a Soviet history book. He saw me looking and slid his backpack over it.

"Yes," I said, picking my words carefully. "My name is Eve Diamond. I'm a reporter for the *Los Angeles Times*. Could you please tell Nick I'd like to talk to him about his brother. . . ." I trailed off. The boy paled and said nothing.

"I know the last thing they probably want right now is to talk to the press. But I have information that may help them find the killer."

"You do?" the boy croaked, then caught himself and added, "I'll let him know." Then, because he just couldn't help himself, he said, "Like what?"

I sat down, leaned in, and said, "The police are looking into possible involvement with the Russian Mafia."

"The Mafia?" he echoed, and I could see the gears whirring in his head. He knew a lot more than he was letting on.

"I don't think that's possible," the boy said, then caught himself. "At least Nick never told me anything like that."

"Was there any evidence that he had angered someone? That someone was out to get him? A fight over a girl, maybe? Did he and Max get into it over Lyuba?"

"No," the boy said hollowly. "Nothing like that. Denny was a good kid." He caught himself again, winced. "That is . . . I met him once or twice."

Ironically, our charade made it easier to question him at this emotionally raw time.

"He wasn't into drugs or gangs, then?" I bit my tongue, rushed on. "I mean, maybe his brother talked to you about him?"

"No," the boy said in a forlorn voice. "Sorry," he added. "It's hit us all so hard."

More urgent now, I dropped all pretense. "What about this phone call he supposedly got right before he went to Griffith Park? Was he meeting someone?"

"I don't know."

"Had you noticed any change in him? Had he become secretive? Was he getting any unusual phone calls? Or letters?" I said, thinking back to how Lukin had asked me whether police had found a note on his son's body.

"That was my father," the boy said dully.

"What?"

He looked at me in panic. "Oh, sorry, I mean Denny's father."

"What about Denny's father?"

"Oh, nothing. I misspoke." He choked out a laugh.

"Pulled an all-nighter for a test early this morning. I'm trashed."

You're trashed and I'm screwed if we don't get any further than this.

"Denny's father was acting secretive?"

He gave me a panicked look. "No. I don't know. I'm just the friend, remember?" His voice pleading to continue our charade. I saw that he was trembling and I wanted to put my arm around him to comfort him. But I didn't, and ever since then, I've regretted it. I never had another chance.

"Maybe I could help Nicolai make sense of everything that's going on," I said.

He licked his lips. "I really have to go now." He grabbed his backpack, stood up, fidgeted.

"Nick," I said softly. "How about it?"

The boy looked steadily at me. "I could ask him," he said.

"Great. Here's my number. Call me anytime. And one more thing."

"Yeah?" His back half turned to me now, walking out of the stacks, out the door.

"I'm really sorry about what happened to your family. I met your father yesterday. I thought he was a really nice man."

The boy's face crumpled. He turned and fled.

I stayed where I was. My gaze fell on the book Nicolai Lukin had been reading. It was called *Jousting in the Shadows: A History of the Cold War 1947–1991*. The authors were a former KGB colonel and an American who had worked for the CIA. Why hadn't Nicolai wanted me to see this book?

Hefting it into my hand, I took it to the desk and asked if I could check it out.

"ID, please," a bored student worker intoned, his head buried in a Java programming text.

Wordlessly, I handed over my California driver's license.

"UCLA ID, please," he said.

"Can I check out a book without one?"

"You must have a valid UCLA ID to check out books."

A long hand reached out to reclaim the book. I grabbed the other end, tugged. Surprised, the student worker looked up.

"Can I read it here, in the library?"

He blinked. "Long as you want," he said, going back to his text. "Next."

I took my find to a trestle table, sat down, and stood the book on its spine. Then I let go to see where it would fall open. It landed on a creased page: "The Purge Years." I scanned but didn't see anything that struck me. This was all too far back in history. I closed the book, examined the leaves. I saw a slight gap, an indentation. Curious, I let the book fall open again. This time, it opened to a page about two-thirds through. Tucked inside was a small receipt. The ink was so faint that I could barely make out the letters. *Thank you for shopping at the Coffee Spot*, it said. The bill was for $2.79. The date was today's. About an hour and a half ago. Nick Lukin's receipt. This was the page Nick had been reading when I showed up, scaring him so much that he slammed it shut. Was it a natural reaction to my coming up on him unawares? Or was this page significant?

I skimmed it, reading about a spy scandal in Russia in the mid-1980s. A U.S. scientific attaché had been detained in Moscow in late 1984, allegedly for helping two Russian scientists smuggle nuclear defense statistics out of the Soviet Union. After being interrogated by the KGB for several days at the notorious Lubyanka prison, the American diplomat had been released. It was rumored that he was exchanged for a Soviet spy named Ludmilla Belyaeva, whom the Americans had been holding. End of story. Except that the two Soviet scientists disappeared and had been presumed executed by the Soviets for treason.

I scanned their names but found none I recognized. I flipped ten pages back and then ten pages forward, scouring to no avail for something that might sound familiar. Checking the index for "Lukin," I came up blank. The index was also silent on the subject of the Russian Mafia, which in those days was only emerging from the shadows.

I sat there, watching students flirt and preen in their study groups, others snoring softly, facedown in their texts. A solitary boy unwrapped food from waxy paper and, glancing around to make sure no one was looking, crammed it into his mouth. The gamut of student life.

I looked back at the book. Was Nicolai Lukin merely suffering from a case of nerves the day after his brother's murder? Or was there something buried here that could help me? I glanced at my watch and saw that another hour had gone by. I couldn't sit here all day. Feeling a bit like a spy myself, I jotted down the book's title and its authors and publisher and the page Lukin had been reading when I surprised him. You never knew when such things would come in handy, all the minutiae and scraps and string you collected as an investigative reporter, then tried to fit together into a narrative like so many puzzle pieces. It paid to be disciplined, organized. Just like in espionage, I thought.

I walked briskly across campus to my car, got inside, and cranked the heat until I grew sluggish from the warmth. I felt disoriented from too little sleep and too much coffee. What was the common thread? What was I missing? It hovered just out of reach.

My cell phone rang, startling me.

"I'm looking for Eve Diamond," a woman's voice said.

"That's me."

"This is Winnie DeCarlo from San Francisco."

In my stupor, it took me a minute to place the name.

"The house? Stepan Domashny?" she said.

"Oh, right. Of course. He's an old friend of my mother's and she's passed on now and I was looking through her old papers the other night and . . ." I stopped, realizing that I sounded like a gibbering lunatic. "I'm just trying to get in touch with people who might have known her. Now that I've got a family and children of my own."

The lies rolled blithely off my tongue.

"Yes, well . . ." DeCarlo said. "It was a long time ago. I had just gotten my first job, and my parents helped me with the down payment. The house was all original. He hadn't done any of those horrible 1960s remodels. Charming man. Quiet, didn't say much. But dignified."

"Was he from here?"

"Oh, honey, no, he was Russian. In fact, that's why he sold. He was going back. As soon as that perestroika came in, he was out like a bullet. I got the feeling he had waited all his life for that."

I swallowed. "Did he leave a forwarding address?"

Another laugh. "That was so many years ago. If he did I might have scribbled it down and stuck it in a file that I dumped when I moved up here."

"Did Domashny also go by the nickname Luka?"

"Not that I know of."

"Did you ever hear from him after you bought the house? Find any of his belongings?"

"You're jogging my memory. Hold on." She spoke slowly, remembering from a long distance.

"He was a widower, if I recall. His children were grown. They lived somewhere on the East Coast."

"Do you remember their names?"

"I never knew them. Stepan just said they were against his going back. But there was something. . . . I had to go up to the attic once to set mousetraps, and I found an old box full of papers. Cards and letters in several languages. Love letters. You could smell perfume."

CHAPTER 17

*W*hat did you do with them?" I asked, my breath catching.

"Oh, honey, I just left them there."

I had to suppress a desire to rush over to the Hollywood house immediately. I wanted it so bad. I just knew that some of the letters had to be from my mother.

"And when you sold the house, did the buyers know about them?"

"I don't know. But they would have found out. There's an apricot tree in the backyard that attracts tree rats in the summer. Horrid things. They get into the attic and you can hear them scratching around, making an awful racket around two in the morning. But you know, I miss Southern California, I have to tell you . . ."

"Oh, Ms. DeCarlo, thank you very much. Is there anything else you remember about Stepan Domashny?"

"No, can't say that there is. But I've got your number if I do."

"Call me collect," I said, my heart warming to this disembodied voice who was such a romantic that she couldn't throw away a box of fifty-year-old love letters.

I hung up and called the family at the Cordoba house. Finally I got a kid who spoke English in a voice that kept breaking. I explained that I had called before and asked if anyone had been up to the attic and seen the box of letters that had belonged to a previous owner.

"Let me ask my mother. I know we had a problem up there with mice last year."

There followed a burst of conversation in what I imagined was Tagalog. The teenager came back on. "She says my dad found a box of papers up there. Really old stuff. He was afraid the mice would use it for a nest so he threw it out."

My heart thudded.

"When?"

"Hold on." There was another conversation in Tagalog. The boy came back.

"Last summer. I hope they weren't important."

Stop! I wanted to scream. You can't do that. It's my life you're throwing away.

I imagined racing over to Cordoba Street, rooting through the overflowing trash bins and pulling out the decades-old letters, stained now with coffee grounds and egg shells and potato peelings. I'd find them moments before the trash truck lumbered up and the mechanical pincers advanced to hoist up the bin and send this priceless link with my past tumbling into the truck's evil-smelling innards.

But I was six months too late. It made me heartsick to think they had lain moldering in a dusty attic for years, only to be destroyed just months before I called. I wondered how many other artifacts met the same end each day, thrown out by people who never suspected they'd just destroyed the last record of someone's life.

"Well," I said, trying for a hearty tone, "If you ever find any other letters or papers, could you give me a call?" I gave him my number.

*   *   *

Finally ready to drive, I spun down the parking structure and through the labyrinth of UCLA. The campus road dumped me out onto Veteran and Westwood boulevards, where I caught the longest red light ever to plague L.A. For the second time that day, I stared at the tall black rectangle of the Federal Building, with its graceless box architecture and tinted windows. Lansing was up there, that cocky bastard.

My cell phone rang. It was Trabuco, asking where I was and when he'd see my sorry ass in the office.

"Hold on a sec," I told him, and put down the phone.

Something Lansing said earlier came flooding back. His scornful comment about Clavendish's liquid lunches at the Hamburger Hamlet bar. I looked at my watch: 4:45 p.m. A time when lots of folks knocked off work and reached for that first drink. Or their sixth.

Clapping the phone back to my ear, I told Trabuco I was in Westwood, about to meet an FBI agent for a drink. "He's a Russian speaker. Does organized crime. I'm gonna pump him about Lukin."

"Call if we need to hold extra space," Trabuco said.

It was dimly lit inside the restaurant and smelled of prehistoric smoke. Several people sat hunched by the bar. I looked for wavy hair, a rumpled suit on a large frame. Yes, indeed, there he was. I sat three seats away and ordered a glass of wine. Clavendish was almost done with a highball. He was shelling peanuts and watching CNN. There had been another hostage taking in Grozny. A hospital this time. The footage showed Russian soldiers running out of buildings, carrying limp bodies of patients. Clavendish shook his head.

"Half of those soldiers are infected with HIV, or will be by the end of their tours. What an end to a superpower. It's Zambia," he said, "with missiles."

I wasn't sure if he was talking to the bartender or to me.

But then he made it clear. Craning his neck in the dim light, he said, "Why did you follow me here?"

And I thought he hadn't recognized me. I should have known better. This guy was practicing tradecraft long before I was born.

I sipped my drink, stared at the TV bolted into the ceiling above the bar.

"They said you knew things."

A sour laugh. "The last time they said that was twenty-five years ago."

"Maybe I want twenty-five-year-old information."

I thought about Nicolai Lukin's book, the one he had slammed shut at the UCLA library. I knew exactly the next name that I had to look up in the index, and it started with a *C*.

"That and a bag of rubles'll get you a shot of vodka in a dark alley. Or maybe just shot." He laughed at his own joke.

"Why does Lansing say you're still fighting the Cold War?" I asked.

"I'm boxing with shadows. In a wilderness of mirrors." He finished off his drink. "That's what James Jesus Angleton called his mole hunts. Know who he was?"

"A spy?"

Clavendish regarded me from under hooded eyes that glinted with malice. I felt suddenly exposed and puny and very naive, enmeshed in a game way beyond my cunning and expertise. Then he blinked and the world tilted and his eyes were deep reflecting pools once more, into which you could gaze and see anything he wanted to reveal. And right now, he was revealing the charming but world-weary FBI agent.

"The CIA's resident paranoid. Head of counterintelligence for decades. By the end he saw moles everywhere. Ruined dozens of careers." Clavendish smiled and the ice in his glass rattled companionably. "Even accused his own wife. He was virtually certifiable. They finally led him off to a padded room. So I consider myself lucky."

"What happened to you?"

Without being asked, the bartender placed another drink in front of him. Clavendish curled his fingers around it, raised it in benediction, and drank deeply.

"Mistakes were made," he said after coming up for air.

"What kind of mistakes?"

"You're the reporter. Look it up."

Another flare of irritation, quickly extinguished. Or was that also an act? To make me feel overconfident and cocky at the thought that I had riled him so easily? The guy seemed to have fifty different personalities, and he slid them on and chucked them off like a practiced actor.

"The Cold War. Spies. That was your specialty, wasn't it?"

Clavendish stared at the screen. A man with half his face blown off appeared on a stretcher. "Jesus," he said, throwing a handful of peanuts into his mouth, "bunch of animals."

Scrawny men with beards were screaming into the TV. Hands came up to block the camera, which shifted to a long shot of the bombed hospital.

"For this we fought the Cold War? So they could tear each other apart? Better that it had never ended." He snorted, took a drink. Looked at me for the first time.

"I could get brought up on charges for saying that.

Except I won't. This is my last week. Pension starts in January, praise Allah." He frowned, considered. "Now we have a new enemy."

He was smooth, I thought. A classic dissembler. Don't want to talk about the past? Introduce a more volatile topic set firmly in the present. But I wanted him back on track.

"So you fought the Cold War. And now you're on the Russian Organized Crime Task Force?"

Clavendish exhaled gloomily. "It's the Eurasian Task Force now," he said. "We learned the hard way it was also Ukrainians, Armenians, Georgians, and Chechens."

"What else did you learn?" I asked, aware he wouldn't tell me anything he didn't want me to know.

There was a long pause. Then he said, "I learned that when you lie down with the enemy, you get up with sickles and hammers in your backside."

"Who did you lie down with?"

"Why, a woman, of course." He chewed a mouthful of peanuts, swallowed. Washed it down with a drink.

"What was her name?"

"Her name was sorrow, because that's what she brought me." He squinted and looked up at the screen, where women in kerchiefs were sobbing and wringing their hands in front of rubble that used to be houses. Clavendish gave a sodden belch.

"And she was KGB? Did she, like, try to blackmail you? Turn you into a double agent?"

I kept my voice breathy and excited. To hide the fact that I really was.

He gave me a sideways look. "You should consider a career with the government. You've got quite a way with interrogations."

I ignored him. "Didn't an FBI agent do that recently? Had a long-term affair with his Chinese source. She's the one who got arrested, not him."

Clavendish shifted on his bar stool. His jaw twitched and his head lowered and I recognized the wounded soul from the file cabinets earlier today. I wondered how often Clavendish wheeled him out and what secrets he concealed within those eyes that gave away too much.

"A fall from grace," he said. "In a weak moment. It can happen to the best of us."

"I don't think it was a moment," I said drily. "In this Chinese case, they had an affair for two decades, while he was her handler."

"The Greek philosophers understood the thin line between love and hate. It's something we seem to have forgotten in our brave new world."

I sighed. We were getting nowhere. But the *Times* archives would have the story. I switched gears.

"A brave new world where the Russian Mafia plies its trade across borders. Do you know a family named Lukin? Russian immigrants, live in Studio City. Their son was shot yesterday in Griffith Park and it looked like a professional hit. Have you run across that name in your, uh . . . work?"

Clavendish was staring at his drink, trying to decode its amber depths. "Doesn't ring a bell," he said without inflection.

"I was hoping—" I began.

"In my day, they didn't hide in caves," he sneered. "Miss the old cat-and-mouse, tell you the truth. There were standards then. Even their villains had style. And their women . . ." He winced.

"You know," I said, "you're the strangest FBI agent I've

ever met. Not that I know many. But aren't you guys supposed to be gray? Faceless. Blend into the woodwork. You're as flamboyant as a drag queen."

And that alone tells me you've got secrets to hide. Because if there's one thing this profession has taught me, it's that what you wear on your sleeve is usually the opposite of your soul.

"They're all Young Turks now," he said, ignoring me. "All anyone cares about is terrorism."

"That *does* seem to be the threat of the day," I said. "So how about the Lukins? You're retiring. You could tell me off the record. I happen to know that your pal Lansing leaks like a sieve to my colleague."

"Perhaps," Clavendish said, sliding off his stool. "But that is not how I played the game."

He laid a twenty on the table. "See you around, Jonathan," he told the barman, tipping an imaginary hat. Then he was gone.

CHAPTER 18

D riving back to the office, I could hardly wait to look up Clavendish in the archives.

I was in the *Times* lobby when the elevator doors opened and the anchovy can emptied. The last one out was Luke Vinograd.

His eyes lit up, then narrowed as he noticed my demeanor. The tightly clutched satchel. Dilated pupils.

"Ah, deadline, is it?" he murmured by way of hello.

It was a logical greeting in a place that lived and died by the clock. Deadline trumped everything. Once the day's stories had been shepherded into their pens, wagging their tales behind them, normal life could resume.

"Not exactly. I need to look something up in the archives."

Luke glanced at his watch and frowned.

"No time for a coffee?"

I raised an eyebrow. "Since when is that your drug of choice?"

"Didn't I tell you? I've reformed my evil ways."

Luke was known to toss them back.

"You're not drinking? Is that, um, hard?"

He sighed, hooked a strand of wavy black hair behind his diamond-studded ear. "Oh sure, sometimes I feel like having a drink after work. But then I remember I have plans for New Year's."

"You were never that bad."

"You never saw me at three a.m."

"I saw you at one."

He gave me a sardonic look. "A lot can happen in two hours."

"That bad?"

"It wasn't just booze. I'm either perfectly fine, or I'm tête-à-tête with the valet at your party, then we disappear for forty-five minutes and come back looking very alert, even though it's four a.m."

"I was going to suggest drinkies at the Redwood after my archive errand but I guess that's out."

"Not at all," Luke said. "I'll have a soda. It's part of my recovery."

I regarded him doubtfully. "I don't know, Luke. I'd hate to . . ."

"It's fine. You can still drink, it doesn't bother me."

Just talking about it, I could already feel the gin singing in my veins.

"I'll just have one, then. I should go on the wagon myself."

"One drink is *not* going on the wagon," Luke said prissily.

I shrugged. "So for tonight it's a three-wheeled wagon. But first I need this archive file. I met an odd duck today."

Luke gave me a bemused look. "They flock to you." He slapped his thigh and chuckled at his bon mot.

"You're proof of that."

Luke crossed his arms archly. "Is this how you worm your way into my good graces?"

"Should I get on my knees?"

"Get that tasty friend of yours, Josh, on his knees, and then we'll talk."

"He doesn't swing from that vine."

"I think he could be persuaded."

"Really?" This made me think of Josh in a whole new way. He definitely had an animal magnetism. With Silvio gone, I was noticing such things more.

We filed into the empty elevator and went back upstairs.

"This odd duck has an even odder provenance," I said once we were in the library. "But it's pre-1989."

The *Times* had computerized its archives that year. Prior to that, librarians had clipped each story by hand and filed it away in yellowing envelopes according to subject. Oh, and for backup there was always microfiche. But I loved holding those fat envelopes stuffed with clips that you had to unfold like origami.

"That's no problem," Luke said.

"Thomas Clavendish," I said. "Name ring a bell?"

He pursed his full lips. For a long moment, there was silence.

"Well?"

"Spies and espionage. A honey pot. Cold War. Before your time, of course." A look down his long lashes.

I thought of the flies I had mistaken for bees yesterday on the hillside and my stomach lurched.

"Honey pot?"

"It's when the KGB used to set people up with hookers, then blackmail them."

"How quaint and Cold War," I said. "Somehow I can't imagine Osama using that strategy. The burka-clad hooker fails to entice. . . . What else?"

"That's all these synapses are throwing up right now. Let's get the envelope."

I followed him through the stacks, where he pushed buttons, and walls moved and revealed other stacks.

Luke ran his finger along a metal file cabinet. At *CA–CL,* he stopped. He opened the drawer and plucked out an envelope, handing it to me with a flourish.

"One more favor," I said. "Can the library get me a copy of a Cold War history called *Jousting in the Shadows?*"

He typed it into the computer and said it should be on my desk tomorrow afternoon.

"Does Her Majesty require anything further before libation?"

"We're set, vassal," I said. "Let's go."

I slipped the Clavendish clips into my bag. I really ought to get home and read them. But whatever secrets they held would have to wait a few hours. I wanted that drink.

It was drizzling outside, headlights reflecting off puddles. Steam rose from manholes. Luke held an umbrella and we clustered under it with an intimacy that only winter can bring.

Two short blocks and we were at the Redwood, an unrenovated downtown bar where newshounds could drink in peace, unmolested by designer furniture, arugula, and microbrews. The financial tides that had swept through downtown, remaking the skyline in glass and steel and tossing up trendy new restaurants like so many maritime treasures, had never reached this unglamorous stretch of Second Street.

A waitress with dangling potato earrings took our order, gin and tonic for me and a 7-Up for Luke.

"So what's new?" I asked when she left.

"Ladies first," Luke said, settling his elbows onto the table. "What does a washed-up Cold War expert have to do with that dead boy you found at Griffith Park yesterday? Is he the abandoned love child of the FBI and the KGB?"

"Five points for Señor Vinograd, and give yourself a raise," I said, amazed, as usual, by his agile brain. Why couldn't the paper see that despite his lack of an advanced degree or formal experience, Luke was an asset that they should cherish and promote?

"I've just gotten a raise, thank you very much. So spill."

I told him what I knew as he sipped his soda.

"Did it ever occur to you that nosing into the past could put you in danger? What if this Clavendish fellow did it?"

"Yeah, right, some disgraced FBI alkie," I said, ignoring a tingle down my spine.

"Okay, then what's with your hunky Latin lover? Tell Uncle Lukey everything."

But Silvio wouldn't be home until tomorrow and all I knew was that the bed was too big without him.

"What's new with you?" I asked, turning the tables.

Luke's eyes gleamed. "I won a contest," he announced.

"Publishers Clearing House, I hope? You gonna buy me that dream house overlooking the caldera in Santorini?"

"Honey, when my ship comes in I promise you all the ouzo you can drink. But this is work related. I'm going to be a food critic for the *L.A.Times*."

"What?" I said, astounded.

"For a day. Remember that in-house contest the food section ran? After the redesign. The winner gets to review anything they want. A restaurant. A flight of wines. They hinted it could be a stepping-stone if they like the review. Well, I won."

"Congratulations," I said, sipping my drink. I hadn't heard about this contest, though I'm sure it had been advertised in "Among Ourselves," the in-house rag, which we regularly reviled as "Among Our Slaves."

"Is this a dinner invitation? Will they fly you to France to review a Michelin four-star joint?"

"We're dining *chez moi.*"

"No offense, but if you can review any place you want, why order in?"

"Or perhaps the *Times* test kitchen would be best," said Luke.

"But what are we going to eat?" I wailed. "Will you have the kitchen duplicate Louis XIV's coronation meal?"

"Even better." Luke grinned. "We're going to eat dog food."

Choking, I spewed gin and tonic across the bar. "What?"

"You heard right. I'm going to taste-test ten brands of dog food."

"You're insane."

"Each variety will get a one-paragraph description. I've ordered up ten silver spoons for the job."

I burst into laughter, then realized he was dead serious about this revolting idea.

"I cannot believe you would subvert the contest like this. Just think of all the fun you could have."

"Don't you wonder what our pets are eating? Our darling doggies who get walked and groomed and treated to the same Prozac and chemo as us?"

"I don't have any pets," I said, thinking that I wasn't home long enough to keep a goldfish.

"Well, I have. Ever since I got Maximilian."

Maximilian was Luke's bichon frise, which he treated as his child. "I'm going to apply the rigorous standards of culinary criticism to pet food. It's the final frontier, Eve. It will revolutionize the food pages of newspapers across the country. We need an objective opinion, not just company touts. Is it salty, spicy, greasy? What's the gristle quotient? Are there subtle tones of fennel and thyme, or a metallic aftertaste? I'm sampling frou-frou and grocery-store brands. And the chow. Is it better dry and crunchy, or does it release flavor bursts when moist?"

"They'll never believe you really ate it."

"That's why we'll do it in the *Times* kitchen. With witnesses."

"What do you mean, we?"

"You're going to help me."

"No, sir! I am *not* eating dog food. You've got the wrong gal."

Just the thought made my gorge rise. Quickly I gulped down a mouthful of booze.

"You don't have to taste it. You can open the cans and announce the brands."

"The paper will never go for it. It's way too . . . high concept."

"They promised. And I intend to tip off the media. It will be great PR. The best-read edition in ages."

Luke mistook my silence for approval.

"Maybe they'll make it a weekly feature. I can review kitty tuna. Rabbit chow. Fish flakes. The possibilities are endless."

He beamed, dead serious. I suddenly understood why the paper had never harnessed his talent. On a very low brainstem level, he terrified them.

"Okay," I said. "I'll do it."

"See," Luke said as we walked out, "I wasn't even tempted to drink. I've got to keep my head clear. I'm drawing up lists of ingredients. Do you know they can put tumors in so long as they radiate them? I wonder if I'll be able to tell. You know, Eve, I could become the Upton Sinclair of the pet food world."

I pictured myself handing him spoons and announcing brands.

"And I'll be Vanna White."

At home, I sat at my kitchen table, torn between reading the thick manila clip file and rummaging deeper through my mother's hatbox. I took a bunch of papers out of the hatbox and shuffled through them. As far as I could see, there were no other letters from Stepan Domashny. I looked at old photos of my mother and father before we were born, then my mother back in France, before she ever met my dad, then unknown relatives wearing lace and furs, staring sternly into the camera, but my heart wasn't in it tonight.

Pushing the hatbox aside, I reached for the clips.

Thomas Clavendish had been big once, the head of counterintelligence for the FBI's Los Angeles field office. His biggest coup had been recruiting a highly placed Soviet informant in Los Angeles in the early eighties who went by the code name Tatiana.

At this, I put down the clips and considered. A spook saga right here in Los Angeles? How incongruous. Spies plied their skullduggery in the government corridors of Washington, D.C., not the languid palm tree haze of Lotusland. What national secrets did we have? The script for the next *Star Wars* flick? The recipe for Wolfgang Puck's barbecued duck pizza? The chemical equation for Botox? It was true that many defense companies were headquartered here but as far as I knew, the Falcon and the Snowman had been the only spies to penetrate that industry.

Intrigued, I picked up the fraying newsprint and kept reading.

Tatiana was a beautiful White Russian émigré business-woman with a French passport and a Hollywood villa who traveled back and forth to Moscow selling art, even during the bad old Cold War days. She seemed to have a special dispensation from the Sovs, and no one could figure it out. Was she just a go-between so the Communists could sell off inferior works to a West hungry for Russian artifacts? Or was something more sinister afoot? In the Bureau, it was widely assumed that Tatiana was a KGB agent. Which made her doubly attractive to Clavendish. He told his bosses that he needed to wine and dine her, cozying up so he could feed her disinformation to pass on to the Russkies. The Feds signed off.

In 1984, the CIA caught whispers out of Moscow that Tatiana was learning real secrets from Clavendish and playing him for a fool. That she had a Soviet lover who was a KGB colonel. The Bureau dismissed the talk as CIA sour grapes for not landing her themselves. But rumors grew so loud that eventually the Bureau launched an internal inquiry. When pressed, Clavendish admitted an affair with Tatiana. Then the speculation started in earnest. Had the KGB wormed its way into the very heart of the FBI's counterintelligence desk in L.A.? And why did Clavendish have top-secret defense files from Southern California aerospace companies lying around his bedroom, documents that were prohibited by his very order from leaving FBI headquarters?

Sensing a public relations nightmare, the Feebs placed the investigation under lockdown. It was the height of the Cold War. Glasnost and perestroika were only fevered dreams in the head of an ambitious regional party chief named Mikhail Gorbachev. But then the Bureau made the fatal mistake of arresting Tatiana, whose real name was revealed as Ludmilla Belyaeva.

Here, I stopped. The name rang a bell. Ludmilla Belyaeva was the spy thought to have been traded to the Soviets for a U.S. embassy scientific attaché in the waning days of the Cold War. Nicolai Lukin had been reading about this very scandal when I startled him at the UCLA library.

What did it mean? I wondered, plunging back into the clips. The U.S. government had indicted Belyaeva for spying and she promptly hired herself a hotshot lawyer named Samson Brenner—a civil rights pit bull I knew from an earlier investigation—who began whispering to the press about subpoenaing FBI records and calling Bureau employees as witnesses. Brenner promised that a trial in open court would blow the case sky high by revealing a third, as-yet-unnamed coconspirator.

A U.S. district judge eventually dismissed Belyaeva's indictment and scolded the U.S. government for "willful and deliberate misconduct" in denying her attorneys access to Bureau files during the discovery phase of the trial. The government maintained it had no choice, since a trial would endanger national security. And the press, drooling at the thought of a cloak-and-dagger spy trial, had its hopes further dashed when the alleged KGB femme fatale flew the coop. It was said she had gone back to the Soviet Union. The *Los Angeles Times* floated a juicier story that in early 1985, Belyaeva had been traded for an American spy in the USSR, which jibed with what I had read in Nicolai's Cold War history. But nobody seemed to know for sure. The whole imbroglio had been hushed up under the National Secrets Act. And

Clavendish? His star only rose further. The Feebs met with hand-picked reporters and explained that Clavendish had risked his job and his reputation on behalf of his country. They wished they could reveal the extent of their man's adroit genius, all the false data he had fed the Sovs. That, of course, was impossible. But the FBI wanted it known that Clavendish would receive a medal for service to his country.

Not everyone bought it. A syndicated columnist and longtime critic of the FBI got into hot water with the administration for speculating that the Bureau was hiding its culpability. Shielding Clavendish meant not having to admit that the FBI's Soviet operations in L.A. were shot to hell because their top man couldn't keep his pants zipped. Inside the Bureau, there were unconfirmed rumors of Stalinist purges. A disgruntled former agent claimed to be writing a book that would reveal all, but was killed in a car accident before it could be published. When his widow cleaned out his desk, she found only rambling, paranoid notebooks.

I read on, fascinated by this tale of Cold War intrigue and anxious to learn how it ended. To my disappointment, the record on Clavendish grew dormant. It wasn't until the 1990s that his name resurfaced in a clip announcing that the FBI was forming a task force to tackle Russian organized crime in Los Angeles. With his language skills and Soviet-era contacts, Clavendish rose, phoenixlike, from the ashes of his Cold War disgrace. In the next decade, his name appeared twice more. The stories made no mention of the KGB spy scandal. It had become ancient history. Reporters who might have remembered it were long gone. And now Clavendish himself was about to retire, taking his secrets to the grave.

Disappointed, I shoved the wad of clips back into the manila envelope. It was late and I was exhausted and no closer to figuring out who had killed Denny Lukin. But there was one more thing I wanted to check. Firing up the computer, I typed Ludmilla Belyaeva's name into a search engine. I got tons of Google hits, even a photo on a female-spy site that showed Ludmilla to be a heavy-lidded Slav with luscious lips and a mane of red hair. But there was no fresh information after 1985, just reams of speculation. It was as though she had fallen off the face of the earth. Others had tried to look her up over the years. There was even a 1994 story on the scandal's ten-year anniversary that mentioned her disappearance and speculated that the Sovs had executed her for failing in her mission. But she could also have become an anonymous hausfrau in Kharkov with a brood of grandkids by now.

Putting on my pajamas, I turned on the eleven o'clock news. The Lukin story had drifted down the lineup, reduced to stock shots of the Lukin house and the body being carried out of Griffith Park as an earnest mustachioed reporter intoned that the LAPD was still investigating. I hoped tomorrow would be different. Tomorrow was Denny Lukin's funeral.

CHAPTER 19

*A*ll night the storm battered the city and winds gusted, splattering my window with sheets of horizontal water. In the morning, it was still coming down, the sodden trees bending under the force of the gale. Looking out, I accidentally pressed my arm against the ice-cold windowpane and shivered. I wondered where Mischa had spent the night, and promptly banished that thought. He was Russian, used to a lot worse than this. He'd cope. And hopefully, he'd disappear into the great immigrant slipstream that was L.A. and I'd never see him again.

I made coffee, popped an English muffin into the toaster, and rooted around the freezer until I found a jar hoary with frost. When I nuked it, the aroma of summer filled the air. Tart, acidic, intensely sweet. Apricot jam.

Unlike peaches, which hang around through September, apricots are a fickle fruit, gone by early July. In my childhood, our backyard tree was often so laden that its branches swept the ground, allowing the fruit-loving dog to graze bovinely until my grandmother shooed her away. Grandmama would pick the low branches and send my brother and I scurrying up ladders fast as squirrels for the rest. In the kitchen her knees resounded with thin, high clicks as she moved from sink to stove, washing, quartering, and dumping apricots into a copper-bottomed pot with lemon juice and sugar, throwing in a few pits for flavor. We'd stir with wooden spoons, then ladle the golden essence onto vanilla ice cream or atop the dough she fried for piroshki.

So intense were those memories that years after my grandmother's death, the urge still came upon me every summer and I'd head off to the Farmer's Market for a case of Royal Blenheims, the apricots of my childhood. They weren't as big and plump as the commercial varieties, tending toward mottled, roseate skin and quick to bruise, but they were sweet and succulent, a testament to California's magnificent agriculture before shelf life and aesthetics began to trump taste.

Standing over the stove, apricot steam rising into my face, I felt transported into a time when the backyard was a mysterious jungle and even the light seemed clearer. It is for moments such as these that we embrace ritual, I thought. To recapture something—a comforting aroma, a cool hand on the brow, a sound borne away by the wind— the alchemy of the past.

And so I ate my jam, the essence of a million sunsets, and after the muffin was gone and the coffee drunk, it was time to go.

St. Cyril's Cathedral was tucked away in an Echo Park neighborhood that was now heavily Latino. But the gold-painted onion domes, carved wood doors, marble statuary, high ceilings, and elaborate frescoes all testified to a once-thriving Slavic community.

The church parking lot was full of shiny, expensive cars with tinted windows. The sky had finally spent its fury, the clouds parted. In the cold morning light, a watery sun reflected off the gold dome but shed no warmth.

Reporters and cops go to funerals for reasons different

from those of the rest of the human race. We're not there to grieve, but to coldheartedly observe, scanning for tics or excessive interest. Even the solitary mourner on the fringes ignites suspicion.

Pathology is what we're after. The more dire the better. One reporter I knew spent slow news days attending funerals of gang members. With so many murders, young men from rival gangs often got buried the same day at opposite ends of the cemetery. When gangbangers spotted one another across the grass as their comrades were lowered into the ground, high emotions could lead to more shootouts. And for my colleague, that meant good copy.

I stood in the back of the cathedral and watched mourners sail like regal ships up the center aisle in search of seats. There were effusive greetings in the pews, especially among the men, who favored bear hugs and loud, smacking kisses on each cheek and a third on the lips, tears streaming unchecked.

Grief brings out strange plumage and behavior, and I soon noticed two distinct types of people. The first wore flashy jewels and furs of fox, mink, and sable. The women's dresses had plunging, ample necklines. Wet, glistening lipstick set off big hair in glossy red and black. The men were packed into dark suits, meaty shoulders straining the fabric. The second group of people were equally dressed up, but these women wore simple black dresses with a strand of pearls and subtle makeup. Their partners favored wool scarves tucked into good coats. It was as if two separate tribes had converged. You could see the demarcations in the pews. Old Russians and their brassy new cousins. The Lukins were definitely Old Russians.

What the two groups had in common was their offspring, who might have been from another planet entirely:

gaunt boys and girls wearing black combat boots and over-size jackets, with wildly styled blue-black hair and silver nose rings gleaming from powdered faces. I felt a flash of sympathy for the parents who had to negotiate across chasms of generation *and* culture to reach their children.

The open casket lay in state, draped in gold cloth. I made my way past, and saw the sculpted face of Denny Lukin, his athlete's limbs concealed inside a charcoal gray suit that set off his waxy pallor and blond hair. His lips were drained of blood, the generous mouth closed, lids shut over the intelligent eyes that had stared out of his driver's license. His head rested on a satin pillow, obscuring the gunshot that had killed him. The puka-shell necklace was gone, replaced by a wool scarf tucked around his neck, as though to keep him warm in the afterlife. I made my way back and found a seat.

Now the grieving family appeared, Irina Lukin supported between her husband and the nervous boy I had last seen in the UCLA library. Nicolai. They made their way to the coffin. Irina bowed her head, made the sign of the cross, and turned away. Her face was hidden behind a black lace mantilla, revealing only a pale outline of lips.

My eye was drawn to movement at the cathedral's side door, which opened to reveal Lyuba, the girl from the deli. She wore a fuzzy pink angora sweater, pink-and-black-striped stockings, and a black skirt with lace-up Doc Marten boots. Beneath a knit skier's cap, her hair spread out in unruly tendrils. I had only seen it pulled back in a hairnet before, and out of her white smock, Lyuba looked less Russian, more like any American high school student. She dabbed a handkerchief against her nose and sniffed morosely. As I watched, a young man came up and took her arm. He was tall, with a smattering of freckles against his pale skin, and I noticed an earring glint under the curly brown hair. The boy led Lyuba to a pew and the teenagers sat next to a man and a woman holding a little girl. The woman was beautiful in a subdued way. The man was slender and rumpled, with longish curly hair, round steel-rimmed glasses, and a distracted, professorial expression, as though he might be using this downtime to calculate pi to the hundredth place. Could this be the elusive Max and his father? The poetry-loving computer programmer? The man craned his neck to adjust his tie, and I was surprised to see he could only be in his mid-thirties. Sasha Lukin had told me he and Max's father were friends, and I expected someone older. This man was young enough to be Sasha Lukin's son.

Our eyes met and he blinked owlishly once, then glanced away. But something must have registered on my face that was not pi. The man scratched his unruly hair and pretended to examine the stained glass above our heads while surreptitiously checking me out. Had Sasha Lukin described me? Or did he simply sense an imposter? Finally the man fingered the metal rim of his glasses, leaned over, and whispered to his son. The boy shook his head.

And then something unexpected happened. As the priest appeared and the congregation stood as one, a stooped man slipped into the church. He might have been waiting for just this moment of distraction. Funerals bring people out of the woodwork who haven't seen the deceased or one another in years, and probably everybody assumed that this man knew someone else there, and that was as far as their curiosity went. Mine went a lot further.

Because the man who had slid unobtrusively into the pews was Thomas Clavendish.

CHAPTER 20

As the call and response of the liturgy got under way, the gold-and-linen-bedecked priest with a long gray beard and Old Testament eyebrows recited incantations and prayers in a rumbling Russian that sounded way more exalted than English.

But my mind was not on the ceremony. It was on Clavendish. What was he doing here? He had refused to talk to me about the case and denied knowing the Lukins, and I had put it down to a knee-jerk refusal to talk to the press. Now I knew he had been lying.

I watched him for the entire hour-and-a-half service while I gripped the missal and struggled to get my mouth around the strange sounds.

Gospodu pomolimsya, intoned the priest.

Gospodu pomolimsya, answered the mourners.

The priest came around with the incense burner on a chain, swinging it, sending the acrid, sweet fumes spiraling to the cathedral's dome.

Clavendish stood, head bowed. He didn't take notes. He didn't glance around or appear unduly wary. It looked like he was there to mourn. At last the pallbearers bore away the coffin, and the family followed, Irina Lukin bent in grief, Sasha's face carved into a stoic mask, Nicolai with downcast eyes and a pallor under his California tan. As he passed me, a red stain spread across his cheeks. Then family and friends fell in behind him and he disappeared.

Outside, it was overcast once more. The wind had an icy bite and cold seeped off the stone steps and into empty pockets and exposed skin. I made my way through the crowd, watching people say hello, that two-handed grasp, then arms flung tight around one another, sobs stifled into thick fur, all of it in Russian, which whirled around me like a roaring current I couldn't understand. Just then, Nicolai Lukin swam out of the crowd. I waved but he averted his eyes and pushed determinedly through the people, away from me.

"Max," I heard a girl cry in English. "Wait up."

It was Lyuba. She was down by the curb, calling out to the boy she had sat with earlier. At the same moment, Clavendish appeared at the cathedral doors. I hesitated. Who should I approach first? The teenagers, I decided. They might take off.

Moving sideways like a crab, I worked through the crowd, smelling incense and aftershave, mothballs and damp wool and French perfume. The girl had reached Max now, and they were deep in conversation.

"Lyuba, how are you?" I said, feigning surprise as the crowd jostled me to her. She wore mascara and garnet lipstick that accentuated her cornflower eyes and pale complexion.

She whirled around and I saw many emotions flit across her face: surprise, suspicion, fear, annoyance, then curiosity.

"What are you doing here?"

I smiled sheepishly. "I'm on assignment. They wanted me to try to talk to the relatives." I lowered my voice. "I know it's really sleazy," I said, defusing any potential accusations by admitting it head-on.

"You a detective?" the boy named Max said, shrinking back.

The cops must have worked him over well.

"Oh no." I gave a deprecating laugh. "Just a reporter."

I thrust out my dog tags and he reached out fingers adorned with silver rings hammered into dragon and wolf heads.

"Eve Diamond," I told him, not wanting the silence to clot too thickly around us.

"Max Golodny. And this is Lyuba, my girl— uh, hey . . . what did you do that for?" Max said, as Lyuba's foot connected with his shin. "My friend," he finished.

Lyuba turned away, red blotches flooding her pale cheeks, and I realized why she had been so reticent at the deli. Max was her boyfriend. In my head, I saw a teenage love triangle. Denny and Max are best friends. Denny loves Lyuba. But Lyuba loves Max. Denny gets angry. He and Max fight over the girl. They scuffle. Then what? Max kills his best friend? Is that what had happened?

"I see," I said, turning to Max. "I understand you were best friends with Denny."

"You don't have to talk to her," Lyuba said. "She's not police."

And then Max did something strange. He grabbed my hand and pulled me around to the side of the cathedral, where he stepped into the shelter of a crepe myrtle bush and leaned back against the stone wall, unseen by the crowd. Squawking with alarm, Lyuba followed.

Max rummaged in his coat pocket and pulled out a cigarette. Lighting it, he inhaled, hooked one leg up, and pressed it against the wall. As he blew out the smoke, I saw the tension leave his body.

"God, I needed that," he said, squinting into the street. "My mom hates my smoking."

He took another hit, then tipped the ash. "You shouldn't be here," he said. "It's dangerous."

I smiled at him, even as fear ran screechy nails down a chalkboard. "So's smoking," I said.

He snorted in disbelief, shook his head.

"Get real," he said.

"Okay," I said. "Why is it dangerous?"

He took a long puff, considered. "The murderer could come after you," he said finally.

I sensed that he was bluffing. "Is Denny's killer here?"

"How would I know?" Max said.

"Who wanted him dead?"

"Max," Lyuba said warningly.

Max looked at the sky, took a toke, blew out a stream of smoke.

"Well, not me, that's for sure. This theory that we fought over Lyuba," he encircled her slender waist and pulled her toward him, "is bullshit. I mean, if Denny thought I stole Lyuba from him, then he'd want to kill *me*. Not the other way around. Right?"

I heard the pleading in his voice and wondered if he was trying to convince himself.

I shrugged. "You could have fought, and it turned to blows and someone pulled a gun." I looked at the terror metastasizing in his eyes. "I mean in self-defense," I said hurriedly. "But as far as I know, the police said there were no signs of a struggle."

I thought back to how Knightsbridge had walked up to the body, how we had added our own tracks and obscured potential evidence. Could they even tell?

"They said whoever shot him was a ways away."

Max just shrugged. "The whole thing is so messed up."

"Is it true he was going to tell the Russian Mafia to leave Lyuba's family alone?"

"That was just bluster," Max said. "He wouldn't have any idea who to talk to."

"And you would?"

"No." Max glared.

"What about this phone call he got at your house before he took off?"

"He said it was about his family. And that he was going home."

"What?"

"Those were his exact words. Like I told the cops, he didn't get any more specific."

"He told his parents he was spending the night with you," I said.

Max and Lyuba shifted their feet but said nothing.

"The cops can trace that call," I said, watching their reaction. "There was no cell phone on his body but they'll subpoena phone company records."

The kids looked more intrigued than scared.

"Good," Max said. "Then maybe they'll catch whoever lured him out there."

"Who would want to do that?"

"Try asking Denny's brother," Max said.

"Max, for the last time . . ." said Lyuba.

"Shut up, Lyuba," Max said heatedly. He spoke in fast Russian and Lyuba fell silent.

"His brother killed him?" I said.

I flashed onto Nicolai's frightened face, swimming upstream through the crowd to get away from me. "Why haven't the police made him a suspect, then?"

"I'm not saying he killed him," Max said. "Just that he might know things."

"Like what?"

Big shrug. "Ask him."

"Did you tell the police this when they questioned you?"

"Of course."

The police reminded me of Clavendish, which reminded me that I couldn't see him anymore, which panicked me. What if he had already left? I had to talk to him. And then Nicolai Lukin.

"Did you know there's an FBI agent at the funeral?"

Max and Lyuba stared in slack-jawed disbelief. Either this was news or they were accomplished actors.

"W-why?" Lyuba stuttered. She looked at Max and a bolt of fear passed between them.

"That's what I'd like to know."

"Is Denny's dad Mafia?" I asked, trying another tack.

A low chortle came from Max. "Mr. Lukin? Hardly. He's a scientist. No head for 'beezness.'"

"Unlike some people you know?" I said softly, wondering if his father's absentminded-professor routine was all a cleverly managed act.

He whirled on me. "I already told you. It's dangerous for you to be here. You should leave now. And don't come back. Stop asking questions."

"That's funny," I said. "A couple of thugs told me the same thing yesterday."

"You should listen. You want to end up floating in a canal?"

A slow shudder went through me. A few years back, five corpses had been found with hands tied behind them and gunshot wounds to the backs of their heads, dumped into the California aqueduct in the bare hills of Tehachapi. They were all Russian. No one had been convicted of any crime, but the victims had common business interests.

"This is a Mafia thing, isn't it?" I said softly.

"No." In agitation, Max threw down his cigarette and ground it into the dirt. He thrust his hands deep into his pockets.

"So what happened the day Denny died?"

"I already told it all to the cops."

"That doesn't mean they'll tell me."

He looked over my shoulder.

"C'mon, Max, don't you want your friend's killer caught and brought to justice?"

He kicked the dirt, and his face got a stubborn expression. Then he spoke in colorless, expressionless tones.

"We drove over the hill to Zuma, smoked some pot. Rode a few waves. Then we came home, got fish tacos for lunch, rented a movie, and fell asleep. Denny got woken up by a call on his cell phone. That's when he told me he was going home. That's the last I saw him."

"Did he seem unusually agitated or upset? Was he meeting someone?"

"No, nothing like that. I already told the cops."

"Was it strange that he would go hiking by himself?"

"I didn't know he was going hiking, remember? He told me he was going home. But he loved the mountains. He talked about being a ranger. Or a Fish and Game guy. He was all into solitude. More than me. I like the city."

"Was he close to your family? Maybe your dad?"

He shot me a quizzical look. "My old man's in computers. Always working. He doesn't even have time to hang out with me."

"What company?"

"Ionix."

"Where's their office?"

"West Hollywood."

"You and Denny ever go there?"

"Why would we?"

"So you don't think Denny was doing anything illegal?"

"Other than smoking a little weed? No."

"Did he have enemies? Did you get into a fight?"

"No, I already told you."

There was something tantalizing, just out of reach, but everyone I talked to was a dead end. Were all these leads just so much tinsel and trappings, when the reality was much simpler? That a boy had been shot dead by a deranged person in the hills?

"C'mon, Lyuba, let's get back. See you later, Ms. Reporter." Max grabbed the girl's hand and yanked her around the corner to the cathedral entrance. I waited a decent interval, then followed.

A quick scan and I spotted Clavendish. He was talking to the Lukins, their body language intimate. He held Mrs. Lukin's slender hand in his two great meaty ones.

He knows them. This isn't just a work thing.

Then he released her and bent his head toward her husband. Sasha Lukin fumbled in his pocket, brought out a white handkerchief, and dabbed at his eyes. Clavendish grabbed Sasha Lukin's shoulders, steadied him, murmured one last condolence. Then, wrapping his muffler tighter around his neck, he turned and walked off. Taking long strides across the churchyard, I caught up with him. The bottom of his overcoat flapped in the wind.

"Mr. Clavendish," I said. "Can I ask you something? I've got this book of poetry by Osip Mandelstam, and I'm wondering, in your opinion, if he's worth reading in English? It seems okay so far, especially when he describes Stalin's 'full cockroach mustache' . . ."

Clavendish turned and a curtain dropped across his face, but not before I saw a flash of anger.

"You again!"

"Yes, sir. The reporter. Fancy meeting you here. I'm covering the investigation into Denny's murder. They sent me to the funeral to get local color, a few fresh quotes."

I stared at the pavement. "But I'm confused . . . what could *possibly* bring the FBI out to the funeral of a Russian-American teenager?"

I caught his eye, dropping all pretense.

I had expected an acidic retort, but to my surprise, Clavendish looked away. He shoved his hands into his coat and stared at the view, two tall palm trees bookending the snow-peaked San Gabriel Mountains.

"It's not just work, is it?" I said softly. "You *know* these people."

Clavendish's brow furrowed. After a long while, he peeled his eyes away from the scenery. "Since when are they mutually exclusive?" he said.

"What is Sasha Lukin tangled up with," I asked, "that someone would kill his son execution style?"

"A very good question." Clavendish bared his lips in a ghastly smile. His teeth were numerous and crooked, the muted hue of old ivory. "One for law enforcement to pursue."

I bounced on the balls of my feet. "Like the FBI? A Russian speaker such as yourself?"

He lowered his head and shook it slowly from side to side.

"I'm afraid not, young lady," he said. "In two more days, I'm officially retired."

"Then what are you doing here?"

"I've come to pay my respects."

"How do you know him?"

But Clavendish was admiring the view again.

"Only in Southern California will you find snowcapped mountains just twenty miles from the sea. Truly extraordinary."

"Mr. Clavendish, was Lukin one of your informants?"

"What's that?" He tore his eyes away. "Let's just say that Sasha Lukin and I had interests once upon a time that intersected in a way that was mutually beneficial."

"Interests? You mean like chess? Caviar? National secrets?"

He gave a wry grimace. "Sasha and I have devoured our fair share of caviar over the years. Did you know they've managed to harvest white sturgeon caviar in Sacramento? Osetra. It's quite palatable. Soon they won't need the Caspian Sea anymore, and it will wither up just like the poor Aral."

"So you go back a long time?"

"Long enough."

"How'd you meet?" I asked stubbornly.

"Trade secret, my dear."

"Don't patronize me."

"Don't ask me questions I can't answer."

"These aren't idle questions. I've been threatened since I started covering this story."

That caught his attention. "Really?" He fiddled with his muffler. "Perhaps you should take heed."

"What do you mean?"

"Reporters get killed in Russia all the time. Mail bombs. Drive-by shootings. Suspicious auto accidents. Poisonings."

I looked up at him. His voice had changed, become more steely and serious. I matched him.

"Last time I checked, this was America, not Russia."

He clicked his tongue against the roof of his mouth. "Look around you. This is an outpost of Mother Russia. Normal rules don't apply."

"Isn't this exactly what the FBI is fighting against, sir? To keep America safe for democracy and all that?"

"I spent my whole career fighting it. That's why I know what I'm talking about."

"But you still haven't told me how you know Denny Lukin. You his godfather? Sent one of his relatives away during the Cold War?"

Clavendish clamped his lips so tight that the blood drained. By contrast, his ruddy, clean-shaven cheeks were marked by red branching capillaries, his nose starting to go bulbous as a tuber from the drink. But his eyes were clear and blue.

"You are quite tedious, Ms. Diamond. Good day." He tipped his hat and strode off.

But I was harking back to what I had read last night in the archives. What had brought about this man's downfall from one of the rising stars on the Russia desk to his ignoble twilight, pushing papers. Because no matter what fancy title they gave him, that's all he did.

I ran after him, planted myself in front of him.

He stopped, affronted. "Look, Ms. Diamond, will you please . . ."

I took a deep breath. "Fine," I said. "Your business with Lukin is a private matter. Let's move on to a public record. Court record, even." I cocked my head. "From 1984. A generation ago, but still, I'm wondering. Just for old times' sake. Ever see her around?"

Clavendish grew still.

"Who?"

"Ludmilla."

He hadn't moved.

"Why would I do that?"

"I did my homework. It was a big deal back then."

His face tightened. The condescension of earlier was gone.

"If you think I'm going to spill my soul to a two-bit reporter who assaults me at a funeral, think again."

"You told me to look it up. At the bar, remember?"

He gave me an inscrutable look.

"Good for you, hack," Clavendish said, already loping down the street. He tossed over his shoulder, "You need anything, go pester young Lansing. He's more your speed."

"No, he's not," I yelled after him. "Lansing wouldn't know Pushkin from Tsvetayeva."

Clavendish stopped in his tracks, and I thought he might come back, but then he shook his head and continued charging into the parking lot. He slowed down at a new, dark blue El Dorado with extra antennas on the roof. Just what an FBI guy would drive. American. Not foreign and flashy. He clicked something in his hand, opened the door, and climbed in. He started the car and drove for the exit. As the car pulled out, I noticed a YMCA sticker on his bumper. That told me one thing. He wasn't in a company car. For the FBI agent, whatever this was, it was personal.

CHAPTER 21

I stood there a few minutes longer, watching the milling crowds. I had gotten very little I could use for the paper. But it hadn't been a waste of time. Sometimes the most tantalizing things don't make it into print. I made my way back to the people on the cathedral steps. I could see Lukin surrounded by well-wishers. I couldn't confront him now about what I had learned. It was indecent. And it would ruin any chance I might have later. I knew reporters who would stride right up, disregarding that it was his son's funeral, and try to wheedle out a new quote or two. But I didn't have the heart. I wondered whether I was losing my edge.

A bony hand closed on my shoulder, and a voice near my ear said, "And just who might you be?"

I jumped and slid my shoulder out from under the grip and found myself looking into a broad Slavic face whose high forehead ended in an explosion of black curls shot with silver. Brown eyes appraised me with probing curiosity from behind the spectacles.

It was Max's father, the man who had stared at me inside the church. He wore a belted tan raincoat that had been buttoned unevenly so one side sagged. A cigarette dangled from his thumb and forefinger, and ash lay sprinkled across the lapel of his suit. He had shoved a tartan cap over his curls but they poked out at unruly angles. His suit pants were a mite short for his angular frame, like they had shrunk at the dry cleaner's, and a mothball smell emanated from his person. His English was good but you could hear his accent in the cropped consonants and odd inflections.

"Eve Diamond, *Los Angeles Times*," I said, forcing a smile. "My paper sent me. . . ." I shrugged, to indicate my discomfort with having to disturb such a solemn occasion.

"Victor Golodny," he said, extending a pale hand with fine black hairs on each knuckle. His palm was smooth and dry. "Call me Vic."

My brain raced to call up everything I knew about him.

"I understand you're good friends with Sasha Lukin. And your son, Max, and Denny . . ."

Golodny adjusted the rounded wire rims behind each ear.

"Yes, yes. My son." He rubbed his chin vigorously. "Now granted, I spend my days talking to computers, not human beings, but still, what kind of manners is this, Ms. Diamond, to speak to the child without getting the father's permission first?"

"Um . . ." I said. So he had seen me sneak away with Max and Lyuba.

"In my country this is the height of disrespect. In your country, it may even be against the law." He leaned in, eyes assessing. "Minors have special protections, eh? Isn't that what your courts say?"

I swallowed drily. This was a gray area. He could make things very sticky for me if he complained.

"My son had nothing to do with this. Do you hear?" He balled his hands and spoke through clenched lips. "Nothing."

"Well, yes . . ."

"Your paper printed lies and innuendo that have disgraced my family and brought down shame and suspicion. The police have cleared him. Absolutely. But am I going to read another story tomorrow saying, 'Extra, extra, Golodny son cleared in murder of his best friend'? Of course not. Because that's not how you people operate. In the Soviet Union, we didn't have this problem. There was discretion."

"You think those days were better?"

"I'm not saying that. But if you're here trying to gather dirt on my son . . ."

"I was just getting background."

"You want background, I will tell you something. Our family is very close to the Lukins, though we are friends of only one year. It is hard to understand if you are not Russian, the soul-sickness. For us, Los Angeles is an alien landscape. The heat. The blinding white sun. Everybody smiling, but clutching daggers as they say have a nice day."

"Yes," I said, flashing on how it must have been for my own parents.

"I must keep my wits about me. I am like your mountain lion that prowls the canyon; ah, what a magnificent creature. I feel a kinship with this animal, which must adapt to survive in hostile terrain."

I couldn't resist sniggering to myself. He was skinny and concave, with the pallor and posture of someone who spent his days over a fluorescent screen. More like an ungainly bird than a predator. He wouldn't last long in the wild.

"For me, America is hostile terrain," Golodny said. "Here the predators camouflage their stripes, hide their tails in fancy clothes. Look at all these computer companies, gobbling up their competition, laying off workers, engaging in predatory pricing."

"And how does Sasha Lukin fit into this ecology?"

"Aleksandr Nicolaievitch—oh, excuse me," he said, noting my confusion, "we Russians confuse everybody with our patronymics—I mean Sasha, is a beacon of light from home. We share many interests despite the difference in our ages. Or perhaps because of it. He says I am like a son to him. And he reminds me of my own father, God rest his soul."

Victor Golodny bowed his head a fraction of a second, and when he looked up, his eyes brimmed with melancholy.

"Did the Lukins have any enemies that you know of?" I asked.

"Enemies? That is a joke." He jabbed his thumb into his chest, scattering ash. "I have more enemies after a year in this country than Sasha Lukin has after twenty."

"I understand that Denny was at your house Sunday. Did you notice anything out of the ordinary? Did you see him before he left on his hike?"

Golodny made a soft clucking sound. "My dear, I am up at five a.m. and in my office by six every day when my company has a project that is nearing deadline. I'm afraid I heard and saw nothing out of the ordinary."

"On a Sunday?"

He breathed in, surprised that I would question this. Then he relaxed and chuckled.

"You are right. On Sunday, I arrive at eight a.m. Among my colleagues, I am one of the later ones. Some do not sleep at all."

"So you didn't see Max or Denny on Sunday?"

"The boys were asleep when I left. I heard no sound, saw no movement. Max was watching TV when I got home that evening. He said Denny left around three p.m.

The police have checked everything out. I suppose they are just doing their job, but it is unsettling. Denny was like a son to me."

Interesting that he would volunteer all this when I hadn't asked.

"Max speaks very colloquial English for a kid who just immigrated," I said.

"Why, thank you, Ms. Diamond. Max is my stepson, you know, but I regard him as my blood. He spent seven years in boarding school in New Hampshire. Last year after much effort I finally obtained the L1 visa for high-tech workers and my wife and I were able to join him."

"Why didn't Max finish school in New Hampshire?"

Golodny peered at me from his spectacles. "My my, these questions are getting farther and farther afield. This cannot possibly have any bearing on your story, can it? Very well, I suppose I have let myself in for it. My wife and I wanted our family together in California. And Max wanted to be closer to his little sister. She is eleven months old and the light of our lives. Do you have children, Ms. Diamond?"

"No," I said, eager to get the conversation back to Denny's murder.

"Children make you rethink everything," Golodny said. "Their frailty, their vulnerability. You realize what a dangerous place the world is. You want to shelter them from evil, to lay down your life for them. But this is not always possible."

"Did Max indicate that Denny seemed at all agitated on Sunday?"

Golodny gave me a bemused look. "Not at all. But then, who can know the mind of a teenage boy? When you crack that mystery, I hope you will share it with us. And how is your investigation going? Have you conducted many successful interviews?"

"Well, yes and no," I said, caution kicking in.

He must have sensed my reticence.

"It's been a pleasure, Ms. Diamond. I must get back to my family."

"Wait," I said in desperation. "Could I get your number, in case I have any more questions?"

He frowned, considered, then jotted something down on a piece of paper.

"Thanks," I said, shoving it in my purse quickly in case he changed his mind.

"Not at all."

And with that, Golodny disappeared into the sable- and cashmere-clad crowd.

CHAPTER 22

U sually I write just fine on deadline, but today I kept getting sidetracked by thoughts of my rendezvous with Silvio. When I glanced at the clock, it wasn't to calculate how many more minutes I had to finish my funeral story but to count down the time until I'd be in my lover's arms.

It was squalling when I left the office. I took the Century Freeway, only to realize I hadn't checked ahead for flooding and accidents. I didn't want to be late, and a freeway pileup on a night like this could bring traffic to a standstill and ruin everything. Suddenly there was an enormous crash against my windshield, followed by a machine-gun patter that sprayed the hood of my car. I braked and the car fishtailed, splashed into a puddle, and began to spin. Was this another freeway shooting? Had I been hit? I wanted to reach out and touch the windshield, see if it had shattered, but I didn't dare take my hands off the wheel. Meanwhile the noise continued, on the hood, on the roof, on my windshield.

My palms were slick with moisture, my heart beating time to the percussive chatter, as I concentrated all my powers on straightening out. The car resisted, then spun a slow 360-degree turn that played like an amusement park ride. Then I was moving forward again in an eerie calm, wondering if I had hallucinated it. Lights flickered outside and I heard horns and squealing brakes behind me, then the crunch of metal on metal. I pressed down on the gas, anxious to escape the mayhem. Miraculously, I hadn't crashed. Another loud thud as something ricocheted off the windshield and bounced onto the hood, and in the flash of brake lights from the car in front of me, I saw that it wasn't bullets after all, it was hail. The sky was disgorging hail the size of golf balls. The frozen chunks of ice rained down on the freeway, terrifying skittish commuters who, like me, probably feared they'd driven into a gang war. The deluge intensified and I gripped the wheel tighter, perfectly calm now that I knew I wasn't under attack. Nature I could deal with.

As I pulled up to the hotel forty-five minutes late for our rendezvous, I realized that the violet camisole I had changed into before leaving the office, with only a raincoat covering it, was completely drenched in sweat. Silvio would have to peel the lingerie off me. So much for sexy seduction. The only good thing was that the heat from my body had ignited the oils in my perfume. I planned to pour myself a stiff drink and collapse into his arms.

I had expected one of the usual airport chain hotels that crowd Century Boulevard, but Fantasia was a total surprise—elegant retro architecture with boxy Japanese kana script unfurling below the English letters. Must be one of those new hipster boutique places.

I pulled into the underground parking and a black-tuxedoed valet wearing spotless white gloves and a white surgical mask sprang to open my car door, avoiding my gaze. I wasn't sure if it was corporate-mandated discretion or the haggard sight I presented after my wild ride. He didn't seem surprised at my lack of luggage either, just tore off a corrugated stub, bowed, and drove off.

In the elevator mirror, I ran my fingers through my hair and reapplied my lipstick, smiling at the knowledge that it wouldn't last long. Stepping into the lobby, I found myself transported into a spare, early 1960s modernist environment done in orange and gray and black. There was a speckled linoleum floor and sculptural Scandinavian furniture but no traditional reception area that I could see. Instead, bamboo thickets, rock sculptures, pebbled koi ponds, and miniwaterfalls were strategically placed throughout the large lobby. Above each nature enclave were green neon signs that said *Reception*. Some were lit up, others banked. The path that led through this jungle was made of green Astroturf. I approached a young, clean-cut man with bland features who waited at attention and I asked for a key to Mr. Aguilar's room, suddenly feeling like a cheap tart. Could he tell I was half-naked under my raincoat? But the reception clerk seemed supremely unmoved. As he scrolled through his list, I saw a fat scrapbook atop the desk that said, "Fantasia, a room to fit every fantasy." While the attendant clicked his computer keys, I flipped it open and saw glossy photos of the different rooms available at this hotel where Silvio had instructed me to come.

The Safari Room had a zebra-skin rug on the floor and the heads of African wildlife mounted on the wall. The bed comforter was a bear pelt and the sheets were tiger striped. A colorful mural of snowcapped Mount Kilimanjaro took up one wall. For an extra fee, you could rent safari gear and order a "big-game" dinner, available only through room service.

Wow.

I flipped to the front of the book and saw in discreet type that rooms were available by the hour or the half day.

Fantasia took most corporate credit cards. For the convenience of guests, there was a twenty-four-hour ATM kiosk. Each room had a chest of adult toys—disposable, I hoped—and the guest's credit card would be charged, much the same way the minibar was inventoried each day by hotel staff.

I went back to the rooms. The Island Suite had real sand, palapa huts, hammocks, a saltwater tub, and a piped-in sound track of waves and mating whales to lull guests to sleep. The dominance and bondage interrogation center had black rubber sheets and handcuffs affixed to the four-poster bed. It came with a closet full of costumes and equipment. Guests were asked to provide proof of insurance and sign forms that said they were consenting adults.

What on earth had Silvio booked us into? What was his fantasy? The hotel employee finally jotted down a number, then handed me an envelope. I could feel the outline of the plastic key card inside. He gestured to the elevator and I felt almost sorry that it hadn't taken longer so I could have checked out each fantasy.

Silvio's room was on the fourteenth floor. I imagined him pacing, wondering what had kept me, checking his watch. I had barely shoved the card in the door when it opened with a robotic beep and I found myself in a space-age bachelor pad suite filled with the strains of languid Tropicalia music. A cobalt blue pitcher of martinis stood at attention at the bar, with orange glasses and silver swizzle sticks waiting by a melting bucket of ice.

Clearly, he was expecting me.

But I didn't see him.

I stepped inside.

"Silvio?"

Could this be right?

I called out again, listened for footfalls. The bathroom door was open and he wasn't there either. The bathroom tiles were orange, as was the modernist couch and the Formica table. The bedspread was made of a shiny quilted silver material that might repel ultraviolet rays and solar radiation. Lava lamps bubbled on bedside stands, and above the table where Silvio had set up his computer hung a chandelier of hollow chrome rods that looked like an atomic particle. The walls were painted a royal blue like the sky at twilight, pulsating with stars and planets and spaceships, the Horsehead Nebula spiraling off into the distance.

I pulled open the closet and saw two puffy white space-suits with, of all things, Velcro crotches. There were also skintight microfiber uniforms that might have looked at home on *Star Trek* and gigantic polystyrene ray guns that hotel guests could, I assumed, use to administer paddlings. This is for serious fetishists, I thought. I walked into the shower, which looked like a decontamination unit, with six showerheads and a bathtub with three-foot-high sides. Just then I heard the door lock click. Silvio stood there, another bucket of ice in his hands.

"What took you so long?" he said, putting down the ice. He grabbed my wrist and pulled me toward him, not waiting for my answer.

He pressed me against the wall, his lips already seeking out mine, his hands worrying the knot of my raincoat belt, yanking the sides apart. My body surged in response to his. Silvio wore a dressing gown and it fell open, and he made an impatient noise and shrugged it off. He was naked underneath. The sight of him made me dizzy with desire. I dropped my purse and it fell with a thud on his toe and he kicked it out of the way, his hands busy. He had my raincoat off now. He stepped back a minute and breathed out roughly. His face was a mask of concentration. There was so much to be done. His penis was erect, a milky pearl forming at the tip. He ran his hands along my front, cupping my breasts, then bent to take them in his mouth, his tongue teasing my nipples through the fabric of my camisole. I reached for him, gripped him, moved my thumb over and around. He gathered my hair in his hands and let it fall through his fingers like water. His hand slid down my inner thigh, twisted and cupped me. I was so wet. For a long moment we kissed, entwined, the heat between us rising, then he put his other hand under my ass, lifted me up, and carried me toward the bed. I thought he would lay me down on it now, and I could almost feel the silver quilt rising up to greet me, when he spied an armless chair by the desk. Still carrying me, he dragged it over, bracing the chair against the foot of the bed.

He sat down on it, legs apart, then placed a hand on either side of my ass and pulled me down on top of him. We shuddered at the first contact. I braced my bare feet against the bed as he slid me up and down, the hot, lubricated friction making me scream. He pressed his mouth against mine until every wet membrane in my body felt like it would explode. And then it did explode, and the week's tension drained out of me like I was a punctured balloon. When his time came, I clung to his shoulders like a shipwrecked sailor as he rocked the chair on two legs and sent us both toppling backward onto the bed. For a long moment, we lay where the chair had tipped us, then Silvio tightened his grip on me. I imagined taking a nap, doing it again, then maybe running a bath and ordering in dinner.

The room was cool in a Disneyland kind of way. I hadn't even explored it yet. We had plenty of time.

"How are you?" he whispered into my ear.

"Mmmmm," I said, too languid to speak.

We must have drifted off, because next thing I knew, Silvio was untangling my arms from his and reaching for his watch on the bedside table. I looked at the clock and saw that twenty minutes had passed.

"I have to go," he said.

"Go?" I pushed myself up onto an elbow. "What do you mean?"

"My flight."

"What flight?"

"Didn't I tell you? I haven't got the producer on board yet; he's a genius, you wouldn't believe what he can do."

"So get him on board."

"He's in New York. I'm meeting him first thing in the morning. I'm taking the red-eye."

"Tonight?" I asked, already knowing the answer.

Slowly, I sat up, pulled the thick cotton sheets up to cover my nakedness, embarrassed, suddenly, at my ardor. A quickie, is that all Silvio had wanted? And me risking life and limb to drive through a goddamn hailstorm to accommodate him? I hadn't even told him about that. We hadn't talked at all. About anything. How dare he? But a voice in the back of my brain told me to get a grip. I had wanted this as much as he, or I wouldn't have come. At this moment, however, I just wanted more than I was getting.

"No, you didn't tell me." I pulled the sheets up tighter, crossed my arms under my breasts, and scowled. The Brazilian electro-Tropicalia music, infused with space-age burbles and beeps, serenaded us in the background.

"I e-mailed you."

"Then I never got it. I just got the one to meet you here. I thought that was a little weird, but then I decided it'd be cool to check into a hotel in your own hometown. Something different and, um . . . *romantic*."

I glared at him, but he was busy putting on his clothes.

"Then I promise we'll do it again as soon as I get back. And book the whole night. But right now, if I don't catch this plane, this contract is toast."

"I'll toast *you*." I threw a pillow at his face. It missed. He buckled his belt, walked over.

"What is this room supposed to be, anyway?" I said. "Captain Kirk's love battleship? I had no idea they had hotels like this in Los Angeles."

He just looked at me and smiled like he was quite fond of me.

"Surprise, eh?" He tucked a stray tendril behind my ear. "You're so beautiful when we make love. Your pupils dilate and get dreamy and a rosy flush spreads up your chest and neck and spills over into your cheeks. A love flush."

"An angry flush."

"You look like the Goddess Diana with that sheet wrapped around you, your hair all tousled like you've been on the hunt. All you need is a garland of leaves in your hair and a bow."

"If I had one I'd shoot you."

He leaned closer, kissed me fully on the lips, and despite myself, my arms went around his neck, pulled him down. His hands cupped my face.

"I'll make it up to you. I promise." He gave me a last look and pulled away. "But now I've got to go."

I flung myself onto the other side of the bed and gave him my back.

He crossed over to the bar. I heard him take two long gulps. He was whistling as he walked out, suitcase in hand. At the door, he stopped.

"Stay awhile. Take a nap."

He looked at the new bucket of ice that had tipped onto its side in our frenzy. "Have a drink. I got fresh ice." He looked at his watch again. "We've got the room for two more hours."

CHAPTER 23

My mood darkened as I drove home. Silvio took me too much for granted. He hadn't even asked about my day, my stories. Not that we had had a chance to talk about his work either. It had been a rendezvous of pure, unadulterated carnality. Which left me wondering what, exactly, I meant to him.

Back in my bungalow, I took to my bed with a box of take-out Thai noodles, spicy comfort food on a cold wet night. The rain outside was an anemic patter now that the sky had purged itself of golf balls.

When the phone rang, I put down the chopsticks, hoping it was Silvio calling from the plane to reassure me that he loved me.

"Eve Diamond, please," a wavery voice on the other line said. A male voice. Trying to sound older and more sophisticated than it was.

"That's me."

"It's Nicolai Lukin." Gulp. "I saw you at the funeral."

"Yes. My paper sent me to cover it. I didn't come over because . . ." and here I lied ". . . I wanted to give you some space and respect. But I'm glad you called. I'd like to talk with you."

I held my breath.

"Thank you. My family and I appreciate your discretion," he said.

I was impressed by the young man's manners, just as I had been with his father's.

"I'm sorry I lied to you yesterday at UCLA," he said.

"It's okay, Nicolai, I understand."

"But I have something to show you. I've wrestled with this and I don't know what to do, who to talk to. I'm afraid to go to the police. I'm afraid . . . for my family. Maybe you'll have ideas?"

"Yes, of course. I could meet you in twenty minutes. Where are you?" I asked, already shrugging off my camisole and pulling on jeans, a shirt, boots.

"It's late."

"I don't mind."

"I need to get some sleep. I haven't been sleeping since . . ." There was a shallow stutter of breath. "I keep going over it, wondering if there's something I should have done differently, that could have prevented . . . and it's eating me up. The funeral today was excruciating. And afterward, at our house. All those people. I've never felt so alone."

"Tomorrow then," I soothed. "What time? I can come to you."

"I have to be at my aunt's house at noon. She's in Hollywood. How about at Xleb. It's a bakery on Santa Monica Boulevard. All industrial-looking, gray and red and black geometric shapes. Say ten a.m."

"Sure, let's do it. Um, Nick?"

"Yeah?"

"What is it you want to show me?"

Silence. I could picture his brow furrowing.

"I don't know."

"Is it a document? A photo? A letter?"

"There's writing."

"Can you read it to me?"

"What, like over the phone? What if this line is tapped?"

"By who?"

"I don't know anymore. I'm so paranoid."

"Your line isn't tapped," I said. "Just tell me the gist of it, then."

I heard a crackle of paper and thought he might have changed his mind.

"My dad barely drinks, but every once in a while, he ties one on. It started last summer. I was home a lot, getting ready for college, and one day he came in from checking the mail and he had a strange look on his face. And when I asked him if he wanted to play chess, which he usually loves, he didn't answer. Just went into his bedroom and closed the door. From then on, he was watching for the mailman, like he was waiting for something. And afterward, he'd lock himself in his study and come out pale and distracted. He'd argue with my mother in Russian, too low for me to hear."

"Yes?"

"Well, one night, I got up to go to the bathroom, and it was two, and all the lights were on, and he was slumped over his desk. I turned off the stereo and tried to get him to go to bed. I tugged at him and pulled him up and put his arm over my shoulder and half carried, half dragged him to bed. When I went back to turn out the lights, I saw a paper on the floor. It was in Russian."

"What did it say?"

"It was the end of a sentence. It said, '. . . reckoning is at hand.' And it was signed, 'the Prisoner of Memory.'"

I forced myself not to ask any questions that would break up the flow of his story.

"And then I hunted around and found another page that

must have slid under the desk. I couldn't make out all the words, I knew I'd have to look some of them up in the dictionary. But it was late and I was tired so I made a photocopy so he wouldn't know, and I put the originals back exactly where I had found them.

"And in the morning, I saw my dad hunting for the missing page. I picked it up from under the desk and asked if that was what he was looking for. He was so relieved. He grabbed it and lectured me and I thought he was going to hit me, my gentle father who has never hit me in his entire life."

"What did the rest of the letter say?"

"There's a lot more, but I can't tell you over the phone. So, ten a.m. tomorrow?"

"Yes," I said. "But can't you give me the gist of it now?"

"I can't. You'll understand tomorrow."

"I could come over to wherever you are, bring coffee if you'd like," I said, uneasy at the thought of waiting. What if he changed his mind?

"See you at Xleb," Nicolai said, and then the dial tone buzzed in my ear.

When the phone rang again, I hoped it was Nicolai, announcing he had changed his mind.

"Eve?" A familiar voice.

"Who wants to know?"

"It's Josh. I was just checking to see how you were doing."

"Oh, Josh," I said, thinking of Silvio and my busted plans for tonight. I sighed. "I'm okay."

"I got to thinking of that Russian cousin of yours and I figured I'd better just, you know, make sure you're okay. Are you okay?"

"Yeah," I said, not very convincingly.

"Did he show up again? Is he there now, holding a big Russian serrated blade to your throat and that's why you sound so muffled?"

I laughed. "No, he hasn't come back. I'm alone."

"Want some company?"

"Oh, Josh, you're sweet, but honestly, no. I'm fine. I just need to sleep. It's been a long day."

"You wanna talk about it?"

"Thanks for calling but I'd better just see you at the office. We can debrief then."

"Okay, but call me if you need anything."

What I needed, Josh couldn't provide. Or could he? Why was he being so attentive all of a sudden? I hadn't told him about my rendezvous with Silvio. But somehow his radar had told him there was a crack in my heart where he might slip in. Even though I understood that business was business, I felt that Silvio had pulled the rug out from under me today. Maybe I just needed a shoulder to cry on.

I opened my mouth, thought about it, closed my eyes, thought better of it, and said, "Thanks, Josh. I appreciate it. Good night."

CHAPTER 24

The green text message pulsing across the top of my computer the next morning said, *See me. (Trabuco, Jon)*.

I dragged my feet walking to his desk. I didn't want anything to derail my 10 a.m. meeting with Nicolai Lukin.

Trabuco looked up from his computer. "Ah, there you are. Let's find Josh and get started."

Get started? What was he talking about?

Josh strolled over and sat down.

"You'll want to take notes, Diamond," Trabuco said, looking with approval at Josh, who sat, yellow legal pad in hand, gazing ardently at our editor.

I crossed my legs. "I have a photographic memory."

Josh snorted.

"Suit yourself," Trabuco said. "Now, Josh and I were kicking this around last night after you left . . ." here he paused and they both looked at me, as though I had bailed early or something, which I absolutely had not, ". . . and there are a lot of rumors about Denny Lukin's murder. I'm talking Russian Mafia. Find a connection and you may break the case wide open. Right now, the Bureau will not confirm or deny they're investigating, is that right?"

Josh nodded. "But my source is being awfully coy, which could be meaningful."

"What do you have?" Trabuco turned to me.

"Denny Lukin had vowed to tell off some Mafia hoods

that were terrorizing the family business of a girl at his school, but I don't know if anything ever came of it. There's rumors that someone might be blackmailing the father, but nobody knows what about. I'm meeting the surviving son, Nicolai, this morning. He claims he's got something hot for me."

I left out the part about the Prisoner of Memory. I wanted only one byline on my next story.

"Good work," Trabuco said, and I couldn't help but beam.

"We can go together," Josh said.

"Eve may have better luck alone," Trabuco told Josh. He scrutinized me. "And she might have stellar luck if she undoes the top two buttons of her blouse."

"Oh, for God's sake," I said.

"Just kidding. Josh, you stay here and work your LAPD sources for Russian Mafia leads."

Josh nodded unhappily.

"What else?" Trabuco asked. The guy never let up.

"L.A. Sheriff's Office has a Russian organized crime task force out of their West Hollywood offices," I said. "I've been meaning to call them."

"We're looking for the Godfather. The Don Corleone of the Russian world."

I cleared my throat. "I don't know if it works that way."

"Why wouldn't it?"

"For the same reason the Soviet Union broke apart. FBI says you've got Armenians, Georgians, Ukrainians, Chechens, ethnic Russians all vying for the same criminal pie."

"I want names," Trabuco said. "Check the clips. Get me criminal records. I want gang affiliations, families. What do they own? Where do they hang out? What rackets do they run? We're going to do a story on Russian organized crime in L.A. Maybe that will flush something out. My gut tells me this was a take-down. Too clean and sanitized to be anything else. If it was a kiddie love triangle, the cops would have squeezed it out of friends and family by now. Hire a translator if you need to. The *Times* will pay."

"We don't need a translator," Josh said. "We've got Eve's Russian cousin. I'm sure he'll resurface soon."

He winked at me.

"Russian cousin?" Trabuco barked. "You mixing work and personal life again, Diamond, I'll banish you to the 'burbs."

I reddened but said nothing.

Trabuco stared suspiciously at me for a long moment.

"Okay, so take the cousin," he said finally. "Call in after you talk to the Lukin kid. I'm anxious to hear what he has to say. Then the two of you can fan out, hit the streets, talk to people, go to restaurants, nightclubs, saunas, wherever these people hang out. We rendezvous by phone at"—he pulled his shirtsleeve up smartly—"fifteen hundred hours. Now go."

There was an accident and traffic was terrible on the Hollywood Freeway. I saw an overturned car and a tarp covering a lumpy object. I shivered, feeling a black cat walk over my grave. I got off at Santa Monica Boulevard and knew I was in West Hollywood when the signage grew more attractive, the paint more colorful. Flowering trees in pots lined the sidewalks and business awnings were draped with fairy lights. West Hollywood has long been known as Boytown due to its gay community but large swaths of it could be renamed Little Odessa today. The Russian immigrants brought their own nightclubs and social service agencies, newspapers, and boutiques, and the two tribes lived in wary détente.

I found Xleb, parked in the back, and walked inside. The bakery was painted red and black and gray, with angular rooms and geometric tables that reminded me of a constructivist painting. Nicolai wasn't there. I checked my watch and cursed. The traffic tie-up had made me fifteen minutes late. What if he had already left? What if he had changed his mind?

In the corner, two old men in dark suits played chess. They wore frayed sweaters and needed shaves. One had huge ears with white hairs sprouting from the lobes.

I sat next to the plate-glass window where I could watch for Nicolai and ordered Turkish coffee. A white ceramic cup and saucer appeared, a whirl of beige foam in the middle. The flour-smeared waitress, a nimbus of teased black hair around her face, also deposited a pastry, oozing with honey and chopped green pistachios.

"Excuse me, I didn't order this."

She scrunched her eyes.

"House special," she said. "You try."

"But—"

"Gratis," she said loudly, then waddled off.

I watched her receding back. *"Spasibo,"* I called.

I looked at my watch. Nicolai was twenty-five minutes late. A nagging feeling passed through me. The kid wasn't coming. I drank my coffee, nibbled the pastry. Baklava, I guessed. I wondered where in the sprawling Soviet Union the proprietors of this shop came from. Baku. Tbilisi. Yerevan. The Soviet Union had been an empire. Way, way bigger than the United States, with cultures and diversity that made us seem homogeneous by comparison. Now it was all adrift, creating a power vaccuum. Were they our friends? Still enemies? Something in between?

Then I saw him. Parallel parking across the street, as

L.A.'s rude motorists honked with annoyance behind him. He got out of his car, stepped into the street, then stopped and walked back to the curb to feed the meter. He dug deep into his pockets, plucked change out of his palm, pushed in coins. Checked his watch and grimaced.

I walked out onto the sidewalk to let him know I was still here.

Clutching a white paper, he sprinted into the street with only a cursory glance at traffic. I called to him. He stopped, scanning for the voice.

At that instant, a black SUV barreled around a residential side street and onto Santa Monica Boulevard. It was an odd kind of car, black, with tinted windows, half Mercedes, half Hummer. It came straight for him. He twisted away but it was too big, and there wasn't enough time. The car clipped his right side. His body flew fifteen feet in the air but the car kept going. I saw Nicolai's expression as he flipped up, eyes dilated with surprise, mouth twisted, hands already reaching for his side. A silver arc of coins rose into the air like a glittering fountain, then rained down. Wicked away by the wind of the speeding black car, something white fluttered in the air and zigzagged to the ground.

License plate, I thought. Get the plate. I squinted at the receding car but the plate was missing. As I pondered the significance of this, a terrible screech of brakes brought me back to the boy, and I turned to see a white Audi fishtailing and skidding, trying to stop but hitting Nicolai's legs, which disappeared under the carriage. I saw a young woman inside, mouth open in a scream.

The next recollection I have is of darting across the street to where other cars had already stopped to make a protective cordon around Nicolai. His body lay torqued at an unnatural angle, not moving. The Audi's owner was on her knees beside him, hands clasped, reciting a prayer in an unknown language. I looked for the SUV but it was nowhere in sight.

I stepped closer. Could he be dead? Where was the blood? Maybe he was just in shock. But his chest wasn't rising and falling. I fought to restrain my emotions, but in a recessed compartment of my brain, Sasha Lukin's as yet unfelt grief washed over me. His second son, killed like the first. This was no coincidence.

"Nick," I whispered.

The body on the asphalt looked like a corpse.

"Nick, can you hear me?"

Nothing. Except puzzled, then increasingly suspicious looks from people gathering around us.

"Hey?" a man said. "You knew him?"

"Yes," I said slowly. "His name is Nicolai Lukin, and he was on his way to meet me. I'm an *L.A. Times* reporter."

A merciful Samaritan was directing traffic and within moments, an ambulance arrived. Then a police car. They hustled us away, screaming instructions to one another. I saw something white on the asphalt, already trampled by feet and bearing black tire prints. Without thinking I bent to pick it up, then shoved it into my pocket. The man who had questioned me was talking earnestly to the cop. He pointed at me. As the cop began walking toward me, I'm not sure what possessed me but I strolled away, pretending I hadn't seen him. When I turned the corner, I ran, fleeing into an alley and down two streets, then into another alley, fingering the paper in my pocket. Could this be what Nicolai had wanted to show me?

It was an overcast day in L.A. In the alley, people chatted in shop doorways, leaned out of second-story windows to shake out rugs. A bum sifted through the trash. But I saw only conspirators whispering secrets. Surveillance experts watching my every move. Get a grip, I told myself. Then I'll go back. Tell them what I saw. Get some quotes. I should call work too. Dictate an eyewitness account for tomorrow's paper. Let Josh sift through what it all meant. But first I had to stabilize my sanity.

And as I loped along, a shop door opened fifty feet ahead and Mischa Tsipin stepped out.

"You!" I screamed, beside myself with rage and adrenaline. What was he doing here, just blocks from where Nicolai Lukin got run over, right before he was going to tell me something important? Any lingering trace of goodwill evaporated. How could I have been so stupid? He was involved in this. It couldn't be just a coincidence. My anger clotted, giving me strength as I ran toward him. Curses ran through my brain, but I figured I'd save my breath until I reached him. He saw me, panicked, and grabbed the door to go back inside. It rattled but didn't open. Mischa yelled in Russian, then sprang into the alley, running away. With a sinking feeling, I saw that the distance between us was opening up.

"Help," I screamed. "Stop him."

Farther up the alley, two old ladies in widow's weeds with black kerchiefs over their heads sat companionably in white plastic chairs, having a chat. They gripped the arms of the plastic as they heard me, then one lady reached for her cane and stuck it out as Mischa pounded by. He had chosen that moment to look over his shoulder to gauge my pursuit. The next thing Mischa knew, he was flying through the air, arms flailing. He landed on the asphalt with a loud grunt. In a flash, he scrambled to his feet, but it was too late. With another burst of speed, I reached him and we collided, my fists pummeling him as we both went down this time, me on top, crying and screaming, hitting him about the head with a ferocity I didn't know I had in me.

"Liar. Sleazebag. Asshole," I roared, straddling him and gripping his squirming torso with both knees to hold him still so I could aim better. With each curse I rained down another blow.

"You almost got me killed the other day. Then you disappeared. And now you're back, right after Nicolai Lukin gets run over? You're in league with them, aren't you? Murderer."

Hands plucked at my coat, fluttered around my arms, and by their black-clad limbs I recognized the babushkas whose quick thinking had helped me land my quarry.

"Devuchka, devuchka," they chided. Then a man spoke in Russian, and I felt my arms grabbed from behind and pinioned.

"Lady, lady, you must stop. Why you are beating this man?"

Facedown on the asphalt, Mischa crooked his neck and spoke in Russian. The man grunted and kept my arms locked. I struggled to break free. Tears of frustration mingled with impotent rage.

"You liar," I screamed, trying to catch my breath. My heart galloped inside my rib cage, and I thought it might leap out. "What lies did you tell now?"

Mischa scrambled to his feet. Several layers of skin had been scraped from his cheek. One eye was swelling where my fist had connected. His trousers were torn at both knees.

He spoke Russian to the man, then the babushkas subjected him to a lengthy interrogation. One raised her veiny, mottled hand to his eye and made a tsking sound. Then it was my turn. The man who held my arms said, "Lady, he steal from you? He attack you? What he do?"

"Nothing like that," I said, struggling to hold back tears. "He showed up at my house saying he's my cousin. He is in debt to the Russian Mafia, and they almost killed me because of it. And now a boy's been run over on Santa Monica Boulevard. And this guy, he knows something about it."

"Kill? Mafia?" The man's eyes narrowed and he let go of me so fast that I staggered forward and had to brace myself against Mischa's chest so as not to fall. Completely misinterpreting the gesture, Mischa put his arm around me.

"Never fear, I will protect you, Cousin Eve."

With my last ounce of strength, I flung his arm away.

"I don't want your help," I spat.

The man spoke then dusted his hands in the air to be rid of us. He turned and disappeared into a doorway. The babushkas hobbled back to their chairs, dragged them inside an enclosure, and shut the door like they were battening down the hatches for an enemy attack.

Still trying to catch our breath, Mischa and I stared at each other.

"What did you tell them?" I asked.

"That I am poor pilgrim smuggle in by criminals. And they must take pity on me."

"And what did he say?"

"He says, I am honest businessman. Go away and never darken my doorstep again or I will call both police and Mafia down upon you."

Mischa put his hand to his eye, probed the swelling skin. "You gave me real shiny."

"You deserve a lot more than that. You're following me.

You're involved with the people who just killed that boy."

The smile ebbed.

"What boy? You call me murderer?" he squeaked. "Your cousin?"

I gave him a disgusted look.

"Why did you run away just now if you have nothing to hide?"

"I see your face, like you are killing me. I am afraid."

"I don't believe you," I said. "And that's the second time. When you ran out on me in that café, those thugs almost killed me."

He hung his head. "I am sorry. But it is me they want. I know you are safe."

"They interrogated me."

"Lucky you know nothing to tell them," he said softly.

"They thought I was lying."

"You deny our blood, yes? You are smart cousin."

"Stop trying to flatter me. Of course I denied it. But look, Mischa, tell me what's going on or I'm taking you to the cops."

"You cannot do that, Cousin Eve."

"Then I'll tell the police *and* the Mafia. And you better hope the INS finds you before the Mafia deports you in a one-way coffin back to Moscow."

"There is other option."

"What? That I get you a job with Microsoft?"

"I can help you. I will upgrade my cousin's home computer."

"No, thank you. The last thing I want is you snooping around in my files. And stop referring to me in the third person. It's obnoxious."

Impervious to my anger, Mischa was already moving on to Plan B.

"I will help you with researches," he said, tapping his nose with one finger. "I know people in Russian community. Is no problem."

I was beginning to notice he said that each time a really big problem surfaced.

"It is a problem. Everyone you know in the Russian community is trying to kill you."

But how many people did he really know? I considered Trabuco's instructions. With Mischa's help, I could interview Russians who didn't speak English. And I could keep my eye on him. I didn't want him roaming loose.

"It's a deal."

Spotting the big white Hollywood sign as we walked back to my car, Mischa gushed with amazement. Meanwhile, I considered the paper in my pocket. Was this the letter from the Prisoner of Memory? Falling back, I pulled it out. It was a piece of bond paper. One side was filled with type. My heart quickened until I realized it was a syllabus for a UCLA Russian literature class. I flipped it over. Nicolai had jotted down a time, my name, and the word Xleb. This paper trail led nowhere. I balled it up and dropped it into my coat pocket.

My thoughts flashed to Sasha Lukin, who was probably on his way to the morgue again, one day after he buried his youngest son. I thought about Denny's funeral. How could God be so cruel? Then I considered the surprise mourner: Special Agent Clavendish. He had some connection to this family. I had felt it radiating off him the way body heat does on infrared cameras. And now, I knew something Clavendish didn't. Perhaps if I sprang the news of Nicolai's death, he'd be shocked into telling me some important revelation. I'd have to plot my psych op with military-style precision. But first I'd better call in.

"So what did the kid have to say?" Trabuco asked when I rang through.

"A man in a monster SUV just ran over Nicolai Lukin," I said.

"Holy shit! Is he dead?"

I hesitated. "It sure looked that way. Josh can confirm it with the cop shop."

"Tell me it happened *after* you talked to him, Diamond."

"He was crossing the street to meet me. I saw him get mowed down. He wanted to discuss a weird letter his dad got last summer that might be connected to his brother's murder. I think someone didn't like the idea."

"Don't go all black helicopter on me. Who knew he was on his way to talk to you?"

I looked at Mischa, who was gazing in worship at the Hollywood sign above us. The expert hacker. Had he been listening in on my line?

"I didn't tell anyone except you and Josh," I said.

"You didn't tell me anything about a letter this morning."

"I wanted to see if it would pan out first."

"You gonna come in and write it up?"

I considered my plan to confront Clavendish. "How about I dictate it? I'd like to try that FBI agent again, the Russian organized crime guy."

Trabuco gave a little snort. "The one you had so much luck with the other night? Good luck, Jane Bond. How's this gonna advance the Lukin story?"

"Special Agent Thomas Clavendish. Ring a bell?"

"No."

"Well, it should. He was embroiled in a KGB sex scandal

in the eighties right here in El Lay when he ran the bureau's counterintelligence unit. Demoted but never charged, presumably since an open trial would have exposed gross Feeb misbehavior, not to mention national secrets."

"How convenient for everyone involved," Trabuco said.

"Act Two: resurrected in the post–Cold War world as a quote 'valued member' of the Eurasian Organized Crime Task Force. Then slowly put out to pasture. He was at the Lukin kid's funeral. It reeks of rotten sturgeon eggs."

"I don't know, Eve. It could be a wild goose chase."

"He's retiring tomorrow, so this could be my last chance. I want to follow him home, to the wilds of Simi Valley or wherever Feebs live."

"Josh has good Bureau sources. Why don't you let him handle this?"

"Josh's source was still wearing diapers when this guy was screwing KGB playmates. And we've already met with Josh's guy."

There was a long silence.

"So how about it, Jon?"

"You know, I've heard worrisome things about you. Jane Sims says you're a hothead and—"

"Jane Sims can go fuck herself. I've brought her more front-page stories than her little brownnosers ever will."

"There's no need for that kind of language."

"Come off it, Trabuco. Is this a newsroom or a church? Besides, in case you haven't noticed, I'm a bona fide guttersnipe. But I'm also good. Let me do my job."

I paused, held my breath.

"I hope you're right," he said. "Because I could use you here at the mothership."

Trabuco rustled papers. "There was another mountain lion sighting this morning in Fern Dell. And they found a dead deer on Mulholland. You write me the definitive puma take-out and I guarantee you it'll go nondupe."

Nondupes, or column-one stories, ran on the coveted left-hand column of the paper's front page. They were regular contenders for prizes and shone the magnanimous light of celebrity on everyone involved. For once, I wasn't interested.

"Sure thing," I said. "Soon's I get to the bottom of these murders."

"I'll give you two days. Now talk to Josh, who's hopping up and down, annoying the crap out of me."

"Josh here," came my colleague's insinuating voice.

I dictated what I had on the hit-and-run, leaving out the part about the Prisoner of Memory because it was too speculative for now. Josh said he'd just gotten off the phone with Lansing at the Bureau, who was hinting around about a Mafia hit, but none of their usual hairy canaries were singing.

"Did they find anything on Nicolai Lukin's body, like a letter or a note or anything?" I asked.

"Why? Was he bringing you a letter?" Josh asked guilelessly.

"Maybe. But he wouldn't go into it over the phone," I lied. "He was scared and wanted to talk in person."

"What sucky timing. By the way, the courier dropped off a history of the Cold War from the L.A. Public Library."

Damn, I had forgotten all about that. Maybe it would shed light on what poor, dead Nicolai Lukin had wanted to show me.

"Want to fill your old droogie in?"

"Just a hunch I'm checking out," I mumbled.

"Be sure and let me know, Anna Karenina."

CHAPTER 25

I worked out the final details of my plan as Mischa and I drove to a sporting goods store on La Cienega.

"A little shopping, Eve?" he asked, staring at the sleek exercise equipment.

"You're not allowed to ask questions."

I went up and down the aisles until I found what I wanted: a pair of cheap but functional binoculars. They were $39.95. I smiled, imagining what the *Times* bean counters would say when they saw it on my expense report. I could list it under "clandestine operations, surveillance." I'd been on stakeouts with the cops before. I saw how they did it and it didn't seem too hard. Most people were too distracted to realize they were being followed. Law-enforcement types were the exception, but Clavendish had checked out a long time ago. Tomorrow he'd turn in his badge and regulation pistol and be home free. I actually fooled myself into thinking I had a chance.

Next, I stopped at Paradise Deli in West Hollywood and bought vodka and a variety of Russian salads, savory pies, and smoked meats. As Mischa's hand snaked to one of the bags, I slapped it back.

"Wait," I said. "We'll either eat this with my source if he talks or you can have it on the way home, 'cause Lord knows I won't have any appetite."

We drove to Westwood. It was 3 p.m. I parked on Veteran Avenue and propped a newspaper in front of me to hide the binoculars as I scanned for people coming out of the building and cars leaving the garage. Mischa read a Russian-language newspaper, occasionally casting mournful glances at the bags to make sure the food was still there. An hour passed. I started feeling nervous, figuring that any car parked near the Federal Building for too long would catch the eye of the roving surveillance cameras and eventually earn me a visit from security.

I leaned forward to change the radio station and almost missed a tall form hurrying from the building into the parking garage.

"I think that was him," I told Mischa.

A few minutes later a Buick El Dorado left the Federal Building complex and turned east onto Wilshire Boulevard. I remembered it from the funeral, clocked the first couple numbers on the plates. Yup, it was him. Slowly, I slid out behind him, keeping two cars and one lane away. The traffic was miserable. Clavendish inched his way toward Hollywood. At Beachwood Canyon, he turned into the hills with the impatience of a man who is almost home.

I had expected to tail him to a remote tract home in a far-off suburb. Maybe he was visiting someone. But no. His car disappeared into an underground garage. I parked out front and we walked up. The building had a name, the Savoy Arms, and a 1930s-style tiled fountain. Banana plants and bougainvillea and date palms grew lush and wild. It was a bona fide hideway. You could still find hidden pockets of old Hollywood like this if you looked hard enough. Except these had been converted to condos with modern security, I thought, noting the wrought-iron front gate. I checked the tenant list on the mailbox but didn't see his name.

I rang a buzzer at random, telling Mischa to let me do the talking.

"Yes," said a gravelly female voice.

I introduced myself, said my brother and I were visiting my uncle Thomas Clavendish but he wasn't home yet.

"Sorry," the voice said, cutting me off.

"It is same in Moscow now," Mischa said. "Too much crime."

"Follow me," I said. I walked to the side of the building, followed the driveway downhill, and met an electrified security gate that sealed off the underground parking lot. I wedged myself into a hedge along the wall and Mischa followed.

"When a car goes in or out, that's our chance to slip inside," I said.

"They will arrest us."

"Nonsense. I've done this loads of times."

We had barely gotten ourselves settled when a car pulled up. The security gate began its long slide open and the car drove inside and disappeared.

"C'mon." I grabbed Mischa's hand and we ran in. I didn't see anyone, but just in case, I pulled out keys and stood next to a car like I was locking up.

"Don't look scared. Act like you live here," I said.

Mischa gave a grunt and followed me in search of a stairwell.

We found it, climbed up, and emerged into a whitewashed courtyard with more tile and jasmine trellises. A fountain trilled in welcome. There must have been about sixteen units, set back from the courtyard. A tiled pool shimmered, blue and unused, a single banana frond floating on its still surface.

I looked around, wondering if we'd have to knock on every door. Mischa examined a giant bird-of-paradise tree, leaning his face close to the angular blue and orange flowers.

"They have no smell," he complained.

"Lesson One of Hollywood: Not all that glitters is gold."

We heard footfalls and Clavendish appeared around a corner, a khaki raincoat draped loosely over his shoulders, the way pickpockets do to conceal their roving hands. An umbrella and a briefcase dangled from his left side. I couldn't see anything on the right.

Clavendish halted. He forced his features into an exclamation of surprise and examined Mischa carefully. Satisfied that his hands were empty, Clavendish's gaze slid to me and my plastic bags. Then he cut his eyes and walked to his unit.

I fell into step with him, Mischa bringing up the rear. "Mind if we come in?" I said. "Got a few things to run by you."

"Fuck off," he said. He faced us full-on again. "And don't think I didn't notice your silly games on the street."

"How did you see me? I was over a lane and several cars back."

Clavendish examined me with what would have been contempt, had his face been less pitiless. I realized he must have lain in wait for us or he'd be inside by now. He shrugged one shoulder and the raincoat rippled and revealed a gun in his right hand, pointed at my heart. My stomach churned. Rogue agents weren't unknown at the Bureau. Neither were those so paranoid that they saw assassins behind every palm tree.

"Sight is the least of it," Clavendish said, his breath coming fast and heavy. "One gets a sense, after so many years. Now both of you. Against that wall."

The hand with the gun swept sideways and we followed without a word. I glanced at Mischa and saw his fear. His eyes were fixated on the gun. I think he would have preferred the Russian Mafia.

Clavendish dropped the briefcase on a doorstep and I flinched at the thud. The FBI agent's mouth curled into a smile.

"A little twitchy, are we? Too bad. Mess with me, you better have trigger reflexes."

He stamped the ground and pretended to lunge at me and I flinched again. Mischa's eyes were closed and he was praying in Russian.

Clavendish laughed. "Isn't this what you came for? Cloak-and-dagger?"

With a little sleight of hand, he produced a key and opened his front door. A stale smell of cigarettes wafted out.

"Inside," he said, the gun sweeping us along like a broom. "You've botched the cloak. Now it's time for the dagger."

There was nowhere to run. Mischa and I looked at each other.

"Let's move it," Clavendish said. "Leave all your belongings outside."

Gingerly, I set my purse down, then the shopping bags. The bottles clinked together. So much for grabbing one by the neck and bringing the glass down hard on his head.

"What have you got there?" Clavendish said, licking his lips.

"Just food and some vodka. My mother taught me it was impolite to show **up** empty-handed."

"My mother taught me it was impolite to show up without an invitation," he said.

I nodded at the gun. "You already knew we were coming."

We walked into a twilit room and Clavendish brought the bags in, then closed the door.

"Sit down." He pointed to a couch, and we sat and slid together on a cold and slippery leather surface.

I heard the chain rattle and the dead bolt slip home. We were locked in.

CHAPTER 26

C lavendish moved through the room with ease. A light flicked on, illuminating the condo. I expected a slovenly mess but the unit was clean and neat, the walls hung with modern art, the furniture displaying a connoisseur's eye for classic lines.

He pulled an electrical wand out of his briefcase and I wondered if it could be a torture device. Holding it like a divining rod, he walked through the room, waving it over furniture and paintings and tables and watching the digital readout intensely as it scanned.

Finishing his rounds, Clavendish turned the machine off and shoved it back into his case.

"Clean," he said.

He sat down heavily in a chair and gave me a searching look.

"It's a crime to harass a federal agent. You clear on that, Ms. Diamond and her sidekick?" His eyes flickered to Mischa. "Now. You will tell me who sent you."

"Nobody sent us. I'm doing a story—"

"Yes, yes." Clavendish rolled his eyes. "And who have you spoken to so far?"

I thought about Lyuba and her terrified family. The Lukins. Nicolai at the UCLA library, then sprawled out on the street. Ludmilla. Golodny. The thugs who had threatened me in the deli. The letter with its odd signature.

"I'm pursuing a Mafia connection in the Lukin case," I began shakily.

Clavendish looked away. His voice grew elaborately casual.

"Those people are dangerous. You don't want to mess with them."

"The ones I've talked to so far seem okay," I lied.

"Don't kid yourself. Vassily's outfit would just as soon kill you as look at you."

"Vassily who?"

"Vassily nobody. Stay out of it, Ms. Diamond. I'm warning you. You have no idea what you're getting involved with."

"And you do?"

"I know these people."

Clavendish glided to the window, lifted a corner of the blind, peered out. Satisfied that there was no one there, he came back. Before he could sit down, his cell phone rang.

"Yeah," he answered. I heard a Russian voice rumbling loudly on the other end. Clavendish said two words back, then punched off the phone. I looked at Mischa but he had a glassy, frozen stare on his face and was examining the seam of the green leather couch with great interest.

"Don't move," Clavendish said. He waved the gun for good measure and disappeared into another room. I thought I heard a bottle unscrew, then a *glug-glug*. Soon he reappeared. His features had relaxed almost imperceptibly.

"So where would I go if I wanted to talk to these folks?" I said.

"To your grave."

There was something jovial in his answer.

"I'm serious."

"So am I. Now what did Lukin tell you that day at the house, when they found the body? I didn't get a chance to talk to him much at the funeral. It wasn't the right . . . venue."

"Nothing. That's why I'm here. And to tell you that something horrible has happened."

"You," Clavendish said, "are a horrible little pest. First thing tomorrow, I'm lodging a complaint with the Bureau."

Oh, and you don't think that I should lodge a cross-complaint about you pulling a gun on me?

He seemed to read my mind.

"I'd just deny it," he said. "So save yourself the trouble."

"Mr. Clavendish, I need your help. Your expertise."

I saw genuine curiosity in his eyes before it was snuffed out by resentment.

"What expertise?" Clavendish said bitterly. "The young Turks who run the Bureau have no use for me. The Russian Mafia's running wild in the city, but to them I'm nothing but a dinosaur."

"Look," I said. "I'm just a civilian, but something horrible's going on. Another member of the Lukin family has just been murdered."

"Is that right?" he said with weary skepticism.

"Nicolai Lukin."

Emotion flitted over his face, but he willed it to disappear. His eyes grew hard. "If you are lying, so help me God . . ."

"He was on his way to . . ." I stopped, thought better of it. "I saw it with my own eyes."

"This is a provocation," Clavendish said. "It's an old trick." His eyes focused warily on Mischa.

He questioned him brusquely in Russian. Mischa answered, stating his name and many other things, based on the length of time that he spoke.

"Is not trick," Mischa added, switching to English. "Just truth. You will help us?"

"No," Clavendish said reflexively. "I'm going to hurt you. Maybe I'll arrest the two of you for harassing a special agent."

"We're telling the truth, sir," I said. "Sasha Lukin's sons have been murdered only days apart. Tell us what you know and the *Los Angeles Times* will splash your name all over the paper. Not like the other time." I paused meaningfully. "You can redeem your name, salvage your reputation. Someone has killed two boys, and you can find him."

"Not so fast." Clavendish raised a finger.

He pulled out two pairs of handcuffs and ordered us to a massive, carved-wood dining table. I got the creepy feeling anything could happen here in this man's apartment. Our decomposed bodies would be found months later dumped in a ravine.

"You, over here," he gestured to me.

"Why . . . ?"

"Shut up," he said matter-of-factly. "I need to secure you while I check your story."

"You don't need to do this."

"Yes," he said, "I do. Sit down. Put your arms around the table leg."

I sat. He handcuffed us to opposite ends of the table, then left the room, whistling a Russian song I recognized from childhood: "Black Eyes."

It was the whistle that scared me more than anything; it was so inappropriate and it told me the guy was completely unhinged.

"He will kill us," Mischa whispered. Sweat dripped from his temples, despite the cold apartment.

"No, he'll see that I'm telling the truth."

We heard him on the phone in the other room, but it was impossible to make out what he was saying, or even if it was in English. Ten minutes later, Clavendish loomed in the doorway, the color drained from his face.

He ran long fingers through his unruly locks, then pinched the bridge of his nose. The raincoat and gun were gone. I didn't think that made him any less dangerous.

"Well, well," Clavendish said. He busied himself laying out the Paradise Deli take-out food and vodka as we sat shackled at his feet, humming a new song under his breath and ignoring our pleas for release.

"All in good time, madam," he said.

To my great relief, he laid out three plates and three glasses, fussing over cutlery and napkins. Only then did he free us.

Stiff from fear and crouching on the cold floor, we straightened up. Clavendish gestured to the chairs and we slid into them. He poured us each a shot, downed his quickly, then refilled his glass. He downed that, too, then sat down and loosened his tie.

"He's not dead," Clavendish said finally.

"What?"

Clavendish plucked at the silver tines of a fork.

"Nicolai's in the hospital with internal injuries, two shattered legs, a broken pelvis, and a severe concussion. Unconscious. But alive."

"Thank God," I said, feeling a surge of relief. I was also glad that Clavendish had released us and stopped acting like a maniac.

"But still, who did this? And why?" I asked, lifting a shaky glass to my lips.

Clavendish's shot glass disappeared in his huge palm. "He's Russian, isn't he? Field's wide open."

"What's that supposed to mean?"

"Either the kids or the dad were involved in something. Mafia. KGB. New enemies. Old friends. Onetime business partners. Someone Sasha slighted on a street corner in Moscow thirty years ago. Take your pick."

"You're just trying to throw me off the track." I groped for the connection I knew existed. Clavendish's use of Lukin's first name. "You ran Sasha Lukin, didn't you?" I said. "For the Bureau. And someone from the other side found out."

"And you, my dear, have been reading too many John Le Carré novels."

"That not make sense, Eve," Mischa interjected. "Then they would just kill father. Not go after sons."

"Good point." Clavendish leaned back.

"But you do know him."

"I already told you that," Clavendish said quietly.

And with those words, the conversation moved to a different plane. The FBI agent's tone was no longer defensive. The shock of hearing about Nicolai's hit-and-run had done its work.

"How did you and Lukin meet?" I said, trying for casual and shooting Mischa a warning. But I needn't have bothered. He was happily spooning purple cabbage salad onto his plate and hoovering up smoked fish. I watched him tear off huge chunks of black pumpernickel.

"In Moscow," Clavendish said absentmindedly.

Holy shit, I thought. The dam has busted and all the water's pouring out at once.

"Really?" I said in my best conversational tone.

Clavendish rolled up a slice of smoked meat and folded it sideways into his mouth. He fished a pickled mushroom out of a jar and chased it with a snootful of vodka.

"Aah," he said, after belching.

Foiled by the food, I tried again. "So the FBI sent you to Moscow? I thought they left that to the CIA."

He regarded me coldly, and I realized my gee-whiz tones didn't fool him at all.

"This was years before I joined the Bureau."

"Oh?" I played with my food, tried to exude only mild interest.

He poured himself another slug of vodka, lifted his glass, and we all clinked.

"*Na zdorovye,*" he said. "To their incompetence, may it never falter."

"Whose incompetence?"

He looked at me like I was stupid.

"The killers, of course."

"Who were the killers?"

He wagged his finger at me. "You've already asked me that, young lady. Better brush up on your Interrogation 101 techniques."

"You wrote the book," I said, smiling with my teeth. "So let's just cut to the chase. Under what circumstances did you meet Sasha Lukin in Moscow?"

He sunk another drink, leaned back, laced his fingers behind his head. The food and booze were making him expansive. But I knew better than to relax.

"Let's see, it was spring 1968. Moscow State University. He was several years older than me."

"You went to school in the Soviet Union?"

It was hard to keep the incredulity out of my voice. My mind jumped like an electrified toad. So that was where he learned his language skills, his love of the literature, the people. But wouldn't the FBI worry that he'd been recruited in Moscow? Told to apply to the Bureau, work his way up, then let the KGB run him as a double agent? And wasn't that, ultimately, what had happened, thanks to a persuasive Slavic femme fatale named Ludmilla Belyaeva?

"You kids have been fed such a load of crap about the Cold War," Clavendish said. "A lot of Americans visited behind the Iron Curtain. Nikita Krushchev came to California and toured Twentieth Century Fox."

"I thought it was Disneyland."

"That's an urban myth. Security officials couldn't guarantee his safety so they nixed that, and he blew a gasket at missing Mickey. But my point is that there were lots of scholarly exchanges. Especially in the sixties and seventies. Even Bill Clinton went. It was a fantastic, hopeful time when great change seemed not only possible but preordained. Before the Prague Spring shut everything down."

A trace of sorrow in his voice for what might have been.

"So the Feebs didn't hold that against you? Consider you a sort of Fifth Columnist?"

"I joined in 1973. Hoover was gone by then, and there was a terrific backlash against everything that had gone wrong under his long and paranoid reign. Plus," he cracked a thin smile, "it was hard to find good recruits then. If the cops were pigs, the FBI was the Antichrist. And I was a patriot, believe it or not. I loved my country. Plus I had the language skills."

Just then Mischa broke in, asking if he could use the bathroom. I felt my blood boil at this interruption, after I had specifically asked him to be quiet. Clavendish clammed up and gave Mischa a penetrating stare.

"Let me show you where it is," he said with elaborate courtesy, eyes darting around the room.

"You can just point," Mischa said, but Clavendish was already halfway to the door, leading the way. They disappeared.

Free to look around, I saw a pile of mail and several gambling magazines on the entryway table. I remembered Lansing's comments about his colleague's fondness for cards. So it was true. I wondered what Clavendish's monthly bank statement would show.

In no time, they were back, Clavendish following Mischa close as a shadow. I tried to pick up where we had left off.

"So you and Lukin met during a cultural exchange in Moscow? And you became friends?"

To my surprise, he started right up again.

"Mikhail and I were part of an international club on campus."

"Who's Mikhail?" I said.

For a long moment, Clavendish fixed me with those large, bright eyes.

"Sorry," he said. "I mean Sasha. For a moment there, I got him confused with another friend." He smiled expansively, but after what had happened earlier, it didn't seem genuine. "The Soviets wanted the world to think they supported international brotherhood but most of it was lip service. In reality, they discouraged fraternization and we were watched and followed. By both sides, probably. Ha! But we didn't care. We'd stay up until two a.m., talking about a new brotherhood. We were the founding members. The two of us and another Russian, a brilliant, excitable fellow."

"Was that Mikhail?"

Clavendish's eyes grew more gauzy and indistinct.

"No."

"Life must have been so exciting then," I said wistfully. "All the hope and fear. Such high stakes. The Cold War so black and white. Everyone knew exactly who the enemy was."

He gave me a shrewd look.

"Things were often more murky than you'd imagine."

"Well, nothing compared to now. So did you keep up your friendship with Lukin and this other guy when you got back home?"

"There were a few letters. By then we had other lives, careers. It wasn't a good idea. But in our own ways, we were all working toward a day when politics would no longer be necessary. We believed in humanity, that was our ideology."

He raised his leonine head, stared out the sliding glass doors onto his patio. Long furrows rippled across his forehead and down either side of his mouth.

"Did the other Russian guy emigrate to America too?"

There was a pause. "No," he finally said.

I could see years of secrecy rising up in Clavendish's face.

"I must be getting old. It was on the tip of my tongue but now it's escaped me," he said. He pulled a grape off its cluster, popped it into his mouth.

"I doubt anything escapes you. And it's not like any of this is a state secret. All right, well, when did Lukin emigrate?" I asked.

"Nineteen eighty-five."

The year Ludmilla Belyaeva got traded back to the Soviets.

"The year Gorbachev came to power," I said.

Clavendish nodded.

"And you renewed your friendship then?"

His head turned back to me with exaggerated slowness. He's about to lie, I thought.

"Eventually." He examined me with large, frank eyes.

"How'd you find out he was here?"

"We . . . ran into each other."

The FBI agent reached for another grape, put it in his mouth.

"Was Lukin ever a spy?" I asked.

A drop of juice squirted out of his mouth and landed on the table. "Oops." Clavendish reached for a napkin.

He scrubbed at the table. I waited for him to finish. Finally he looked up. His eyes were liquid pools you could drown in.

"Was Lukin ever a spy?" I repeated.

"For which side?"

"Either."

Clavendish moved his tongue between his teeth, probing for bits of grape skin.

"I'd only know about one side," he drawled.

"Yes, and you've been so forthcoming. But rumors do have a way of getting around, even if they can't be proven."

"Disinformation can be a powerful tool in the wrong hands," Clavendish said cryptically.

"Was Lukin a double agent or something?" I said softly.

Like Ludmilla, I wanted to add.

"There's nothing like hitting a man when he's down," Clavendish said.

"I didn't mean—"

"Of course you did."

Clavendish gave meticulous attention to smoothing out his place mat.

"Before you go casting aspersions . . ." He stopped, changed tack. "Sasha's having a tough time of it right now. No one deserves what he's been through."

I filed away his words for later.

"What drew you to Russian studies?"

"Studied it at Berkeley. Under Czeslaw Milosz. Tremendous man. Fired me right up for a doctorate in Slavic studies. I was ABD."

"ABD?"

"All but dissertation. Then I discovered criminal justice. And got a hard-on for the Bureau. When they found out my background, well . . . the Cold War was in full swing and the CIA was trying to encroach on their domestic turf. So the Bureau wanted its own in-house Russian experts."

He offered me the platter of zakuski, his head wobbling slightly. I was struck by his exaggerated solicitousness, the way he gripped the platter in both hands. His enunciation, with too-long beats in between. He was getting pickled.

"I can't see you as a Fed, frankly," I said.

"I love my country. Make no mistake. But I broke the Bureau's cardinal commandment. I allowed myself to doubt."

"Doubt what?"

"The mission."

"You mean the Cold War?"

"If you wrap yourself in moral righteousness, you feel you can do anything you want. But it isn't so."

"You mean the end doesn't always justify the means?"

He gave a sad smile. "There is something truly frightening about a lack of doubt, don't you think? It's what makes us human."

"So this is about humanism? Not spying?"

"It's about a fall from grace," he said.

"How's that?"

"You couldn't understand," Clavendish said.

"Try me," I said. "'Cause all I know so far is that Nicolai Lukin was run over by an armored car on his way to show me a letter that someone sent his dad. And you're mumbling cryptically about falls from grace."

Clavendish got very still.

"What did the letter say?"

"I don't know." I pretended not to notice his scrutiny. "He never got a chance to show it to me."

"I wonder if the police found anything on his person," Clavendish said, and I could tell that he intended to find out as soon as we left.

He lifted his glass but his hand shook and vodka sloshed out. He moved his elbow to cover the stain. Then he pushed his chair from the table and stood up.

"Thank you for coming, Ms. Diamond. Mr. Tsipin." He inclined his head to me, then Mischa.

"I have nothing more to say. I grieve for Sasha Lukin's loss. Please do not torment him during this time with requests for interviews. Some things are best left to the past."

CHAPTER 27

W hy didn't you tell me the Lukin kid was still alive?" I screamed into the phone at Josh as soon as we were back in my car.

"I thought you knew," my colleague said mildly.

"Last thing I saw they were loading him onto a stretcher. I swear they pulled the sheet over him."

"He's not out of the woods yet. He's got head trauma and they're doing brain scans."

"I heard it was a concussion." I stopped to consider. Maybe it was good I hadn't known. It had allowed me to bluff Clavendish with utmost sincerity. "The cops will have a lot of questions when he wakes up."

"Hospital says it could be a while," Josh said.

"They better post an armed guard. Someone wants him to take the big sleep."

"LAPD's there around the clock," Josh said. "What a pisser. You were so close to learning something. Now they're not going to let us near him."

I already had something important—the Prisoner of Memory. But I needed to talk to Lukin to learn more. He was the only one who knew the whole story. Besides the killer. What a scoop it would be if I could lay out the entire story in the *Times*. But for now, I wanted to keep it to myself. It was a decision I'd live to regret.

"One last thing," I said to Josh. "Can you call your

friend Lansing and ask him something about Clavendish, that older FBI guy who's the Russian expert?"

"Sure. You want to date him?"

"Your attempts to pry personal information out of me are pathetic. I want to know if he's really got heavy gambling debts or it's just a nasty rumor."

"Why would they keep an agent who's made himself vulnerable?"

"Maybe that's why they're retiring him."

"What's this got to do with the Lukin kid?"

"Just a hunch. I'll tell you everything soon."

"Okay, Lois. But keep your phone on. Honestly, I don't know why I let you lead me around by the nose."

"Because you want to get in my pants and you delude yourself into thinking you have a chance."

There was a long silence.

"You don't know the half of it," he said.

As we drove back to Silverlake, I considered what I was going to do with Mischa now that he was back in my life.

Reading my thoughts, he stirred.

"A pity he accompany me to bathroom," my cousin said.

I shot him a pensive look. "Clavendish? Why?"

"I want to search apartment."

"Really?" I smiled at the oncoming traffic.

Mischa shrugged. "He is FBI. We are in his flat. You are distracting him while I . . ."

He mimed sneaking around and rooting through papers.

"Why do you think he went with you, sport?"

Mischa's face fell.

I patted his knee. "But I appreciate the effort," I said.

"In the bathroom was something," Mischa said. "Maybe nothing but . . ."

"What did you see?"

"A paper pad near sink. It is yellow. Much writing. Man from FBI grab it as we walk in."

"Could you read any of it?"

"Maybe one word. It was large, yes? And lines underneath."

"What word?"

"Something about prisoners."

I gripped the wheel tightly.

"Prisoner of Memory?"

Mischa repeated it in Russian, trying it out on his tongue.

"Yes. Maybe. I am not whole hog." He looked at me hopefully. "It is help?"

My mind went skittering in different directions. I was sure I hadn't mentioned this term to Mischa. I had only heard it the night before from Nicolai Lukin. Why had Clavendish gotten all intense when I mentioned the letter? And why did he have a phrase like that written on a notepad? Was the FBI also on the killer's trail and just not making it public? Or, I thought with welling dread, could it be Clavendish himself?

"It's a help," I said finally.

"What means this?" Mischa asked.

The eagerness in his voice pulled me up and I hoped I hadn't been thinking out loud. From now on, I would have to be very careful around FBI Special Agent Clavendish. And while Mischa had somewhat proved his usefulness, the less I told him, the better.

"I don't know yet," I said, then added darkly, "I wish you knew more about the city's Russian community."

"Is not problem. What you wish to know?"

"Where do the Russian Mafia hang out?"

He snorted. "You want I should take you? To that house from which I am running? Many Russian Mafia there. They see me. They catch me again, maybe kill me. Maybe kill you. No problem. We will go."

"I guess you're right. You can't help me with that one," I said.

When we pulled up to my house, I realized I had made up my mind a long time ago that Mischa could spend another few nights on my back porch. But he had a point about the Mafia problem, and we had to get that resolved.

"Tomorrow we're going to make an appointment with a good immigration lawyer. Meanwhile, you can stay with me. Now, where are your things?"

Mischa reddened.

He walked to the window and pointed to the banana tree.

"Please do not be angry. I come to house when you are at work and I leave my knapsack behind plants. I know is safe here."

I looked at him. Sneaking around behind my back. Suddenly, I wasn't so sure anything was safe.

CHAPTER 28

A t home, Mischa slipped in a CD and settled himself onto the couch with the remote. I grimaced as the falsetto tones of Freddie Mercury filled my living room.

Eyes closed, Mischa sang along with the reverence others devote to church hymns. When it ended, he sighed blissfully and hit "mute."

"What genius he was. So tell me, Eve. You are important newspaper reporter?"

"I'm a reporter, yeah."

"You have interviewed many famous people?"

"Some."

"You have interviewed Freddie Mercury?"

"The singer from Queen?"

Mischa gave a fervent nod. "He is kind of hero for me. Lyrics are poetry. True genius."

"You're kidding, right?"

"I have translated his songs into Russian for friends, who are publishing them. 'We Will Rock You.' 'Under Pressure.' These are brilliant songs for our times. Do you not feel under pressure?"

"All the time. But when I think of genius, I think of Ella Fitzgerald. Billie Holiday. Even Bob Dylan. But not Freddie Mercury."

I stopped at his hurt look. He stabbed the remote and

the sound swelled, giving me a second chance to catch the staggering brilliance.

I groaned. In the land of Dostoyevsky, Lermontov, Tolstoy, Shostakovich, Rostropovich, and Tchaikovsky, I had to land a cousin who thought Freddie Mercury was God. This is what happens when a society is locked away from Western culture for too many generations. They embrace pop culture without discrimination.

As the strains of "Bohemian Rhapsody" swelled, I threw myself into the rocking chair.

"Oh God," I muttered. "What have I gotten myself into?"

But Mischa had an uncanny knack for knowing when he was skating on thin ice. He came over and gave my shoulder awkward little pats. "I am here. Your cousin. I will protect you. I will help you find killer of Russian boy. I am not afraid. You will tell me everything, slowly now, and we will birth plan. But first . . ."

He stood up, stretched, and patted his belly. "I have need of nourishment. Please, where you are keeping sour cream?"

While the Bottomless Pit ate, I reread the Clavendish clips, looking for clues I might have missed the night before. When the scandal hit, Ludmilla Belyaeva had been living in West Los Angeles. Just for the hell of it, I checked the phone company, but found no listing. I knew others had tried to find her, and the trail was ice cold, but maybe they had missed something. Maybe enough time had passed that she had gotten careless. With open borders, maybe some of her relatives had immigrated and knew where she was. I got listings for every Belyaeva in four counties and called, but most of the ones I reached had no idea what I was talking about. Some didn't speak English. This was where Mischa would earn his room and board.

"C'mere," I called, and Tapeworm bustled in with a bowl of chips and a plastic tub of sour cream.

I told him what I wanted and handed him the list.

But after an hour of grilling people in Russian, he had nothing to report.

"Did you get the feeling they knew but were lying?"

"No. They are suspicious by nature but they speak truth."

"So you're a human polygraph?"

I stared out the living room window, where steam was condensing.

Mischa snapped his fingers.

"What is last known address of Gospoja Belyaeva? And age?"

"It's not even an address," I said bleakly. "Just an area. And she'd be about . . ." I checked the stories and did a quick calculation, "about fifty-five."

"Please may I use computer?"

I realized what he had in mind.

"You're going to hack into databases, aren't you? Track her down. Well, it won't work."

Mischa coughed and cleared his throat. "I prefer to call it research."

"I already Googled her. The trail goes cold after 1985. Several journalists and Cold War historians have tried to find her over the years but never turned anything up."

"When was most recent try?" Mischa asked.

"Nineteen ninety-four. For the ten-year anniversary."

He dismissed me with a wave of his arm. "Databases were in infancy then," Mischa said. "Many new ways to cross-reference. And please know Google is just for beginning."

He drifted toward the computer, sat at the chair, fingers flexed over the keys.

"And so?" he said, waiting for my approval. His eyes were unfocused, already moving through electronic pathways beyond my ken.

I hesitated, licked my lips. Could he really turn anything up?

"How are you going to . . . ?" I began. "Oh, never mind. It's better if I have plausible deniability. Go ahead."

I made a pot of coffee, put on a thick sweater, and went onto the back porch with a steaming cup to clear my head.

When I came inside ten minutes later, Mischa was muttering in Russian. He scratched the side of his head vigorously. *"Da, da,"* he said, fingers scampering over the keys, the monitor scrolling lines of data.

He hit "print" and pulled the sheet off.

"Here she is," he said, stabbing with a greasy forefinger. A blotch spread across the paper.

I took the sheet, flicked off granules of oily salt, and read: "Milly White. 862 Fruitland Terrace, Sunland, California 91506."

"What makes you so sure this is the same person?"

His face got that angelic look. "You said is better not know."

I dangled the printout between us. "So this notorious KGB spy wasn't traded to the Soviets after all? She just changed her name and retired to the Valley?" I laughed at the incongruity.

"She is not changing much."

"What do you mean?"

"Milly. Milla. Ludmilla. You see?"

"Maybe."

"And in Russian, Belyaeva means white." He looked away with modesty. "Simple powers of deduction," he said.

I whistled in admiration. "Even if you're wrong, it's a hell of a guess."

"You must think like Russian," he said. "A *shpion*. Use mnemonic tricks."

"How would you know to think like a spy?" I asked suspiciously.

"I read paperback novels," he said. "Now. We must have telephone number." He peered at me mischievously. "Shall I also show her bank balance?"

"Mischa," I said. "You have to stop this."

"I am only try help," he protested.

"I don't want to break any more laws," I said, shuddering at the idea of security experts tracing the break-in back to my computer.

"Is not problem," he said. "No electronic footprints. All is routed through Singapore."

A few more clicks and he brought up a phone number. He handed me the mobile, jumping up and down like a small boy on Christmas morning. "You call?"

"I'm not going to call. We'll go to her house." I looked at my watch. "Right now. Do you realize that the kid they ran over today was looking up the Ludmilla-Clavendish spy scandal in a Cold War history book when I found him at the UCLA library? Except somehow Clavendish's name got left out. Maybe because nothing was ever proved." I paused, realizing that in my excitement, I was telling Mischa way too much about the case. But I couldn't stop. "Nicolai slammed the book shut when he saw me," I continued, "but there has to be a connection.

Why else would he be looking it up right after his brother got killed?"

"For a school paper, maybe? You say his *spezialnost* is Slavic studies."

"No way, Mischa. It's too much of a coincidence. You're the one who told me to think like a spy."

We took Interstate 5 north, playing bumper tag with all the other commuters. To our right, the Verdugo Mountains were obscured by night. We got off at Sunland Avenue and headed into a land of parched hills and low-slung housing that had once been a rural outpost of Los Angeles. A pioneer aura still clung here, amid the rolling horse country and canyon creekbeds where tumbled stones gleamed white as dessicated bone.

But the intervening years had brought ragged urban sprawl, and it was enough to make an angel cry. The commercial area was a disgrace: run-down strip malls, cement plants, and scrap metal yards. In the residential streets, pit bulls patrolled the perimeter of ragged horse barns. Trucks plastered with biker decals rusted on cinder blocks in front yards, testament to short-lived spurts of meth-fueled tinkering. Even in winter, there was a scorched, bleached quality to the landscape. Paint peeled off the houses and shrubs grew stunted and brown, as if the sun shone more fiercely here and the rain battered without cleansing.

We pulled onto Fruitland Terrace. The properties were set back from the road, with mailboxes standing at attention by the curb.

Milly White lived in one of the older homes, made of rough-polished river rock that the spring torrents had once sent tumbling in abundance down Southern California's arroyos. The lot was deep, with a ramshackle barn and dog runs in back. The fragrance of orange blossoms drifted in the air, and we saw a mini-orchard, the dark green leaves and pendulous fruit glowing in the street-lights. Someone here cared.

"I dunno, Mischa, I hope you're right about Milly White. This is an odd place for a Soviet spy to hole up."

"Not at all," he murmured. "Look at mountains, dirt streets, horses, fruit trees. I am remind of Caucasus. Not at all like Los Angeles."

"Ah, but this is exactly what Los Angeles looked like eighty years ago," I said. "An empty, semi-arid paradise. Stake your claim and put down roots. In tiny pockets like this, you can still see old L.A. if you squint. But it's dark. Which obscures the iron smelter five blocks away, and the miles of crappy concrete apartments and fast food joints."

"We must embrace dark, then," Mischa said.

We set off up the path to the front door. It was heavy oak with a copper knocker molting in five shades of green. I banged with increasing strength, feeling a perverse pleasure in the rising decibels.

Inside, a small dog began to bark, and was immediately joined by a faraway chorus of deeper howls and yelps behind the house. I knocked again. The barking got closer and claws scrabbled on a wooden floor.

"Anybody home?" I yelled.

"Just a minute," a voice inside said, and Mischa gave me a thumbs-up as the unmistakable cadence of a Russian accent filled the air.

"Who is it?" the voice called from the other side of the door. A tiny metal grate opened and an appraising blue eye, its lid greasy with color, beheld us.

"Ms. White," I said, "I'd like to talk to you. I'm with the *Los Angeles Times* and—"

"Not interested," she said. The eye withdrew and the metal grate began to close.

"Gospoja Belyaeva," rang out Mischa's voice.

With a creak, the grate halted its journey and the eye zeroed in with hawklike intensity.

"Please, Ms. Belyaeva," I said. "Ludmilla. I need to speak with you. I'm a reporter."

The eye studied us.

"There is no one here by that name. Go away or I will call police."

It was a standoff. We held our ground, and so did the eye.

"You don't really want to call the police," I said.

"You have two minutes to get off my property," she said. "Then I release the pit bulls."

The grate slammed shut.

So the police had morphed into pit bulls. It made me think that Mischa was right. I recalled the ramshackle barn in back and the far-off baying. It probably wasn't an idle threat. I calculated quickly. The kennels were in the rear of the property. She'd have to walk out her back door to get to them.

"C'mon," I told Mischa. "Let's head her off."

We tiptoed off the porch, ducked under windows, and slunk along the side of the house like Indian scouts. I told Mischa to keep his mouth shut and let me do the talking. I didn't want him bungling this interview. We passed the window of what looked like a converted garage. I peered through a slit in the ruffled curtains and saw it was a garage—just large enough to hold a new-looking gold Cadillac Seville. We continued around. At the back door, I knocked again.

"Ludmilla," I said, "I've read all about you. I know

what happened in 1984. With Clavendish. That's why I'm here. Something has come up from that time long ago. Please open up. It's important."

On the other side of the door, there was a silence, then the footfalls of someone moving inside. We saw a corner of curtain rise, a face in the half gloom.

"There's nothing to be afraid of," I said. "I'm just a reporter. And this is my cousin."

The curtain dropped. We heard the measured tread of someone moving away, then returning. I practically felt her weighing her options, crouched behind the kitchen door.

Then a frantic scrabbling started up on the linoleum and a snuffling growl came from ankle level just inside the house. My heart galloped and I thought about how fast I could sprint to the car. Oh God, I've miscalculated, I thought. The pit bulls are inside, not in the kennel. She's going to sic them on us. I looked around wildly for something to use as a weapon. Then I realized the growl was too shrill for a pit bull. This was a smaller dog.

"Sharik!" Milly White's voice said from inside. Then a command in Russian, and the growl tapered into a high-pitched whine.

The kitchen door opened. A woman in her fifties stood there. She was tall and haughty, with a high broad forehead and dramatic Slavic cheekbones. She had the long, wavy hair of a girl, dyed an unnatural crimson that clashed with her pale skin. She wore lipstick to match, some of which had smeared into the crevices above her lip. But her bone structure had held, giving her a severe elegance light-years removed from the taut, polished visages of Hollywood. She was more a gnarled limb of driftwood, scoured white and austere by the tides. Her eyes, large and deeply recessed in that magnificent face, outlined in thick black mascara, were riveting and hypnotic. She wore long dangly earrings and a dozen necklaces looped around her neck and was clad in a crimson velvet dressing gown with hanging sleeves. For a moment I thought she had her arm extended in greeting.

Then I realized she was gripping a gun. It was pointed at my head, and as this thought registered, she released the safety with a loud click.

he head is a smaller target than the body. It can bob and weave, which makes it harder to hit, I thought, as I stood paralyzed, Mischa silent behind me. The thought offered little solace. As a KGB operative, Ludmilla's nerves would be iron, her aim flawless, and I'd be dead before I hit the ground.

"I invite you inside to tell me what this is about," she said, motioning with her head but keeping us covered. Her accent was thick as clotted cream. With pounding heart, I complied, and Mischa shuffled in behind me while a small brindled dog with toenails painted hot pink sniffed at our heels. We walked through a cheery yellow kitchen into the gloom of a living room with a stone fireplace that smelled of ashes and wet dog.

I prayed Mischa wouldn't say or do anything sudden. Twenty years of retirement had done little to dull Ludmilla Belyaeva's professional instincts. There was no longer any doubt about Milly White's identity.

"Sit," she ordered, her chin inclining toward an overstuffed couch by the window. Immediately, the dog's ears went back and its rump hit the floor. Reaching the couch, Mischa and I complied too. I felt my rear end beset by uneven lumps of what felt like horsehair.

"Speak," she said, and the little dog lifted its head and barked.

Never taking the gun off us, Ludmilla Belyaeva chuckled and lowered herself into an easy chair. She patted her lap and the dog gave a gleeful yelp and leapt onto her bony knees. She caressed it with one jeweled hand, keeping the other trained on us.

"What brings you to my house?" she said. Her accent was wobbling all over the place now, changing from heavy to light within a sentence. It made me wonder if her outward composure hid the fact that she was as scared as we were.

"It's a long story." I glanced at Mischa, whose complexion had turned a shade of rancid grease.

Ludmilla Belyaeva crossed her legs, kicked up a foot, gave a fast laugh. "Take your time. I don't get many visitors. So I intend to get my money's worth out of you people."

"Maybe you could put down that gun. It's making me nervous."

I was stalling and thinking hard. She must be freaked out to have us land on her doorstep, calling her by a name she had shed years ago when she disappeared into a new life. It was a good bet that we were the first to track her down, or else I would have read about it online. She was just a two-bit KGB honeypot living out her retirement in the boonies of L.A. Nobody cared anymore, did they? And yet her fear suggested she still had plenty to hide, and a strong desire to stay lost. Or was it merely tradecraft precautions, still second nature after all these years?

"Depends what you tell me," Ludmilla said slyly. "How do I know you're really a reporter?"

"Check the credentials in my purse."

"I warn you, do not move."

Unceremoniously dumping the disgruntled Sharik onto the floor, Ludmilla advanced. Her knees clicked as she walked, legs extended in outward rotation in the manner of models, ballerinas, and ducks. Her brocaded house slippers were sliced open at the toes, the better to accommodate her bunions.

But her right hand slid into my purse with the agility of a world-class pickpocket's. Up close, she smelled of lilacs and face powder. Still covering us with her gun, she pulled out my California driver's license and dog tags and glanced quickly at them. Then she walked around the couch to Mischa.

"Excuse me, darling," she said, snaking her hand into Mischa's pocket. She spoke in Russian, watching my face for signs of comprehension. Then she switched to English.

"A Russian and an *Amerikanka*," she said in wonder. "Showing up on my doorstep after all these years. What can it mean?"

She glanced at Mischa's documents and a look of disgust crossed her face.

"Fake," she spat out, throwing his ID at him. It hit him in the nose and bounced down his front to land in his lap. He made no effort to retrieve it.

"You think I don't know false documents when I see them? Who are you? Who sent you? Was it Pavlik? That KGB pig? I'll send your testicles back to him in a pouch."

A squeal of protest erupted from Mischa and he spoke in rapid-fire Russian.

"So you deny knowing him? I will find out the truth, of that you can be sure. Now let's hear from the *devuchka*.

"That's you," she said, waving her gun at me. "Speak."

Sharik barked again, then looked at his master for approval.

"Oh, for God's sake." Ludmilla reached in her dressing gown pocket and threw her pet a dog treat.

"Four days ago," I said, "a teenage boy named Denny Lukin was shot dead in Griffith Park while hiking. He might have been going there to meet someone. His parents are Sasha and Irina Lukin, Russian immigrants from Moscow."

I stopped and pretended to catch my breath, studying her reaction to the names. I thought I saw her pupils dilate, but then she squinted her eyes.

"I covered the funeral yesterday for the *Times,* and I noticed an unusual guest paying his condolences to the Lukins. A man you once knew well, in another lifetime. FBI Special Agent Thomas Clavendish."

"That worm," she erupted. "I spit on his mother's grave."

I looked at her and gambled.

"That's not very nice."

"He sold me out. To save his hide."

"Hadn't you been selling him out to Moscow Central for years?"

She began pacing. I didn't think it was good to get her excited with a loaded gun in her hand.

"Can you at least put the safety back on that thing?" I said.

She looked from me to the gun in her hand.

"Yes, please, Gospoja Belyaeva," said Mischa, finding his voice at last. The little dog wandered over and sniffed Mischa's pants. Then it reared up and began humping his leg.

"Sharik!" Ludmilla Belyaeva screamed. "How many times have I told you? Stop that."

She pointed the gun at the floorboards directly in front of Sharik and fired. The smell of cordite and scorched wood rose up as the dog yelped, its long pink nails scrabbling for a toehold on the slick wooden surface as it scampered away.

"Jesus Christ," I said, feeling as though my heart might explode. Would we be next?

Mischa gave a kind of moan and bent over. A string of yellowish saliva ran from his mouth to the floor. Ludmilla looked at him in disgust.

"Here," she said, throwing him a handkerchief from her seemingly voluminous pockets. It landed on his face and he flinched, making low, unintelligible sounds.

"Wipe your mouth," Ludmilla said a touch more kindly.

For a long moment, we both watched him. Then Ludmilla looked at my dog tags again and made an appreciative noise. She turned to me. Under her withering gaze, I wanted to flinch and shield my face, but didn't dare. Then, a change came over her. Her eyes continued to appraise me hungrily, but I realized she wanted something from me.

She moved her thumb and I heard a click. The gun's safety was back on.

"Great. Now can you please put that thing down?" I said.

"All in good time," she said. "But first, Ms. Diamond. Mr. Tsipin. You must please accept my apologies. This is no way to treat guests."

She smiled garishly. My head spun at the complete turnaround. In the blink of an eye, she had gone from homicidal harpy to tittering hostess.

Oh, she definitely wanted something. But then, so did I.

"Why did you pull a gun on us?" I asked.

"A woman living alone cannot be too careful," she said demurely. "Especially in a neighborhood such as this."

"What are you afraid of? Has someone threatened you?"

"No," she said, eyes glinting.

"Someone out of the past, maybe? From when you were a . . ." I licked my lips. "An agent."

There. It was on the table. The next move was hers.

Ludmilla walked to the far wall of her living room, adjusted the frame of a painting. She stepped back, cocked her head, tilted the frame an infinitesimal degree more. Then she nodded. Turned. The gun had disappeared into her pockets. I could see its outline, a hidden still life nestled against the red velvet of the dressing gown.

"It was a complicated time," Ludmilla said. "Clavendish knew I had to report back. It was part of the job, or they would have gotten suspicious. But he knew I never told the Moscow directorate anything that would compromise him. The FBI knew that. That's why they didn't pursue charges."

"That's not what I read," I said.

This is too easy, I thought. She's playing me, just like she played him all those years ago.

"Of course they hushed it up, flooded the case with disinformation and made me the femme fatale," Ludmilla said. "Ha! That was a good joke. Thirty-five years old, with varicose veins and laugh lines. I was really the victim, when it comes down to it. Used and then cast aside.

"And where did it get me?" she went on bitterly. "He claimed he loved me but when things got hot, he betrayed me to save his hide."

"I heard there was another spy. One who was never caught."

A caul fell over her eyes. "That's rubbish," she said at length.

"So do you know the Lukins?" I said, changing the subject. "Were they spies too?"

"No," she said scornfully. "Of course not."

"No, you don't know them or no, they're not spies?"

"We met once or twice. Clavendish knew Sasha. Says they met at Moscow State University when he was on an academic exchange there in the late 1960s."

That fit with what the FBI agent had told me. But I suspected that was her strategy. Throw in enough truth so that the lies slid past with ease.

"I still find it hard to believe the FBI would recruit someone with his background."

"It was the Prague Spring. Before the crackdown. Everything was détente, love and flowers." She shrugged. "Or so they tell me. It didn't trickle down as far as the Urals, where I grew up. But I can tell you that there were many times during its history when the Cold War was not so cold."

Yeah, like when you and Clavendish were rolling in bed, swapping pillow talk about national secrets.

"Are you still in touch with Clavendish?"

"I have not seen him in twenty years."

"Do you know anyone who would have wanted to kill the Lukin boys?"

"No," she said.

"What about the Mafia?"

She looked up with curiosity. "Sasha Lukin was Mafia? This I do not believe."

"And why not?"

"He is not the type," she said in a condescending voice. "He does not like to get his hands dirty."

"And you?" I asked, wondering if I was pushing her too far this time.

"I steer clear of that nest of vipers. Why do you think I live here, so far away from everything? I want nothing to do with any of them. I'd rather starve alone."

I looked around. The furniture in Ludmilla's living room was old, shiny with use, threadbare in places. There were lace doilies on every surface and an array of knick-knacks, dried flower sachets, gloomy oil paintings in dark wood frames.

"What do you want from me?" she asked.

"Prisoner of Memory. Was that a code name from your KGB days?"

"No." Her voice was flat, without affect.

"Was Lukin the third spy? To round out the triumvirate?"

"Oh." She laughed. "That is too much."

"How did you meet Clavendish?"

Her eyes got a faraway look. A small spring came into her step as she walked back to the easy chair and sat down, smoothing the folds of her dressing gown over her knees. I wondered if it was like asking a ballplayer to recall the time he slammed it out of the park.

"I approached him at a bar. I had spent months getting to know his daily rituals. He was very good at covering his tracks then. Anonymous in that way of spies. Hair a mousy brown, cropped but not too short. Off-the-rack suits, nothing flashy. A rubbery face and muddy brown eyes."

I thought back to Clavendish's outsize personality, long, wavy hair, intensely blue eyes. We could be talking about different men.

"But his eyes . . ." I began.

She laughed. "Yes. It wasn't until I slept with him that I found out. Contact lenses. To hide that brilliant blue. He was a master at self-effacement. It was one of the tricks of the trade. You could meet him five times and never recognize him. It was like trying to cup water in your hands. But it didn't come naturally. That's why he drank. To ease the pressure."

She stared at me with the clinical coldness of a coroner.

"The Clavendish I met this week is the opposite of everything you just described."

Her eyes narrowed. "Then something has slipped," she said.

"Maybe with his retirement in sight he's no longer making any effort to disguise himself."

She looked at me with surprise.

"This is his last week with the Bureau," I said.

She shook her head. "He's a professional," she insisted. "It's out of character."

Her comment should have made me wonder. Instead, I dismissed it as the paranoia of an old spy.

CHAPTER 30

*L*udmilla gave me a large, predatory smile.

"What else can I tell you?" she asked sweetly. "Because if we're done, I have a story of great personal importance to discuss with you."

I knew it!

"Would Clavendish have any motive to kill Lukin's sons?" I asked.

"He's a spy, isn't he?"

"He was. But the Cold War's over."

She looked disappointed at my naivete.

"Such things are never over. They rage on, in a parallel universe. People want to settle old scores. Avenge honor. Feather their nests with a little blackmail, perhaps." Her voice grew petulant and she patted down the sides of her hair. "Whereas I just want enough to see me into old age, nothing like *some* people." She batted her mascaraed lashes at me.

"You think Clavendish was blackmailing him and Lukin stopped paying so he killed his son?" I asked. But then why would Lukin have greeted Clavendish so warmly at the funeral? Unless he had no idea that Clavendish was behind the letter and the blackmail attempts.

"That man is capable of anything," Ludmilla said, and I caught the twenty-year-old sulfur of a scorned lover.

"What do you mean?" I said, thinking that she had aptly described herself.

"Look. Some people become spies for the money," Ludmilla said. "Some are addicted to the adventure and thrills, even the danger. Then there are those who do it for the power. The detached intellectual game. They aren't cold-blooded. There's no blood at all in their veins. It's ice. We called them 'the bloodless ones.' And Clavendish was the best we ever saw."

"Well, he's not the only bloodless one. Someone ran over Nicolai Lukin today. He's in a coma at the hospital under armed guard."

Ludmilla put her hand to her mouth. Was it possible to fake the shock in her eyes?

"Did Lukin have enemies?" I asked. "Someone he might have offended, now or in a previous life? In Russia, maybe."

Her eyes got far away.

"There was a rumor—"

"What?"

"I can't remember," she said, coy and transparently false.

It was like bargaining in a Turkish bazaar, but instead of carpets I was buying information. Her stock in trade.

"I'm eager to hear about your matter of great personal importance, Ms. Belyaeva. But first we must finish up here. What do you recall?"

"At home, Lukin was some kind of scientist."

"Yes," I said. "What of it?"

She licked her lips, tasting victory.

"So you don't know, then?" She leaned back in her chair.

"Know what?"

"This I will tell you. Lukin came from a closed city in the Urals."

"What do you mean, a closed city?"

"They did special work there. Government work. Once upon a time, your Lukin worked for Sakharov."

"Andrei Sakharov? You mean Lukin was a physicist?" I said in disbelief.

"This is what I heard," she said primly, dabbing at her mouth with a napkin.

Now it was my turn to lean back. My fingers drummed on the table. "I'm not a Soviet expert like you," I said, "so forgive me if I've got my history wrong, but if I recall the Sovs weren't exactly handing out exit visas to physicists back in 1985."

Ludmilla pulled herself a little straighter.

"Depends what area of physics they specialized in," she said, choosing her words carefully.

"Wasn't there just one area back then? National security? Nuclear bombs? Isn't that why they wouldn't let Sakharov go?"

Ludmilla's mouth curled in disgust. "That was trumped up. Andrei Sakharov was a brilliant scientist and father of the Soviet hydrogen bomb. But once he became a dissident, they cut him out of the loop of anything sensitive. Any national security issues would have been so old as to be irrelevant."

"But Lukin was never a dissident," I said softly. "So they wouldn't have had any reason to cut him out of the loop, would they?"

"I cannot speculate," Ludmilla said, examining me from behind lowered lashes.

"So why would the Sovs have let Lukin emigrate?" I said. "Unless . . ."

Ludmilla was picking at the hem of her robe.

"I don't believe it myself," she said. "But you asked

and so I am telling. Lukin was back in Moscow by the late 1970s. We heard he began distancing himself from anything sensitive years before he applied to emigrate."

"Would that have been enough?"

"I was not privy to such things," Ludmilla said. She leaned in toward me, her hawk's face sharpening. "But they let him go to conferences abroad. And you know what that means."

"Tell me."

She got a cagey look.

"My friends," she said. "I am a terrible hostess. Please, you must join me in some refreshments. It is long past time for tea."

I felt her old instincts stir. She was playing us. Yet we had no choice but to go along. She would tell us when she was ready.

Outside the kitchen window, an overhead light now illuminated the backyard. In the recesses of the property was a pounded-earth dog run where a dozen animals lounged and frisked. Maybe six more sat in dog pens, peering out. They were all breeds and sizes.

Ludmilla Belyaeva clicked over to the kitchen and poured milk into a cracked bowl that might once have been Limoges china.

While Sharik lapped at his milk, Ludmilla put on the teakettle. On a table laid with oilcloth, she set out thick slices of rye bread, tiny pale green cucumbers, and cold herring swimming in pickling juices. A plastic bag held dried leaves and blossoms. Soon the cheerful sound of a singing teakettle came from the two-burner stove.

Ludmilla reached into the bag of dried herbs, pulled out a fistful, and dumped it in the teapot. Then she carried it to the stove and poured in boiling water to steep. Five minutes went by while we made strained small talk. Then Ludmilla poured the tea, squeezing in juice from a cut lemon and adding a spoonful of blackberry jam. There was no polite asking how I took it. In Stalinist fashion, this had been decided for me.

"Is this herbal tea?" I ventured.

"It is mountain tea," Ludmilla said. "With healing properties."

"Then it can't be from our local mountains," I joked.

She looked at me sharply.

"It is from the Caucasus. Made of special plants. You must ride on donkeys, up the mountainside. The trail is very steep. For this tea," she lifted the steaming cup to her lips, "I pay good money."

"Ah." I inhaled my own. It smelled like chamomile, a hint of mint. I pictured dizzying gorges, mountains glinting with snow. Then armaments, decomposing corpses. The Chechen war.

"Do you breed dogs?" Mischa ventured.

"You know how Muscovites are about their dogs," Ludmilla said with a conspiratorial smile. "When I bought this property in Sunland," she went on, "I started taking in strays. It's terrible, the overpopulation in the United States. Soon I found myself running a dog rescue operation. I nurse them back to health first; most of them are mangy and worm-infested. Then I get them fixed and try to place them.

"Yes," she said, her voice brimming with affection as she looked out the window at her charges. "I've had to learn to do everything." She tore off some bread. "I castrate the males myself."

A green chunk of cucumber went flying across the room as Mischa choked.

"You don't!" I said, appalled but not surprised.

"But how do you know you are doing it right?" Mischa asked, hands dancing nervously along the front of his pants.

"I always wanted to be a vet. But my parents were Cheka. It ran in the family. What could I do?"

She toyed with her herring, took a bite. Wiped her mouth delicately with a napkin, leaving a red kiss.

I speared a cucumber and crunched it solemnly. "So what can you tell me about Lukin's standing in the Russian community?" I said.

She looked out the window. "Pah," she said. "What Russian community? Put two Russians together and you have three arguments."

"Because there are so many different groups?"

"Of course," said Mischa, who was busy gobbling up pickled herring, little cucumbers, and black pumpernickel bread. He seemed to have forgotten the trauma of having a gun leveled at his head.

"Speaking of the Cheka and their successors, the KGB," I said, eager to get the conversation off dog castrations and back to spies, "What did it mean that they'd let Lukin go to conferences in the West?"

"There was only one way they let people visit the West back then."

She picked up a dainty morsel, popped it in her mouth.

I put my fork down, swallowed. Wiped my mouth. I wanted to be ready.

"You mean if they agreed to spy?" I said carefully.

She looked steadily at me but stayed mum.

"He didn't tell me that," I persisted.

"Of course he didn't tell you." Her voluptuous mouth curved in a sneer.

Outside a dog barked. Farther away, the whir of a rotary drill resounded off fresh wood. A hammer rang, its pounding synchronized to the beating of my heart. Ludmilla was suggesting that Lukin had been a spy, and she was in a position to know, having been one herself.

"Sasha Lukin was a spy?"

"I never said that."

She pursed her lips like a cat that has swallowed an enormous canary and fears it might burst out of her mouth in a shower of feathers and fly away. Then she bent her head and flicked crumbs of bread off her lap.

"You think someone's trying to blackmail Lukin about his past. And killing his sons because he won't pay up."

"There was a rumor about his son," Ludmilla said.

"Which one? He had two. Denny's dead and Nicolai was on his way to meet me when a large armored-type thing ran him over."

"That's what the Mafia drive," she said immediately.

"Really?"

"In Moscow. You see them everywhere."

"But we're not talking about Moscow. We're talking about America."

"Of course." Ludmilla reached for a cucumber and a knife. Faster than my eye could follow, she sliced the thing into perfectly even discs. "And what did Nicolai Lukin want to speak to you about?" she asked, placing a cucumber slice on her bread and balancing herring on top.

"I don't know," I said, acutely aware of the knife palmed in her hand. She probably knew many ways to kill people. She could have poisoned our food. I ran my tongue along the inside of my mouth but came up only with the sour taste of my own bile.

"But surely the boy said something?" Ludmilla popped

the bite-size sandwich into her mouth and reached down to scratch Sharik under the chin. In her other hand, the knife glinted.

Could Ludmilla be the Prisoner of Memory?

"Nope," I lied. "I'm as in the dark as everyone else."

"And did they find anything on the body?"

"Not that I know of," I said.

Disappointment flashed across Ludmilla's face, but she immediately masked it.

"Well, I'm sure the police will pry it out of him when he wakes up." She gave me an arch look. "Bad timing for your story, wasn't it?"

"I'm just glad Lukin has one son who's still alive," I said stiffly.

Ludmilla began clearing away plates.

"I'm sorry I frightened you earlier," she said. "But I cannot be too careful. And as we are sitting here talking, I am thinking of a little thing, a mere trifle, that you may do to help a poor old lady."

As if the thought had just occurred to her. When I knew she had been buttering me up for this since she read my dog tags.

"Perhaps I should not hide myself away in this old house," she said.

"What can I do to help you?" I asked, greedy to have her in my debt.

"You could write about me," she said. "Memoirs of a modern-day Mata Hari. My life story. It's never been told, you know." She eyed me craftily. "We could get a book proposal, sell it to Hollywood."

Of all the things I might have envisioned, this was the last. I was speechless.

"I've always thought Jennifer Garner should play me,"

Ludmilla went on. "She has the right cheekbones. I would split half the profits with you, of course. We could write the screenplay together."

I laughed nervously. There was still the gun in her pocket. And this woman was clearly living in a fantasy world. How could I believe anything she said, about her past or Lukin's or anyone else's?

"Do not laugh. The KGB is in fashion again, haven't you heard? My former bosses are writing memoirs and histories that land on the *New York Times* best-seller list. Our very president, Vladimir Putin, wears his KGB past proudly. But do you know what it's like to make ends meet on a KGB pension? There is not money enough for Sharik's dog food. All these years, I have been selling off my artworks. But I have almost nothing left. It is time to exploit my past."

Ludmilla was crying poverty. And none of the dusty old things in the house contradicted that. But then, what about the shiny Seville parked in her garage? Had she recently come into money and didn't want us to know? Was Ludmilla feathering her nest with blackmail money provided by Sasha Lukin?

"I'm a little confused, Ludmilla. You're selling off your precious paintings, but you've got a spanking-new American luxury car parked in your garage?"

If I expected to catch her in a lie, I was disappointed.

"A temporary loan from a generous friend," she said smoothly, not missing a beat.

We'll just see what DMV records say about that.

"What happened to you after 1984? Where did you disappear to?"

She sat up straighter and her chin rose. "I was traded," she said. "For an American embassy official in Moscow."

So it was true!

"The Americans shipped you back? I thought you had a French passport," I said, flashing back to the clips I had read.

"It was a very good forgery."

"Then how did you get back here? Why did you even want to return?"

She looked at me with disbelief. "But I spent years here. It became my home. Besides, what is left for me in Moscow? It is not the Russia I knew. With perestroika and the end of the Cold War, it was easy to get new papers. I still had friends."

"But wouldn't customs have stopped you at our border? Wouldn't your name be on a list?"

"Names are not a problem," she said, waving a hand in dismissal. "And nobody cares about the Cold War anymore, except as entertainment. I tell you, it will make a magnificent epic."

I shook my head.

"You're unbelievable, you know? First you greet us at the door with a loaded gun and threaten us, and then you serve us tea and propose we write a script together."

"Of course. You are my friend now." She seemed offended.

"Haven't you lived in this city long enough to know what the odds are of selling your script? It's more likely that the KGB would try to recruit you again."

"Do not say that," she said, crossing herself, then kissing the ornate Orthodox cross that hung from her neck. "You do not know. The organs grow ever stronger."

"The organs?"

"The security organs. The KGB."

"Ah. Which reminds me. I'd love to sit down and hear

your stories. Special Agent Clavendish was not forthcoming about your time together."

"Do not trust him," she boomed. "He has a traitor's heart."

Oh, and I should trust you?

"How about Sasha Lukin?"

"Another one you should not trust."

"So the whole world's my enemy, huh?"

"It is dangerous to trust. Betrayal waits in the shadows. Among those you least expect."

Her eyes gleamed with that hawklike intensity. "But I am not your enemy," she said in the honeyed tones of a coquette.

I snorted. "I forgot. You're my friend."

"You will see. I will help you."

She beamed at me, and I knew there wasn't a sincere bone in her old courtesan's body. But we each needed something from the other, and that gave things an odd symmetry.

"Fine," I said. "I won't trust Lukin. "What about his wife? She trouble too?"

"His wife," Ludmilla echoed. "Yes, that's it." She leaned closer and examined my features and it seemed she was peering into the faraway past. Then she blinked and recovered.

"You know, I didn't notice until just now. It's odd. But you . . ."

She stopped and shook her head.

"What?" I said too quickly.

But she had picked up on my enthusiasm and now hoarded her memories.

"Oh, nothing. It's ridiculous."

"I remind you of someone?"

She gave me a significant look.

"We will talk more," she said. "When you come with a tape recorder for our first interview."

The old she-devil, I thought, knowing I would get nothing further until I crossed her palm with my own brand of silver—the newspaper profile.

Ludmilla clutched her orange coral beads, pursed her lips, and turned away with a satisfied smile.

CHAPTER 31

W hat do you think?" I asked Mischa when we were back in the car.

"In Russian, we have saying: *'Bereghis!'* Means 'danger, watch out.'"

"We've got the same one, and I agree."

I turned my cell phone back on. *Eighteen missed messages,* said the screen.

And I bet seventeen of them were Josh, frantic to know what I'd been up to. But I was wrong. Two were from a detective working the Lukin case. Detective James Hudock wanted to find out why Nicolai Lukin had set up a rendezvous with me. Damn. I had blurted out who I was to a man at the accident scene and he must have told the police. Detective Hudock left a number and said he'd be working late.

I called Josh back first.

"I thought you were dead," he said.

I thought about Ludmilla Belyaeva waving around her revolver. "I did too there, for a while."

"Trabuco's gonna have your ass. He told you to keep in touch."

"Not if I throw him some raw meat by tomorrow."

"You'll have to throw me some tonight. Or I'll tell him about your disappearing act. I've been covering for you."

"Buy me a drink and I will. What's up with the police? Any leads on the hit-and-run?"

"Negative."

"Nicolai Lukin wake up yet?"

"Briefly. But the doctors won't let the cops in. They're hoping tomorrow."

"Any word on that call Denny Lukin got on his cell right before he left Max Golodny's?"

"Traced it right to a pay phone," Josh said in disgust.

"Well, here's something. Can you run a DMV check for me? Milly White."

I gave him the address and her approximate age so he could find out what cars were registered in her name.

"Sure," he said. "If you clue me in."

"I'll tell you everything this evening. By the way, one of your detective buds wants to know what Nicolai Lukin was on his way to tell me when he got run over."

"Well?"

"How about I tell you both over that drink tonight?"

"Okay. I'll let him know. What time?"

I glanced at the passenger seat, where Mischa was staring ahead, pretending not to listen. I didn't want him eavesdropping as we discussed the latest theories on the case. Neither did I want him skulking around my duplex alone.

"One hour. I've got to drop off some, um, groceries."

Mischa made an outraged noise.

"Where?" Josh said.

"Golden Gopher?"

"Slumming tonight, are we?"

"Not really."

"On Hill and Eighth? That's a little too scary even for me."

"Haven't you heard?" I said, pleased to have the drop on Posh Josh. "A trendoid renovated it. It's now blue margaritaville."

"They need to tear down the whole block. The hotel next door is a public health menace."

I smiled. "The Bristol? Some German guy bought it and kicked out all the junkies and whores. It's going to be a boutique hotel. Where have you been?"

"Working too hard to keep up on all the hot spots, unlike some people."

I hung up and sneaked a look at Mischa. His crossed arms told me he was upset.

"Even after I find Ludmilla Belyaeva, my cousin not trust me," he said.

"I took you with me to meet her, didn't I?"

"I am not invited for drinks tonight?" Mischa said.

"I can just see it now. 'And by the way, Mr. LAPD detective, this is my Moscow cousin, Mischa Tsipin. He was smuggled illegally into the U.S. last week by the Russian Mafia and now they're trying to kill him because he escaped without paying. Know where he can get authentic-looking papers?'"

"Maybe you are right." Mischa slumped in his seat.

"At least I'm letting you stay with me again. I don't suppose you have anywhere else to go."

"I have bike," Mischa said stiffly. "I will find elsewhere."

I took my eyes off the freeway traffic. Mischa looked like a whipped dog.

"Where'd you spend the last couple of nights, anyway?" I asked.

"Is not important."

Yes, it is. Because if the Russian Mafia's set you up in a cozy flat so you can report back on me to pay off your smuggling debt, I'm going to drop-kick you from here to Vladivostok.

"Okay, I'll beg. Mischa, please sleep on my porch again tonight."

A calculating look came into his eyes. "How about inside? You can see I am no harm."

I don't see any such thing.

"My offer or nothing. I'll rig you up with a light and some books. But I can't have you in my house when I'm not there."

By the time we pulled up to my house, he had agreed. But he was still mad.

"You think I am only idiot cousin with funny accent. You not treat me with respect. That is mistake."

I examined him as we walked in. Was I being foolish?

It's not like I have that much to steal, I thought, looking around. My gaze fell on the hatbox and I reconsidered. He could steal my past. I showered, then hid the hatbox in the recesses of my closet and shooed him out onto the porch.

Twenty minutes later, Josh and I were standing inside the newly renovated Golden Gopher, scanning for empty seats. Detective Hudock would join us at 10 p.m. I wanted one of the red leather booths, each with its own gopher lamp set permanently on dim, but they were full of laughing, drinking night crawlers.

In the bad old days before the beautiful people arrived, I had frequented a taco stand on this street run by a passel of short, squat Yucatecos who made the best *cochinita* in the city. But they had decamped along with the poor families, winos, old men, crackheads, and teen whores as the neighborhood was pulled out from under them. Now it had gentrified to the point where their whole SSI check would barely buy a round of drinks at the Gopher. Not that they'd be able to get past the bouncer. I wasn't sure how I felt about all this.

"There," I told Josh, as a couple slid off their bar stools and made their way out. The woman had that slick, buffed beauty of TV soaps and could have been anywhere from twenty-five to forty-five. Her date, scruffy in a motorcycle jacket, had the requisite sideburns and goatee.

We nabbed the still-warm seats and I heaved a sigh of relief. On a cocktail napkin where the man had just been sitting were two small blue pills.

"That guy's gonna be sorry," I said as the bartender came to take our order. "He forgot his medicine."

The bartender just grinned and swept the pills into his palm. "My tip," he said.

"Whaddya mean?"

"The big V," Josh said.

"Say again?" I felt like my chain had slipped a gear.

"Viagra," Josh said, looking away.

The bartender winked at Josh. "Come in handy tonight. If I get lucky."

"How do you know that?" I asked Josh after we ordered and the bartender left. He reddened.

"From being around. Now why haven't you returned my phone calls?"

"That's right, change the subject," I said, remembering what Luke Vinograd had said and wondering whether young Josh popped pills recreationally to enhance his performance. Whether he had a few in his pocket right now, just like the bartender. In case he got lucky. A curious warmth crept up from my abdomen. Luke was right. Josh did have an animal magnetism. And I was still annoyed with Silvio, who hadn't called or e-mailed all day. I felt my allegiance catch, waver. It would serve him right if I hooked up with Josh. I turned the idea around in my brain. Imagined what it would be like, after so many months of simmering tension. I had no plans to act on our mutual attraction but I could fantasize, couldn't I?

And so that's how it started.

"Strike-out on the Caddie," Josh said. "The only car registered to Milly White in Sunland is a 1994 Volvo station wagon."

I got a home movie image of Ludmilla bumping along the dusty roads in a beat-up Volvo filled with barking dogs. Of course she wouldn't use the new car for that.

"That doesn't mean it's not hers," I said darkly. "It could have been a gift."

"You get a license plate, we can find the owner."

Why hadn't I jotted it down? It had been clearly visible. I squinted, trying to visualize the right combination of letters and numbers. But my cerebellum was on strike.

"What kind of reporter are you, anyway?"

Josh nudged my ribs, leaning into me in a way that was not unpleasant. He was like a small boy who can only show his attraction to a girl by pestering and rough-housing.

"I can get it," I said, thinking I'd send Mischa out to Ludmilla's house. He'd just have to avoid getting shot in the process.

"So why did Nicolai Lukin want to meet with you today?" Josh asked. "And why did someone want to stop him?"

I hesitated for a moment, then decided I couldn't keep it to myself any longer. Slowly, I sketched out the details of Nicolai's late phone call the night before, his father's strange behavior. The nebulous talk about a letter.

"He said it was signed 'the Prisoner of Memory.' Cops say anything about that?"

"Damn it, Eve. This is big news. Why didn't you tell me earlier?"

He was furious. But it wasn't just about work. Scolding me about the case was the only legitimate way he had to vent larger frustrations about our relationship, or lack thereof.

"Because I need to find out more before we put it in the paper."

"Tell the cops then. Let them investigate. People have to talk to them."

"Spoken like a true cop reporter," I said. "But actually, people don't have to talk to the cops. Especially if they've got something to hide. For God's sake, Denny Lukin got killed the other day, and his father still hasn't told the cops a thing about this letter."

"How do you know?" Josh shot back.

"Because, Mr. I'm So Tight with Law Enforcement, they would have told you. And this is the first you're hearing about it, right?"

His silence confirmed it. Then he said, "So you gonna tell Hudock?"

"No. And you're not either."

Despite all his hipster posturing, Josh was basically a straight arrow and now he looked worried.

"Please keep quiet about it for now," I said, "or I'll never tell you anything again. If the cops can have a code of silence, the hacks can too."

"But how are you going to advance the story if Lukin won't talk?"

"I'll do a write-around if I have to. Don't you want to know where I went right after the Lukin kid got run over?"

Josh sipped his drink, unwilling to ask.

"I followed FBI Special Agent Clavendish to his apartment in Hollywood and we had a long talk."

"You're joking. That lush?"

"Don't write him off. He knows Sasha Lukin. He was at the funeral the other day. I'm trying to figure out how it all connects. Oh, and I ran into Mischa in a back alley in Hollywood right after Nicolai got run over."

"Your goofy Russian cousin?"

"Turns out he's not so goofy. He's the one who helped me track down Ludmilla." I recounted what we had learned.

"Why didn't you call me? I could have come too."

"I wanted to spare your shiny hiney. Mischa's research tactics were less than legal and Ludmilla pulled a gun and we had to talk her out of killing us."

"No kidding," Josh said, wavering between disappointment and relief. "Trabuco's gonna shit. He told you to deal me in. On everything." He gave me a significant look. I drained my drink, signaled for another.

"This is my story, Brandywine. You can help but only when I say so. I found Denny Lukin's body. I was there when his brother got run over. And I've got a strange connection with the dad. You have to let me play it out. I've only got one more day. Then Trabuco's bringing me back to chase mountain lions. So just humor me, will you?"

Josh eyed me speculatively. "Let me think about it," he said. "Oh, by the way, I checked out that rumor for you about Clavendish's gambling."

"Why, thank you. What'd you find?"

"Lansing says he lost big at one of the clubs last year."

CHAPTER 32

A tingle went through me. This might be an important development.

"Word is Clavendish was having a hard time keeping his head above water. Bureau saw that as a liability and finally cut him loose."

"So he might have borrowed money from loan sharks?"

"Or be ripe to sell out for a quick buck."

"To a Russian mafioso awash in cash and eager to have a Feeb in his pocket?" I said.

"Exactly, but I still don't see what this has to do with the Lukin kid."

"Neither do I, but I'm getting closer. Improbably enough, Lukin and Clavendish are friends."

"Then why would Clavendish betray his friend?"

"It wouldn't have to be anything personal. Just a matter of saving his own skin."

"Okay. I'm with Trabuco. You've got one day to chase it down, Evie D. But I don't approve. And if someone else gets killed, I want to be clear it happened on your watch. Where is this cousin of yours, by the way? Why didn't you bring him along?" Josh paused. "Not that I mind spending time alone with you." He scooted his bar seat closer. "Maybe you planned it this way."

I blushed. Had it been in the back of my mind all along? If so, I'd never admit it.

"Mischa is at home because I don't fully trust him," I

said firmly. "He helped me find Ludmilla, I'll give him that. But he also landed on my doorstep right after Denny Lukin got shot, claiming the Mafia were after him. Then he showed up again right after Nicolai Lukin got run over. Where has he been the last two days, anyway? Lastly, I'm not sure we're related or that's trumped up too."

"Why would someone go to the trouble to get him to spy on you?"

"They might not have all the cards they need yet."

"I'll protect you," Josh said, inching his stool over so that our thighs touched.

I'm not sure how I would have responded, but just then LAPD Detective James Hudock arrived, dooming our tête-à-tête. We shucked our coats back on and found a table on the covered patio, under the heat lamps. Hudock wore a black turtleneck under a black suit and black cowboy boots. He had a neatly trimmed goatee and a shaved head with sunglasses perched atop his shiny dome, even though it was nighttime. It made him look tough in a Hollywood sort of way.

Hudock made me run through it several times. When I got to the UCLA visit where I tracked down Nicolai, he said, "And he was reading a spy book that he slammed shut when you approached?"

I gave Hudock the citation and mentioned my Cold War theory. Then I told him about Nicolai Lukin's late-night phone call to me but kept it general, saying the boy had promised details when we met in person.

Hudock made me describe the car and draw a diagram of how the hit-and-run went down. I told him the license plates were missing and he zeroed in on that, saying they might want to hypnotize me to see if they could jog my memory. I did an imaginary eye roll and insisted there weren't any. After about an hour, Hudock ran out of questions. Then it was our turn.

"Do you think this could be related to Lukin's job?" I asked. "I keep meaning to look up Rathburn and see exactly what they do. I think he's a scientist there. Maybe a physicist."

"We've interviewed employees," Hudock allowed.

"Did he have a security clearance?" Josh said.

"No. We've already checked that out."

It was looking less likely that Lukin was a spy or had ever had any secrets to sell. I felt gullible for letting Ludmilla manipulate me into thinking so in the first place. The old femme fatale had never actually said he was, just hinted and arched those dramatic eyebrows of hers. But I knew she was hoping to trade information about the Lukin case for a newspaper profile, and so the more knowledgeable she acted about clandestine Cold War operations, the more valuable she became to me as a source. The spy in her wanted me beholden.

"Are you working with other agencies on this?" Josh said.

"Like who?" Hudock said, bristling.

"Sheriffs. The Feds. Both of them have Russian organized crime task forces."

"We've been in contact. Nothing's panned out so far. We're investigating everything."

"Was Lukin hooked up with the Mafia? In debt, maybe?"

"Doesn't fit the profile. He's an old Russian. Came over in 1985. First gasps of perestroika. No criminal record. Homeowner since 1994. That was the bottom of the market, after the L.A. riots, the first Gulf War, the

Northridge earthquake. All that really spooked people. Bad things in threes. Everyone was getting out of Dodge. You could pick up nice properties for a song."

"Did you check their credit, their property holdings?" I asked, marveling that, in L.A., even the cops were real estate experts.

"Bought that house on the hill for three hundred eighty thousand. Checked the records. They've taken out a couple of additional mortgages over the years, but it's got to be worth one and a half million now. Shrewd, those Russians. They just refinanced again, took out some equity. Lukin says they're using the money to remodel. No evidence of fiscal impropriety."

Remodeling, I thought. I hadn't seen any evidence of that. Though I hadn't exactly gotten the grand tour.

"Pay their bills on time, do they?" I said, my mind still on the purported remodeling. "That's unusual in itself for L.A."

"Credit report shows they had a rough patch last year. Lukin says he loaned a friend money for a business venture in Russia and it didn't pan out."

"You got confirmation of that? Bank transfers and such?"

The cop looked at me in disbelief. "You don't know the first thing about these folks, do you?"

"You mean they only deal in cash?"

"Couriered it to Moscow with a friend."

"How much we talking about?"

"Fifty thousand."

My interest piqued. "Currency declaration on file with customs?"

The cop snorted. "What do you think?"

"You gonna pursue that?"

The detective sucked his teeth. "My, she's a bloodless one," he said to Josh.

"Isn't it a crime to ferry big buckets o' cash around the globe?" I said.

"We're trying to catch his son's murderer, not nail him on a currency violation."

I looked at Josh. "Imagine," I said. "A cop with a great beating heart where his badge should be."

"Leave that shit to customs," Hudock said, hunkering down over his rum and Coke. "Not my bailiwick anyway."

"Have you at least talked to the friend?"

He raised his head. "You think we don't do our job?"

"What's his name?" I asked, readying my pencil.

"Nolo commento." Hudock grinned.

"What, it's a state secret?"

"We checked it out with Interpol. Nothing there. Don't waste your time."

"Well, what was the money supposed to be for?" I said stubbornly.

"Gas futures. Someone knew someone whose second cousin was something with the ministry. It was all hot air. The money evaporated in bribes and invalid contracts and broken promises. It's a kleptocracy over there, doncha know?"

"You got backup on any of this?" I pushed.

"Blew out two fax machines," he said in disgust. "None of it worth the paper it's written on. Ministry says it's all bogus."

"Doesn't sound like the thing a law-abiding Russian immigrant would do," I said.

"Says he got caught up in the fever, just like anyone else. Rather sheepish about it now."

"So what, then. One son's dead, the other's lying in a coma, and this is all a freaky coincidence?"

"I did a story once, about an immigrant family," Josh said. "Two sons. Parents slaved away at a liquor store in a bad part of town. One day the older son got mowed down by a drunk driver. Dead on impact. The parents got active in MADD. That's Mothers Against Drunk Driving. Five years pass. Then, in a perfectly sadistic convergence, the surviving son was killed by a drunk driver. We investigated both the suckers. No connection. Sometimes the most obvious explanation is the right one."

"Tell me you believe that, and I'll show you a reporter who'd better find a new profession," I said.

"Of course it's connected," Detective Hudock said. "But we're still putting together the pieces. And I don't know about you, but I work better after a few hours sleep."

He stood up, threw some bills on the table, and left.

I told Josh that I should get home too. We rustled up money for the rest of the bill and stood on the nighttime street in a light drizzle, waiting for the valet to bring our cars around. The thermometer read forty-five degrees.

"I think I should follow you home," said Josh, who lived all the way across town in Venice Beach. "That cousin of yours seems harmless enough, but I'd feel better knowing he's really on your back porch, and not waiting inside to ambush you."

I thought about it for a minute and shivered, from the cold or from the prospect of an ambush, I wasn't sure.

"You really have a way with words, Josh. When you put it in those terms, I think I'll let you."

On the drive home, I tried to clear my head but my thoughts kept going back to the previous night with Silvio and how unsatisfying our quickie date had been. With him it always felt like we were snatching love on the run. I was getting tired of that. I wanted something deeper.

At the front door, my arm brushed against Josh as I pushed my key into the hole and a jolt of electricity passed between us. He stepped in front of me and we collided. Then he grabbed my arm to straighten me and for a moment, his head bent over mine and I felt dizzy.

"Let me go in first, check it out," he said, his breath warm and fragrant on my cold cheeks.

I stepped aside and he went in, flipping on the light. I half expected to find that Mischa had wormed his way inside and onto the couch but it was empty. Slipping in after Josh, I walked with him, inspecting the length of my house, blushing as he stepped inside the bathroom and saw a torn red camisole hanging to dry.

Josh stuck his nose up against the windowpane, where we could see the outline of a capped head at the end of the sleeping bag.

"See," I said gaily. "Nothing to worry about."

We turned to extinguish the kitchen light at the same time and our hands touched. We each pulled away, then stood in the cold darkness for a moment, embarrassed about our embarrassment. Josh turned to me.

"Eve," he breathed, and his hand went out to the wall, making an arch over me. "I worry about you."

"I can take care of myself," I said huskily. Yes, that was definitely a quickening in my blood. It was comforting to feel his solid presence in the dark. All my competitive feelings spilled over into something else. I thought of Silvio, far away in New York. Josh and I worked together. This was wrong. We'd had too much to drink. The excitement and tension had gotten to us.

"Maybe I should stay awhile longer, make sure everything is okay," he said. He leaned in toward me. His face loomed close in the dark. At the last second, I turned aside and his lips grazed my cheek instead.

I didn't know if I'd be so strong the next time. I wanted to be held, comforted. This man was a known quantity. I admired him. Competed with him. Resented him. Such hot, sizzling emotions. I imagined us coming together. It would be a conflagration, both of us fighting to the little death, being reborn. How would his body feel against mine? I felt I knew already, that we had already done it, traced each other's limbs.

He stepped closer. His hand reached out, cupped my chin. I leaned in.

The phone rang. I froze, caught in my indiscretion, listening to it jangle with mounting certainty that whoever was on the other end of the line knew exactly what I was up to.

My machine clicked on. How odd my own voice sounded on the recording. Like a stranger's. Then Silvio spoke, and I was flooded with alertness in every pore of my body.

"Hello, *querida*. I'm sorry I had to run out on you yesterday. My meeting today went great. We're getting together again tomorrow to iron out the details. I should be home Tuesday at the latest, though I'm going to try to catch an earlier flight. If you pick me up at the airport, we can go straight to my house. I heard there's a cold snap in L.A. and it's been raining nonstop. I guess I picked a good week to be gone. But no week is a good week without you. I miss you terribly. Sleep tight, love. I'll try you again tomorrow."

I turned away, astonished that I could think of betraying

this man, who loved me so completely, so steadfastly, and was unafraid to say it. If only he knew. But then Josh broke the spell for good.

"He probably had some Mexican hooker giving him a lap dance while he was leaving the message."

"He's not like that," I said, pushing him away. "And he's not in Mexico anymore, he's in New York."

"Don't you know rule number one of the road?" Josh persisted, smiling lazily. "What happens on the road stays on the road. And that goes both ways."

"Well, nothing's going to happen on this road," I said, gaining control of my jellylike legs and sitting down, far away from him. "I adore you, Josh, but I'm involved. That counts for something."

"Funny," he said, padding over to me like a big, patient cat stalking its prey. "It didn't seem to count for too much a minute ago."

He sat down beside me, gave me that boyish look.

"That's not true," I said, hotly denying it. Had I been about to fall from grace? I thought, remembering Clavendish's odd turn of phrase.

"It's not because I'm not attracted," I said. "Silvio's gone. And I miss him. But this isn't going to happen. Thanks for coming in, for being worried about me. But I'm fine."

With that I turned on the light. Josh blinked, his pupils constricting, disappointment writ large over his features. For a moment he said nothing.

"Would you like coffee before you go? Tea?" I busied myself at the sink, then the stove, glad to have my back to him so he couldn't see the prickly heat spreading across my cheeks.

"I can be very patient," he said, a new inflection in his voice. "You're worth waiting for."

I put the teakettle down on the burner, turned.

"Don't, please. Let's just forget about this. Besides," I said, striving for levity, "we've got to keep up that creative tension between us. It makes us better reporters."

"Okay, Diamond," he said. "You win this round."

He finished his tea, walked across the room, stood at the door, hand on the knob.

"Later, dollface," he said. "It was sweet while it lasted."

CHAPTER 33

*J*osh was already at his desk, headphones on and typing furiously, when I arrived the next morning. He gave me an enigmatic smile and went back to his computer.

A moment later, an e-mail flashed across the top of my screen: *Tell Mischa not to bother going out to that KGB lady's house. I felt a little too wide awake after I left you last night so I drove over to Sunland to get that license number. Already DMV'd it.*

I looked up. He wouldn't meet my eye, but I saw his cheeks crease into dimples.

Jumping up, I walked over.

"I should spurn your advances more often," I said. "It makes you work harder. So who owns the car?"

"Hold your horses, hot stuff."

Josh scrolled up with modest pleasure and we both peered at the screen.

The gold Cadillac Seville was registered to one Galya Pankova of West Hollywood. She was sixty-seven years old.

Josh and I looked at each other.

"This must be Ludmilla's friend," I said.

"So she wasn't lying," Josh said.

I brought out the old Dorothy Parker line: "Everything the woman says is a lie, including *and* and *the*."

"Maybe this is on the level. Two old Russian broads,

getting together to have tea with lumps of sugar and talk about how they used to stroll their toy dogs along Nevsky Prospekt."

"Let's go," I said.

"Give me five minutes," he said. "I have to clear something with the Desk."

"Hurry," I said.

"I love it when you beg."

I walked back to my desk and began to pack up my things. A moment later, another message flashed across my screen.

I dreamed about you last night. It was so vivid, I was devastated when I woke up and you weren't there.

I looked over. Josh's brown head was bent over his keyboard. I decided to ignore him.

Instead, I checked the wires and saw that Nicolai Lukin's condition had been upgraded to stable. A surge of relief went through me. At least one son was going to make it.

On my desk sat the Cold War history I had ordered from the library. I flipped to page 278. Out of the corner of my eye, I saw Josh heading over to the City Desk. I frowned and willed myself to concentrate. The spy scandal might make more sense now that I had met some of the players. The green message light flashed and another e-mail unfurled across the top of my screen.

Wanna grab a bite when we're done this evening?

He must have sent it right before he walked away. I decided to answer him right away and make things clear.

I'm flattered. But I'm also taken. Which I told you last night. So please. Stop ruining my concentration when I need to focus all my energies on this story.

I stopped, reread what I had written. That last part was

no good. It implied he was getting to me. I erased the last sentence.

Rain check in another life, OK? I typed, then hit "send."

Josh strolled back to his desk. He put on his headphones and I saw him check his mail. For a moment, he stared at the screen. Then he hunched furiously over the keyboard.

Good thing I believe in reincarnation, he wrote a moment later. *But with my luck you'd probably come back as a porcupine. Still, I would embrace you, spines and all.*

It wouldn't work, I wrote. *Because you're sure to come back as a toad.*

Where there's a will . . . Josh wrote.

You ready yet? I typed back. *Or should I do this solo?*

Two more minutes, he wrote. *I'm on hold with the LAPD's media flack.*

I turned off the message function on my computer and went back to the history book, stopping when I got to the part about Ludmilla. I recalled the *L.A. Times* clips mentioning a third spy, an "unindicted coconspirator" who had never been identified or caught. Could Lukin be the third man? Is that what Clavendish was hiding? But Lukin hadn't even emigrated until 1985. It didn't make sense.

I pulled my head out of the densely printed volume and saw my voice mail light was blinking. Hoping Josh hadn't stooped to leaving me phone-sex messages, I slipped on my headphones and dialed in while avoiding his end of the newsroom. Instead, I watched CNN on the City Desk TV. This far back, there was no sound but the images were perfectly vivid. A devasting earthquake had struck Iran, 8.6 on the Richter scale, which always got

Californians riled up. Living on our own fault line, we felt their pain.

I punched in the code and a familiar, accented voice spoke into my ear.

"Ah, yes. I would like to leave a message for Eva Diamond. This is her machine, yes?"

There was a rustle, then the voice started up again in cultured and precise tones. "This is, ah, Sasha Lukin, we met the other day, as you will no doubt remember."

A pause, then a sniff.

"Ms. Diamond, I am calling to apologize for our rudeness. My wife was not thinking clearly. . . . But I would like to . . . ah . . . to say . . . thank you. The television people told us what you did. That you, ah, lied and pretended to be our daughter. At first we were outraged. But then we realized you wanted to help us, how shall I say, make our escape. The TV reporter plans to complain to the *Times*, but we know you meant no mischief, so what I propose is that, ah, I also will write a letter to the *Times*, extolling your professionalism in our time of grief. Now. There is one more thing. The police told us that Nicolai was on his way to meet you when the car hit him. I did not know. Ah, well, I am sure the police will clear up this mystery soon. Nicolai continues to improve, thank God. If I can ever be of assistance, please call. Good-bye."

I slapped the "off" button. In Qom, veiled women were picking through rubble. Outside the third-story editorial windows, the rain had stopped battering the city. I played Lukin's message back, straining for subtext. His choice of words. His accent. The emotional breaks in his voice, cracked yet persevering. It was extraordinary that he had called. It also didn't quite make sense. Wouldn't he be overwhelmed with hospital visits? Police interviews? His mind trying to absorb the staggering tragedy of one son's death, the other's narrow escape. And yet he *had* called. And left a long message. At a time when the entire city's media were clamoring to talk to him, to wring out the sorry details of his family's anguish, he had called *me* and left the door open for me to call back.

He's afraid Nicolai told me about the letter, I thought. He wants to find out what I know. But there was something else too, I could hear it in his voice, and it dated back to when he first saw me on his doorstep. There had been a shock of recognition, a bolt of blue light crackling between us. Ludmilla had implied yesterday that I reminded her of someone. Someone they both knew in Russia. An old lover of Sasha Lukin's? Was that why his wife found me so threatening?

But I couldn't exactly call him up and say that, or confess that I was drawn to him, too, because he reminded me of my father, with his Old World melancholy and cultured air. No, I had a job to do, and I had to keep my own feelings under wraps. But yes, Mr. Lukin, there *is* something you can do for me, something my paper and I would like very much. I'd like to interview you. We can talk in a civilized way about your victimized sons, and perhaps you can explain what business you and FBI Special Agent Clavendish had together, and whether you knew Ludmilla Belyaeva, and about that Russian investment that fizzled, and your purported house remodeling project, and any enemies you or your sons might have incurred, and then we can catch the killer and bring him to justice.

I picked up the phone and dialed, wincing when I saw it was only 7:58 a.m.

The Lukins' machine picked up. I was halfway through leaving a message when the phone clicked into life.

"Yes?" said Sasha Lukin's tremulous voice. "Ms. Diamond? Is that you? Forgive me, it took me a minute to find the telephone buried under all this rubbish. And to be truthful, I am screening calls."

A woman's voice cut in, shrill and emotional. Lukin spoke to her in Russian. Irina. She didn't want her husband talking to me. Her voice verged on hysteria. What was she scared of? I wondered.

"I know this is a terrible time for you," I began.

"Yes," he said, and his voice quavered again before finding its tonal center and righting itself.

"I'm sorry to call so early. I hope I didn't wake you. Frankly, I'm surprised you even picked up."

I could sense weariness on the other end. "I sleep only sporadically," he said. "I have terrible nightmares, only to wake and find they are real."

"I can't imagine what you're going through. How is Nicolai?" I asked, wanting to change the subject. I hoped he'd give me more than a hospital supervisor's terse report. A personal update by the grieving father would play nicely in tomorrow's paper.

But Lukin would hear the keys clicking if I typed. And the *Times* was almost a paperless office these days. Stealthily, I flipped over a thick Fish and Game report on mountain lion sightings in Los Angeles County that Knightsbridge had given me before our fatal hike. I pulled the top off a marker, put the felt tip to the paper, and waited.

"He is awake," Lukin said with satisfaction. "The nurse said he ate Cream of Wheat this morning and told us he loved us. But he is disoriented. The doctors say there is a problem with short-term memory. The police have been unable to interview him."

There was a long, quivering pause and I knew it was taking all his willpower not to ask what Nicolai had told me.

"Is the guard still there?" I asked.

"Around the clock," Lukin said firmly. "It is wise, with everything that has happened."

I wrote it down. I wanted to ask him about the Prisoner of Memory but knew I had to do it in person.

"That's such great news, Mr. Lukin. I'm glad."

"I must stay busy," he said. "I force myself to put one foot in front of the other. To go through the motions. It helps me forget, at least for a few seconds."

I let him talk, knowing from experience that it was therapeutic. Not to mention part of the job description. You cried with them, clutched the mug of coffee they handed you, flipped through their photo albums, admired the drawings and sports trophies, but you always kept your eyes trained on the prize—the story you were there to get. And you never, ever walked out the door until you had it.

"And somehow I feel that we know and understand each other," Lukin said.

There it is again.

"I'm glad, Mr. Lukin. It's the same for me."

If we were in a bar on a Friday night and he was some young, slick guy, I would be extremely skeptical. But coming from a seventy-year-old man, it felt more complicated, though no less a manipulation, I had to remind myself.

"And let me assure you. If you sat down with me, I'd write an extremely sensitive story about your sons," I said.

"We can only trust our instincts," Lukin said. "In my line of work that's important. And my gut tells me that you are a good person."

"Mr. Lukin, when could we meet?"

Just then, Trabuco walked into the newsroom. Briefcase in hand, he looked around, noting the early birds who might deserve merit raises when the time came. Then he saw me and his face tightened. With a purposeful glint, he strode over.

"How does your schedule look?" Lukin was saying into the phone.

"Today?" I said, surprised and distracted by the sudden appearance of Lumbering Bull.

Trabuco was at my desk now. He banged his briefcase twice against his knee for emphasis. I bent my head and ignored him.

"Yes," Lukin was saying. "Will you come to my house?"

Deadline reporting is all about triage. You're constantly revising and prioritizing as new leads roll in. And this was a big one. Galya Pankova and her gold Cadillac instantly shifted to the back burner.

"Of course I will, Mr. Lukin," I said, enunciating his name loudly for Trabuco's sake. "I can be there in half an hour. Just let me write down your address again."

SASHA LUKIN, I wrote in big capital letters. INTERVIEW. I shoved the paper toward Trabuco.

The tightness left my editor's face. He gave a thumbs-up and motioned that I should see him when I got off the phone.

"Let's make it eleven," he said. "Irina and I are going back to the hospital for a few hours, and then I shall return home and she will stay with Nicolai."

His last words did not escape me. He wanted us to be alone.

*   *   *

Five minutes later I walked over to the City Desk with a triumphant swagger.

Trabuco ignored me.

"I want a story for tomorrow's paper," he said, squinting into his computer screen. "And I want it in plenty of time so we can add whatever Josh gets from the cops. Say, three p.m."

I bugged my eyes out at him.

"Of all the ungrateful, obnoxious . . . I just bagged an interview with the guy everyone is screaming for, the guy who's living out an unspeakable Greek tragedy with his family, who hasn't said shit to any reporter in this city besides me since it all began, and that's all you have to say to me?"

Trabuco socked me playfully in the shoulder. "Just jamming you, Ace," he said. "Good work. We'll hold space."

CHAPTER 34

B
ack at my desk, I took stock of my morning. It looked like Josh and I had time to visit Galya Pankova after all.

We drove two cars so I could go to Lukin's from there. Galya Pankova lived in a part of West Hollywood where modest prewar bungalows gave way to two-story houses with more elaborate lawns. But that hadn't been enough for Galya Pankova. Whatever had once stood in gracious symmetry and proportion to the open space had been replaced by a McMansion that squatted like a giant malevolent toad within a foot of the property lines. Two gold-painted lions sat on pillars at the bottom of the driveway, their right paws raised in feline welcome or attack, depending on what kind of day you were having. An electrified fence ran alongside the grounds. As we got closer, we saw a two-story-high entryway with marble columns and a sixteen-foot carved wooden door, large enough for old Slavonic giants to enter without stooping. A picture window above the door revealed an enormous and aggressively modern chandelier hanging from an industrial-strength gold chain.

"How do we get in?" Josh said.

"We ring the intercom, like everyone else," I said, spying the metal box attached to the fence.

I pressed down, released, waited. Shifted feet. Looked

at Josh. Stared at the house. Did it again, keeping my finger depressed a little longer this time.

"State your name and business," came a robotic voice from inside the intercom.

Josh stepped up.

"Eve Diamond and Josh Brandywine, reporters for the *Los Angeles Times*. We'd like to speak with Galya Pankova, please."

We waited some more. The recorded voice came on again—"No one is available at the moment. Please leave a message"—followed by a loud beep.

"It's about Ludmilla Belyaeva and the gold Cadillac in her garage that we understand belongs to you," I said.

"Thank you," said the robotic voice. "Good-bye."

We heard a click, then the machine disconnecting. Josh and I looked at each other. Now what? Ludmilla may have lied about steering clear of other Russians, but she had been right about one thing. Her "friend" could afford to be generous if she lived in a place like this.

I looked at my watch. Nine a.m. I'd have time for coffee and a bite to eat before meeting Lukin.

"Guess that's all she wrote," Josh said.

"Nice try, smart guy," I said. "We can try again this afternoon. Or stake the place out, see who's coming and going. 'Course, it might end up being nothing . . ."

We began walking back to our cars. Josh said he was going to Parker Center, the cop shop, to see what was new.

Just then a shriek of electronic feedback erupted from the intercom, followed by Russian. Then again in accented English: "Hallo, hallo . . . this horrible machine . . . what did he tell me? . . . It's one of these . . . hold on . . . oh, it's no good . . . I can't remember. . . . Ah . . . just a minute . . ."

Josh and I almost collided, racing back to the front gate.

"We're still here," I called out. "Can you let us in?"

"My dear young people, I am trying. But you must be patient."

How did she know whether we were young or old? Startled, I looked up and saw the eye of a video camera on top of the gate, recording everything.

"We will wait," Josh said.

There followed an excruciating five minutes, while the woman inside alternately cajoled and cursed the security system.

"I must find the instructions. He wrote them down somewhere. In the meantime, my dears, you are reporters?"

"Yes, ma'am," Josh said.

"Are you Galya Pankova?" I asked.

"I am indeed. Now. Could you please hold up your identity cards so I can see them?"

We fumbled for our dog tags and displayed them. The security camera rotated and pointed.

"A little higher, please."

We stood on tiptoe and held them as close to the camera as we could.

"Thank you, children. Splendid. Now, if you will excuse the delay, it should only be another moment or so. . . ."

Finally, she must have pressed the right sequence of buttons because the electronic door swung inward on noisy hinges and we stepped inside. I resisted an impulse to high-five the golden lions and we walked up to the front door. A plump older woman with white hair done up in curls with old-fashioned bobby pins stood there, watching us. She wore a dressing gown similar to the

one I had seen on Ludmilla but her jewels looked real
and her hazel eyes crinkled with interest.

"Come in," she said.

After the killer security, her hospitality caught me off
guard. We walked inside, Josh staring at the gaudy splen-
dor of paintings, chandeliers, rugs, and heavy furniture,
me scanning for hidden traps or weapons. If this woman
was Ludmilla's friend, it paid to be on my guard. But the
only danger I foresaw was choking on clouds of L'Air du
Temps perfume.

Galya Pankova led us into a large living room with
slick marble floors that must have been hard on older
knees. The furniture was oversize—sectional couches in
forest green that could have seated a battalion. Galya
Pankova perched birdlike on the edge of a poufy chair that
threatened to swallow her.

"Would you like tea?"

"No, ma'am, we came for information."

"Is Ludmilla in trouble? Has there been an accident?"

"No, nothing like that. Tell me, Mrs. Pankova, how
long have you known Ludmilla?"

"I have known her several years."

She smiled enigmatically and said no more. Could
Galya be a retired KGB agent too? I looked at her, sending
out spy feelers, but got nothing back except frank curiosity
and openness. She seemed eager to welcome two
strangers into her house. Too eager. And that made me
suspicious.

I gave her my own Mona Lisa smile and waited for her
to elaborate. Galya hesitated, then said, "We met at the
apartment of a mutual friend. She had invited us both for
tea and we hit it off. Ludmilla is so independent. I admire

that. I wish Vassily wouldn't do everything for me."

"Is Vassily your husband?" I said.

She laughed merrily. "Not at all. He is my son. He built this house for me once his businesses began to do well." Her eyes shone with pride. "He went through Harvard Business School, you know. On a full scholarship. Now he wants to enjoy life. It doesn't do any good to tell him my tastes are simple. He won't listen."

"This doesn't look too simple," I said. "Especially the security system."

"I'd prefer a small apartment in a building full of Russians where the halls smell of cabbage and cooking oil and I can hear children playing, just like back home. Where I could go across the hall and visit friends or walk to the Farmers' Market." Her voice grew brittle. "But Vassily says it's undignified. He wants us to live according to our station. And he's worried about crime. So I must live here. And I can't get used to it. Too quiet."

So that's why she had let us in so readily. She was lonely. In trying to protect his mother and lavish her with every conceivable luxury, Vassily had, in fact, made her vulnerable. I wondered if Ludmilla's befriending of this wealthy, lonely Russian woman was more calculated than Galya Pankova knew.

"And Ludmilla reminds you of home?" I prompted.

"Oh, she's wonderful. Such a support. Especially as I've been having these tests . . ."

Galya put her hand to her hair and smiled brightly. "Well, I'm sure you haven't come here to talk about my health. Are you doing a story on Ludmilla's dog rescue operation?"

I smiled. "Actually, it goes further back than that."

Galya nodded knowingly. "She's lived here since the 1980s. She helps me a lot. For us who have just come, it is more difficult."

"But you've been very kind. I understand you loaned her a car? The Cadillac?"

"Vassily got me that car, even though I told him I don't like to drive here." A note of pride crept into her voice. "His beeznis has been very successful, and now he spoils his old *mamochka.*"

My stomach did a little flip.

"What kind of business is he in?"

She waved her arm. "A little of this, a little of that. Import-export, mainly. And now restaurants and a night-club. Really, it is too complicated for me to keep up with, he's always buying and selling them. But come, I will show you. And I can do my duty as hostess."

She led us into a cook's kitchen with a twelve-burner stove and wood-burning pizza oven and stainless-steel appliances out of a design magazine. Then she threw open the fridge. One shelf held a jar of pickled herring, wrinkled apples, and a container of sour cream. The shelf below was stuffed with jars of Beluga caviar. There must have been tens of thousands of dollars' worth of sturgeon roe in that fridge, all of it illegal, since trade restrictions prohibited the importation of Russian caviar.

"Please," she said, scooping out handfuls of the flat round jars and dumping them into our arms. "Take as much as you want. Give it to your family. Your neighbors. He brings me more every week and I've gotten to where I can't stand the smell of it."

Mafia, I mouthed to Josh over Galya Pankova's bent back. He nodded.

"Really, thank you," Josh said. "But we can't accept gifts. It's against the rules."

Galya looked insulted. Shook her head. "Strange, how you Americans operate." She paused, thought a moment. Clapped her hands. "Then you shall eat your fill here," she said. "I will make toast."

Five minutes later, Josh and I were heaping mounds of the briny, irridescent blue-black eggs onto white toast spread thick with sweet butter.

"Amazing," Josh said between bites. "This is the first time I've eaten caviar during an interview."

"Would you like vodka?" our hostess asked, hovering anxiously. "I understand journalists are partial to spirits."

Josh laughed. "In the old days, maybe. Now we run mainly on caffeine."

"What's the name of your son's nightclub?" I asked off-handedly. "Maybe I've been there."

"No doubt," she said. "An elegant girl like you. Only the finest people are allowed in. There is wild game on the menu every night, and delicacies flown in from Russia. The band, the singers, everything is first-class."

"Yeah," I said. "I think I recall now. Is it White Nights?"

"Nyet." A haughty tone crept into her voice. "That one I do not know. My son's nightclub is the Last Czar."

I memorized the words, intending to pay Vassily a social call very soon.

"Have you been there?" I asked.

Gayla thrust her chin forward.

"But of course. Vassily invited me for opening night. No expense was spared. There were dancing bears, snow machines, imported birch trees to make a Russian forest. Ice sculptures fifteen feet tall embedded with bottles of vodka. Every guest received a shapka—a Russian fur hat, mink, no less."

"How could I have missed such a spectacle?" Josh said reverently.

Galya's white brows beetled. "I will tell him to invite you both to his next nightclub opening. I have your names. Maybe you will write about it for your newspaper."

And maybe the story won't end up in the society pages, but in the news section under "Mafia Don Arrested in Boy's Killing."

"That would be lovely, Mrs. Pankova. We'd very much look forward to that."

I could just picture the look on her mobster son's face when Galya told him about the pair of sweet American journalists she had regaled over caviar with tales of her successful "beeznisman" son. Maybe then he'd realize he would have been a lot safer esconcing his *mamochka* in a noisy, overcrowded, rent-controlled apartment building crammed with Russian immigrants where everyone gossiped to their heart's content but kept it under the big Russian tent instead of blabbing to outsiders.

"Has your son met Ludmilla?" I asked after we had all observed the requisite moment of awe about the nightclub opening.

"He thinks highly of her. Such a cultured woman. She helped him with one of his beeznis ventures. Ludmilla is very clever."

I shot Josh a look.

"What was that?" Josh asked casually. "Another night-club?"

"She did some research for him."

"Oh?"

"Located documents that he needed. Vassily was so

pleased. And to be perfectly honest, he's the one who gave her the car, not me. A little thank-you. He was exasperated that I wouldn't drive it. But I barely know how. Back home, there was no need. That's one thing that always worked well, our metro. Anyway, I just call a car service when I need to go out. Vassily has an account."

"So the car isn't just a loan, then?"

"It was a gift."

Caught up in my salty fish orgy, I hadn't kept tabs on the time. With a start, I realized it was ten-thirty and I had half an hour to get over the hill and into Studio City to meet Sasha Lukin. I gave a last, longing look at the open jars littering the table. It was unlikely that I'd ever see such bounty again. Then I tapped my watch meaningfully at Josh and stood up.

"We've got to get going, Mrs. Pankova. Thanks so much for your hospitality," Josh said.

Galya stood up, flustered. "So soon?" she said, then caught herself. "Well, I know how it is with you young people. My Vassily is the same. Always running. I hope I've been of help. . . ." Her voice trailed off in puzzlement. She wasn't sure that she had told us anything important, and she'd never know how important what she had told us would prove to be.

CHAPTER 35

*J*osh walked me to my car.

"She has no idea, does she?" I said.

"Maybe she just doesn't want to know."

"But Ludmilla sussed it out."

"Or Vassily sussed her out."

"I think I know what kind of 'documents' she helped him with. She had something on Lukin. From her old KGB days. And she sold it to this Mafia guy in exchange for the car."

"It's an interesting theory," Josh said. "Be sure to ask him. Now hurry or you'll be late."

"You just want to get rid of me. I swear, if you go to that nightclub without me I'll kill you."

"Wouldn't dream of it." He smiled, showing shark teeth. "Besides, without a glamorous bauble like you on my arm, they'd never let me in."

"Maybe they'll throw us both out. In pieces. But we have to try."

"That's what I like about you, Evie D. You keep going long after a smart, rational person would give up."

"I think you just insulted me. Twice. And stop calling me Evie D. It's Ms. Diamond to you."

"Go do your interview, Jeweled One. Work your magic. And call me when you're through. I'll be at the cop shop. Maybe Nicolai Lukin woke up long enough to tell the detectives something."

* * *

My heart was in my stomach and my stomach was somewhere behind my knees when I rang the doorbell of the Lukin home at eleven, glad that Irina the dragon wife was busy at the hospital ministering to their son.

Lukin answered so promptly that he must have been hovering just inside. He led me through the living room and I felt like I was walking into a doctor's office for an unpleasant examination. But the dread was shot through with hyperawareness that I was finally going to get somewhere if I negotiated this right.

To my surprise, Victor Golodny was sitting at the kitchen table, drinking a glass of tea. His hair looked even wilder than when I had last seen him and a colorful woolen scarf encircled his neck. He jumped up when he saw me, then pumped my hand vigorously.

"Hello, Ms. Diamond. I have told Sasha I am against this meeting," Golodny said briskly. "But he insists upon it. You have some power over him, it seems. And I am just a friend."

Switching to a scolding but affectionate Russian, Golodny placed his hands on either side of the older man's face, pulled him close, and planted kisses on each cheek. Then he grabbed his hat, gave a slight bow, and excused himself. A moment later, we heard the front door shut.

"How is Nicolai?" I asked.

Lukin rubbed his eyes. "He is still sleeping a lot. The concussion is severe. And the impact of the car fractured his pelvis and both his legs. But the internal bleeding has stopped. And he recognizes us. He knows what year it is, who is president. Other things are more fuzzy." He sighed, shook his head. "The brain is a supple organ. But it needs time to heal."

From the kitchen window, low winter light illuminated a terraced garden. Stacked towers of clay pots stood sentinel over red-tinged hydrangea leaves and brown seed stalks; purple berries and orange persimmons hung from skeleton trees. A more subdued palette than summer but appealing in its own way.

"And the police?"

"My son is in no state to be interrogated. They must wait. We must all wait."

So Josh would find nothing new on that front. It was up to me.

We sat at a 1950s chrome table, close enough to feel the stove's warmth but also the cold emanating from the picture window. Lukin made Turkish coffee, ladling four spoons of coarsely ground beans into a metal beaker. In a pan, he heated milk until a skin formed. He brought over a plastic bag stamped with the word *priyanik* in red Roman letters and shook its contents onto a plate. Out tumbled iced cookies that smelled of cardamom and vanilla.

I forced myself to ignore the roar of impending deadline. It was still early. I knew I had to let him ease into the more sensitive topics. All this kitchen voodoo was just a preamble for him to work up courage. Maybe it was due to the long winters stuck indoors, but with Russians, everything seemed to happen around kitchens and food.

As he moved about the room, Lukin stole secret glances at me. I felt he was pulling my features apart and realigning them in a more familiar configuration.

"I must tell you," he said at last, "that it seems unreal. I walk to Denny's room to call him for dinner, or remind him about homework. Yesterday, I asked the housekeeper to make his favorite soup and she looked at me like I was insane. Which I believe that I am slowly becoming. And why not retreat into madness? Only the thought of Nicolai restrains me."

I wanted to reach out and touch him but that would break an invisible code. I had to play hardball, even though it hurt me to see him in such pain.

"Ms. Diamond," he said, his voice going mournful and low, "do you have any idea who wants to kill my family?"

He seemed even more fragile than before. He was like an exotic butterfly that had blown thousands of miles off its migratory course and now quivered with exhaustion, the powder on its wings smudged and damp. But I suspected that just like those butterflies, Lukin's eggshell surface hid a core of steel.

"No," I said, looking him steadily in the eye. "But I think that you do."

He blanched, plunged his teaspoon into his cup, and stirred, the metal scraping rhythmically against the china.

"We have gone over everything with the police," Lukin said, "and found no answers. They have grilled me about the boys, our life here, my work, our income, our debts. They asked whether I noticed any change in the boys recently—secrecy, new friends, unusual requests for money or new purchases."

I watched his face, waited a beat.

"Well, there was that Soviet army watch," I said.

The liquid membrane of his eyes shimmered. He blinked and turned away.

"The police asked about that. I explained it was a case of adolescent rebellion and they were satisfied."

"Are *you*?"

It was such a thin filament, but it was all I had to cling to at the moment. Let him think I knew more than I did.

"Of course not," Lukin retorted. "Denny's murderer is

still at large. Nicolai is in critical condition. I want these people found and brought to justice."

I didn't doubt his pain. But his outrage rang hollow. He knew more about the perpetrators than he let on. If they were hauled into the light, what other secrets might be revealed?

"Mr. Lukin, could this be a payback for something you or your sons have done?"

He shook his head. "The police have discussed that with me too."

"Denny had a crush on a girl at school whose family was being extorted by the Russian Mafia," I said. "He had vowed to track them down and tell them to lay off. Perhaps your sons . . ." I paused for effect ". . . or you got mixed up with them?"

At the word *Mafia*, a wariness flashed over Lukin's face.

"Our family would never have dealings with common criminals," he said after a long moment.

"What makes you so sure?"

"Such people are devoid of culture, beliefs. For them there is just one god, and that is money. These are not Russians. These are twisted examples of *homo Sovieticus*. Degraded to the point of animals. We have nothing in common."

His vehemence surprised me. I also found it a little unseemly. His culture, his education, had been born of privilege. Not everyone in the Soviet Union had gotten such breaks.

"Do you know a woman named Ludmilla Belyaeva?"

I watched his face closely for a reaction. He didn't deny it immediately, but seemed to diligently search his memory banks—or he was choosing his next lie carefully.

"She was a KGB agent in the 1980s," I said. "She's retired and living here in the San Fernando Valley."

At the mention of the KGB, Lukin's face tightened. I wondered if it was the knee-jerk reaction of anyone who had lived under communism, or something more personal.

"I am delighted to say that I never made her acquaintance," Lukin said in a scornful voice.

That could very well be true. But Ludmilla had known who Lukin was. Maybe they had been on the periphery of the same Moscow circle. And it was Ludmilla's job to collect information and secrets that might one day prove useful.

I went for the jugular.

"What can you tell me about the Prisoner of Memory?"

At those words, Lukin pushed away from the table. He walked unsteadily to the stove and stood with his back to me.

"Ms. Diamond, may I offer you more coffee?"

"Yes, thank you."

I wanted him to turn so I could see his face. I felt I was on extremely precarious ground and he might stop talking at any moment.

But Lukin fiddled at the stove, composing himself. My gaze strayed to the window, where a split pomegranate hung from a leafless tree. From its shrunken husk spilled a withered essence, ruby red in the wash of winter light.

Then Lukin was before me, pouring. He placed the beaker on the table and sat down.

"I mentioned the first time we met that you remind me of someone," he said, changing the subject.

"Yes?"

"She looked remarkably like you. Certain mannerisms.

The way you hold yourself. The frank appraisal in your eyes. It has stirred many memories."

"Who was she?" I asked, wondering what this had to do with the attacks on his family.

But Lukin just shook his head.

I thought of Mischa's tales about my long-lost Russian family on the other side of the Curtain. The secrets buried in my mother's silk hatbox. Ludmilla's odd comment from the previous day hinting that I reminded her of someone in Russia. Someone connected to Lukin.

"What was her name?" I persisted.

He shook his head and murmured, "Her name does not matter anymore."

The windows had steamed up from the kitchen heat. I rubbed a patch and looked out, transported to a land of icicles hanging from windowsills and snow falling in silent flurries, blanketing the onion-domed city in white and muffling the sobs of a woman who cried, alone in a room.

"Did you betray her?" I asked softly.

His eyes pulsed with light.

"We betrayed each other."

"How?"

But Lukin only shook his head. I waited to see if he would go on, but after several long moments of silence, I tried another route.

"I understand that you were a physicist in the Soviet Union."

"Who told you that?" he demanded.

"Someone who knew you in Russia."

"For many years now, I have dedicated myself to particle physics in America. Not defense work," he emphasized, banging his fist on the table.

He took a *priyanik* and began pulling it into tiny pieces, which he arranged neatly on his plate. Then he told me about his life in the closed city of Sarov, working under the father of the hydrogen bomb, Andrei Sakharov, and how the cloistered life had finally gotten to him and his family and he had left for a less prestigious but lower-pressure job at a scientific institute in Moscow, retooling himself as a particle physicist. I wrote it all down greedily, not content to rely on the tape recorder whirring in my bag.

"And they let you leave, just like that?" I snapped my fingers.

He gave an odd little grimace.

"I was never entrusted with the most sensitive projects," he said. "Our work was compartmentalized on a need-to-know basis. I was a medium-security cog in the great defense wheel. There was more mobility under the regime than people imagined. And my wife had an all-important Moscow residence permit."

I noticed that he never referred to his homeland as the Soviet Union. Always Russia, and if there was no way around it, "the regime." Vladimir Nabokov could never bring himself to utter those hateful words, either.

"Mr. Lukin," I said, struggling to get back on topic, "you said on the phone that in your profession, you go on instinct. But wouldn't you rely more on proof? Reason? You're a scientist, after all."

"I was." Pause. "But I served a different master. One who no longer exists."

I took a sip of coffee, barely able to swallow.

"You mean the Soviet Union?" I said.

"I mean God."

"God?" I echoed, disappointed. "You were a believer?"

"No longer. He took my beloved sons. How could I stay loyal to such a one?"

"I'm so sorry," I whispered, wondering why he had said *sons* when Nicolai was still alive and improving with each bulletin we received. I picked my words with care.

"You feel responsible for Denny's death, don't you? You think he'd still be alive if you had stayed in Russia?"

Lukin stared somewhere above my head. A cat appeared, trilling hello. He patted his knee and it jumped up, settled itself in a tortoiseshell ball. His hand curved, caressing it.

"Ironic, is it not?" he said. "We fled a disintegrating superpower, hoping for peace and stability in America. And for a long time, we found it. A fantasy of golden beaches and suburbs and sunshine. But in the end, it was just that . . ." He choked up, squeezed his eyes shut in a grimace.

"My Dennitchka." He rocked back and forth. "How can you ever forgive me?"

I let him grieve. The day outside grew dark with impending rain. Light seeped from the room.

"Why was your life here just a fantasy?" I asked at last.

The fine wrinkles around his eyes deepened but he said nothing. I sighed to myself, growing increasingly frustrated. Every time I opened up a fruitful path of discussion, he shut it down.

"I understand you got to travel abroad when you were in the Soviet Union," I said.

"Yes. But that was a long time ago, another life. Why must we speak of such things?"

"Did the KGB ever ask you to report back?"

He hesitated. "Of course not."

I could see anger overtaking grief and knew I had hit

a nerve. Quickly, I searched for a less radioactive topic.

"Did you ever go to France? My mother was from a White Russian family in Nice. Maybe that's why I look familiar to you."

"Only once did I visit France," Lukin said, getting a dreamy look. The portal creaked wider.

"Tell me," he said, leaning in, "did anyone else in your family have a mark right here?" His finger went to the beauty mark on my cheek.

"No," I said, thinking about the landscape of my mother's face, so familiar and now achingly distant.

"And did anyone in your family have a beautiful voice, like a nightingale when they sang?" He was transported now.

"No," I said, bewildered. "And certainly not my mother. She couldn't carry a tune."

He shook his head, leaned back in his chair.

It was odd, his talk of a songbird as one son lay freshly dead, the other in intensive care. But in grief, strange flowers bloom. He'd be at an emotional ebb. I should hit him now with my next question.

"Mr. Lukin, how do you know FBI Special Agent Thomas Clavendish?"

His head snapped to the name, then he went very still.

"Eh, Ms. Diamond, I don't know what . . ."

Why would he want to keep their friendship secret?

"I saw him at the funeral," I said, saving him the trouble of lying. "I understand you met at Moscow State University years ago."

He relaxed. "That's right."

"So how'd you get back in touch in L.A.?"

"He showed up at my apartment one day."

"He knew where to find you?"

Lukin gave a wry grimace. "Security organs are the same the world over."

"And then?"

"We had a drink. Just like old times in Moscow."

"And after the let's-get-reacquainted drink, you got down to business," I said.

"Yes," he said warily.

"There's nothing to fear," I said, with a reassuring smile. I locked eyes with him, submerging my own identity, willing myself to be reborn as his long-lost love. He would have internalized her every movement and mannerism, the inflection of her voice, the planes of her face, until they were imprinted upon his synapses. Slowly and with great deliberation, I raised my hand to my cheek and touched the beauty mark above my lip.

"I met with Clavendish the other day," I said. "He told me. He needed your help, didn't he?"

"Yes," Lukin said hoarsely.

"And you agreed."

"I wanted to prove my devotion to my adopted country."

"A wise idea."

I placed an elbow on the table, cradled my chin in one hand, and smiled crookedly at him. "So what did you do?"

"It involved my job."

I nodded. "Rathburn, isn't it?"

He shifted uncomfortably. "It was unofficial."

"I see. So what did you do?"

Lukin squirmed. I was losing him. "I think you should hear the details from him."

"You know how he is." I sipped my coffee. Bit into a *priyanik*. "I'd rather hear it from you."

"Still," Lukin said, sounding worried that he had said too much.

I leaned forward. Gave him a dead-serious look.

"Mr. Lukin," I said, "is there any possibility that what's happening to your family is connected to your work for Mr. Clavendish and the FBI?"

"No," he said flatly.

"How can you be sure?"

"I just am," he said dully.

As though he knew it was something else entirely.

"Mr. Lukin," I persisted, "I know you received a letter last summer. One that said, 'Reckoning is at hand' and signed 'the Prisoner of Memory.' Do you have any idea what that might mean?"

His face closed down like a beach boardwalk in a hurricane.

"I don't know what you're talking about."

"Of course you do," I said, exasperated. "Nicolai told me on the phone the night before he got run over. That's why he wanted to meet."

A low moan escaped from Sasha Lukin.

"You can never know . . . it isn't possible . . . all my life I have tried to do right, to protect the ones nearest and dearest to me, my family."

I rubbed my palms against my knees to hide my red-hot irritation. I was tired of his hand-wringing, his obfuscations. I wanted to shock him into important revelations.

"Whatever you're hiding, whatever you've done to incur the vengeance of this killer, you've got to tell us, Mr. Lukin. Me, the police. Because look where all your secrecy has gotten you. Denny's dead. Nicolai's in the hospital with severe injuries. You or your wife could be next. They're not going to stop. We need to know why."

But Sasha Lukin had composed himself.

"Ms. Diamond," he said with renewed dignity, "perhaps you should leave now. I have nothing more to say."

I looked at my watch. It was twelve-thirty. I thought about the tape recorder in my bag, and how I'd have to tease a story out of our maddeningly elliptical conversation. Except there was no story. Oh, there was plenty of heavy emotional weather, and lots of color for a heart-tugging couple of grafs about the immigrant family that comes here for a better life only to watch their dreams die. But it was a *situationer,* not breaking news. I needed facts. I needed two sources to confirm anything I wrote, the old journalistic rule of thumb. Deadline screamed in my ear. I had exactly four and a half hours to find and write a story that would advance the Lukin murder case.

I stood up.

"I need to know about the Prisoner of Memory, Mr. Lukin," I said. "If you won't speak to me, then I have no choice but to go to the police, tell them what I've learned." I paused for emphasis, then stole a line from Josh and intoned, "I can't have any more blood on my conscience."

I waited to see if my little ploy would work. But he sat still as a stone, unmoved by my threat, his eyes far away, locked in a frozen grief where I could not follow.

CHAPTER 36

I roared off, pounding the steering wheel in frustration, screaming obscenities at the radio personality whose warm baritone filled the car. Trabuco was bellowing for copy. And what did I have? A bunch of cryptic leads that went nowhere. The Mafia don Vassily knew Ludmilla Belyaeva the ex-KGB agent, who used to be involved with FBI Special Agent Clavendish, who was friends with Russian physicist Lukin, who was slowly losing his family to a killer. There were patterns here that I wasn't recognizing. The whole thing was an intricate spider's web into the past that I had to unravel before anyone else died.

But I needed more time. And that was exactly what I didn't have. The killer was out there, waiting to strike again. My editor was in the newsroom, ready to pull me off the story if I didn't deliver. But what could I give him? I also had to call Josh. So that we could plot our visit to . . . the Russian Mafia, I thought with satisfaction. That's what I'll give Trabuco. Organized crime, exactly what he had ordered. And Josh could back me up. I didn't know where it would lead, but it was the sexiest lead we had. And it would get Trabuco off my back for another day.

Because in the end, journalism is like poker. You exaggerate your strengths and minimize your weaknesses, concede on points you don't care about while fighting savagely for the bottom line. And all the while you bluff like crazy.

I called Josh, eager to enlist him in my plot, but he wasn't answering. Leaving a message, I sped back to the paper on the Hollywood Freeway, dodging in and out of traffic. I had done this particular stretch so much lately that it felt like my personal Indy 500 racetrack. As I drove, I composed the lead of my Lukin interview and called it in to Trabuco, who was practically pawing at the ground in anticipation.

"As police investigators work overtime to discover who might have killed seventeen-year-old Studio City resident Denny Lukin and whether that murder is connected to the hit-and-run injuries sustained by his brother, Nicolai Lukin, the boys' Russian émigré father sat down for an exclusive interview with a *Times* reporter and recounted his secret work as a Russian physicist during the Cold War, his emigration to Los Angeles in search of a better life for his family, and his new career in a nonclassified scientific job at Rathburn International.

"'Who is trying to kill my family?'" the distraught father asked plaintively, saying he and the police have held numerous talks and come up empty."

"That's all you've got for me?" Trabuco said incredulously. "A thumb sucker? We need to advance this story, Eve. What the hell were you doing all morning out there to bring me back this shit?"

"This is just the background," I said coolly. "Josh and I have another interview this evening that's gonna bag it."

"Who with?"

"A Russian nightclub owner who's thick with an ex-KGB operative and is up to his glacier-sharp cheekbones in illicit activities."

I heard a gulp. "So the Russian Mafia is mixed up in this?" Trabuco said, falling neatly into my trap.

"Could be." Pause. "But we need another day."

"Call me when you've got something we can print," Trabuco said, hanging up.

I got off the freeway in Hollywood and wondered where Josh was. I left another voice mail for him at the office and on his cell phone. I sure as hell hoped he hadn't gone to the nightclub without me. I dialed information to get a number and address for the Last Czar nightclub. The operator tapped away.

"There is no listing."

"Did you just check West Hollywood? How about the city of Los Angeles?"

More tapping. More time went by.

"Sorry, nothing's coming up."

A flare of panic. Was it possible I had heard the name wrong? "Could you look under just 'Czar'? Try spelling it *cz* and also *ts*. There's got to be something."

"Ma'am, I've checked every possible combination, for all of Los Angeles County."

"Try Orange County. Ventura. Riverside. San Bernardino."

"Ma'am, I can only do three requests."

I thanked her, then jammed off the phone and called back. I tried for ten minutes, with six different operators. There was no listing for a nightclub with that name or anything like it. Damn. It was probably one of those underground nightclubs, or so exclusive that it wasn't in any book. You had to be in the know. But I'd find it sooner or later. I smiled, relieved to know that even if Josh tried to double-cross me, he'd run into the same wall. We'd have to do this together, or not at all.

Now what? I thought about my frustrating conversation

with Lukin, the fitful stops and starts that left me no wiser than before. I needed someone close to him who could tell me more. Clavendish? No, he would only spin more webs of deceit. Ludmilla? Highly unlikely. Who else might know Lukin's past? Someone here, in L.A., preferably. I flashed on Victor Golodny, with his wavy hair, his long, aquiline nose, and his distracted air. The absentminded professor who had been sitting right there in Lukin's kitchen earlier today. The two of them were like gangly cranes, huddled together against the elements as the pond froze and turned to ice. Would he talk to me?

I had nothing to lose. I took out the scrap of paper he had given me and called.

It was a work number. Golodny was there but the secretary put me on hold for so long I thought she had forgotten. Finally he came on. I explained that I wanted to talk to him.

"But you spoke with Sasha this morning," Golodny said. "Surely you have enough information for your story."

I hesitated. "Sometimes friends and colleagues can offer details that the person might not think to bring up."

"But this is highly irregular. I told you this morning I was against this. I don't want to say anything that could compromise Sasha."

Does he know things that would compromise Sasha?

They might have talked, over drinks, at their sons' school. During summer barbecues by the pool. They were both Russian. Lukin would have confided his fears. His dilemma. Asked for advice, even. Who better than a fellow Russian who had lived under the regime?

"But it could help him too," I said.

"I must think about it."

"I don't have much time."

"I will call you back in five minutes."

He hung up. I waited, praying he wouldn't call Lukin to ask if it was okay. Realizing suddenly that this was *exactly* what he'd do, I stabbed Lukin's number into my cell phone. His machine picked up. All I had to do was keep the line engaged and Golodny wouldn't be able to get through. But I would still hear the incoming beep of call waiting if Golodny called me back.

Lukin's recorded voice came on asking the caller to leave a message. The machine beeped and began recording dead air as I held the phone to my ear, trying to breathe soundlessly. Five excruciating minutes went by. Then five more. The tape ended and a dial tone rang in my ear. I called Lukin back and reengaged the phone. Fifteen minutes had passed. In my cold car, I was clammy with sweat. When eighteen minutes had gone by, my phone beeped with a waiting call and I hung up and depressed the button to hear the incoming call. With relief, I heard Golodny's voice.

"I am sorry for the delay. But I have considered your request and concluded that there is nothing I can tell you," he said. "And now I must go. The lunch break here is not so long, and I must stretch my legs."

I lowered my head to the steering wheel. So much for all that subterfuge. It was another dead end. My nerve endings misfired. My skin felt itchy, the clothes I wore were too constricting in places, too loose in others. Time was slipping away. I was failing to follow the logic of this case. I needed to be more intuitive and stop darting like a jackrabbit down the first trail that presented itself. One-fifteen. Lunchtime. My stomach growled ferociously at the thought of food. Caviar didn't stick to your guts the way potatoes and buckwheat did. It was for the rich, not serfs who pulled plows from dawn to dusk. I felt momentarily sorry that I hadn't taken Galya up on her generous offer. I could use a jar of caviar right now. Normal people were eating sandwiches at their desks, sitting in restaurants, taking a postprandial stroll, stretching their legs.

Yes.

That was it.

A stroll.

I grabbed my notebook and read back through my notes. Golodny was a computer programmer. Where did he work? Someone had told me. I closed my eyes, concentrated, got a mental image of a cocky boy leaning against a cathedral in Echo Park. Max Golodny. Talking about his father. Who worked at . . . flipping furiously now, I found it: Ionix Company. It was worth a shot. I called information and got the address. They were in West Hollywood, on Santa Monica Boulevard.

I put the car in gear and drove there. It was a bare-bones industrial space, above a retail store, that looked out onto the nonstop Russian carnival that was Plummer Park. On this greensward, you could find Russian mothers pushing strollers and crooning nursery songs. Apple-faced Russian retail clerks enjoying their lunch breaks. And picnic benches filled with old Russian men in threadbare dark suits and jaunty hats, playing cards and feeding the pigeons. On holidays honoring the veterans of the Great Patriotic War, these palsied and bewhiskered men pinned colorful medals to moth-eaten uniforms and rode with quiet dignity and straining seams in parades honoring their unspeakable sacrifices of so long ago.

I parked in front of a tiny Armenian grocery, bought a bag of pita and a container of roasted eggplant dip, and hauled my booty through the park, scrutinizing every thirtyish man I saw strolling alone or chatting with his fellows.

Then I saw a man sitting on a bench. He had a brown paper bag in his hand and a textbook on his lap. Probably a computer-programming manual. He seemed oblivious to the world around him. It was Golodny. As he ate, he plucked crusts of bread from his sandwich and flung them to the pigeons that milled, just out of kicking distance, waiting for handouts.

I got close enough to see that the book on his lap was not a computer text after all, but a survey of Southern California wildlife. Then the pigeons scattered with a flutter and Golodny looked up. When he recognized me, a curtain fell over his eyes and his demeanor grew cold.

CHAPTER 37

"M s. Diamond, I have no idea what you are doing here, but I told you I have nothing to add to your investigation."

I pretended to do a double-take, then made a big show of removing the sunglasses I wore even on overcast days to keep off the glare and stay as anonymous as possible.

"Mr. Golodny, what are you doing here?"

"I work across the street," he said stiffly.

"Do you really? Oh gosh, and my favorite Armenian market is just over there," I said, dangling my plastic bag. "Well, we both have to eat, don't we? May I join you?"

"Of course," he said, as though nothing would pain him more.

I sat down and immediately the pigeons closed in again.

"I see you're studying our native fauna," I said.

"Yes," he said, relieved I wasn't asking about Lukin. "It's amazing the diversity, especially so close to an urban setting," Golodny said. "Your coyotes, for instance, and how they've adapted. In Russia we have wolves. But what really fascinates me are the mountain lions."

He reached into his bag, removed a second sandwich and a cucumber, and took alternating bites.

"You will excuse me if I eat while we talk," he said.

"Of course."

He must have been nervous, because soon he blurted out, "As I mentioned on the phone, I really don't know what more I can tell you."

That gave me all the opening I needed.

"Mr. Golodny, did Sasha Lukin ever talk about why he emigrated?"

Golodny considered my question carefully.

Finally he said, "For a better life, as we all did. And to think . . . It is outrageous. Do we live in a civil society here, or a barbaric wasteland where anyone can get away with murder? This is why we all left Russia."

"Did Sasha ever talk about his life back in Russia? His career?"

Golodny struggled unsuccessfully to hide his dismay. "No," he said.

"What about his family?"

"He used to say that for many years, he was too married to his career to think about a family."

"Did he ever talk about a guy named Thomas Clavendish?"

Now Golodny's face showed disapproval. "I have met this man. He and Sasha are friends."

"Did you know he was an FBI agent?"

"You are sure of this?"

"Did Sasha Lukin ever talk about spying, even in jest?"

Golodny shoved the remains of his sandwich into his bag.

"For us such things are not a joking matter."

He grabbed his book.

"Did he ever say anything about the Prisoner of Memory?" I asked, watching him closely.

The book tumbled out of Golodny's hands and hit me on the toe. "Ouch," I said, bending down to rub my bruised digit. The fact that Golodny's next words were not an apology struck me as significant.

"Ms. Diamond," Golodny said, struggling to keep his voice under control, "what did Sasha tell you about this matter?"

"He told me he was receiving letters," I fibbed, using what Nicolai had told me.

Golodny let out a sigh of relief. "He spoke to you about this, then."

"Briefly," I hedged.

"Sadly, I am aware of the situation. Sasha is terrified to go to the police."

I wondered if Lukin had told his old FBI pal. It would give a legitimate explanation to why Clavendish had a notepad scrawled with the words.

"And now look. Just look what has happened."

"What did the letters say?" I asked quietly.

He shot me a piercing look. "He did not tell you?"

"Just in general."

"It is not my place . . ." Golodny began. He began to gather up his things again.

I grabbed his arm. "I am writing a story for tomorrow's paper about these letters. I need as many details as possible."

A throttled sound came from him. "No. You cannot. It is too dangerous."

"I don't think so. In fact, I think the more people know about these letters, the safer Sasha will be. No one will dare attack his family once this is out in the open. And the police, the FBI, are very efficient. They'll find the killer."

I wasn't sure I believed this myself, but it seemed like a reasonable thing to hope for.

Golodny balled up his brown paper bag and lobbed it

into a nearby trash can. "I don't know what is the right thing."

"What did the letters say?"

He lit a cigarette, crossing his long, thin legs. "This will be in the paper tomorrow, then?"

"Yes," I said, easing my notepad onto my lap.

"You will use my name?"

"I'd like to."

Golodny scratched vigorously at his ear and grimaced.

"It is impossible. Sasha will see it as a betrayal of our friendship."

I hated using unnamed sources. But he was getting more agitated by the minute and I feared he might run off and leave me with nothing.

I gave him my most reassuring smile. "How about if I call you a family friend?"

Golodny looked at me shrewdly. "Then it is sure he will know."

"It could be Clavendish. His FBI buddy."

Golodny's face soured and he turned his head and spit at the ground.

"I do not like that man. He knows many secrets, and he is too close to Vassily Grigorovich."

"Is he the nightclub owner?"

"It is said that when Vassily Grigorovich goes to the bathroom, this Clavendish accompanies him."

I wanted to ask him more about that. But first I had to find out what he knew about the letters.

"So it's okay if I call you a family friend, then?"

He ran the burning ash of his cigarette along the cast-iron bench, honing it to a reddish-gray point.

"I do not know. It is so confusing. Even in translation, the letters make no sense."

"How so?"

"They are full of rants and garbled talk of revenge. They ask for money, which Sasha has given."

So Lukin was being blackmailed. This was why he had refinanced his house.

"How long has this been going on?"

"Since summer. He paid quietly at first. Then several months ago he asked me for a loan." Golodny shrugged. "I gave him what I could, but it wasn't enough. The letters keep coming. Filled with demands and threats."

"Threats about what?"

"Sasha will not say."

"Does it refer to something recent? Or from his life in Russia?"

"Sasha is an upstanding American citizen."

"From his old life in the Soviet Union, then. But what could he have to hide?"

Golodny grew impatient. "Ms. Diamond, you cannot possibly understand. Under the old regime, everyone was guilty of crimes against the state. It was only a matter of matching the person to the crime."

Nicolai Lukin's roommate at UCLA said the same thing.

"But I don't think we're talking about a little black market trading or samizdat literature," I said. "Someone must have damaging information on him."

"And when he ran out of money, they went after his family," Golodny said grimly.

"Who could it be?" I said, thinking about Clavendish and his secrets, his clandestine ops, his facility with all things Russian, his high-stakes poker games and his debts.

"We believe it is a former KGB operative with access to secret files."

Ludmilla, then.

"But it must be true if Lukin is paying. Did he tell you what he did?"

Golodny's eyes grew veiled.

"I am his friend. I have not pressed him."

I felt the lie reverberate in my bones. Golodny was willing to reveal pieces of the puzzle that painted his friend as a victim. Anything that veered from the script, I'd have to learn elsewhere.

"Have you actually seen these letters?" I asked, my inner journalist punching back in for work.

"He showed me a letter, yes."

"Did you read it?"

A long pause. Then: "It was full of accusations."

"About?"

"I told you. They were rambling. Incoherent. The work of a tortured mind."

My bones vibrated again. Lukin's friend knew exactly what the letter said. I should have listened to my instincts then and pressed him. I might have avoided what came later. But in my hot pursuit of the larger story, I didn't want to risk angering him. Because there was one more thing I absolutely needed him to confirm.

"And they were signed 'the Prisoner of Memory'?"

He hesitated, nodded, and threw a crust to the pigeons.

Bingo. I had enough to satisfy journalism's hallowed two-source rule. Both Golodny and Nicolai Lukin had confirmed the existence of letters signed "the Prisoner of Memory." Golodny was on record as saying they were blackmail letters. And Sasha Lukin himself had grown visibly alarmed when I mentioned the name and then refused to discuss the topic.

I allowed myself a moment to gloat at the chaos that

would be unleashed as my story hit the paper. Especially if I could tie it back to the Mafia. The cops, the Feebs, the city's electronic media—it would be a free-for-all and I'd have to grab ahold and ride the news flow, jockeying to stay front and center.

CHAPTER 38

I got lost hiking back to my car and ended up by the tennis courts, where the old Russian men congregate to play cards. I checked my phone, but Josh hadn't called. Since I was here, I thought I'd ask the park habitués what they knew about the Last Czar nightclub.

But first, I looked at my watch: 2:45. I'd better call in what I had so far.

"Now we're getting somewhere," Trabuco crowed. "Connect it up the line all the way to the Russian Mafia and I can promise you and Joshua page one."

I told him I'd do my best. Hanging up, I heard loud music, and it wasn't coming from a passing car. In fact, the din of traffic had been replaced by wild, swirling music—ancient flutes and bouzoukis, clapping and roars, as a bride in a snow white, floor-length dress danced into sight, surrounded by her wedding party and musicians. At first I thought it was a Hollywood film shoot. It was so unscripted on this overcast winter afternoon that it just had to be fake.

I looked around for someone to confer with but saw only a teenage girl with overdone blue eye makeup, torn black clothes, and purple hair lounging against a tree. She took a drag on her cigarette. In the bored tone of teenagers the world over, she said in Russian-accented English, "They are from the Caucasus. Very primitive."

"I rather like it," I said, caught up in the pageantry and

spectacle as elderly men with peaked and tasseled hats danced jigs, and matrons held up their skirts to take dainty steps in high-heeled sandals, and small children romped and threw flowers, and the entire brocaded, corseted, behatted wedding party danced past, trailing fumes of expensive perfume, high-proof brandy, and sweat. The bride's huge brown eyes were rimmed in kohl and her long black hair fell in ringlets below a tall, beaded headdress. The bridegroom had a fierce, beaky nose and high cheekbones. He wore an embroidered shirt tucked into a plaited leather belt that held up billowy black trousers and was surrounded by young men who roared and pranced like goats.

The wedding party swept past, exhilarated and wild. The girl just gave me a glazed stare.

"Spare any change?" she said halfheartedly, which made me wonder if she was homeless and had run away from strict immigrant parents.

"Spare any change?" she repeated, and then a lightbulb went off in my head.

"You speak Russian?"

She looked around, uncertain as to where this was headed. I had diverged badly from panhandling etiquette and we both knew it.

"Why?"

"Wanna make a fast twenty?"

She pulled her neck in like a turtle and I realized that in her lexicon, that meant sex. I saw her checking me out, weighing the possibility.

"No, no, no," I said. "I need a translator. To talk to those old men over there. I'm afraid their English isn't so good."

The girl considered, then nodded.

"Police?" she asked.

"Reporter." I flashed her my ID and she pushed herself off the tree and came round to inspect it with the first burst of enthusiasm she had shown so far.

"Cool." She handed it back. We walked toward a sea of old men in dark overcoats, hats, and mufflers. They sat at picnic tables, playing cards, deliberating chess moves and murmuring ecclesiastically in Russian. A steady stream of sunflower seed hulls flew out of their mouths, leaving a wet and messy trail of parrot litter on the ground.

"Please ask if they know a Russian guy named Vassily Grigorovich. He supposedly owns a nightclub called the Last Czar but there's no listing for it in the phone book."

She looked at me dubiously. As I said the name, the rumble died down and forty pairs of beady eyes fastened upon mine. I heard phlegmy coughs and marveled that they could sit outdoors and immobile for hours on such a cold day. You never saw the old babushkas sitting on picnic benches. They were too busy at home, sweeping floors, chopping onions, shucking beans.

The girl stood but said nothing.

"Go on, ask them."

She stammered out something. I heard the name and the word *czar* repeated in Russian. For a long time, there was silence, with only the occasional sound of sunflower hulls being ejected from wet mouths.

"Nobody knows him, huh? Or his club? Why don't I believe that? Okay, next question." I turned to the girl. "Could you please ask if anyone is familiar with the case of that Russian kid they found killed up in Griffith Park?"

I knew she did as I asked, because I heard her mangled Russian pronunciation of *Gree-fit*.

At once the bench erupted with debate. Calloused,

black-nailed fingers came out and stabbed neighboring shoulders as they argued. One elderly man in a beret gestured so violently that his cigarette left his fingers and flew through the air.

I noticed that we were attracting a crowd of listeners and hangers-on. Two young men with lank hair and red-rimmed eyes drifted into the nearby trees. A young mother with a toddler stopped pushing her pram. Two middle-aged women carrying net bags stuffed with dark green crinkly kale yelled back at the men.

"What are they saying?" I asked.

The girl looked disgusted. "They say teenagers have too much freedom today. That they don't respect their elders."

"What has that got to do with this kid getting killed?"

The girl shrugged with a "What did you expect?" motion.

"At least they're talking. Now ask them about Vassily Grigorovich again."

She did, and one of the women with the kale put down her produce bag and began an angry speech.

I raised my brows at the girl.

"She says they don't have enough money to buy meat, and that only the Mafia and those corrupt bastards in government ever get rich. She says she's in America now and she can speak her mind."

"Great. Ask her if she knows where the club is."

The girl asked and another debate erupted. One man lifted his hand and rubbed his thumb and forefinger together, then spat at the ground. Another ran his finger along his throat in an unmistakable gesture.

"No one is answering the question," the girl said airily.

"Tell them I'm a reporter and I'm trying to find out

who killed the boy in Griffith Park. Is there anything they can tell me?"

"It is Russian business," the girl said. "You should leave it."

At that, the woman with the bundles of kale whirled on my translator.

"Why you are coward?" she scolded in broken English. "Tell her truth. People say Mafia angry with family."

"Why?"

The woman raised her shoulders and pushed her lower lip down in the classic "Who knows?" gesture.

Now one of the chess players stood up laboriously, fingered the brim of his hat. He looked at his fellows, who egged him on.

"You stop question," he said. Then he sat down and his fellows nodded in agreement. A bottle was produced and everyone took furtive sips as it made its way under the table. Soon it reached us. With many winks, it was offered. I saw a gleam of saliva on the glass mouth and declined. Now a handful of sunflower seeds was pressed into my hand. An elderly man slid off the bench, walked over with the rolling gait of deteriorating hips.

"Danger," he said, waggling his forefinger at me. He said something to the girl in Russian.

"He says you must not go asking about that nightclub," she intoned. "He says, 'There are bad ones among us.'"

The old man nodded severely. Then he caught my eye, repeated his admonition, and walked off.

A moment later, the girl and I did too. There was nothing further to be learned.

I opened my purse and gave her the twenty. I expected her to go away but she hovered. Maybe she had seen the green of other bills in my wallet. Maybe she was just bored and lonely and this was as exciting as her day was going to get.

I sat down glumly on a bench and looked at the clock: 4:40. I should get back and write up what I had. I wondered what Josh was doing and why he hadn't called. I could make a perfunctory call to the cops to see if they had a comment on the Russian Mafia allegations, but I didn't think I could put that in the story yet. It was too speculative.

Shoulders sagging, I thought about my latest dead end. How would I ever penetrate the murky confines of the Russian Mafia?

I forced a smile at the girl, who perched on the other end of the bench, studying me. "Well, thanks a lot for translating," I said. "Sorry it didn't get us anywhere. This Vassily guy must be pretty scary if they won't even talk about him. Maybe his nightclub doesn't even exist."

The girl looked at me. She popped a piece of gum into her mouth and seemed to consider.

"I know where to find him," she said finally. "For sixty dollars, I'll take you there."

CHAPTER 39

R eally?" I said.

"My old boyfriend used to run errands for him."

"So is he really a big wheel in the Russian Mafia?"

She shrugged. "So they say."

"I guess if we're going to be working together a while, I'll need to know your name."

"Julia," she said, pronouncing it *Yu-lia.*

"Nice to meet you, Julia. I'm—"

"I know. Eve Diamond. You showed me your press pass."

"You'd make a fine reporter, Julia. Sharp mind. Good memory. So let's see what you remember about Vassily. He has this club?"

She nodded emphatically. "I've been there once."

"Where is it?"

"On Croyden." She saw my blank look. "That's off Santa Monica Boulevard. Here in West Hollywood."

"What's it like?" I said, thinking of Galya Pankova's glowing description.

"There's gambling in private rooms out back. Lots of flashy women and thuggish men. It's not my thing. I'm more into the punk aesthetic."

I glanced away so Julia wouldn't see me smile at the incongruity of her Russian accent and her slangy American teen-speak. Luckily for me, she had been here awhile and knew her way around West Hollywood's nightlife. If there was gambling at the club, it would go far in explaining why it was underground. But the New Russians liked to strut their wealth. Wouldn't Vassily Grigorovich want everyone to know how rich and powerful he was?

"And it's called the Last Czar?"

She scrunched up her face.

"I think that was the old name," she said.

"What's the new one?"

She popped a bubble.

"Prisoner of Memory."

"What!" I exploded. The noise in my head was the last remaining puzzle piece clicking into place.

"You wanna go there or not?"

"I do." I paused. "But I have to call my colleague. I promised him I wouldn't go alone."

"Smart to have backup," she said.

"You think? Have you ever met this guy?"

"Sure."

"He scary? Like a stone-cold killer?"

"He takes care of business."

"What does that mean?"

"It means he doesn't kill anyone he doesn't have to. But he does a lot for the community, too. Donates to Russian charities and shit. The Russian paper said he gave five hundred thousand dollars to the Kirov last year."

"Real balletomane, huh?"

"He just does it for the status. He's more the 'let's go shoot Asian tigers that have been flown into a Montana safari compound and sedated so they can't run away' type. He did that once. Swear to God. Cost him a hundred thousand dollars. Had the head mounted. My ex told me."

"That's disgusting."

She just shrugged. The winter twilight shrouded her face, obscuring any expression.

My cell phone rang.

"Sorry," Josh said. "LAPD kept me busy all morning treading water. Then Lansing called to invite me on a crash raid he and the INS were doing in Canoga Park. Russian Mafia smuggles blue-eyed illegals up from Mexico, crams them into a safe house, then ransoms them out to family or the highest bidder. You cannot imagine the stench. Trabuco wanted a daily and I just got off deadline."

"I wonder if these are the people Mischa escaped from."

"They'll never say. FBI has two low-level operatives in custody but suddenly they're deaf-mutes. Stoic, these Russians. Take the fall, suck it up, do their time. Like they're marching off to Stalingrad all over again."

"You could have called."

"I was busy. But I did call the nightclub. And Houston, we have a problem. There's no listing for this place."

"That's because it's not called the Last Czar anymore. It's called the Prisoner of Memory."

I waited for the significance to sink in.

Josh sucked in a breath. "Sweet," he said.

"And I've got a young lady here who is going to lead us to it."

I could almost hear the drool dripping off his chin. "Where are you?"

"Plummer Park. Corner of Fountain and Vista."

"Don't move. I'll be there in forty minutes."

Julia sat in the front passenger seat and directed us through traffic. We pulled up to a red canopy with gold trim. The club was in a building that someone had remodeled with a lot of money and very little taste. The walls were Travertine marble, inlaid with little alcoves where statues of saints, cherubs, and half-naked angels could look down upon the crowd lined up outside. Imposing white columns framed the door, supporting nothing. The designer had gone a little Japanese with the roof, which was laid in shiny blue ceramic tiles. There was no sign out front.

"Welcome to the Prisoner of Memory," Julia said.

Two doormen in red and gold livery, complete with caps, stood by a velvet rope, guarding the entrance. It was only 6 p.m., but there was already a line to get in. The dinner crowd, presumably. They were mainly couples, the women in heels and glittery dresses, the men in expensive, boxy suits and slick haircuts. I heard the thumping of Russian techno music reverberating on the sidewalk. When the thuggish-looking valet leaped out to take our car, I waved him away and zoomed off. The last thing I wanted was to lose possession of my car and keys in case we had to leave in a hurry.

We parked on a residential street two blocks away. I gave Julia her sixty dollars and she waved good-bye and began hiking away.

"You're not coming with us?" I said, wishing I hadn't already paid her.

"Are you crazy?" she shouted, then turned the corner and disappeared into the night.

Josh and I smoothed down the wrinkles in our clothes and approached the line. Josh was dressed okay, in his khakis and button-down shirt with red tie, but my black wool pants should have been tighter around the ass, my heels way higher, and my shirt exposing more flesh and jeweled necklaces.

A bouncer with the neck of a Minotaur was escorting in three bleached blondes with plunging necklines who had not been waiting in line a minute ago. The couples ahead of us shifted and murmured to themselves, but nobody protested. Maybe after decades of communism, patience in line was embedded into the Russian genetic code. The bouncer patrolled the length of the queue, appraising everyone with dead eyes. In another era, he would have carried a bullwhip and worn shiny black boots.

There must have been something in our body language that told him Josh and I weren't a couple.

The bouncer stopped next to me. "You are alone?" he asked, trying to look down my blouse.

Uncertain, I sneaked a glance at Josh while the bouncer's gaze was occupied. He nodded almost imperceptibly.

"Yes," I said.

The bouncer walked me to the front, the rope parted, and I waltzed in, ignoring the subdued murmur that rose behind me. After depositing a twenty with the metal-caged cashier, I stepped into the club.

Inside, the decor screamed 1970s Moscow bordello. The walls were upholstered with red velvet, from which hung gilded icons with the heads of Stalin and Lenin instead of the usual melancholy Orthodox saints. A glittering disco ball twinkled from the ceiling, reflecting shards of light. Dim figures huddled around tables, wreathed in clouds of bluish smoke.

On the parquet floor, couples danced. I moved into another room where a buxom blond singer stood onstage belting out turbo folk songs accompanied by a synth-heavy band. Her cleavage was pushed up almost to her chin. She wore a tight, curvy dress and four-inch heels with straps that bit into her thick ankles. People sat at tables laden with food and bottles of vodka on ice, listening stony-faced. No one seemed to be having a good time.

I made my way back to the bar and sat down, feeling the murmur and hum of activity around me. Several men in suits appeared and offered to buy me drinks. I declined.

"You are alone?" The same question over and over.

"Yes."

"You are here for a good time?"

"I am here for information."

"That is more difficult," my latest suitor said. "Information is power."

"I want to talk to Vassily."

The man melted away. Suddenly no one knew me.

Then two more men appeared. Heavyset, like bulldogs.

"We go now," one of them said, leading me swiftly up a flight of stairs and into a room that had a perfect view of the bar and stage downstairs. Video cameras attached to the ceiling recorded everything.

I sat between them like a game show contestant waiting for her moment onstage. One of the thugs heaved my purse onto his lap.

"Hey." I reached out. "Give it back."

"Security," he said, restraining me. In the semidark, I watched his stubby fingers manhandle my compact, lipsticks, brush, and wallet. He opened it, pulled out the bills, licked his fingers to count them, and folded them neatly. With a ghoulish smile, he raised one meaty haunch and slid my money into his back pocket.

"That's my money," I said, but he ignored me. Now the thug went laboriously through my credit and ID cards. He stopped at my LAPD and sheriff's press pass, held them up to the light, and ran his finger along the laminated plastic edge.

Then he said something in Russian to his friend.

"That's right," I said. "I'm a reporter with the *Los Angeles Times*. I have many friends in the police." I paused. "Sheriff. FBI. Homeland Security. I know many people. So you better give me back my money."

My self-appointed banker just grinned and slapped my thigh.

"Okay, Yeva Diamanda," he said.

"Can I speak to Vassily?" I asked.

From inside my purse, my cell phone rang, and I knew it was Josh. He was probably inside by now and wondering where I was. I reached for the phone but the thug pulled it away. We all sat and listened to it ring. Finally, it stopped, but started up again like a lovesick bird.

A third man came into the room now, spoke in Russian. My escorts stood up. Strong hands gripped my arms. I wondered where they were taking me, and if the nightclub patrons would see what was going on. Then I realized it was one-way glass. Probably soundproof, too. They led me down a corridor that smelled like old grease. We stopped at a door and they said something into the intercom. A buzzer sounded. The door opened and we walked in. After the twilight of the nightclub, I blinked at the bright office lights.

A large, powerfully built man sat behind a heavy wooden desk, toying with a gold pen. His hair was closely cropped to his skull. He had deep-set eyes, a long, straight Slavic nose, narrow lips, and a piercing gaze. I looked for a resemblance to plump Galya, the jeweled bird in her golden cage. I thought I detected the same widow's peak.

The life-size stuffed and mounted head of a tiger with a snarling mouth kept watch on the wall above us. This man must be Vassily Grigorovich. He was deep in conversation

with a shabby, suited figure who perched deferentially on
the edge of his seat, holding a thick, grimy envelope
bound with rubber bands. He handed his envelope to the
Mafia don and picked up his hat. When he turned, I saw it
was the Russian card player from Plummer Park who had
warned me to stop asking questions.

His mouth opened in reproach when he saw me, then
clamped down in a resigned way. He shrugged and walked
out, and I knew for sure I was in the presence of Vassily
Grigorovich.

He leaned back in his chair and smiled.

"They must tithe," he said in lightly accented English.
"In the beginning, they resisted. But now they see the wisdom of the system and the protection it offers."

I wasn't sure what to say, so I stayed quiet. Behind
him were shelves filled with industrial-size canisters of
roasted eggplant, tahini, and olive oil. Casks of wine and
Armenian brandy. It took me a minute to notice the
machine gun, propped among the cartons, its muzzle
saluting the ceiling.

It was warm in the room. Vassily Grigorovich unbut-
toned the neck of his finely tailored white shirt and cuffed
up the sleeves. He sat like a general in a war room con-
templating his next battle.

The door opened and with a jolt of nerves I recognized
one of the disheveled, glassy-eyed men from Plummer
Park who had listened to me question the elderly Russian
card players. He spoke to Vassily Grigorovich in Russian,
avoiding eye contact with me.

"Thank you, Pavel," the kingpin said. "As you can see,
she has already found her way here. You may go now. A
token of our esteem awaits you at the back door."

The stool pigeon slid out and the ransacker of my purse

stepped inside and deposited my press tags on Grigorovich's desk while all variety of lesser thugs bunched in
the doorway. They were like Russian nesting dolls, but
instead of the ever-smaller *matrioshka* peasant women,
this set went up the criminal ladder, culminating in the
man who sat across from me, although doubtless there
was someone behind him, who might not even live in
L.A., preferring to run his empire from a villa in Cyprus
that overlooked the Mediterranean.

Vassily Grigorovich nodded his head, dimissing the
others. He examined my dog tags.

"I see you have friends with the police, Miss Diamond."

"Yes," I replied, "and I demand that—"

Vassily Grigorovich placed his elbows on the desk and
clasped large hands together. "So do we," he said pleas-
antly.

CHAPTER 40

A glacier formed at the top of my spine and crept all the way down to my toes. This was a more intelligent, educated, Westernized criminal than I had seen before among the Russians. The guy had polish.

"And let me remind you, you're in no position to demand anything right now," he added.

He reached for a silver cigarette case, flipped it open, offered me a hand-rolled one. I hesitated, wondering if I might shove the lit end into his eyes and escape. When I declined, he sighed and indulged alone. The room filled with smoke.

"It's a filthy habit. You Americans are light-years ahead of us on this. But it is my little vice. A man must have at least one vice, don't you think?"

He gave me a rakish smile.

"You must be Vassily Grigorovich. The Godfather, or however you say that in Russian."

"I am a businessman," he said modestly. "I invite you to check our city permits, tax rolls, property deeds. Everything is in order."

There was a slight sibilance to his words, which gave him the air of a snake, coiled and menacing, despite the open face and elegant manners.

"May I offer you coffee? Tea? Vodka?"

He must have given an invisible signal because the door opened and a stunning, six-foot blond Amazon in a

Chanel suit appeared. Wordlessly, she set down a filigreed silver platter with Turkish coffee, black tea, and vodka, pivoted like a runway model, and strode out. I gratefully sucked down the caffeine, passed on the spirits.

Vassily Grigorovich blew a plume of smoke. "I must apologize for not seeking you out before this. My people told me you made inquiries. But it has been a long day with some unexpected . . . complications," he said, massaging his temples.

My thoughts flashed to Josh's story about the FBI raid on the Russian safe house operation and I knew, even if I could never prove it, that I was staring at the man at the top of the smuggling pyramid. I wondered if he had any idea that he had smuggled my cousin illegally into the United States and that I was now harboring his valuable "property."

"Your *people*? I thought Czar Alexander liberated the serfs in 1861."

The smile widened. "Ah, you are a student of Mother Russia. My poor, benighted country. Such human potential, wasted. First by ignorance and poverty and medieval attitudes. Then the ravages of totalitarianism. And now transition. The post-glasnost years have created certain . . . opportunities for those with agile minds. But even now, it is not a normal life. Billionaires on trial in cages. Whole provinces abandoned and left to rot. Politicians gunned down in broad daylight. Do you realize we are the only developed nation in the world where the mortality rate marches backward? And yet we are a normal people. Put us in a normal country, and we, too, thrive and prosper."

He looked about the room to illustrate his point.

Yeah, I thought. You prosper by ripping off and exploiting immigrants poorer and less ruthless than yourself.

"Vassily Grigorovich, I'm not interested in your business right now. I'm investigating the murder of a Russian-American boy in Griffith Park, and since some people have raised the possibility of Mafia involvement, my editor asked me to check it out. I'm here with a colleague. He's either waiting in line outside or he's gotten in and is looking for me. We're just normal people too, trying to live and do our job."

His face tightened, and all of a sudden it wasn't a jovial history lesson anymore.

"Mafia? And so you came to me? What kind of insult is this?"

Afraid he'd throw me out, I tried for common ground.

"I have Slavic blood too."

His eyes narrowed. "Oh?"

Now I had to walk a tightrope. I didn't want him resenting me because my family had made the wise decision to flee St. Petersburg as the Red Army advanced. Not everyone had been given that choice.

"My great-grandmother came from Russia," I said.

"Then we are the same, you and I."

"I'm just a reporter on assignment. I've been interviewing people who might have known this kid and why he was killed. Maybe the real killer is using the Mafia as a smokescreen. But whoever's doing this is sending the Lukin family blackmail letters signed 'the Prisoner of Memory.' And I want to know why."

Vassily Grigorovich studied me for a moment. Then he said, "Do you really think I would be stupid enough to sign a letter with the name of this club if I were blackmailing Mr. Lukin?"

He had a point there.

"I'm sorry you came here on this wild goose chase. We have read about this unfortunate boy and his family. We know of him. But we did not kill him."

I flashed on what Lyuba had told me in the deli.

"Did you ever meet him?"

Vassily Grigorovich hesitated. He tapped his pen on the table. "No," he said.

"But someone who works for you did."

"I will tell you something. I want you to understand that we are not animals. But if you repeat the story in public, I will deny it. Is this clear?"

"Yes."

"The boy tried to interfere with one of our collection businesses. He came here, approached Volodya, one of my more . . . excitable associates, and it would have gone badly for him had I not learned of the situation and pried him out of Volodya's hands. The boy went away, shaken but unharmed."

"When was this?"

"The day before he was shot."

"What exactly did Volodya do?"

"He whetted a rather large knife that he carries about his person at all times and threatened to chop the boy into little sausages. But that is as far as it went. I questioned Volodya and am confident that neither he nor any other of my employees had anything to do with the boy's murder. I run this corporation on sound business principles. I read all the latest books. We want to stay nimble, increase market share, and slash costs. But we are not in the business of killing innocent boys."

I wasn't sure why he was telling me all this, unless it was the truth. I remembered his mother boasting about her son's Harvard MBA. I was glad he had put his education to such good use. Or was his story an elaborate ruse to throw me off the track of what had really happened?

"Well, someone is," I said. "And I think it goes back to what Denny Lukin's father did in the Soviet Union, during the Cold War. Ring any bells?"

"No."

"Is the name Ludmilla Belyaeva familiar to you?"

A cautious flicker behind the lizard eyes.

"She is a friend of my mother's."

"And you gave her a gold Cadillac recently?"

"I appreciate everything she does for my mother."

"Is that the only reason?"

"I am a generous man."

"Your mother told me this morning that you and Ludmilla did business together."

Vassily Grigorovich reached out across his desk and made a minute adjustment to a paperweight.

"I do not know how you met my mother, nor would I recommend you having additional conversations with her." His focus shifted from the paperweight to me. "But if you have spoken with her, then you know that she is a garrulous woman who is getting on in years and sometimes grows confused."

She had seemed perfectly lucid to me.

"You know, of course, that Ludmilla was a KGB operative," I said. "During the Cold War, she was privy to many secrets."

"They are worthless now."

Had he already examined everything that Ludmilla was selling and found it wanting?

"Listen to me, Ms. Diamond," he said, stabbing at the paper with one outstretched finger. "Go back to your newspaper. Forget we ever had this conversation. And do not stir things up."

Curiosity overcame fear. "What do you mean?"

But he only reached under his desk and pressed a buzzer. The door opened, and the thuggish thief appeared, carrying my purse, which he deposited on the chair next to me.

"I'm not leaving until he gives back the cash he stole from my wallet," I said.

Vassily Grigorovich spoke sharply in Russian and the foot soldier sheepishly reached into his back pocket, removed the folded bills, and placed them on top of my purse.

"Please accept my apologies for Volodya's deplorable conduct, Ms. Diamond."

My head swiveled. So this was the notorious Volodya. Low brow. Bad skin. Piggy eyes. I should have guessed. Vassily Grigorovich stood up, walked over to his henchman, drew back his arm, and hit him hard in the jaw with an uppercut. I heard a sickening crunch. The man crumpled to the ground and lay without moving. Two other men, hearing the commotion, ran in and began dragging the unconscious Volodya out.

Grigorovich looked pensively at their bent backs. "I do not allow such things in my business. First the Lukin boy. Now you." He tsked and shook his head. "A liability must be dealt with swiftly, like a cancer, before it contaminates the entire operation. I can assure you that Volodya will not bother anyone again."

As the implications of Vassily Grigorovich's words sank in, I shuddered. Then I shuddered again. Because in the instant that the Mafia don had pulled back for the punch, I had seen something dangling from the underside of his upper arm.

It hung from the dark hollow of his armpit, where the cuffed shirt had gaped open for a second. It was an IV shunt. Vassily Grigorovich was either so sick that he needed a steady supply of medicine dripping into his veins or he was an illegal drug user who had found the ultimate way of feeding his addiction.

I didn't want to stick around long enough to find out.

"My men will escort you out now and you will not return," Vassily Grigorovich said. At the door, he cleared his throat. "But Miss Diamond," he said softly, the *ss* hissing, "take heed. We will be watching you."

I looked around frantically for Josh as they led me through the crowds. Soon we were at the back of the property, where a door opened out onto an alley. Hands pushed me through and the door closed behind me.

The alley was brightly lit but I didn't linger. I walked briskly around the corner and back to the front of the nightclub. Shivering on the sidewalk, I scanned a new line of partygoers waiting to get inside. Josh wasn't among them. The doormen spotted me and began moving toward me in a decisive manner, trouble in their eyes. They had already gotten their orders that I was persona non grata. Cursing, I walked back to the alley to call Josh, and as I did so, I saw a familiar rumpled figure slope through the back door. I was pretty sure it was FBI Special Agent Thomas Clavendish.

"Eve," Josh's voice said in my ear, "where did you disappear to? They kept me cooling my jets outside for forty minutes. I threatened to call the police but they said it was a private club and they had the right to refuse admittance to anyone. Why didn't you answer?"

"Oh my God. I think I just saw that FBI agent go inside the club. Through the back entrance."

"Maybe he's working undercover," Josh said.

"Working off his gambling debt is more like it."

"Why don't you follow him?"

"I can't."

"What happened in there?"

"I had a private meeting with Vassily Grigorovich and he denied everything, then kicked me out. I'm around the corner from the club now, in the alley."

"And I'm at your car. Come on over. Oh man, I wish I could have gotten inside. What did he say before he kicked you out?"

"He claims Denny Lukin showed up at his place to defend Lyuba's family's honor and got threatened by one of his henchmen the day before Denny was shot in Griffith Park. But he swears the guy didn't kill Denny. In fact, I get this awful feeling that Vassily Grigorovich is going to kill the henchman, if he hasn't already," I said, telling him about the blow that had knocked Volodya unconscious.

"Wouldn't that be a brilliant move if this guy did kill Denny? Get rid of the only eyewitness."

"It *was* pretty creepy in there. Oh, there you are. Good."

I hung up, relieved to see Josh's figure in the dark. I ran up and his arms enveloped me. It was so comforting, especially now that the adrenaline had worn off and I was starting to feel quivery. I stood for a moment, absorbing his warmth. Then his arms tightened and I thought better of the whole thing and broke free. I just wanted to go home.

This evening had misfired and gotten me nowhere. If the Russian Mafia was involved, we'd never find out, or get killed trying. It was a dead end. Like everything else. I was frustrated, unsure of what to try next. But Clavendish had turned up again. How did he fit in?

Mischa was already zoned out on the back porch when I got home and the light was out. I put on my pajamas and walked into the bedroom closet to lay out clothes for the next day. Immediately, I thought of the silk hatbox. Drained but too wired for sleep, I got the box down and took it into the living room, flipping through documents until I came to a 1946 letter on cheap gray paper that felt almost greasy with age. It was in Russian. Near the bottom the handwriting changed to a child's block printing. What was this? My mother's writing? I put it aside to ask Mischa in the morning and kept looking.

I was in the early 1960s now. I could tell by the clothes and the hairstyles of sultry French teenyboppers. All of a sudden I stopped cold at the image of a striking young woman. She stared into the camera, drop-dead serious in her red kerchief and white blouse, a thick belt encircling her slim waist. It was like looking at my teenage self in the mirror. Except I had never had such presence. She had something of my mother, too. All three of us had the straight classic nose, the large, expressive eyes, the strong curve of jaw. I held it closer, noticed a speck of dust. Brushed it off with my hand. The box had deteriorated over time, sloughing off flecks of cardboard, strands of silk, crumbs from leather frames. But this speck didn't go away. I held the photo up to the light. There, above the young woman's lip, off to the side. It was a beauty mark.

CHAPTER 41

W ho was this woman who resembled me so strikingly? Her features, and her presence in my mother's hatbox, suggested a blood connection. I turned the photo over, hoping for an inscription, but the back was blank.

Frantic now, I plowed through the stacks. Once I thought I saw her posed in front of a sixties car, all fins and chrome and sleek curves, but upon closer inspection, it wasn't her. It took many photos before I found the young woman again. In her twenties now, and in the full bloom of beauty. My mother was with her, the two of them with their arms slung around each other's necks, beaming into the camera. The Eiffel Tower stood in the background. They were in France. I flipped it over. Saw my mother's spidery handwriting. One carelessly tossed-off line, in Russian. I could make out only the last word, deciphered the Cyrillic letters as *Katya*. All of a sudden, I had to know what it said.

I hurried to the kitchen door, flipped on the porch light, ran to the bundle of blankets, and shook Mischa roughly by the shoulder. He sat up immediately.

"Shto, shto?" he said groggily. "Huh, what?"

"What does this mean?" I shoved the photo under his nose.

"Oh, hello, Cousin Eve. I was just dreaming of our dacha, in the south, where each summer—"

"Read it to me," I said ferociously. "Now."

A hurt tone crept into his voice.

"Ah, a pretty woman. She looks like you. But not as angry."

"What does it say?"

He looked at the photo, squinted. Turned it around. Yawned. I felt like strangling him.

"It says, 'Beloved sister Katya.'"

She was my aunt. A beautiful woman named Katya I had never known. I cast back to my earliest memories, but the face stayed maddeningly elusive, out of reach. So like mine and yet not. I couldn't believe it. My mother had a sister she had never talked about. Did this mean I also had cousins, uncles, other relatives? Where did they live? What had become of them?

And why had my mother hidden this away? It might have been instinct. My house was full of ghosts and secrets. The legacy of a lifetime of subterfuge, for fear of the Nazis, for fear of the Sovs, for fear that the FBI would find out my family had Russian roots and deport us. You might laugh, but for my mother it wasn't such a paranoid idea in the early 1960s, with red-baiting U.S. Senator Joe McCarthy on the rampage. After a while, it became a normal state of mind. To dissemble. To be ever vigilant. To be ready on a moment's notice to flee or take on a new identity. I think that adaptability made me a good reporter. It just didn't make me an emotionally healthy human being.

I remembered being invited on a school trip to Central Europe while barely in my teens. Brimming with excitement, I ran home to tell my mother, only to have her burst into tears.

"Why are you crying?" I asked in bewilderment.

"They'll find out about us and put you in a gulag. I'll never see you again."

I had laughed with relief at her great ignorance of world events.

"Aw, Maman, it's 1991, there's nothing to worry about anymore. They're all democracies over there."

But that had only made her more resolute.

"They'd like everyone to believe that. But inside, nothing has changed."

Luckily, my father's logic had prevailed and I'd gone and had the time of my life. Yet in retrospect, I wondered if there had been more concrete reasons for her fear. What had become of Katya and what did she have to do with Sasha Lukin?

"Mischa, do you know this woman? Is she one of our relatives from Russia?"

I was begging him so hard I was crying. I held the photo under his nose and my hands shook.

"I am sorry, Eve. I am not seeing her before."

"Think, Mischa," I said, willing a different answer from him. "She'd be a lot older now. She would have had a hard life. You never heard about a Katya?"

He shook his head.

I should have questioned his response then. If he was my cousin, wouldn't he know? But I was so frantic to learn the truth that I wasn't thinking straight. If Mischa couldn't tell me, I had to find someone who could. And that person was Lukin. He had described Katya to me perfectly, down to the beauty mark. Lukin held the key. Shrugging out of my pajamas and into jeans, I threw on a jacket and drove like a bat out of hell back to Studio City, the two photos of Katya clutched in one hand.

* * *

I had calmed down by the time I pulled up the winding street to his house. I checked my watch. Midnight. But the living room light was on. A shadow moved behind the drapes. Someone was still awake.

Stomping my feet against the cold, I rang the doorbell. The porch light went on.

"Who is it?" came Sasha Lukin's voice.

"Eve Diamond. I know it's late, but I have to show you some photos. It's important."

The spy hole opened and he peered out. "Just a minute," he said.

A series of deadbolts peeled back, then the door opened and he ushered me inside. He had a yellow legal pad filled with Russian writing tucked under one arm and looked distracted.

I followed him to the couch and we sat down. He flipped the pad to a blank page like he was going to take notes, then seemed to decide against it and shoved the pad under some coffee table books.

I laid the portrait of Katya on the table, hoping he wouldn't notice the tremor in my hands. The photo of the Eiffel Tower girls stayed in my purse for now.

"This is who I remind you of." My breath came fast. "Who is she?"

There was no answer. All the blood seemed to drain from his face.

"Her name's Katya, isn't it?"

His lips moved but nothing came out.

"Look, all I know about my mother's family is they were Francophile Russians who settled in Nice after the revolution. Then, the same day that I cover your son's murder"—here I had the grace to flinch—"a guy lands on my doorstep claiming he's my Russian cousin and you start making moon eyes like I'm your long-lost love from across the generations. And this Katya, who I've just learned I'm related to, is the missing link. It all comes back to her, somehow, and I need to know how."

I picked up the portrait and slapped it back down. It made a satisfying sound, like a winning card in a Vegas poker game.

"Who . . . is . . . she?" I demanded, punctuating each word with a slamming fist on the wooden table.

"My . . . my wife," Lukin said.

"This isn't your wife." I was furious with contempt.

"Yes."

"No. Your wife's name is Irina. And even when she was younger, it's not the same face."

"My . . . my first wife."

He touched the photo timidly, caressed its scalloped edges.

"Katya. Yekaterina." He spoke in low, soft Russian that needed no translation, because endearments are the same in any language.

For a long time, he stared at the photo. A lone tear welled and he wiped it away with the sleeve of his cardigan.

"You look so much like her. The same blood-and-milk complexion."

"Blood and milk?"

"It's an old expression. Skin so pale you can see the veins beneath. She had it too. You could be our . . ."

"Daughter," I said.

Our breath caught. A question formed in his eyes.

"How did you come by this photo?"

I opened my mouth to speak but the words lodged. I cleared my throat. Tried again. Gave up. Pulled out the photo of my mother and Katya at the Eiffel Tower and laid it down next to the portrait. We bent to observe the two young women smiling prettily into the camera, arms draped around each other, the wind tugging open their coats and exposing dresses that ended at their knees. They wore high heels on the cobblestones, and purses and scarves dangled from their shoulders. Their hair was styled in those flips popular at the time, and even through the black-and-white print, you could see the flush in their cheeks, the glow in their eyes, and the glossy dark of their lipstick. After a time I turned the second photo over so he could see the inscription.

"The other woman was my mother."

Lukin scrutinized the two young women. How young and happy they looked, lips parted slightly in excitement. I had seen her only as a suburban Valley housewife, but my mother had lived another life in a faraway country before my brother and I had been born. Before her naturally high spirits gave way to domestic drudgery, a chronically depressed husband, the displacement of immigrant life in sunny Southern California.

Lukin heaved a sigh. "I remember your mother. I remember every detail of that trip."

"What?" I burst out. "You knew her? You were there?"

Lukin nodded. "It was 1962. Katya and I had been invited to Paris for a scientific conference. It was our first trip to the West. We were giddy, feverish. We left a drab, gray world and emerged into Technicolor. You can't imagine what it was like for us. Merchandise piled high in the stores, like riches from a pirate's chest. Food shops overflowing with *fromages* and salami and fruits and vegetables. Billboards and ads and fashion. It was sensory overload. We'd go back to our hotel room and draw the curtains, catch our breath. We were consumer-autistic."

"Was Katya Russian, then?" I said. "I mean born there?"

"She was from St. Petersburg," Lukin said.

Then she couldn't be my mother's sister, I thought.

"An old artistic family that had suffered much in the Stalin years," he continued. "Katya's mother was dead. Her father died at hard labor in the gulag. He had been captured by the Allies during the Great Patriotic War and spent time in an American POW camp. Stalin had it in for those poor bastards when they got home, he thought they were Fifth Columnists. And it was known she had family in the West."

Well, that took care of that. My grandfather had spent World War II doing forced labor in German factories and ruining his health. He had come home to France and died in 1946. My grandmother had told me so during our endless card games. And as far as I knew, my mother had no siblings. How could a sister have ended up in Russia, anyway? The whole thing was ludicrous, a fantastic trick of bone structure and lighting that made two women a generation and a continent apart look related.

And yet. Other things did track—the relatives in the West, the old family in St. Petersburg. And the ache of intimacy in Lukin's voice, his genuine shock at seeing the photo. But if Katya really was my aunt, why didn't Mischa recognize her? A second flicker went through me then, that something was not right. But I was being bombarded by heavy emotional revelations, and I so *wanted* to believe.

"I was urged not to marry her because her family was politically unreliable," Lukin went on. "But we believed that love would conquer everything."

"How did Katya know she had family in the West?"

"Her father told her, right before the KGB took him away. She was five. He made her memorize an address in Nice and some names. Like a secret prayer she could never say out loud. When and if the time came, she was to look them up."

"And the time came in France?"

"She posted a letter our first day in Paris. Your family must have been long gone from that address, but someone remembered them and got the letter to your mother. Anya, wasn't it?" he said with a shy, sideways look.

"Yes." I nodded, feeling a warm flush of certainty. No one outside the family called her Anya. To everyone else in her adopted country, my mother was Anna.

"The last day of the conference, your mother showed up at our hotel, clutching Katya's letter. She was all of seventeen. She'd taken the train from Nice. She was trembling, fearful of a KGB trap. She hadn't known she had a sister, you see. Until she got Katya's letter. And she didn't tell anyone she was coming. She feared they would have forbidden it. Those were tense times. Khrushchev was blockading Berlin. Kennedy had just given his famous speech. For all anyone knew, a third world war was looming. And your mother's family was terribly anti-Communist."

"They sure were."

"It's not like we would have tried to recruit her," Lukin said mildly.

"Maybe from their perspective, it wasn't such an outrageous assumption," I said.

"Not everyone in Russia believed."

"But you were a party member!"

"You had to be, to work, to travel. Don't you understand? No, of course you don't." He shook his head rue-fully. "You're too young. Everything has come too easy to you. You're like my sons."

His eyes grew glassy and he stared at the floor.

"So what was it like, this reunion of the sisters?" I asked after a time, still not sure they could *be* sisters.

"They clutched each other the whole time. We strolled through the Latin Quarter, St. Germain. We ate ice cream in a café. We talked nonstop."

"And you visited the Eiffel Tower?"

"Yes," Lukin said. "Your mother had a camera. She asked me to take this picture."

He touched it reverentially and we stared at the cellu-loid image, incontrovertible proof, more than a half cen-tury later, that the afternoon had really happened.

"Katya gave her sister this portrait," he said, fingering the edges of the other photo. "Of herself as a Young Pio-neer."

"Did you and Katya ever see my mother again after that trip?"

"We had given our KGB minders in Paris the slip to meet your mother and when they realized it, they feared we had defected and there was hell to pay. They didn't let me go abroad again until the early 1980s."

"Why *didn't* you and Katya defect in Paris? You could have gone to the French police and demanded asylum."

Our easy camraderie evaporated.

"It is not so easy to abandon one's country, Ms. Dia-mond. And anyway, they knew we would never do that."

"Why not?"

"They made us leave Yuri behind."

"Who?"

"Our son. He was their insurance we'd come back."

I recalled my grandmother's story about Natasha at the villa in Nice, tearfully explaining that she had to go back because her husband was in St. Petersburg, a semihostage to assure her return. The Communists didn't need chains when they could bind people so tightly with love.

But I was confused.

"You and Katya had a child together?"

With his newest revelation, I had gained a cousin.

"Is he in America too? He must be middle-aged by now."

Lukin went to the window, stood at the curtains, and yanked them apart. He stared into the twinkling darkness and I thought I heard the faint strains of "God Rest Ye, Merry Gentlemen."

"First let me finish telling you about the Paris trip and your mother."

He paced the room. "Your mother was engaged to her childhood sweetheart. A Frenchman of Russian descent like her. They were emigrating to America and she told us it would be too dangerous to correspond."

Reluctant to abandon this intriguing new topic of Yuri, but seduced by tales about my mother, I expressed surprise that she didn't want to stay in touch.

"You have to understand the times. She was a creature of the Cold War."

"But the Cold War ended long before she died. And she never said a word. She left me thinking I was alone in the world." I paused as something registered. "You said my mother was engaged to a French Russian in 1962. But my father was from Eastern Europe. And they didn't marry until the early 1970s."

I tried to remember how my parents had met. Mutual friends, they always said. Had I ever asked for the details?

"Did she mention his name? Show you a photo?"

"She only spoke of how happy they were."

I leaned against the couch, squirming in frustration.

"What happened to Katya?"

Lukin stared at his hands. "Eventually we divorced. It was not my choice. I loved her very much."

"Then why . . ." I blurted out.

"She blamed me for something that happened," he said softly.

"I'm sure it wasn't your fault."

He gave me a long, speculative look. "That's not the way she saw it. She couldn't stand the sight of me. She had a nervous breakdown. I cared for her as best I could, but eventually I conceded defeat."

"I'm sorry."

He shrugged. "Not a day goes by that I don't think about it. But that was another life."

"Is Katya still alive?"

He turned away. "We aren't in touch."

"But as far as you know, she never left Russia?"

My aunt. She'd be in her sixties now.

Sorrow pooled in his eyes. "I just don't know."

CHAPTER 42

"Come to the kitchen," Lukin said, "and I will make tea."

He retrieved the notepad from beneath the books and padded off.

Quivering with nervous exhaustion, I followed.

"Is it mountain tea?" I asked, thinking of Ludmilla.

He put the water to boil, slid the notepad into a drawer, and pulled out a canister of loose tea leaves.

"Darjeeling. I hope that is all right," he said.

We sipped our tea in silence, all talked out. My brain was spinning like a top, gyrating around half-remembered stories. But I also had a job to do and it was clear that Katya had opened the floodgates to this man's psyche.

"Mr. Lukin?" I began.

"Sasha. We must do away with all this formality. We are practically related."

"Then you must call me Eve." I gave him a wan smile. "But Mr. Lukin, oops, I mean Sasha, forgive me if this is painful but in light of what's happened to Denny and Nicolai, I'm just curious about Yuri. . . ."

I trailed off. His head swiveled and his features grew sharp.

"He was drafted into that abomination called the Afghan War, where so many families lost sons. In battle, of course, but also through hazing. Their army is barbaric, cruel, and corrupt."

"I thought most of the intelligentsia were able to get draft exemptions. Pay off the right person. Keep the kid in college. Or at least away from the frontlines? You were *nomenklatura*. It should have been a slam dunk."

Lukin hugged his elbows.

"I tried, God knows I tried. But under communism, who ever knew? Maybe I angered someone high up in the party hierarchy."

"Did Yuri want to enlist?"

"He was terrified."

"Then why couldn't you pull some strings? With your contacts and clout."

"It was exactly because of that that I couldn't."

He sat next to me and lowered his head.

"There are things you don't know about me, Ms. Diamond."

"Eve. We're practically family, remember?"

"It is only because you remind me so much of her that I can even speak of these things."

"I'm honored at your trust."

"She never understood," he said, "why I had to do it."

"But I'll understand." I grabbed one of his hands. It was cold and knobby and I rubbed it with my warm ones.

"What happened to Yuri?" I said softly.

There was a pained silence. When he finally spoke, it was with the detached tone of a man reciting a story that happened long ago to someone else.

"When they told me I could go abroad again in the early 1980s," Lukin said, "I was ecstatic. Then representatives of the security organs came to me. They made polite propositions. I turned them down. They returned several days later with fewer smiles. Again, I said no. To my surprise, they let me go anyway. A scientific conference in

Jakarta. Such a weight lifted off me when I stepped from that plane into the humid air.

"But they just wanted me to taste freedom before approaching me again. They were so clever that way. When the next conference invitation came, they paid me another visit."

"What did they want?"

"They wanted me to report on colleagues."

"I heard that's how they did it. The quid pro quo for going abroad was a debriefing by your neighborhood KGB troll."

"Again I refused," Lukin said. "I was so disillusioned by then. The system was morally bankrupt and we all knew it. But they made threats. No more trips abroad. A demotion. They'd take away our privileges at the special stores. They seemed almost frantic. Later I learned that they suspected one of my colleagues was passing on information to the Americans. A good friend of mine from Moscow State University. But I am getting ahead of myself. All they told me at the time was that everyone did it. My colleagues reported on me, too. It was just the way things worked. But Katya and I agreed that I couldn't compromise."

"It must have been a difficult decision."

"No," he said with simple dignity. "There are things more important than Western chocolates and trips abroad."

"Bravo."

"But they came back. They had learned that luxuries and trips had no hold on me. So they asked themselves, what is most precious to him? And there they began to apply pressure."

A feeling of dread was creeping up my throat. "Where?" I asked, already half knowing.

"Yuri," he said. "They threatened to send him to the frontlines in Afghanistan. It was 1984. Russian boys were dying like flies in the most horrible ways, or returning home in wheelchairs, critically burned, missing eyes and limbs.

"Katya begged me to do as they asked. But I explained calmly why I couldn't. It was evil. A Faustian bargain that would only lead to more evil. The next thing we knew, Yuri was seized from his dormitory at Moscow State University in the middle of the night and put on a cargo plane to a military base in the Far East. Like in the worst of the Stalin years.

"Katya couldn't eat, drink, sleep. But I held firm. I banged my head against the wall until it bled but I didn't waver. Instead, I made secret pacts. *Please God, let him live. And I will dedicate myself to you. I will renounce science and everything that I love.* It did no good.

"Yuri's unit came under heavy fire outside Kabul. He was killed by a mortar round. They assured us that death had been instantaneous."

Lukin slumped in his seat. His body curled like a caterpillar that has been poked with a stick. A long time passed before he continued.

"After we got the telegram, nothing mattered anymore. Katya and I should have turned to each other for comfort. Instead, our marriage fell apart. She wouldn't speak to me. She just reproached me with huge, gaunt eyes. Eventually she moved out, screaming that she hated me, that I had destroyed the family with my pride, that she hoped I suf-fered as much in life as Yuri had suffered in death. Despite all this, I still loved her. I followed after her like a dog. I begged. And she just stared through me. 'In my heart,' she said, 'you are already dead.'"

"That's horrible."

Lukin turned away. "Eventually I went to the organs. I told them I wanted to emigrate and that they owed it to me, after what had happened. I was desperate to leave Russia. I saw Yuri's ghost on every street corner, in each room of our flat. Every brown-haired woman standing in line with her net bag reminded me of Katya. The organs agreed. They let me go."

I studied him. "Just like that, huh?"

"Yes."

This was it, I thought. The unraveling has begun.

"I'm afraid I know too much about the KGB to believe that," I said. "How exactly did you buy your freedom?"

Lukin looked away.

"You must tell me."

There was a silence.

"Mr. Lukin, someone's trying to kill your family. Don't you want them caught?"

He looked extremely pained. "Yes," he said.

"So then, what's the motive? Why is someone doing this?"

"It dates back to those days of which I am just telling you," he said calmly.

"How are you so sure?"

"Because whoever murdered Denny sent a message."

"What? A phone call? A letter? There was no message found on his body, we've already gone over that."

"Oh, but there was. Something whose significance only I would recognize."

"What?"

"The watch."

The Red Army watch. I'd fixated on it, but never discovered its true significance.

"Denny would never wear such an odious thing," Lukin said. "Not even in jest. He knew what it meant to me."

"So he didn't buy it at a swap meet several weeks ago?"

"I never saw it before."

"Is it possible he got it from Max? As a joke?"

"Whoever killed him strapped it on his wrist after he was dead. As a sign to me."

"But of what?"

"That the past has come alive again."

"Can you be more specific? What in the past?"

"As soon as you told me about the watch, I knew I could never go to the police," he said hoarsely.

"Your kids are getting killed, Sasha. Why the hell not?"

He stood up. Walked back into the living room and up to the big picture window. Stared into the black night. I followed him, sat on the couch. Waited.

Lukin turned. His face was a hollow mask.

"Because there is no statute of limitation on treason."

CHAPTER 43

What do you mean, there's no statute of limitation on treason?" I said.

He sighed heavily and turned to me.

"You have to understand that all the things that had been dear to me—discretion, moral elegance, irony, respect for ideas, an aesthetic sense of life—became impossible in the world where I found myself after Yuri died and my wife left. I became an animal."

"You became a spy."

He winced, buried his face in his hands, and was silent for a long while. Far away, a dog barked. A car gave a soft whoosh as it passed, its headlights illuminating the sky like heat lightning.

I waited.

"I became privy to information that certain people wanted and I conveyed that information," Lukin said.

"How, exactly?"

"Two months after I arrived in Los Angeles, word came from Moscow that I was to apply for a job at Rathburn International."

"But you were a Russian émigré. How could you get a security clearance?"

"This particular job didn't require it. Rathburn also does nondefense work. Once I was hired, another employee would make contact. One who did have a security clearance and wanted to pass on documents. For the right fee. They would be left in waterproof containers inside the toilet tanks in bathrooms near the cafeteria. Simple, but effective."

"So this employee fed you documents and you passed them on to Moscow?" I asked, aghast.

"Yes, but not the real ones."

"What do you mean, not real ones?"

"I had my own plan by then. Clavendish and I met and he doctored them. Only then did I pass them on."

Was Clavendish a good guy after all?

"He was in on this too?"

"I told you he came to visit me soon after I arrived in the United States. Somehow he had my address. And he knew."

"He's FBI. That's what they do." I leaned back against the couch, considering what I had just learned. "So you and Clavendish cooked up a plan to pass on fake defense secrets to the Sovs? You agreed to become a double agent?"

"I don't know how Clavendish altered the documents," Lukin admitted.

"Yeah, because, wait a minute." I struggled to sort things out in the battered road map of my mind. "During all this, he was playing his own double game. There was a scandal with a female KGB agent. They were having an affair. And they found top-secret defense documents in his bedroom."

"Of course they did," Lukin said.

I recalled the newspaper stories and something slid home.

"You were the third spy, weren't you? The one who was never caught."

"I was working for *your* government, remember?"

A new and startling possibility arose. Maybe the FBI had been telling the truth all along back in 1985. What if Clavendish was clean but they just couldn't make it public because it would blow his cover?

"How did you pass on the documents? It wasn't a matter of posting them to Moscow, KGB directorate. Were there dead drops?"

"Yes, and a cutout."

"Which is?"

"A third party. An intermediary. Who passes on information to and from Moscow. So there's no direct connection."

"And who was this cutout?"

"I have no idea. We only spoke on the phone."

Was this the third spy, then? A bona fide mole and KGB agent. Who had sat incognito on the West Coast, plying his trade unnoticed for years.

"What was his name?"

"I knew him only as Luka."

Oh, please, let me be wrong, I thought.

"My mother has a letter in her papers, from before I was born. It's from a man named Luka," I said, afraid of the door I had just opened.

I felt the molecules in the air tighten and charge with energy.

"Luka is a common nickname," Sasha Lukin said offhandedly.

I tried to match his level of cool disinterest. "Did you ever learn his real name?"

"I cannot say that I did."

Every fiber in my body screamed that he was lying.

"I'm sure this is the man who knew my mother," I said.

"Your mother," he echoed.

"I have a love letter he wrote to her," I repeated. "You must tell me the truth. Please. This is my family's history, not just politics or a story. And I know nothing."

Lukin sighed. "I suppose it can do no damage anymore. The Cold War is long over. And we have learned that the cutout himself recently passed away in Moscow. Probably thinking, to the very end, what a service he provided to his motherland and at great personal risk. When it was all doctored lies. His name was Stepan Domashny."

The world exploded into a million fragments.

So much for no damage. Stepan Domashny had been my mother's lover. He was a KGB spy. Was that what lay at the root of my mother's paranoia?

"You must tell me everything you know," I said, wondering whether life as I knew it was about to be turned completely upside down.

"I wasn't allowed to know anything about him. There would be phone calls. We always spoke in code. From his accent, he was French."

"This must have been the fiancé my mother mentioned in Paris back in 1962."

Had Stepan Domashny already been a Communist back then? Had my mother known? How could she have stomached it?

Unless . . . Unless my mother had been a spy too.

I swallowed hard.

"Did you ever deal with a woman cutout? Or did you ever hear rumors about a woman who worked with him?"

"Never." He shook his head for emphasis. I exhaled with relief. Did he know how badly I needed to hear that?

But I still couldn't picture it. The United States didn't let in Bolsheviks, so Stepan Domashny must have lied about his political affiliation. They would have arrived in an era when the FBI was so paranoid it even videotaped worshippers at the local Russian Orthodox church. At what point had he told my mother the truth? Or had she stumbled across a radio transmitter and cipher book hidden in a closet?

I imagined the volcanic fights that would have ensued. Unable to reconcile her beliefs with her lover, she would have left him. Eventually she met my dad. Married him. I hadn't been born until the late 1970s. And from a very early age, I recalled my father's silent presence. I didn't think I was Stepan Domashny's daughter.

"I'd leave a preset number of milk bottles on the front porch, and he'd know a package was coming," Lukin said. "It went on that way until shortly before the regime collapsed."

Stepan Domashny had continued spying for the Soviets until the bitter end. And my mother had taken his secret to her grave.

Another car zoomed past. Far off, I heard the drone of a small plane, the tentative calling of a songbird. Dawn must be at hand.

"What happened to the Rathburn employee who fed you the documents?" I asked.

"He was arrested in 1987 and sentenced to twenty-five years in prison."

"I don't remember a trial."

"That's because he pled out. In Washington, D.C. He had been asking for more money but Moscow directorate was cheap and refused. He had debts and was getting desperate, so he flew to Washington to ask the Soviet embassy directly, if you can believe such stupidity. The

FBI found documents in his hotel room that night and arrested him."

"What was his name?"

"Chip Johnson."

"Is he still in prison?"

"The United States Supreme Court overturned his conviction in August 2001. Johnson wasn't a bright man, but he had extremely savvy lawyers who claimed his FBI interrogators in Washington had coerced and beaten him into pleading guilty. They used the loaded word *torture*."

"A month later, that argument wouldn't have stood a snowball's chance in hell," I said. "But if he's alive and he's out, could he be the Prisoner of Memory?"

"I looked into it. He's housebound. In poor health. I do not think so."

"He could be directing others."

"He's got dementia praecox on top of everything else. It's not him."

"But we have to do more digging, make sure some relative of his isn't coming after you for revenge. Because it sounds like whoever's blackmailing you could be Russian or American. But I still don't understand why. From what you've told me, you're an unsung Cold War hero. What have you left out?"

There was a long silence. Then Lukin said, "The letters mention things that only a KGB operative would know. Back in Russia . . . I cooperated . . . there was . . . I caused . . . the regime made me—"

He broke off.

"Wouldn't your later work for the Americans exonerate you of treason?"

He stared at his hands. "I don't think so."

This kind and gentle man made me want to scream with frustration.

"So what you're saying is that even though someone is killing your family, you can't go to the police because they'd arrest you for something you did a generation ago on behalf of a Cold War superpower that no longer exists?"

He looked at me, eyes filled with pain.

"It would destroy everything I've built so carefully over the past twenty years. I was a broken man when I came here. Irina put me back together, piece by piece. We made a life. I got a second chance. My poor Denny is gone but I must be a father to Nicolai, a husband to Irina. All that would be taken from me. Yet again."

"We've got to find the murderer ourselves, then," I said.

"We?"

"But you have to tell me everything."

"How do I know you're not just using me to get a story?"

"Because I am the blood," I said, recalling Mischa's words. "Or as close as we can get. Because a week ago, I didn't have any relatives in the world and now there's Katya, and you. And your family. So I've got to help. I'm your niece by marriage, Sasha," I said. "I care about you. But I need to know exactly what you did during the Cold War."

Still he didn't say anything.

"Look," I said in desperation. "I tracked down the spy who brought Clavendish down. Ludmilla Belyaeva. She's living here in L.A. and she supposedly had a lover high up in the KGB. Maybe they've reunited for one final filthy Cold War trick. Or maybe she's teamed up with the Russian Mafia to blackmail you," I said, thinking of the gold Cadillac.

Was that why she had been so skittish and gun-happy when we showed up?

"But why would they wait so long?" I mused. "They could have gone after you years ago."

Lukin's voice quickened. "Maybe it was not possible. Maybe this person was in prison. Or didn't emigrate until recently."

That made me think of his gangly computer friend.

"How well do you know Victor Golodny?" I asked. "Could he have worked for the KGB as Ludmilla's handler?"

"Golodny was a teenager in 1985. A brilliant, absent-minded child. He is like a son to me. He reminds me of what Yuri might have grown into."

"Well, okay then, but I think we do have to pursue the Chip Johnson angle," I said.

My thoughts returned to Thomas Clavendish. His checkered past. His affair with Ludmilla. His gambling debts. How he had played both sides of the Curtain and recast himself once the Cold War ended as a Russian Mafia expert. What had he been doing in Vassily Grigorovich's nightclub tonight?

"What about your FBI pal?"

"Impossible. What would the motive be?"

"Maybe he needed the money. I've heard—"

"I have known Thomas Clavendish for decades," Lukin said, looking like he might cry. "He is a man of integrity."

"Okay, you're shooting down everyone I can think of. But I'm at a disadvantage here. Level with me, Sasha. It's our only chance."

Lukin looked around for a way out. But it was only me and him, with the blackness of night crouched outside, the grandfather clock ticking its way toward dawn. Its gold-tipped hands stood at 4:09 a.m. The hour when defenses are at their lowest ebb, when the human body and psyche are weakest and most vulnerable. It was the hour of betrayal, when knives plunge into hearts and murderers swear oaths of secrecy, only to break them before the light.

Lukin looked glumly at his shoes. "I couldn't let him die," he began.

"Who?"

"Yuri."

My jaw dropped, my brain buzzed, a jillion questions swirled in my head. Was this another one of his subterfuges? I took a breath to begin my next question, but the words never left my mouth. There were four sharp pops, then breaking glass, the whiz of bullets, and a car screeching away. Next to me, Lukin jerked back against the couch, making a gurgling noise. Still holding his hand, I dove for the floor, yanking him down with me.

CHAPTER 44

*T*oo late, I realized that as Lukin had paced in front of his living room window, the curtains had been open. Anyone who drove past would have seen us, deep in conversation. I flashed back to the cars I'd heard whooshing past at such an odd time of night in this quiet neighborhood. Someone hadn't liked what he'd seen.

I tensed, listening for the sound of someone trying to break into the house, realizing that one kick from a booted foot would shatter the rest of the picture window. But all was silent. We had just become victims of L.A.'s most odious criminal export: the drive-by shooting.

I looked over and saw that the front of Lukin's broadcloth shirt was splattered in crimson. His hand had tightened around mine like a claw.

"Don't leave me, Katya," he gasped, then lapsed into Russian.

I patted his hand. With the other, I reached into my purse and called 911. Neighbors had beaten me to it. From outside came the sound of sirens, then the aborted wail as they were switched off. Crazy patterns of red light danced on the ceiling. I ran to open the door and it was only when I raised my arm to release the deadbolt that I noticed the streak of red across the forearm of my sweater.

"Over there," I called to the ambulance technician, pointing to Lukin, who lay beside the coffee table, writhing in pain. I feared he might die of shock, or have a heart attack, before they could get him stabilized. Another paramedic came at me, brandishing what looked like poultry shears, and I shied away from him, saying I was okay. He ignored me and cut away my sweater, exposing a bullet streak that ran up my arm like a highway carved into my skin.

"It's just a flesh wound," I said.

"You're not dead yet?" he asked in delight, adopting a mock British accent from *Monty Python*.

I let him apply a stinging salve and then ointment and wrap my arm up in a bandage.

Over on the other side of the living room, two paramedics were loading Lukin onto a gurney, already hooking him up to an IV.

He managed to get out that he wanted to be taken to Queen of Angels Hospital in Hollywood, where his wife and son were.

"Bad night for the family, or what?" the paramedic said.

"Bad week," I said, and left it at that. "Can I ride with him? He's a . . . we're distantly related."

But they said another ambulance was coming for me. I started to tell them I was perfectly fine, then stopped. It wouldn't hurt to be in the hospital. That would put me closer to the Lukins, and to getting some answers. But I told the paramedics I'd drive myself, holding up my perfectly fine right arm.

Then the police arrived. I explained I'd been interviewing Lukin when the shots came through the living room window.

"At four-oh-nine a.m.?"

"It was a long story. About forty years' worth."

When I told them Lukin's name, they looked at each other. They knew all about Denny's murder, the hit-and-run on Nicolai.

"Someone really has it out for this family," they said, shaking their heads and getting on the phone to the detectives.

"He was about to tell me something important when the shots came," I said. "He said he was a spy during the Cold War."

"They're gonna want to talk to you. Get a look at your notes."

I had rushed out of the house in such a hot panic that I hadn't even brought a notepad. For that I was now glad. My eye fell on the two photos from my mother's box still lying on the coffee table.

When the cops went outside, I sauntered over to the table and scooped them up, slipped them into my purse. Unless you were family, they didn't mean a hell of a lot.

"Think he'll make it?" I asked the cops innocently when they came back in.

"EMTs say the bullet missed most of his vital organs. But it's still in there. They'll know more after X-rays. They may have to reroute part of his gut."

The ambulance tore off, lights and sirens blaring. Outside, neighbors massed like shoals of fish. The bolder ones crowded around the front door, asking respectful questions.

"This is a crime scene," the policeman intoned, after a bare-bones explanation of what had happened. "Please go back to your homes."

While the crime techs were busy in the living room, I was suddenly acutely aware that none of the Lukins was home. What if I could find one of the Prisoner of Memory letters? I'd get it translated, and it might give me a clue about the murderer.

I drifted to the edge of the living room to see if anyone would stop me but they all seemed busy with their own tasks. I took a step into the kitchen. Still nothing. I walked to the window, pretended to look out, half expecting to hear a voice call me back, but there was only a low murmur from the other room. I turned around. The kitchen was empty. I pulled out a drawer and grabbed a tea towel, pretended to dab at my forehead in case anyone was looking. Then, still holding the towel, I walked through the kitchen and into what looked like a spare bedroom. If anyone asked, I'd say I was looking for the bathroom. But I made my way unchallenged through that room and up a set of stairs into a glass-paneled room that appeared to be Lukin's office. I froze, listening for voices, footsteps. Still nothing. Now I ran to his desk and used the tea towel to pull out drawers and flip through papers with my knuckles, an annoying and laborious task. I didn't see anything that looked remotely like a letter from the Prisoner of Memory, just neatly labeled files with bills and documents. Where would he keep them? I tugged on another drawer but it was locked. Pulling open the center drawer, I looked for the key. Then I felt under the desk with the tops of my fingers to see if he had taped it to the underside, but the wood was smooth and bare. It didn't really surprise me. The letters probably weren't there anyway. Lukin would have stashed them in a more secure place where Irina couldn't get hold of them. I cast my eyes around. If I were Lukin, where would I hide the evidence of my treason?

I walked over to the fireplace mantel, plunged my arm

deep inside vases, came out with only sticky cobwebs. After a while, I gave up. They could be anywhere in this big house.

Creeping back down the stairs, I made my way to the kitchen, and opened the freezer, because I had read that people sometimes keep important documents there. But the Lukins' freezer was the usual conglomeration of frozen vegetables and meats plus plastic baggies filled with homemade pelmeni.

I was giving up, ready to walk out, when I remembered the yellow legal pad Lukin had dropped into a drawer as he made tea. Ears cocked for approaching footsteps, I pulled it open, found the notepad, and saw a salutation and three pages of a letter. It was in Russian. Sasha Lukin had been in the middle of a letter when I pounded on his door and interrupted him. I tore the corrugated pages off, folded the letter into a tiny square, and stuck it down my bra, where it poked unpleasantly against my flesh. In the living room, the police looked at me with surprise and I knew they'd forgotten I was there. They told me I'd better get to the hospital and I agreed and murmured that I had been in the bathroom.

As I pulled away from the curb, I transferred the offending paper to my purse. I'd get Mischa to translate it as soon as I got back home. I thought I heard a car engine start up on the hill above me, so I drove slowly, waiting for it to appear in my rearview, but although I sat at the bottom of the hill for two minutes, it never did.

Queen of Angels is an old dowager of a hospital in Hollywood. In the dawn emptiness of a Saturday morning, I got there in twenty minutes. Whoever was behind me had long ago evaporated. I recalled the Mafia don's threat and wondered if he had set a tail on me. But then I put my paranoia down to sleeplessness and walked in.

After sitting in the emergency room for an hour and a half, I got a nice plastic intake bracelet and a new bandage from a taciturn doctor who assured me how lucky I was that the bullet had missed the bone. I also learned that surgery to remove a bullet near the stomach could take three hours or more.

My bracelet and bandage were the perfect costume. I looked like I belonged. I walked down a long corridor to get to the other side of the building, then took a random elevator upstairs and found myself on the brain injuries floor. I tried again, figuring that Sasha was probably in surgery on an internal medicine ward, and that I might as well go and see if I could find Nicolai and Irina, who I knew would be sleeping on a cot in his room on the fifth floor. Dawn had come and gone hours ago, leaving the low gray winter light of tundras and humpback whales, lichen and sealskins.

I took the elevator up and stepped out.

Hospital attendants in scrubs scurried by on obscure errands. Janitors pushed mops. My cell phone rang, absurdly loud in that hushed place, and I grabbed it quickly.

"Eve?" I recognized Mischa's voice. "Where are you? I am worry."

"I'm fine," I said.

"Is good to hear. But your bed . . . you not come home last night?"

"Right. I'm at Queen of Angels Hospital. Someone tried to kill Sasha Lukin early this morning as I was interviewing him. They shot through his living room window. He'll live, but the bullet lodged in his stomach."

"Bozhe moi!" Mischa said. "Eve, you must be careful. Will you come home now?"

"No. I'll be tied up here for several hours. I want to find out how Lukin is doing after surgery."

"I see."

"Mischa? I still don't know who's behind this. Stay home and wait for me. Okay?"

I heard his smirk through the phone line. "Where you think I am go?"

"I don't know. But just sit tight, I've got a letter I need you to translate."

"Of course, Cousin Eve. Is no problem. I await your return."

I had been squatting in the hallway while I talked. Now I straightened up and saw someone turn the corner and move down the hall in a manner I could only describe as skulking. What was Ludmilla Belyaeva doing here, on a weekend morning in a hospital miles from where she lived?

CHAPTER 45

Ludmilla," I called. She whipped around, gave me a fearful look, then hurried down the hall. I put on a burst of speed to catch her. I grabbed her plump upper arm and she gasped and pulled back.

"What are you doing here?"

"Visiting a friend," she squeaked.

"At . . ." I looked at my watch ". . . eight-thirty on Saturday morning?"

She had been on her way to the elevators. What mischief had she gotten up to?

"I'm calling security," I announced, tightening my grip. "Let me go."

"What are you doing on Nicolai Lukin's floor?"

"Nicolai Lukin?" Her face drew a momentary blank, then recognition kicked in.

"Nice try," I said. "Security!" I bellowed. Then to her: "He better be alive."

I remembered the gun she had pulled on me last time. Yanking a very large and heavy bag off her shoulder, I heaved it across the floor. It skittered like a bowling ball.

"You're going to break it," she cried, reaching into her pockets.

"Oh no, you don't," I said, figuring she must be hiding the gun there.

I pinned her wrists together.

"Security!" I screeched. "I need security!"

A drowsy-looking janitor peered from around a corner and saw a young woman manhandling an older lady.

"Help," I pleaded. "She could be a murderer."

With one well-aimed kick, Ludmilla Belyaeva sent me flying. She ran down the hall, snatched up her bag, and took off.

A full five minutes later, two uniformed security guards came panting up, followed by the janitor, who pointed at me.

"She's the one," the janitor said. "Arrest her."

"Me?" I said. "It was that lady. You don't realize, she's a former Soviet spy, a KGB operative." I stopped, realizing how insane I sounded. "Oh, never mind," I said. "We've got to get to Nicolai Lukin's room. Quick. She may have poisoned him. He's supposed to be under twenty-four-hour armed guard; you know about this case, right?"

I filled them in.

The security guards checked on their walkie-talkies and got a room number. We ran over there, but the LAPD officer at the door—and I was happy to see there was one—wouldn't let me through.

"What's going on?" I heard Irina Lukin say from inside. There followed a muffled conversation to make sure that Nicolai was still alive.

"He is sleeping," Irina announced. "See. The machines are on. A nurse came in and checked twenty minutes ago. Everything is fine."

She shuffled out in her slippers to find the cause of the commotion, and when she saw me her lip curled.

"What are you doing here? Go away and leave us in peace. You have caused enough trouble."

"I'm sorry to be the bearer of bad news," I said, "but someone tried to kill your husand and me earlier this morning. Sasha was shot. He's going to live, but he's in surgery right now. He asked the ambulance to bring him here."

Irina's face froze in shock.

"Talk to ER if you don't believe me. But the reason I called the guards is because as I was walking down the hall, I saw a former KGB agent named Ludmilla Belyaeva. And I was afraid she had come here to harm your son. I'm sorry."

Irina Lukin blinked in disbelief. "Why would a KGB agent want to harm my son?" she said, looking over her shoulder to the room where Nicolai slept.

"I don't know. That's what I'm trying to find out."

I wanted to ask if she knew her husband was a spy during the Cold War, but I bit my tongue and kept quiet. Everything would be coming out soon enough, once the police got hold of him.

Irina Lukin's nostrils flared and a muscle in her jaw twitched.

"Out," she said. "Get out of my sight and don't come back."

"I'm going," I said. I probably would have done the same thing, in her shoes. And she didn't even know the whole story yet about her husband's Cold War activities. But then, as it turned out, neither did I.

Driving up Cove Avenue, I did my usual scan and saw a car pull out several houses ahead of me. It was a dark blue American car and I wondered if it could be Clavendish's. But I had also been an entire night without sleep and didn't trust my instincts anymore. Why would the retiring FBI agent be waiting outside my house? As a precaution, I drove around the block but didn't see anyone familiar.

"Honey, I'm home," I called to Mischa as I opened the door. It was 10 a.m. and I was eager to learn what the letter said. But the house was cold and empty. I tiptoed to the back porch. I couldn't see his head but the sleeping bag looked lumpy and his knapsack was there too. I gave the sleeping bag an experimental poke. It collapsed like a tent. I poked harder. It was empty. Mischa was gone.

I thought about the car I had seen, pulling away from the curb. Could Mischa have gone somewhere with Clavendish? After I had specifically told him to stay put? I wondered, too, about his phone call. Had he been checking what time I'd be home so he could sneak out without my knowing?

Something else finally hit home. It should have registered much sooner, but I had been derailed by Lukin's intense revelations and these last crazy hours. If Mischa was my real cousin, he would have known about Katya. I had learned more about my Russian family in four hours with Lukin last night than in a week with Mischa.

A second memory rotated to the front of my brain. Again I saw Ludmilla reaching into Mischa's pockets for his ID and then throwing it at him with a scream of "fake." That alarmed me now. Mischa had asked for my help in getting a fake ID. But as far as I knew he didn't have one yet. So what was Ludmilla talking about?

Nervous at what I was about to do, I picked up Mischa's backpack, looked through it, and found a California driver's license with his picture. It looked real, down to the hologram and state seal. But it couldn't be. Where had he gotten it? What had he done for it? I swallowed with fear, answering my own question. He had sold me out.

My phone rang.

"Hello?"

"Diamond? It's Trabuco. What's new? You okay?"

His voice brimmed with tension. He must be working a Saturday shift and had read the wire story about Lukin. I liked the way he asked what was new before inquiring about my health. Well, at least he inquired.

I stifled a yawn. I desperately wanted sleep and knew I couldn't have it.

"Someone tried to kill Sasha Lukin last night at his house while I was interviewing him," I said. "It was a drive-by. The paramedics said the bullet missed his vital organs. He was in surgery when I left the hospital."

"You gonna come in and write it up?"

"Yeah. But I was up all night. I could use a quick nap." I looked at my watch. Deadline was still hours away.

"Josh says the Russian Mafia angle didn't pan out."

"I'm still working on it," I said, feeling a flash of panic. I needed to track down Clavendish. Officials at Rathburn International. Released felon Chip Johnson. Golodny. Anyone who could confirm Lukin's story. And I needed to get Lukin's letter translated ASAP.

"Give me a rundown," Trabuco said.

I hesitated. Could I really sell out Lukin for a lousy story? I thought of the tremor in his voice, the shame and humiliation as he revisited the past. The fear. And in the end, it was the fear that brought me around. Lukin thought he was doing the right thing for his family by keeping his secrets, but I knew none of them would ever be safe unless the whole story came out into the open.

So I conjured up Sasha Lukin's image and begged forgiveness for what I was about to do. And then I told my editor everything that Lukin had told me.

"It's a fantastic Cold War spy saga," I concluded. "If it's true."

"Holy shit. Are you shitting me?" I heard him typing excitedly. "You'd have to confirm everything before we can run with it."

"I know," I groaned. "And fat chance of that. They don't exactly leave a paper trail, spies. Oh, and Lukin used to be married to a Russian relative of mine. An aunt I never knew about until last night. He says I look just like her. That's why he's been willing to talk to me. And here I thought it was my charm and superior investigative skills."

"You're losing me, Diamond. Your Russian *aunt*? Was she a spy too?"

"No. Maybe. I don't know. I told you it was complicated. I've got a lot of investigating to do."

"I want this thing airtight before you turn it in. And then, don't argue with me, Josh is going to reconfirm every single fact. You're too close to be objective and all we need is another journalism scandal. Bring me what you've got on Monday. You blow this and you're back on mountain lion patrol."

I hung up, staring blindly. Now what?

Lukin and his son were at the hospital and unreachable. Irina Lukin wouldn't speak to me. Rathburn International was closed but I left an emergency message and prayed someone would call me back. Then there was Clavendish. He was the natural choice, but thinking of the car I had seen pulling away from my house this morning, combined with Mischa's disappearance, made me wary.

I thought of Victor Golodny. Who better to understand Lukin than a fellow Russian who had lived under the regime? But he had made it clear he didn't want to see me again. He might even blame me for what had happened. But he probably didn't know yet. Which gave me a perfect excuse to call. I'd pretend I just wanted to let him know the horrible news. And then maybe I could keep him on the line for a while. I picked up the phone and dialed.

"We've only just heard," Golodny said in response to my greeting. "It's unbelievable. Someone wants to wipe the entire family off the face of the earth. I am on my way to the hospital."

"How is Mr. Lukin?" I asked, relieved that he hadn't cut me off. He was probably too upset and distracted right now to even remember our last conversation.

"Irina says the surgery was successful. There are guards posted in both Sasha's and Nick's rooms. They are on different floors and Irina must run from one to the other. And now if you will excuse me, I must go."

I hung up, annoyed that I hadn't gotten in more questions. I was still holding Mischa's driver's license and I realized that in my rush to investigate everyone else, I had never really probed Mischa's story. For my own safety, it was long overdue.

The L.A. County sheriff had a Russian organized crime unit in West Hollywood and I'd been meaning to visit them, even though the crimes had happened on L.A. city territory, not county. Now I drove to their headquarters on Santa Monica Boulevard and pretty soon I was ushered into the office of Detective Paul LaBonge. I laid down Mischa's fake California driver's license and asked what he could tell me about the document.

LaBonge picked it up, scrutinized the photo. I thought I saw the corners of his eyes tighten.

"Hmm," he said. "A very good fake."

"Have you ever seen this guy before?"

"I can't say that I have."

"Who in the Russian community could make these?" I tapped the license.

"Leave it with me and I'll find out. Who is he?"

"He showed up on my doorstep Monday, claiming to be my cousin Mischa Tsipin from Moscow. He knows details about my family's history that only a real relative might."

"Your family was Russian?"

"My mother's immediate family left St. Petersburg in 1917, during the Russian Revolution. They settled in Nice, France. But I had relatives who stayed behind. Anyway, this guy Mischa has old photos. He knows their names. But something doesn't sit right. And now he's disappeared."

I hesitated, not wanting to tell LaBonge about the Mafia connection, the smuggling into the country, the car that might be Clavendish's driving away this morning. If it was all legit, Clavendish would make sure Mischa was protected. If it was the tip of a criminal iceberg, they both deserved to be thrown to the wolves.

LaBonge listened with sympathy. "I think you got taken," he said.

"What do you mean?"

"It's a scam we've seen recently in the community. They forge papers, get ahold of old letters, and claim kinship. American relatives who can sponsor them for immigration and help them get on their feet once they arrive."

I swallowed drily. His words confirmed my worst suspicions. I couldn't meet his eyes.

"I feel like an idiot. Me of all people. Tough, skeptical reporter. I mean, in some ways he was nice. Sweet. There was a warmth . . . oh, I don't know."

"Don't beat yourself up," he said. "These people prey on the good intentions of folks like yourself. But they're just using you. You shouldn't feel bad about turning him in."

But I do. I feel like I'm betraying someone in my family.

"I'll give you a call when I get something," LaBonge said. He stood up.

I fidgeted, the letter burning a hole in my purse.

"Look, um, you don't happen to speak Russian, do you?"

"Wish I did," the detective said brightly.

"Anyone in the office maybe who—"

"Sure, tons of them."

"Could you—"

LaBonge shook his head. "They don't work Saturday."

CHAPTER 46

I had barely gotten back in the car when Luke Vinograd called.

"Monday, eleven a.m." he whispered in the hushed
tone reserved for state secrets.

"What's Monday at eleven a.m.?"

"Not so loud, I'm at work," he said with indignation.

"Okay," I whispered back, humoring him, "but why all
the secrecy?"

"In the *Times* kitchen," Luke murmured. "Taste-testing.
We're on. I've tipped off all the media. CNN has promised
to send a crew so pray we don't declare war on Iran next
week."

"Oh my God, Luke, you're really going to eat dog food
on national TV?"

"Shhhh," he erupted.

"Okay," I said. "I'll be there. They're probably pulling
me off this murder saga on Monday anyway."

"Wear your fanciest frock, Vanna," he said. "Heels are
always good. And I like your hair upswept, away from
your face."

When the phone rang again I thought it was Luke with
another fashion directive. Steering with one hand, I
groped for the cell phone again.

"I've made inquiries," said my new friend, L.A. County
Sheriff's Detective Paul LaBonge.

My brain hiccupped from dog food to Russian cousins.

"That was fast."

"I didn't want to say anything until I checked. But it's the same person. Different name."

My palms got sweaty and I took my hands off the wheel one at a time and wiped them on my pants, cradling the phone on my shoulder. "What do you mean?"

"I asked a colleague in Moscow. This Tsipin fellow is a petty con artist and crook, a confidence man."

Even though I had been skeptical from the beginning, the news hit me hard. Part of me still wanted to believe. He's never stolen anything from me, I wanted to say. And he's helped me track people down. He's enthusiastic. Sincere. Brimming with optimism. Even his bumbling could be endearing.

"If you see him again, call us or LAPD or the INS immediately."

"Is he dangerous?"

"He will feel cornered. Desperate. Such men are always dangerous," LaBonge said ominously.

He made me promise to call him back if Mischa reappeared. I was touched by his concern, but also a little alarmed. Now that I had drawn the full scrutiny of the L.A. County Sheriff's Department Russian Organized Crime Unit down on my head, I wasn't sure I liked it.

I pulled back up to my house and sat in the car for a long while, trying to figure out what to do next. I considered finding a Russian store and asking whoever was behind the counter to translate the letter, then realized I didn't want just anybody reading it. Besides, that might take hours. And it was already twelve-thirty. Finally I got out and trudged up the steps.

As I opened my front door, I heard energetic Russian singing in the bathroom. Mischa was back. He could read the letter for me. But what if the sheriff's detective was right and he really was dangerous? I backed out slowly, wondering whether I should call LaBonge and be done with it. I recalled everything he had said about the scam. *Let them take him away.* But as I listened to the water splashing, the throaty hum of bloodthirsty Cossack songs, my own blood heated up. He had taken advantage of my hospitality, lied to me, wormed his way into my sympathy, played me for a fool. I wanted a showdown. I wanted to watch his face as I told him that I knew the truth. Despite the detective's warning, I didn't think he would hurt me. Oblivious to my presence, Mischa sang on. I pictured him luxuriating in my tub, feeling completely at home, and I grew infuriated. Suddenly all that mattered was that he was in my house and I wanted him out. Now. I grabbed my cell phone, ready to dial 911 if I needed to, and pounded on the bathroom door.

"Mischa, I need to talk to you."

"Yes, yes. I am coming now," he called gaily.

In a few minutes, he emerged, his skin pink from the bath, his hair wet. He wore my white terry-cloth bathrobe and looked a little too comfortable.

"Ah," he said. "That was divine. Even without birch switch and sauna. And how was your morning, cousin?"

"Fine." I crossed my arms. "And what did you do today, Mischa?"

He toweled his hair thoughtfully. "I watched TV. I sat outside. And you?"

"You're lying. I came home this morning and you were gone. After I told you not to leave."

He hung his head. "Oh, my cousin is angry. Please calm down. I can explain."

"Stop the charade, Mischa. I know you're not my

cousin. This is all a scam, and I'm finally wise to you. I'm sick of you abusing my hospitality, eating my food, wearing my bathrobe!" For some reason this outraged me more than anything. I would have yanked it off but I didn't want to see what lay underneath. I glared angrily and continued on my tear.

"I found someone who knew you in Moscow and says you're nothing but a two-bit thief."

"But, Eve, this is slander on my person. It is lie!"

"It's not. I showed him your photo. Your *fake* California driver's license. Where did you get that, huh? From the same people who told you to come to my house and spy on me? To get information about the Lukin killing? Did the Prisoner of Memory set this all up?"

"This is not to believe. Who tells this?"

"A detective in West Hollywood," I said, stomping onto the back porch, grabbing his jeans and sweater. I threw them at him.

"He is bad man who knows nothing," Mischa said.

"Why? Because he uncovered your lies? You came here, took advantage of my ignorance, my neediness. You're a con artist and I fell for it because I wanted to believe."

Now my face was hot and it was all I could do not to break down crying in front of him. Mischa stood there, his wet hair plastered against his head, gripping his rumpled clothes. Without his glasses, his face looked naked, owl-like.

"I can explain."

"Change," I said, "then get out of here."

I pushed him back into the bathroom, grabbed his stuff off the back porch, and threw it out the front door.

A moment later, Mischa appeared, fully dressed, his glasses askew on his face and fogged from the bathroom's steam. He wrung his hands and told me whatever I had heard was a pack of lies. He vowed allegiance and recounted all the ways he had helped me.

"I would never harm you, Cousin Eve," he said in his earnest schoolboy fashion.

"Stop calling me cousin."

But his words reminded me that I was alone with him. In my anger I'd disregarded the detective's warning and broken my own personal safety rule—I'd left myself vulnerable.

"But I like you. You are nice lady. We can be cousins. I know things about your family. I will share them with you. For instance, the man—"

"No," I screamed. "You betrayed me. You lied to me. Now get out or I'll call the cops."

I brandished the phone, ready to dial 911.

"Wait," he said. "Yes, I lied. But I needed help. I am good person. You will see."

"You really believe that makes it okay? That you can use people? That, that"—I recalled Clavendish's words—"that the end justifies the means? Well, it doesn't."

"You are in danger, Cousin Eve," he said.

"Don't call me cousin. Don't you dare do it."

"But I can help you. I know things about the case. Clavendish told me."

"Clavendish?" I choked, my suspicions blooming tenfold. Again I saw his car pulling away from the curb. "When did you talk to him?"

"He gave me cell phone other day in his flat. And card, too. See?" He pulled it out. "So we stay in touch. He say not tell you. But now I tell."

"Give me that." I snatched it, read the card, shook my head in disbelief.

"His last week on the job, and he just can't help recruiting one last source. What did he promise you? Citizenship? Money?"

"He ask me watch over you. He say you are in danger, asking so many questions. Prying into past. He say I must make sure you don't get into trouble."

"I don't believe you. You're a congenital liar. Thank God our ancestors never swam in the same gene pool. Now go get your bike," I said, "so you don't have any excuses to come back."

I marched him through the tall grasses to the back of the property, where the stolen bike still leaned against the banana frond plants. Mischa regarded the green bananas queasily but plucked tangerines from the tree and hurriedly shoved them down his shirt, where they settled in lumpy bumps by his belt. It would probably be his dinner tonight, but I didn't care. I was tired of being taken advantage of by this creep. Now that I knew we weren't relatives, guilt had flown out the window.

As he wheeled his bike uphill, struggling to balance the bags dangling on either end of the handlebars, I followed him, my shoes squelching in the mud. A gray drizzle had started up again.

After Mischa pedaled away, I went inside and locked the doors. Who could I trust? I was outraged that he and Clavendish had gotten together behind my back. What could this mean? Safe in my locked and empty house, I realized I was still clutching Clavendish's card. I called his cell phone. I was giving his machine a piece of my mind when he picked up.

"You have to stop this, Ms. Diamond," he said. "You have no idea how much danger you're in. You could have been killed last night."

"Are you threatening me? You'd like to see me stop, wouldn't you? And what's the big idea of setting Mischa Tsipin to spy on me? This is not another of your little Cold War intrigues. It's my life."

"And I'm trying to save it. Just promise me you'll stay home tonight, do nothing. I'm very close to catching him."

"How do I know you're not the Prisoner of Memory?"

A long pause. "You'll have to take it on trust. Now let me speak to your cousin."

"He's not here, and I've just learned for sure that he's not my cousin. I kicked him out," I said with satisfaction.

"Who told you this?"

"A detective from the Russian Organized Crime Unit of the L.A. County Sheriff's Department. He checked with colleagues in Moscow."

There was a sharp intake of breath. "Mischa's got a few blemishes on his record but he's really an okay guy. You shouldn't worry."

"Oh, right, and I should believe you? Besides, it's not just that. There are too many other things that don't fit. For instance, there's this Soviet spy, Chip Johnson, who passed defense secrets on to Sasha Lukin and spent fourteen years in federal prison before his conviction was overturned. And then there's Golodny—"

"Ah, Golodny. Do you know what his name means in Russian?"

"No."

"Hungry. An apt name, if I ever heard one, because our Mr. Golodny is very hungry. For what, I am not yet sure. But he has an unnatural power over Sasha. I don't trust him."

"Funny, he said the same thing about you. Maybe it takes one operator to recognize another."

"Jesus," I heard Clavendish say. "So wait a minute. If Tsipin's gone then you're alone. You're sitting in your house all alone?"

"I'm fine," I said, before realizing that might not be such a great thing for him to know.

I heard a muffled curse in the background.

"Oh no! Oh no! Don't go anywhere. I'm coming right over."

The phone went dead. And then I got really worried. Clavendish hadn't asked where I lived. So how did he know? Because he had been staking out my house this morning? And suddenly I didn't want to be home, where a disgraced FBI agent who was unraveling before my eyes was coming to "protect" me.

The only one who knew the whole truth was Lukin. I had to speak to him again, or at least try. Surely he realized now how dangerous it was to keep silent. I knew that Irina Lukin would be shuttling between her husband and son on different floors. I'd have to slip in when she was gone and see if I could get past the guard at the door. I really was a relative. Sasha Lukin would vouch for me. But I'd have to plan it with split-second military precision. And for that I'd need a physical layout of the hospital. But I had to hurry, Clavendish would be here soon. I ran to the computer and within a few strokes I had the floor plans. Clutching them, I grabbed my purse, unlocked the deadbolt, and ran to my car, throwing everything onto the passenger seat as I roared out of the driveway.

CHAPTER 47

D rumming my fingers with frustration at a three-way light on Glendale Boulevard, I saw a familiar bicycle pedaling toward me. Oh no, not again. It was Mischa.

"Eve," he called, pulling up alongside my car, his face red with the effort. "How are you? What's going on?"

As if I hadn't just kicked him out of my house.

I rolled down the passenger window and leaned across.

"If you want to see your pal Clavendish, he should be at my house in about twenty minutes. He apparently doesn't want me alone or off investigating, which I find highly suspicious."

"Will you meet him?" Mischa said.

"You don't need to know."

"You must wait for Clavendish."

"What, I should trust you, who has lied to me from the moment we met? No, thank you. And I've called the police, too," I lied. "They see you, they'll pick you up, turn you over to the INS."

"Please allow me to accompany you. I will explain everything."

He stared through the window into my car, then fell silent.

And I pulled out and left him in my dust.

* * *

In the hospital parking lot, I studied my maps with Talmudic intensity. Then I walked into the lobby, called the hospital operator, and asked for Sasha Lukin's room. That got me the nursing supervisor on Lukin's floor, who said she couldn't put any calls through.

"That's okay," I said apologetically. "Actually, I'm looking for Irina. I'm her next-door neighbor and I noticed her cat was out so I brought him to my house. She can pick him up when she gets home. We have a lot of coyotes in these hills and I thought she'd like to know."

"That's very kind," the nursing supervisor said. "I'll give her the message when she gets back."

"I hope she's not on her way home right now, because I have to run my nine-year-old over to—"

"She's still here. She just went to check on her son."

I told the nursing supervisor thanks. So Irina must be in Nicolai's room right now. This was my chance. I ran my finger from the boy's room to the father's, finding the most direct route. I figured that's what Irina would take. Then I sketched a more circuitous path that required going down a long corridor past the cafeteria to a second lobby in the west wing and taking the back stairs up instead of the main elevator.

I set off, walking briskly but not too fast. The corridor turned left. I passed the cafeteria entrance and saw two familiar figures pushing through the glass doors. It was Irina Lukin and Victor Golodny, paper cups of coffee in their hands and glum expressions on their faces.

Irina saw me and her mouth opened in disbelief, then anger.

"You again," she said. She would have pummeled me with her fists if Golodny hadn't grabbed her. She flailed impotently and their cups collided.

"Oh," she cried as the scalding liquid splashed her legs. "Now look what's happened. Let me go, Victor. That woman is a ghoul, always popping up at the worst possible times. We must call the police this instant."

People were starting to gather. Soon security would arrive.

Then Irina's hand went to her mouth. "Sasha," she said. "He's up there alone. She's probably snuck in there already and stirred him up with her infernal questions. It's not good for his heart. I'd better—"

"Hang on, Irina, it's okay." Golodny patted her arm. "You're going to give *yourself* a heart attack if you don't stop. Why don't you go check on Sasha? I'll take care of this reporter."

Irina turned, and I thought she might spit or curse me. Instead, she pulled her shawl close about her shoulders and inclined her chin.

"Thank you, Victor," she said, and walked away.

We watched her leave. A maintenance worker was already wheeling over a yellow bucket and mop to clean up the spilled coffee.

"You shouldn't have come here," Golodny said. "It's upsetting the family. They don't want to talk to you."

"Then you talk to me," I said. "Lukin must have confided in you."

"What if he did? Why should I tell you?"

"Because someone almost killed him last night. And they're going to keep trying until they succeed. Right now, the killer's able to skulk around in darkness because nobody will discuss something that happened a generation ago. Expose it to the light and you expose the killer."

Golodny pursed his lips, trying to decide something.

"Yesterday, I would have gone to my grave determined not to say a word. But after last night"—Golodny twitched—"I am beginning to think you may be right."

It took all my willpower not to say anything. Let him come round to it on his own.

"Let's go get a drink and sit and talk like normal people, shall we?" Victor Golodny said.

I followed him back into the cafeteria. We got our coffees, paid, and walked onto the outdoor patio to the farthest table, where no one was likely to disturb us on this bleak and cold afternoon. It was only 3:45 but twilight was already pooling in the shadows.

Golodny blew on his steaming cup.

"What is it you think I can tell you?" he said.

I decided to start out slow, right where Sasha Lukin had left off.

"Last night, right before he got shot, Sasha was telling me about the son he had with his first wife, Katya. His name was Yuri."

Golodny's head jerked up. "He told you about Yuri?"

"Yes, but I didn't understand. First he told me Yuri died in the Afghan War. But the very last thing he said before the glass shattered was that he couldn't let his son die. So I'm confused. Is he dead or not?"

"Hmm," said Golodny, looking worried. "I didn't realize he had told you so much."

"Sasha said the KGB wanted him to report back, to be a stool pigeon."

"In Russia we call them *stukach*," Golodny said with derision.

"But Lukin said he refused. It was against his principles. As a result, the KGB ordered Yuri shipped off to fight in Afghanistan. Where he got killed, like so many others."

"Ah," said Golodny. "This is where a new story begins."

"Okay. Let's hear it."

Golodny settled into his chair and took a sip of coffee.

"For all Sasha's noble talk about not caving in to the KGB, Yuri was his only son. He loved him more than life itself."

He paused and gave me a meaningful look.

"Go on," I said.

"So Sasha Lukin went to the organs and said he'd cooperate if they promised to let Yuri go."

"And what did they want?"

"They wanted him to betray a good friend and colleague."

I forced myself to exhale. "Go on."

"The KGB suspected that Sasha's friend was passing defense secrets to the Americans when he went abroad. That's why they had put so much pressure on Sasha to report on this man earlier."

"You knew about that too?" I said wonderingly.

"Ms. Diamond," Golodny said, "you should know by now that there are no secrets between Sasha and myself."

"Well, you certainly kept this story under wraps," I said, then raced forward, nervous that he might realize the magnitude of what he was telling me and stop. "So how did it go down?"

CHAPTER 48

"T he KGB ordered Sasha to make overtures to this colleague," Golodny said. "He was to say disparaging things about the regime and suggest that communism was doomed."

Golodny laughed loudly and hysterically at this. "Such irony. Since that was precisely how Sasha felt, when he allowed himself to feel anything at all besides paralyzing fear for his son."

"They wanted Lukin to entrap his friend?"

"The friend trusted Sasha, you see. He was an idealist. They would stay up all night, drinking and talking about fraternal brotherhood. The real kind, not the bullshit Soviet kind. A world where all men would be free and equal."

Golodny's voice was suddenly thick with emotion.

"What was his name?" I said, recalling Clavendish's talk about his bloodstone days in Moscow.

Golodny paused, and I could see him struggling with the revelation. His voice lowered and grew even more husky.

"The man's name was Sergei Krasnov."

I waited in vain for the name to resonate in my memory. Nothing.

"Go on," I said.

"Krasnov knew from his trips abroad that the Soviet people were living a sham. The regime was a house of cards, held together by power-mad old men, drooling over their dinners in the Kremlin. Brezhnev, Andropov, Chernenko. He saw the rot at the core."

"Lukin told you all that?" I barely dared to breathe.

"The two of them discussed it on long walks through the forest, to avoid any listening devices that might have been planted in their apartments. Krasnov told Sasha about the clandestine meetings he'd held with the Americans. The opportunity they had to weaken the regime, maybe even hasten its downfall. He wanted Sasha to join him. He was very brave, Krasnov. And foolhardy."

"But why would this Krasnov trust Lukin? Didn't he know the anguish Lukin was going through with his son? Didn't he suspect a setup?"

"Krasnov thought their commitment to justice overrode all else. Even the fate of Sasha's son. His fatal mistake," Golodny went on, his voice cold and precise, "was to believe that Sasha still felt the idealism of his college years. But twenty years in, the only thing Sasha Lukin cared about was saving his son's life. And so from the strength of Krasnov's conviction were sown the seeds of his own destruction.

"Sasha has spent years convincing himself that the KGB would have caught Krasnov even without him," Golodny said. "He insists Krasnov's enthusiasm had already spilled over to the wrong ears and that he just sped things up. But whatever the case may be, the KGB caught the two of them red-handed, passing documents to a scientific attaché from the U.S. embassy in Moscow in late 1984."

"What do you mean, the two of them? I thought Lukin refused."

"Lukin had to be in on it too, or Krasnov would have

suspected. The KGB arrested them both and took them to Lubyanka."

Stalin's notorious prison from which so few returned, I thought.

"There they were separated. It was the normal procedure. As they dragged him off, Krasnov wrenched his head free—his hands were restrained, his shoulders bound—and shouted that Sasha should not be afraid of death. That he should rejoice that their sacrifices were building a better world."

"Oh my God. Poor Krasnov never figured it out, did he? That Lukin had betrayed him."

"No," Golodny said.

"And then what happened?"

"The two of them were executed as traitors in February of 1985."

A chill went through my bones then that had nothing to do with the frigid cafeteria patio at Queen of Angels Hospital in a Los Angeles winter. It was a chill that no tropical heat, no heavy wool sweaters, no hot showers would ever fully chase away. I finally understood the black sorrow that clung to Sasha Lukin, the haunted look that burned in his eyes. The man who had stood before me and poured tea in his beautiful hillside house could never be fully alive because he was a ghost, a KGB construct.

"So after they buried the bodies, a new man named Sasha Lukin rose from the ashes," I said hoarsely.

"You see how it is, then." Golodny gave me a tortured smile. He grasped his bony elbows and stared at the floor and spoke like he was reciting an ancient Slav song cycle that had no end.

"After they led Krasnov away at Lubyanka, they brought Sasha into a room. A nice room, in that miserable hellhole, with rich wood paneling and woven car-pets. A KGB colonel shook his hand, congratulated him for his work on behalf of the motherland, and promised that Yuri would be home in a week. They'd send the fam-ily abroad with new identities, to join the slipstream of dissidents settling in the United States. Then they'd acti-vate him."

"As a spy!" I said.

Golodny looked annoyed at the interruption. Surely this was self-evident to anyone with half a brain.

"So what happened with Yuri?" I prompted.

"His unit was stationed in the Far East," Golodny said. "The KGB had promised Sasha that Yuri wouldn't be shipped to Afghanistan, even if his unit deployed. And as soon as the arrests were confirmed, Yuri would be released and sent home. Sasha certainly held up his end of the bar-gain. But someone at military headquarters got drunk and fell asleep and didn't do his job and the order about the Lukin boy was never relayed to the right people. Yuri Lukin was deployed with his unit to the frontlines in Afghanistan. He was killed on February 17, 1985. Two days after his father betrayed Sergei Krasnov."

The bleakness of Golodny's face confirmed that we had finally hit the rock-bottom truth.

I sat stunned, and was struck with the most horrible irony.

"Mikhail Gorbachev came to power just a month later, in March," I said, remembering Agent Lansing's Russian-history tutorial. "If Lukin could have stalled them a few more months, none of this would have been necessary."

"For those like Sasha who grew up under the Soviet sys-tem," Golodny said, "it was inconceivable that things would ever really change."

"I had no idea the Soviet Union was still executing spies that late in the game."

Golodny shook off his lethargy and came awake.

"For high treason? Absolutely. And you must remember that it took time for Gorbachev to implement his reforms. The old military-industrial machine never succumbed. Yeltsin was still battling them in the 1990s."

"And what happened to the U.S. scientific attaché?" I asked.

"Sasha heard he was traded for a Soviet spy in L.A.," Golodny said. "I don't know the particulars."

Ludmilla Belyaeva.

"Nicolai was looking up this very spy case at the UCLA library the day I met him," I said. "He was on his way to figuring this out. I think that's why the killer tried to run him over."

"He was getting close, but he would never have put the names together," Golodny said darkly. "He didn't have his father's birth name. Few remember anymore that it was Mikhail Grushkin."

A memory clicked into place. Of FBI Special Agent Clavendish recounting his budding friendship with a young Russian named Sasha Lukin.

Mikhail and I joined an international club on campus, Clavendish had told me.

Who's Mikhail? I had asked.

Sorry, Clavendish had responded slickly. *I mean Sasha. For a moment there, I got him confused with another friend.*

Clavendish had tried to cover up his slip of the tongue. Now I finally understood its significance.

"That FBI agent who's friends with Sasha? He knows," I said.

"I don't think so," Golodny said immediately.

"How are you so sure?"

"Unless he is the Prisoner of Memory," Golodny said softly.

"Clavendish called me not long ago," I said. "He was on his way to my house. He was worried about me being alone."

Golodny frowned.

"You were wise to leave." He took a final gulp of coffee, put his cup down on the table.

"I must say it's a relief to unburden myself of these secrets after so long. I feel almost light-headed."

"But . . ." I said, studying him in the dusk.

It was true, a heaviness had lifted from Golodny's face and he looked almost childlike. "You only met Sasha Lukin last year."

"That's right."

"So why do you say you've been carrying these secrets for so long?"

"In Russian it's a figure of speech," Golodny said, turning around to take in the empty patio, the gloomy cafeteria.

"I don't think so," I said, my mother's ancient paranoia rearing up. Flee. Fire. Foes. Something wasn't right.

I swallowed hard.

"Your descriptions . . . the details . . . it's almost as though you were there. But that's impossible. You're way too young. . . . Lukin really told you all this?"

"He didn't."

"Then who did?"

Victor Golodny scooted over like he wanted to tell me a secret. Something hard and metallic pressed against my left side.

"Sergei Krasnov was my father."

CHAPTER 49

A nd now," he said, "stand up. We're going to your car."

Even though the patio was deserted, there had to be lots of people nearby. I'd have a chance to break free, scream, push a table into him. I couldn't let him drag me into a dark parking lot or drive me away. But I hesitated a second too long.

"Now," he said, and released the safety.

He wasn't crazy enough to shoot me on the patio of a hospital cafeteria, was he? Security would be on him right away. Even if he made it to his car amid the melee and drove off, he'd be a wanted man, and it was just a matter of time before he got caught. But then I saw the red dots pulsing in his eyes and knew that I couldn't count on his capacity for reason. Anyone who had spent twenty years obsessing over his father's betrayal and meticulously plotting revenge against his enemy, going so far as to cultivate a warm friendship with the man and his family, was completely, irrevocably driven, and maybe insane.

I did as he ordered.

"Follow that path," he said, placing one arm around me and keeping his gun hand jammed against my side. His bulky overcoat would hide the truth from passersby, except there were none on this frosty evening, and so we made our way past the shrubs that gardeners had artfully clipped into topiary animals and out to the parking lot.

"Where's your car?" he said, reaching into my bag for the keys.

"I . . . don't remember," I said, wondering how long I could lead him through the endless car aisles until someone came to my rescue or I could dive behind a vehicle and escape.

"Liar," he said. He pulled out my keys and with it came a folded yellow square with Russian writing.

"What is this?"

Keeping the gun trained on me, he unfolded the papers and scanned the top.

"A letter from Sasha Lukin," he said, his face breaking into a wolfish grin. "I recognize the script. He writes to his good friend, FBI Agent Clavendish. How interesting. In a moment we will see what he has to say. But first . . ."

Holding out my keypad like a divining rod, he pressed the "unlock" button and looked around for lights and telltale clicks.

Unfortunately, I had found a close spot for once and my car nickered in metallic welcome as the lights flashed.

My legs felt rubbery as the possibility of escape receded.

"Get in, you're driving." He opened the door.

He held out the keys and I reached for them, trying not to show hope. How quickly could I start the engine, barrel out of here?

Golodny laughed and snatched the keys away.

"You think I am stupid," he said. "You don't get the keys until we're both inside. Now I'm going to walk around. And remember, I've got you covered."

I tried to control my breathing and slow everything down to a crawl. *Keep alert. Do as he says, for now.*

"Get on the Hollywood Freeway north, get off at

Barham, and take the Cahuenga Pass. Turn right at Forest Lawn Drive."

He must have seen the look on my face. Forest Lawn was a cemetery.

"Don't worry, I'm not going to dump your body there. We're going for a little hike in Griffith Park. Lots of stars. Owls hooting. So beautiful on a winter evening."

He fell silent as I drove, each of us locked in our thoughts. *When I get out of the car,* I thought. That will be the time. Meanwhile I should keep him talking.

"Aren't you going to read me Sasha's letter?" I said. "You know I can't read Russian."

"Yes, the letter," Golodny said, pulling it out of his pocket and making himself comfortable. As he began to read, I could hear Lukin's intelligent and cultured voice bleeding through the gravelly rasp of his enemy, and it gave me a flash of hope that beauty could still triumph over ugliness in this world, even in the most unlikely circumstances.

"'My dearest Thomas,'" Golodny read, "'I know it is old-fashioned to write letters these days, but what I have to say doesn't belong on a computer, as it recounts things that happened before they came to prominence, in a world that has long ceased to exist except in our memories and perhaps also our nightmares. And so it is only right that it should be committed to paper so that you can read it, dear friend, and then burn it, as these words should never be seen by other eyes.

"'As you know, events of recent days have brought me to my knees in black despair, and I have racked my brain to imagine who might hate me enough to unleash such cataclysm on my family. And thus it is with a heavy heart that I must ask you.'"

Golodny laughed. "Poor, misguided fool," he said. "He really had no idea, did he? Well, neither did my father. One good turn deserves another."

I didn't answer. It couldn't be much past twilight, but the sky was black as midnight and we were locked inside a metal cocoon, hurtling into the past. The city slid past on either side, canyons and mountains and serpentine streets with only the intermittent glow of civilization.

"'When I revisit the events of several decades ago,'" Golodny picked up again, "'it occurs to me that you have always had good reason to despise me. And so I want to lay out the facts as I remember them and explain what I did and why, and obtain your reassurance that we do, indeed, retain a place in each other's heart despite all that has happened, and that it is not just an old man's sentimental dotage that makes him see things this way.

"'If you will indulge me for a moment, I will take you back to our first reunion in America in the year 1985. I was in the flower section of my local market, holding a bunch of daffodils, when a man spoke in Russian, asking which I thought an old friend would appreciate more, a potted narcissus or an iris.

"'I turned at the familiar voice, and there you were, half obscured by the ferns, giving me that look that reaches deep into people's souls and dredges up all their secrets. Then you stepped forward. I hadn't seen you in many years and you'd put on a few pounds and your face was redder and more jowly and you wore a suit instead of the blue jeans you used to go around in back in Moscow, but other than that, you looked exactly the same.'"

Golodny's voice cracked as he read. He rustled the letter violently and said, "This is what the traitor Grushkin stole from my father. The chance to reminisce. To live through the end of the regime and meet old friends in a new land. All this was taken from him because he was a true patriot."

Golodny gave a ghastly smile. "But let us go on."

"'For a long time, we just looked at each other,'" Golodny read. "'Then you cracked a smile and swiped the daffodils from my hand and lifted them to your nose.

"'"I see you were expecting me," you said gravely. "But is this any way to treat an old friend? Aren't you going to ask me back to your apartment?"

"'Then you rattled off my address. A Kolyma wind blew through me then. I had heard whispers, over the years, about the path you had taken, but this was the first time I knew for sure. Fearing that the KGB had bugged my apartment, I stammered something about getting fresh air. You gave me another piercing look. "Of course," you said. "How silly of me. Why would we want to be cooped up inside on such a glorious day?"

"'You suggested a walk to the park. Then I said it was great to see you again and we began to catch up with each other's lives.

"'"So you're Sasha Lukin now?" you said under your breath as we strolled. "No more Mikhail. How am I ever going to get used to that?"

"'Letting me know that you knew about that, too.'"

Golodny broke off at this point and the gun listed against my side. "He speaks here of my father. I shall read it to myself first."

We were on Forest Lawn Drive, a long, dark, sinuous road that hugged the mountains of Griffith Park. If I jerked the wheel to the right and then hard to the left, could I slam his side of the car into the dirt hills? Would he manage to shoot me first?

Golodny murmured in Russian, shook himself, and the gun took up position once more against my ribs.

"I cannot grow distracted," he said. "I have waited too many years. Still, it is so eerie, to read the traitor Grushkin's words about my father. Now I will continue."

Golodny cleared his throat and went on.

"'Eventually, my dear Thomas, our conversation came round to Sergei Krasnov, as I knew it would. And I had to stick as close to the truth as possible, explaining that our mutual friend had recruited me to pass secrets to the Allies and we had taken a great chance and been caught.

"'At this, your eyebrows shot up. And when I got to the part where they separated us in Lubyanka and Krasnov cried out to me, your brows positively did a jig.

"'Do you recall your words, my friend? Because I cannot forget them. "What an extraordinary piece of luck then," you said in your lazy drawl, "that you made it out of Lubyanka and Krasnov didn't." And you cocked your head at me. "They gave you a reprieve, didn't they, old boy?"

"'We were walking down Van Nuys Boulevard and a bus roared past and blew a piece of grit into my eye and I was blinded and cried out.

"'While I rubbed at my eye, you examined me. You were always a clever devil, and I could tell you had concluded there was only one possible reason the KGB had kept me alive and sent me west—to become a spy.

"'"I would have come to you eventually, Thomas," I told you, holding a tissue to my weeping eye. "You know that."

"'"Then I have saved you the trouble, haven't I, Mikhail?" you said.

"'I remember our conversation like yesterday. It was a glorious spring morning and the butterflies were everywhere. Black and white and orange with scalloped edges. Painted ladies. They slammed into the windshields of buses and cars, then fell to the asphalt and were ground into an orange paste. It was a fine day to betray one's country.

"'I told you then I'd do whatever you wanted. And I begged you to forgive me. I wanted your absolution, you see. For agreeing to spy. You would forgive that, once you knew the circumstances. But at all costs, I couldn't let you find out I had betrayed Krasnov.

"'So I explained that our mutual friend had rejected the *comitet*'s offer to become a spy and save his life. And you gritted your teeth and said, "Sergei was always an idealist. And in our business, one must learn pragmatism. Isn't that right, Mikhail . . . er . . . Sasha?"

"'I wondered if that was your way of saying that you, too, were a pragmatist, aware that I had betrayed Krasnov but able to sublimate your revulsion in order to work with me for the good of the cause.

"'You at least suspected, Thomas. You grilled me, and I was so emotionally exhausted that sometimes I told a lie for the right reason and a truth for the wrong one.

"'You asked me then what the KGB had in mind and I said I didn't know. But I swore I'd be your man once the dirty business started. Two months later, Moscow sent word that I was to apply for a job at Rathburn International.'"

Golodny shuffled the papers. "It ends there," he said. "Something must have interrupted the traitor."

"Me," I said. "I showed up at his house. He was starting to tell me all this when you shot him."

"It's lucky I missed the vital organs," Golodny said. "Now he will suffer more."

"You really hate him, don't you?"

"He destroyed my life."

The gun jiggled angrily at my side. "Everyone sees him as an éminence grise. A benevolent and charming old man. But he is a killer. A traitor. He deserves to burn in a living hell. And that is what I have provided."

"But—"

"You have heard Sasha Lukin's story, Ms. Diamond. Now it is time to hear mine. Only then can you understand how fully he ruined me."

In my rearview, I thought I saw headlights. They had been there awhile, staying constant even when I slowed or speeded up. I didn't want Golodny to notice. I wanted him to get lost in his tale.

"Maybe I can write your story for my newspaper," I said.

"It is a great pity that will not be possible, because it is a Dostoyevskian tale of good and evil. When I was a young child in Russia," Golodny began, "I lived in a happy cocoon. My father was a scientist. He had access to special stores. He brought my mother and I fantastic gifts from his trips abroad. Then one day my father went away and did not come back.

"At first, I didn't know he was dead. I just knew my mother cried all the time and the school chums who once fought to share my Western treats now shunned me and called me traitor. Can you imagine how devastating that might be to a small boy?"

"It must have been horrible."

"And when I came home crying, my mother pulled me close and I felt her tremble.

"'Your father is a hero, not a traitor,' she'd say. 'He stood up for what was right. Someday everyone here will realize that.'

"Her words scared me. 'That's fine, Mama,' I said, 'but when is he coming home?'

"And she sniffed and said that sometimes ideals were more important than individuals and people had to sacrifice, and that I'd understand when I was older but I should never, ever doubt that my father was terribly brave and loved me very much, and had taken a great and noble chance so that I and millions of other children could grow up in a safer world.

"'But I don't care about millions of other children,' I said. 'I just want Papa back. That's what makes my world safe.'

"'Feodor,' my mother said, gripping my shoulders, 'you must be brave like your father.'"

The man called Victor Golodny smiled. "You see, I was called Feodor then. Feodor Krasnov."

"Yes," I said. "You couldn't very well emigrate to the States and introduce yourself to Sasha Lukin with your real name."

"After the state executed my father," Feodor Krasnov said, "my mother lost her job and then she got sick. The doctors said it was cancer but I know she died of a broken heart. I didn't cry at her funeral, all my tears had been shed for my father. The state put me in an orphanage where the older boys beat me because I was the son of a traitor. So I ran away. It was 1986. The nation was in ferment. Everything was turned upside down. The social order became frayed. Soon I was running with a criminal gang on the Arbat. Those were the glasnost years. Perestroika. Everything was opening up. America was no longer our enemy but our friend, and it confused me that my father had been executed for helping our friend. What kept me alive was the thought of revenge. It became my obsession. The state had taken my father's life. So I would take the real traitor's. But it wasn't an even trade, because I had lost everything. I had become something twisted and lame, with a shriveled lump where a heart should beat.

"Still, I vowed to find him, and for that I needed money. I had little formal schooling but that didn't matter in the new Russia. I was good with numbers and computers so I found a job with a high-tech company. Then another. I saved my money. It gave me power and I liked that.

"It took years to bribe the right people and get my father's secret file. His case had been erased from official history, become part of the shameful past. The day I learned the name of the animal who betrayed my father, I sat in my flat with a bottle of vodka and made a toast. To Mikhail Grushkin, aka Aleksandr 'Sasha' Lukin. Finally I had him."

CHAPTER 50

Golodny's breath came fast. He was exultant, his face glowing. With a cry of triumph, he crumpled the letter in his hand, then dropped it into the foot well, where he stomped rhythmically, pulverizing it.

"Soon," Golodny continued, "I knew my father's betrayer was no longer in Russia. He had emigrated to America. Within months I had his address in Studio City. At first I thought I would dispatch a hit man to kill him. But ultimately, this idea didn't satisfy me. He should know why his life was ending. He should tremble and fear and feel the agony, the howling emptiness, that his betrayal had created.

"Around that time, the Los Angeles branch of my company needed more programmers and I received a high-tech work visa. Max was already in the States, attending boarding school. We moved to Los Angeles.

"I knew my father's betrayer wouldn't recognize me. I have my mother's cheekbones and coloring—she was Georgian. On the day we arrived, I drove past the traitor Grushkin's house for the first time.

"He had done well. I saw two teenagers unloading sports gear. Boys who would now grow up without a father, just as I had. I concocted elaborate scenarios of revenge, in which I tortured him slowly. Grushkin would pay. I stalked him as a mountain lion stalks a deer. In the

Russian deli he frequented, we met for the first time. You can't imagine my perverse joy when we became friends. What I didn't count on was that our sons would also draw close. I had no desire to hurt my stepson. My quarrel was not with him."

"But you did cause him pain," I said, seeing an opening where I might reach him. "Max is devastated by Denny's murder. You've got to stop this cycle of evil before it escalates any further." My words tumbled out. "The years of being consumed with revenge have twisted you in horrible ways. But you can end it. Do you want your kids to grow up without a father, as you did? You're mad if you think you won't get caught."

"Do not interrupt me," Golodny said, brandishing his gun. "Where was I? Ah, yes . . . Then my wife and I had a child together. And as I cradled my newborn daughter, I was filled to bursting with love. You might have thought it would cleanse my black heart, but instead it showed me what the perfect revenge would be. To take not Lukin's life, but that of his sons."

The man was truly insane—to murder the sons for the sins of their father.

"But he had to know why. So I sent blackmail notes signed, 'the Prisoner of Memory.' There is a nightclub owned by the Russian Mafia with that name, and I thought it would sow confusion if he showed it to the authorities."

"It worked," I said.

Golodny allowed himself a tiny smile. "It was a good choice," he said. "All my life, I have been tortured by memory, by thoughts of how different my life would have been had my father lived. Now, I would imprison the traitor Grushkin."

"You're mad," I said. "And wrong. You're slaughtering innocent children. You lured your son's friend out onto the trail and killed him in cold blood."

Like so many criminals, Golodny felt the need to boast about his crime. "I left my office by the service exit, and no one even knew I was gone. I called Denny from a pay phone and disguised my voice and told him I had information about his dad. He was to come alone to the lookout a half mile from the trailhead on the Valley side. He did as I asked. He's a good kid. I waited in ambush and shot him."

"Didn't anyone hear the gunshot?"

"I had a silencer," he said. "Then I left a memento. So Grushkin would know it was the handiwork of the Prisoner of Memory."

"The Soviet army watch," I said.

"I wanted to wait before going after Nicolai," Golodny said. "Let the traitor Grushkin grieve and then begin to think he could put his life back together with his surviving son. Then when the moment was right, when it was most painful, I would strike again. But I had bugged Nicolai's phone—oh, I am very thorough—and I knew he had learned something and was going to tell you. I couldn't let that happen. So I ordered the hit. I was surprised at how easy it was, how cheap. But you called to him at the last minute and he turned and it saved his life. I thought that would scare you off. But you kept sniffing around. And Grushkin was growing attached to you. You reminded him of his first wife. He felt he had found a daughter. There was joy in his heart. So I have to remove that joy. Sasha Lukin will live. Everyone around him will die. That's my justice. Those shots into his living room were meant for you, not him. Meanwhile, as his world collapses, I sit with him, hold his hand, share his pain. It's such exquisite torment that sometimes I must excuse myself and lock the bathroom door and examine my face in the mirror to ensure that my elation doesn't show. Then I allow myself a moment to gloat. But no more. My work is not yet finished."

We pulled into Griffith Park. It was deserted. Golodny got out first, ordering me to stay in the car. He came around to the driver's door. Opening it, he took my arm and led me to the trailhead.

"We will take a hike," Golodny said, pushing me onto the muddy trail. He put the gun against my back and fell in behind me. "If you try to run away, I will kill you."

We hiked in silence. The mud sucked at our shoes. It was a cold, clear evening. The rain had stopped, and the sky above us was dark blue with the moon shining intermittently through the clouds. With the end of the rain had come a more piercing cold. I slipped and fell and he yanked me up roughly. Behind me, I heard the rustle of raindrops sliding down leaves. A wet branch slapped me in the face and I flinched. Was it my imagination, or were there sounds behind us? We hiked higher. He carried a flashlight, shining it on the muddy path.

"We're leaving prints," I said, hoping that he would change his mind. "They'll track you by that."

He laughed and gestured to his sneakers. "I plan to throw these into a reservoir before I head home. Along with your car keys and the gun. No one will ever find them. Besides, these are common enough shoes, produced by the million."

We were in a clearing. Without warning, he pushed me onto my knees. "Don't move," he said. He took a few steps back. I guess he didn't want my blood to splatter on him. The mud was freezing through the knees of my pants. The smell of rancid meat filled my nostrils, like déjà vu from Denny Lukin's death. His decomposing body.

"I promise I won't say anything," I begged. "I'll give you twenty-four hours. You can be in Moscow by then. You've already gotten your revenge. Sasha Lukin is a broken man."

"Say a last prayer," he said. "I will give you twenty seconds. But do not waste your breath arguing with me. When I finish off Nicolai, my life's work will be complete. And then Feodor Krasnov can disappear forever. I find it quite suits me to be Victor Golodny, Russian-American computer programmer."

I looked at him and saw only dead fish eyes, staring up from a slab of ice.

"You have ten seconds left."

I turned to run, figuring I had nothing to lose anymore, and so it was that I heard only a wordless *umph* and a deep, terrifying growl at the same time that the gun discharged with a quiet pop. As I threw myself down, a bullet whistled near my left ear, then something heavy hit the ground. My head exploded with such pain and blackout adrenaline that it took a moment to realize I was still alive, writhing in the mud, groping for nonexistent wounds and mistaking the sticky mud for blood. A primal fight was taking place behind me as two creatures struggled for their lives. I heard tussling and strange, inhuman shrieks and gurgles and inched laboriously away on my belly, propelled by a preservation instinct I hadn't known I possessed.

The moon cleared from behind the clouds just then and I turned and beheld a large and sinewy animal with a feline muzzle and a long tail that dragged on the ground, crouched over the body of Victor Golodny. I tried to scramble to my feet but only succeeded in burrowing further into my mud trap, moaning and groveling in terror.

"Eve, I am here," came a familiar Russian-accented voice.

Mischa.

I scrambled onto all fours and saw him. He was advancing on the mountain lion, carrying a heavy branch that the storm had wrenched off a tree. The cat had Victor Golodny's head in its mouth and was slowly dragging him into the brush.

Reaching them, Mischa beat at the mountain lion's head with the branch.

"Eve, help me!" Mischa called. With great effort, I pulled myself free of the mud and ran in a half crouch to where Mischa bashed away at the big cat.

"He had a gun," I sobbed. "Find the gun. If he comes to, he'll kill us both."

"He can do nothing. You must take legs"—Mischa gestured to Golodny's bottom half—"and pull."

"He deserves to die," I said, but got hold of his ankles as Mischa ordered and engaged the mountain lion in a fearsome tug-of-war with Golodny's body as the spoils. The cat was six feet away, its yellow eyes lit up and giving off their own light. It smelled rank and feral. Its muzzle was flecked with blood. Again, I smelled decomposing flesh. I was deathly afraid it might decide to release Golodny and lunge for me.

"Look for the gun," I screamed. "You can shoot the lion. You can shoot them both."

"Gun is buried in mud," Mischa said, panting. "Impossible to find in dark."

He continued to smash at the cat and I tugged and we

shrieked and yelled like rabid wolverines to scare it into letting go.

Suddenly, with a fluid leap and a rush of air, the lion vanished into the dark mountainside. Still holding Golodny's ankles, I fell into the muck.

"Is he alive?" I panted, pushing myself back up. "We've got to find that gun. He'll kill us all. He's completely insane."

But clouds had obscured the moon again.

We heard a groan that confirmed Golodny was still among the living. I crawled over to touch his head and my hand came away bloody.

Mischa was standing over Golodny, holding the branch and panting. Despite the cold, we were drenched with sweat. Puffs of steam came out of our mouths like in a cartoon.

"He cannot kill," Mischa said. "He is lucky to survive."

"It was Golodny all along. He brought me here to kill me, just like he killed Denny. Just like he tried to kill Nicolai. To revenge himself upon Sasha Lukin. For betraying his father to the KGB during the Cold War," I panted to Mischa. "Golodny was the Prisoner of Memory."

Just then, we heard people in the distance, crashing through the underbrush.

"Thank gods they come," Mischa said.

"How did you know we were here?"

"I see *gospital* floor plans in car and know you go to speak with Lukin family. I call Clavendish and tell him, then steal car and drive fast to *gospital*."

"You stole a car?"

"I have many black skills," Mischa said. "In Moscow, is pure survival. I am not proud. I am not want live this way. But is good I know such things or you are not alive. At *gospital* I see Golodny force you into car. I follow you Griffith Park and call Clavendish but he is at *gospital* by then. He thinks Golodny takes you to same clearing where he kill Denny Lukin. 'I not arrive in time, Mischa,' Clavendish say. 'Is up to you to save her. Follow them onto trail. That is best bet. Attack from behind.'"

Mischa held up the tree branch. "So I follow you. I hear him talk. I look for weapon. I am ready to beat him over head when lion jump. From what zoo such creature escape? Never mind. I am ready fight for you, Eve. Because even if we are not cousins, there are other ways to be the blood."

"Everybody freeze," said a stern voice.

Mischa and I put up our arms.

"Sirs, we are already freezing," Mischa said. "But at least we are alive."

CHAPTER 51

At the police station, the detectives gave us blankets and hot coffee and made us answer questions for hours, our clothing stiff with caked mud, our hair bristling with twigs and dried leaves. Clavendish sat on a folding chair with his legs crossed and said nothing. I knew he could have observed it all from the one-way glass, so I took his presence as a sign of mute support. When there was a break, I turned to him.

"You knew about Sasha," I said. "You knew all along that he had betrayed Krasnov."

Clavendish wrapped his long fingers around his coffee mug and hunched over it like he was protecting something.

"Yes," he said, discreet to the last.

"Then how could you . . . ?" I began.

"I also knew *why*."

"But . . ."

He watched me trail off.

"What they did to him, the choice they put before him, was something no man should ever face," Clavendish said. He rubbed at his jaw, thought for a moment. "And lest you forget, there was a war on. Despite his earlier, uh, lapses in judgment, Mikhail Grushkin was useful to us. He was a conduit to the enemy. And lastly," Clavendish said simply, "he is my friend."

"But he betrayed your other friend."

"You are young. Things are still black and white for you. In time you will see the gray. The shadows and flaws. We are all imperfect vessels."

"You're talking about yourself now, aren't you? And that spy scandal with Ludmilla."

Clavendish only turned away.

"But you really were on the straight and narrow all along. She never seduced you into working for the KGB, that was just your cover, wasn't it?"

"I told you once that I was a patriot," he said softly.

"And I bet all those rumors about your gambling debts were planted too."

"I needed to be susceptible to Vassily's overtures. So I trotted over to his nightclub and lost seventy thousand dollars of the Bureau's money. It was painful." He shook his head. "Because I'm a better player than that."

And humble, too.

"And the Russian Mafia believed it?"

"Why wouldn't they?" He examined me with those frank, inquisitive eyes that could hide so many things.

"Were you working on the Lukin case too?"

"As you know," he said gravely, "I'm a special agent with the Eurasian Organized Crime Task Force. My job was to take down Vassily and his people. The Lukin murder case, that was different. It was personal. Though for a while, I thought they might intersect."

"Me, too. So you weren't really retiring, were you? That was just a cover."

He gave a belly laugh. "Lansing certainly hoped I was."

"I guess we're all glad you didn't. Especially Sasha Lukin. When did you realize that his blackmailer was Golodny?"

"We have Mischa to thank for that. After you kicked

him out, he pedaled to an Internet café and looked up Golodny, only to find that the Russian records didn't go back more than a few years. The identity was a construct. But for what? Mischa asked some of his hacker friends in St. Petersburg and they found a faint trail to a man named Feodor Krasnov. The name didn't mean anything to Mischa, but it did to me. I only hoped we could get to you in time."

I looked at Mischa, sprawled on a plastic chair, scratching his elbow. Flakes of glazed sugar from a half dozen doughnuts clung to his stubbled chin.

"Yeah," I said. "He saved my life."

When I looked back, bursting with a jillion questions, Clavendish was halfway out the door.

"Be seeing you," he said, tipping an imaginary hat.

Then he was gone.

A moment later, Detective Hudock arrived, looking as slick and camera-ready as he had at the Golden Gopher. He had been at Queen of Angels Hospital, interviewing Sasha Lukin, who had finally decided after his near-death experience to tell the entire Cold War story.

"Did he tell you about betraying Golodny's father so the KGB would let his son out of Afghanistan?"

"We're going to check that out."

"Could the U.S. government still put him on trial for treason?"

Hudock's eyes glinted. "That's not for me to say. But Special Agent Clavendish has already put him in touch with a good lawyer. Guy who used to work for that firebrand Samson Brenner. I pity the poor U.S. Attorney who has to go up against that rabid liberal lot."

I recalled how Clavendish had sat silently in the corner while the detectives interviewed me.

"I guess he thought Brenner and his firm did okay by Ludmilla Belyaeva some years back," I said. "Speaking of which, did you check out what she was doing at the hospital? I'm sure you got a report from your security people."

"Bizarre story," Hudock said. "She was visiting a friend named Galya Pankova who was there for tests. The nurses confiscated a birch branch and a humidifier from her. She had Pankova's gown off and was beating the poor thing with it. Heater up as far as it would go. The patient declined to press charges. Some witchy Russian thing, I guess."

"And how's our pal Golodny?" I asked.

Golodny was in the hospital with severe head injuries, and it was too soon to know if he'd make it. I thought with sadness about his son, Max, doomed one way or another to grow up fatherless just like his dad. Because even if the Prisoner of Memory lived, he'd be going away for a long time. And the poisonous legacy would cycle through another generation.

They had found Golodny's gun in the mud. The bullet must have gone wide when the cat jumped him; they found that, too, embedded in a nearby tree trunk. Based on the trajectory and where I was standing, the crime techs thought it had missed me by two inches. They also found the partially eaten carcass of a deer, half buried off the trail, which accounted for the awful smell. The big cat must have been hiding out nearby, guarding its dinner.

The words of Fish and Game tracker Jeff Knightsbridge came back to me: *If it killed recently, the puma will perceive anything that gets too close as threatening its meal.*

Would Mischa have reached us in time if the big cat hadn't? I would never know.

It was 4. a.m. before they let us go, sending us home in a cruiser. The crime techs would need my car for a few days. There was no question Mischa was going home with me. The guy might be a liar, a car thief, a computer hacker, and a con artist, but he had saved my life.

Mischa let me have the first shower and I tried to hurry, even though I wanted to stand under the hot jets for an eternity.

Freshly bathed and finally warm, we sat on the couch at dawn and sipped mugs of scalding coffee, left with the awkward task of sorting out what we meant to each other. For the first time ever, we were embarrassed and at a loss for words. He because of his lies, me for treating him so shabbily.

"One thing I still don't understand," I said after a long silence, "is why, out of the millions of people in Los Angeles, you landed on my doorstep. How did you know I had relatives in Russia?"

"I want tell you last night but you kick me out," Mischa said, his eyes darting away.

"I'm sorry," I said quietly. "I'll listen now."

"In our Moscow building was old man who live alone. He had the cancer, and my mother and aunt cook for him and I deliver him food. He is very lonely. He live long time in America, returning after perestroika to die in homeland. True Communist believer. Sometimes when medicines too strong, he is delirious, tell us stories that he is *shpion* in Los Angeles."

A tingle started up near my belly.

"One day my aunt bring *shtchi*. Is cabbage soup. Very hearty in winter. He is in armchair. Natural death.

"We not know if he has relatives, so Mother and I, quick quick, we go through papers to look, to write and tell sad news. We find many old letters. Photos of children. We write to addresses on envelopes. Get no answer. The state take body away and new tenant moves in. We keep his things. That winter, I read everything more slowly. I learn about this lonely man. And I think, I will look up relatives in United States. And that is how it begins. With Internet, anything is possible."

"But you still aren't telling me how my name came up." I said, although I thought I knew.

Mischa looked at me with curious cunning.

"I find a letter he never send. To woman name Anya Diamond. It is long, many pages, and goes back in time, remembering years together, great-aunt name Natasha, childhood in Nice, and engagement. This is sorrow of his life. That Anya marry other man, this Mr. Diamond, and had child with him. Girl name Eve. He saw them once, daughter so pretty, miniature of mother. Old man has great sorrow about this. He, too, marries and has children, but marriage fails and he divorces. He is sad. Letter has, how do you say, many cross-outs and splotches, like he is crying while writing."

"What was the old man's name?" I said hoarsely.

"Stepan Domashny."

A second person had now confirmed that my mother's lover was a Communist spy. I had satisfied the two-source rule of journalism in tracking down this story from my own life.

This was the burden my mother had carried. The reason for her melancholy. The fear I had dismissed with American arrogance, growing up in an anodyne suburb, bliss-fully unaware that spying and treason weren't just things that happened in movies. That there were people out there who risked their lives for their beliefs, even if they were wrong. My mother's heart had belonged to a traitor. And when his services were no longer needed, this man, who had lived so long in exile, sold the house on Cordoba Street and shuffled back across the globe to his homeland and died.

I thought back to the letter from Luka I had found in my mother's things, and the hot embarrassment that had flooded my cheeks at reading such intimate words: *If I could only persuade you of the nobility and integrity of my intentions, then we could always be together. Do not say I am wrong, or misguided. I am passionately committed, and what I wish for, every waking moment of my days and in my dreams at night, is that you will join me in this life.*

Stepan Domashny hadn't been talking about marriage. He had been talking about his work for the USSR. His work as a spy. He might have loved my mother, but he was "passionately committed" to the cause of Lenin.

"Why didn't you tell me the truth?" I said hoarsely.

"How I can do this?" Mischa said. "Then you know I am not real cousin."

"But the photo. Of the girls outside the dacha in 1904. Where did you get that?"

Mischa waved his hand in dismissal. "At Moscow flea market. Izmailovo. There are many such things for sale now." He hung his head. "I am sorry."

"So you wove in bits of truth from this old man and bits of lies patched together with someone else's history and photos?"

"It is wrong. But I am desperate to come to America.

You cannot understand. So I contract with Mafia to bring me to Los Angeles and hope I find you fast. Then I have opportunity to run away. Is pure truth, what I say."

Something struck me. The San Francisco woman had told me Domashny had grown children. And Mischa's story confirmed it.

"You said there were photos of children? Addresses? But that you got no response when you wrote? Well, you managed to track me down, why not them?"

"You are best hope for me. Old man's children would immediately know I was not real relative."

I crossed my arms. "So I was your ignorant American," I said.

"Please, Eve, I not mean insult . . ."

Suddenly, I grew elated.

"Mischa, do you still have the letters and addresses in Moscow? Could you have someone fax over the letters or photocopy them and mail over the box?"

"Yes, but why?"

"Don't you see? I need to find Domashny's kids. I want to know all about this man my mother almost married. He could have been my father. And I haven't had a chance to tell you this yet, but I may have an aunt in Russia. Sasha Lukin's first wife. Katya. I think I have to take a trip there."

"You can stay my flat," Mischa said immediately. "I have very good connections. We will track everybody down. Is not problem."

I scowled at him. "If we're going to work together, you have to promise me never, ever to say those words again. With you, *everything* is a problem."

"No problem," Mischa said.

He got up for a coffee refill. At the table, he stopped, picked up a ratty sheet of paper. It was the old Russian letter I had pulled out of my mother's hatbox the other night.

"Oh gosh, I've been meaning to ask you," I said. "Will you please read that to me?"

Coffee cup in hand, Mischa carried the letter to the couch and sat next to me.

"Date is fourteenth April in year 1946," he announced.

"'Dearest Valentina and Anya' . . ." Mischa raised his head. "You know these people?"

"My mother and grandmother," I said, wriggling impatiently on the couch. "Keep going."

"'I love you both very much and send you warm greetings from our motherland,'" Mischa read. "'Glorious things are happening and I want us all to be part of this historic time. Valentina, can you find it in your heart to forgive me for taking Katya? She has just gotten to know her Papa again after our separation during the war and she begged and pleaded to accompany me. I'm sorry I didn't tell you ahead of time, but you would have forbidden it. I trust you found the note I left on the kitchen table. You will be pleased to know that after just two days here, Katya is already wearing the red scarf of the Young Pioneers and learning the songs of our beloved Comrade Stalin. There is no hope for us in France. The West is a dead institution. Here in the Union of Soviet Socialist Republics, we are building the future of mankind. Please sell everything and come as soon as possible. We await your arrival.

"'With all my love forever, your Aleksandr.'"

Mischa looked up, frowned.

"There is more," he said. "Two lines, in child's writing."

I peered over his shoulder and saw block Cyrillic letters wavering across the page.

"'Dearest Mamochka and baby Anya,'" Mischa read,

"'please come soon. We miss you terribly. The sun is shining and the butterflies are everywhere.'"

Suddenly I was no longer in my cozy, heated living room in Silverlake. I was flailing in black, icy waters and I couldn't breathe.

"Eve, what is wrong? What does it mean, sun and the butterflies?"

But I could only hear my grandmother's words, bitter as they recounted what lay in store for Francophile Russians who returned to Stalin's worker paradise.

Here, finally, was proof that Katya was my aunt. That my grandfather hadn't died of disease and poor health after the war as my grandmother had always claimed. He may have been disillusioned by the West, but he still retained faith in his homeland. And one day in 1946, he had taken my aunt Katya, a mere child of five, and joined the throngs of pilgrims headed home at Pied Piper Stalin's behest to rebuild the motherland. No wonder my grandmother claimed his ideals had killed him.

Sasha Lukin said my grandfather had been shipped to the gulag shortly after he arrived and died there of overwork, one of millions caught between the maws of Nazism and communism. In his misplaced zeal, he had wrenched Katya from her safe home in France, dragged her thousands of miles east, then abandoned her to be raised by distant relatives in a strange land. But Katya had survived and grown up and married Sasha Lukin. And they had found happiness together before the system came crashing down on them again, setting off a chain reaction that was still radiating its poisonous half-life today.

Slowly, I came back to the present. Mischa put his arm around me and I leaned into him, comforted by the rough cotton nubs of the bathrobe against my cheek. My anger against him had long ago flamed out into feelings so complicated it would probably take years to sort them out.

The doorbell rang. Probably a detective, back to ask us more questions. Then the door opened and Silvio stood in the entryway, backlit by the orange and purple streaks of sunrise.

I jumped up.

"I was so thrilled to get an earlier flight," Silvio said, the anticipation on his face already fading as he saw the twin tracks of my tears, the half-clad figure behind me.

"*Querida,* what's going on?"

With great deliberation, Silvio stepped farther inside.

He looked past me to the bathrobe-clad Mischa, hair still wet, sitting on my couch. Silvio blinked in disbelief, shook his head. I saw muscles tighten in his face.

His voice, when it came, was stiff and formal.

"I tried to call from the taxi but you didn't answer," Silvio said. "I felt bad about our abrupt parting the other day. I wanted to make it up to you. So I came right from the airport. Which in retrospect seems to have been a mistake."

I remembered now, too late, how I'd turned off my phone yesterday so I wouldn't have to hear Mischa's pleading after I had kicked him out. How much had changed since then. In the mad rush of days, I hadn't even realized the holiday was finally upon us. Today was Christmas Eve. For the first time since my parents had died, I had relatives to help me celebrate Christmas. Even if we had to do it at Queen of Angels Hospital. But if I didn't do something soon to defuse this situation, Silvio wouldn't be joining me.

My boyfriend stood with his arms crossed, his jaw set in a way that meant trouble.

"Eve, will you please tell me what's going on?"

Blushing, Mischa leaped off the couch and advanced toward Silvio, one arm outstretched for the ceremonial American handshake. Silvio planted his legs apart and wound up to take a punch at him.

I ran between them and grabbed Silvio's arm. Looking from one to the other, I smiled through wet lashes.

"There is a perfectly logical explanation for what you're seeing here at six on a Sunday morning," I said. "Silvio, this is my, uh, sort of cousin, Mischa Tsipin. Now let me start at the beginning."

AUTHOR'S NOTE

This book was inspired by stories my mother told me over the years about her family in St. Petersburg and Nice, France. My mother's maternal family was from St. Petersburg, and she had at least seven aunts and uncles, many of whom were members of the Mariinsky Theatre. One of my great-aunts, Sanya Kosloff, was a dancer for the Kirov Ballet in her youth, as was her husband, Feodor Kosloff. When they emigrated to Los Angeles in the 1920s, they opened up a ballet school in the basement of the Hollywood Roosevelt Hotel on the Sunset Strip and counted many Hollywood actors among their students. Feodor Kosloff also played small roles in many movies of the time.

The recollections of Eve's grandmother in this book are drawn directly from stories my mother told me about her glamorous Russian aunts who would come to the villa in Nice for visits but always returned home to Russia because their families had been forced to remain behind. Sometime in the 1920s, my mother's aunts stopped coming to France. Letters were returned unanswered. After World War II, my mother learned that three of the aunts had starved to death during the nine-hundred-day siege of Leningrad. With the start of the Cold War, it grew difficult to renew contact with any relatives that might remain. In 1949, my mother and grandmother left France for Los Angeles, where my mother met my father and settled in the San Fernando Valley to raise three children.

I've often wondered what happened to the Russian branch of my family and for much of my life have felt a strong connection with Russian people, culture, literature, and language. Many of my childhood touchstones involve Russia, and it was the language my mother, aunt, and grandmother spoke at home when they didn't want us to understand. After I grew up and became a *Los Angeles Times* staff writer, I spent months living and reporting on life behind the Iron Curtain and covered the collapse of communism and the emergence of the former USSR republics as independent nations. In my journeys, I often fantasized about meeting my long-lost relatives and, conversely, what might happen if one of them showed up at my door in America. This book, then, is partly an attempt to imagine what such a reunion might be like and how Eve might respond to learning about her own Russian history—filtered through a murder mystery lens, of course.

ACKNOWLEDGMENTS

I want to thank George Q. Fong, supervisory special agent with the FBI, for his generosity and help.

My dear friend Lienna Silver read the manuscript for Russian continuity and provided emotional sustenance. Any errors are solely mine.

Thanks go to Terry McGarry, my former *L.A. Times* colleague, who took me on a Cold War tour of the San Fernando Valley and packed a picnic lunch that we ate in the hills overlooking the defense-industry plants.

Thanks go to my lovely agent, Anne Borchardt, and to my extraordinary editor, Sarah Knight, whose incisive editing and keen mind improved this book tremendously.

Snaps to Susan Moldow, Louise Burke, and Maggie Crawford for believing in the series and to Suzanne Balaban and Erica Gelbard for tirelessly promoting it.

Thanks to my copy editor, Karen Richardson, and production editor, John McGhee, who went over the manuscript with a fine-tooth comb.

Thanks to my writing group, whose camaraderie, support, and heaped tables nourished body as well as soul.

Last, thanks to David, Adrian, and Alexander, who provide regular reality checks and love.